Dear Friends,

So here it is—the third and final installment in the Manning series. I hope you've enjoyed the stories thus far. I wrote *Bride on the Loose* in 1990 and dedicated it to my friend Ginny and her husband, Dean, for their fiftieth wedding anniversary. Ginny was a special reader who inspired me and I came to love her feisty nature and her zest for life.

As is often the case with a series, I thought I was finished. I'd written about all five of the Mannings and was happily moving on with my writing schedule. Yet every now and then, James Wilkens, the man who was once Christy Manning's fiancé, would drift into my mind. I was touched by the way he insisted that since he was the one to put the engagement ring on her finger, he should be the one to take it off. Nearly four years later I decided to give James his own book, and that was how *Same Time, Next Year* came about. So although James isn't *really* a Manning groom, his story belongs with theirs.

Like my own family, the Mannings are a close-knit group. At the time I wrote these books, my four children were teenagers. Now, like the Manning sisters and brothers, they're all married with children of their own. It was a joy to write the Mannings' stories and it's been an even greater joy to see them come to life a second time.

My wish is that you'll enjoy this last installment. I love hearing from readers! You can reach me at www.debbiemacomber.com or you can write me at P.O. Box 1458, Port Orchard, Washington 98366.

W9-BLJ-222

DEBBIE MACOMBER

The Manning Grooms

MIRA®

MIRA®

ISBN-13: 978-0-7783-2602-1
ISBN-10:   0-7783-2602-0

THE MANNING GROOMS

Copyright © 2008 by MIRA Books.

The publisher acknowledges the copyright holder
of the individual works as follows:

BRIDE ON THE LOOSE
Copyright © 1992 by Debbie Macomber.

SAME TIME, NEXT YEAR
Copyright © 1995 by Debbie Macomber.

www.MIRABooks.com

Printed in U.S.A.

CONTENTS

BRIDE ON THE LOOSE

To Virginia and Dean,
whose fifty years of love have inspired me.
Happy Golden Wedding Anniversary!

One

It was one of those days. Jason Manning scrubbed his hands in the stainless-steel sink, then applied ointment to several scratches. He'd just finished examining and prescribing antibiotics for a feisty Persian cat with a bladder infection. The usually ill-mannered feline had never been his most cooperative patient, but today she'd taken a particular dislike to Jason.

He left the examining room and was greeted by Stella, his receptionist, who steered him toward his office. She wore a suspiciously silly grin, as if to say "this should be interesting."

"There's a young lady who'd like a few minutes with you," was all the information she'd give him. Her cryptic message didn't please him any more than the Persian's blatant distaste for him had.

Curious, Jason moved into his book-lined office. "Hello," he said in the friendliest voice he could muster.

"Hi." A teenage girl who seemed vaguely familiar

stood as he entered the room. She glanced nervously in his direction as if he should recognize her. When it was obvious he didn't, she introduced herself. "I'm Carrie Weston." She paused, waiting expectantly.

"Hello, Carrie," Jason said. He'd seen her around, but for the life of him, couldn't recall where. "How can I help you?"

"You don't remember me, do you?"

"Ah…no." He couldn't see any point in pretending. If a cat could outsmart him, he was fair game for a teenager.

"We're neighbors. My mom and I live in the same apartment complex as you."

He did his best to smile and nod as though he'd immediately placed her, but he hadn't. He racked his brain trying to recall which apartment was hers. Although he owned and managed the building, Jason didn't interact much with his tenants. He was careful to choose renters who cared about their privacy as much as he cared about his. He rarely saw any of them other than to collect the rent, and even then most just slipped their checks under his door around the first of the month.

Carrie sat back down, her hands clenched tightly in her lap. "I—I'm sorry to bother you, but I've been trying to talk to you for some time, and…and this seemed to be the only way I could do it without my mother finding out."

"Your mother?"

"Charlotte Weston. We live in 1-A."

Jason nodded. The Westons had been in the apartment for more than a year. Other than when they'd signed the rental agreement, Jason couldn't recall speaking to either the mother or her daughter.

"Is there a problem?"

"Not a problem...exactly." Carrie stood once again and opened her purse, taking out a thin wad of bills, which she leafed through and counted slowly. When she'd finished, she looked up at him. "It's my mother," she announced.

"Yes?" Jason prompted. He didn't have a clue where this conversation was leading or how long it would take the girl to get there. Stella knew he had a terrier waiting, yet she'd purposely routed him into his office.

"She needs a man," Carrie said, squaring her shoulders.

"I beg your pardon?" The girl had his attention now.

"My mother needs a man. I'm here to offer you one hundred dollars if you'll take her out on a date. You are single, aren't you?"

"Yes...but..." Jason was so surprised, he answered without thinking. Frankly, he didn't know whether to ask which of his brothers had put her up to this, or simply to laugh outright. He couldn't very well claim he'd never been propositioned before, but this was by far the most original instance he'd encountered in thirty-odd years.

"She's not ugly or anything."

"Ah...I'm not sure what to tell you." The girl was staring at him so candidly, so forthrightly, Jason realized within seconds it was no joke.

"I don't think my mother's happy."

Jason leaned against the side of his oak desk and crossed his arms. "Why would you assume my taking her out will make a difference?"

"I…don't know. I'm just hoping. You see, my mom and dad got divorced when I was little. I don't remember my dad, and apparently he doesn't remember me, either, because I've never heard from him. Mom doesn't say much about what went wrong, but it must've been bad because she never dates. I didn't care about that before, only now…"

"Only now what?" Jason asked when she hesitated.

"I want to start dating myself, and my mother's going totally weird on me. She says I'm too young. Boy, is she out of it! I'm not allowed to date until I'm sixteen. Can you imagine anything so ridiculous?"

"Uhh…" Jason wasn't interested in getting involved in a mother-daughter squabble. "Not being a father myself, I can't really say."

"The ninth-grade dance is coming up in a few weeks and I want to go."

"Your mother won't allow you to attend the dance?" That sounded a bit harsh to Jason, but as he'd just stated, he wasn't in a position to know.

"Oh, she'll let me go, except she intends to drop me off and pick me up when the dance is over."

"And that's unacceptable?"

"Of course it is! It's—it's the most awful thing she could do to me. I'd be mortified to have my mother waiting in the school parking lot to take me home after the dance. I'd be humiliated in front of my friends.

You've just got to help me." A note of desperation raised her voice on the last few words.

"I don't understand what you want me to do," Jason hedged. He couldn't see any connection between Carrie's attending the all-important ninth-grade dance and him wining and dining her mother.

"You need me to spell it out for you?" Carrie's eyes were wide, her gaze scanning the room. "I'm offering you serious money to seduce my mother."

For a wild instant, Jason thought he hadn't heard her right. "Seduce her?"

"My mother's practically a virgin all over again. She needs a man."

"You're sure about this?" Jason was having a hard time keeping a straight face. He could hardly wait to tell his brother Rich. The two of them would have a good laugh over it.

"Absolutely positive." Carrie didn't even flinch. Her expression grew more confident. "Mom's forgotten what it's like to be in love. All she thinks about is work. Don't get me wrong… My mother's an awesome person, but she's so prim and proper…and stubborn. What she really needs is…well, you know."

Jason felt sorry for the kid, but he didn't see how he could help her. Now that he thought about it, he did recall what Charlotte Weston looked like. In fact, he could remember the day she'd moved in. She'd seemed feminine and attractive, more than a little intriguing. But he'd noticed a guardedness, too, that sent an unmistakable signal. He'd walked away with the impression that she was as straitlaced as a nun and about as warm and inviting as an Alaskan winter.

"Why me?" Jason was curious enough to wonder why Carrie had sought *him* out. Apparently his charisma was more alluring than he'd realized.

"Well, because…just because, that's all," Carrie answered with perfect teenage logic. "And I figured I wouldn't have to pay you as much as I would one of those dating services. You seem nice." She gnawed on her lower lip. "Being a veterinarian is good, too."

"How's that?"

"You've probably had lots of experience soothing injured animals, and I think my mother's going to need some of that—comforting and reassuring, you know?" The girl's voice became fervent. "She's been hurt…. She doesn't talk about it, but she loved my father and I think she must be afraid of falling in love again. I even think she might like another baby someday." This last bit of information was clearly an afterthought. Carrie cast him a speculative glance to be sure she hadn't said something she shouldn't have. "Don't worry about that—she's probably too old anyway," she added quickly.

"She wants a baby?" Jason could feel the hair on the back of his neck rising. This woman-child was leading him toward quicksand, and he was going to put a stop to it right now.

"No—no…I mean, she's never said so, but I saw her the other day holding a friend's newborn and she had that look in her eyes… I thought she was going to cry." She paused. "I shouldn't have said anything."

For one brief, insane moment, Jason had actually considered the challenge of seducing Charlotte Weston, but the mention of a baby brought him solidly back to earth.

"Listen, Carrie," Jason said, "I'm sorry, but this isn't going to work."

"It's got to," she pleaded urgently, "just for one date. Couldn't you ask her out? Just once? If you don't, I'll be humiliated in front of my entire class. I'd rather not even go to the dance if my mother drives me."

Jason hated to disappoint her, but he couldn't see himself in the role of rescuing a fifteen-year-old damsel in distress from her mother's heavy hand, even if Carrie did make a halfway decent case.

"Is it the money?" Carrie asked, her eyes imploring. "I might be able to scrounge up another twenty dollars… but I'm going to need some cash for the dance."

"It isn't the money," Jason assured her.

Wearing a dejected look, Carrie stood. "You sure you don't want to take a couple of days to think it over?"

"I'm sure."

She released a long, frustrated sigh. "I was afraid you were going to say that."

"Good luck." Jason held open the door. He had no intention of asking Charlotte Weston out on a date, but he he did feel sorry for Carrie. Although he hadn't been a teenager in years, he hadn't forgotten how important these things could seem. Things like the ninth-grade dance.

* * *

Charlotte let herself into the apartment at six that evening. She slipped off her heels and rubbed the tense muscles at the back of her neck.

"Hi, Mom," Carrie called cheerfully from the kitchen. "How was work?"

"Fine." There was no need to burden her daughter with how terrible her day had been. Her job as an executive assistant at a large insurance agency might have sounded high-powered and influential, but in reality it was neither. Charlotte worked long hours with little appreciation or reward. For six months, ever since Harry Ward had taken over as managing director, she'd been telling herself it was time to change jobs. But she couldn't give up the security of her position, no matter how much she disliked her boss.

"How was school?" she asked.

"Good. Tickets for the dance went on sale today." Her daughter looked hopefully at Charlotte, as though expecting her to make some profound comment.

Charlotte chose to ignore the pointed stare. Her stand on the dance issue was causing a strain in their relationship, but she refused to give in to her daughter's pressure. Carrie wasn't going on an actual *date*. She was interested in a boy named Brad, but as far as Charlotte was concerned, Carrie could attend the dance with her girlfriends and meet him there. Good grief, the girl was only fifteen!

"Mom, can we *please* talk about the dance?"

"Of course, but…"

"You're not going to change your mind, right?" Carrie guessed, then sighed. "What can I say to prove how unreasonable you're being? Every girl in my class is going to the dance with a *boy*. And Brad *asked* me."

Charlotte reached for an apron, tied it about her waist and opened the refrigerator door. She took out a package of ground turkey for taco salad. She wasn't up to another round of arguments over the dance.

"Did you buy a dance ticket?" Charlotte asked, forcing an artificial lightness into her voice.

"No. I won't, either. I'd rather sit home for the rest of my life than have my *mother* drop me off and pick me up. Brad's father said he'd drive us both... What am I supposed to tell Brad? That my mother doesn't trust his father's driving? You're making way too big a deal out of this."

Ah, the certainty of youth, Charlotte mused.

"Will you think about it?" Carrie implored. "Please?"

"All right," Charlotte promised. She hated to be so hardheaded, but when it came to her daughter, she found little room for compromise. To her way of thinking, Carrie was too young for a real date, even if the boy in question wasn't the one driving.

The meat was simmering in the cast-iron skillet as Charlotte started to wash the lettuce. The faucet came off in her hand, squirting icy water toward the ceiling, and she gasped.

"What's wrong?" Carrie asked, leaping up from the kitchen table where she was doing her homework.

"The faucet broke!" Already Charlotte was down on her knees, her head under the sink, searching for the valve to cut off the water supply.

"There's water everywhere," Carrie shrieked.

"I know." Most of it had landed on Charlotte.

"Are you going to be able to fix it?" Carrie asked anxiously.

Charlotte sat on the floor, her back against the lower cupboards, her knees under her chin. This was all she needed to make her day complete. "I don't know," she muttered, pushing damp hair away from her face with both hands. "But it shouldn't be that hard."

"You should call the apartment manager," Carrie said. "You've had to work all day. If something breaks down, he should be the one to fix it, not you. We don't know anything about faucets. We're helpless."

"Helpless?" Charlotte raised her eyebrows at that. The two of them had dealt with far more difficult problems over the years. By comparison, a broken faucet was nothing. "I think we can handle it."

"Of course we can, but why should we?" Carrie demanded. "We pay our rent on time every month. The least the manager could do is see to minor repairs. He should fix them right away, too." She marched over to the wall phone and yanked the receiver from the hook. "Here," she said dramatically. "You call him."

"I...I don't know the number." They'd lived in the apartment for well over a year and until now there hadn't been any reason to contact the manager.

"It's around here somewhere," Carrie said, pulling

open the top kitchen drawer and riffling through the phone book and some other papers. Within a very brief time, she'd located the phone number. "His name is Jason Manning. He's a veterinarian."

"He's a vet? I didn't realize that." But then, Charlotte had only met the man once, and their entire conversation had been about the apartment. He seemed pleasant enough. She'd seen him in the parking lot a few times and he struck her as an overgrown kid. Frankly, she was surprised to learn he was a veterinarian, since she'd never seen him in anything other than a baseball cap, jeans and a T-shirt. Dressing up for him was a pair of jeans that weren't torn or stained and a sweatshirt.

"Are you going to phone him?" Carrie asked, holding out the receiver.

"I suppose I will." Charlotte rose awkwardly to her feet in her straight skirt. By the time she was upright, her daughter had dialed the number and handed her the receiver.

"Hello," came Jason Manning's voice after the first ring, catching her off guard.

"Oh…hello… This is Charlotte Weston in apartment 1-A. We have a broken faucet. I managed to turn off the valve, but we'd appreciate having it repaired as quickly as possible."

"A broken faucet," he repeated, and although she knew it made no sense, he sounded suspicious to Charlotte, as though he thought she'd purposely interrupted his evening. She resented his attitude.

"Yes, a broken faucet," she returned stiffly. "It came off in my hand when I went to wash some lettuce. There's water everywhere." A slight exaggeration, but a necessary one. "If you'd prefer, I can contact a plumber. Naturally there'll be an additional charge for repairs this late in the day."

He muttered something Charlotte couldn't decipher, then said, "I'll be right over." He didn't seem too pleased, but that was his problem. He shouldn't have agreed to manage the apartments if he wasn't willing to deal with the hassles that went along with the job.

"What did he say?" her daughter asked, eyes curious, when Charlotte hung up the phone. "Is he coming?"

"He said he'd be right over."

"Good." Carrie studied her critically. "You might want to change clothes."

"Change clothes? Whatever for?" Surprised at her daughter's concern, Charlotte glanced down at her business suit. She didn't see anything wrong with it other than a little water, and in any event, she couldn't care less about impressing the apartment manager.

"Whatever." Carrie rolled her eyes, returning to her homework. No sooner had she sat down than the doorbell chimed. Her daughter leapt suddenly to her feet as if she expected to find a rock star at the door. "I'll get it!"

Jason considered the whole thing a nuisance call. It didn't take a rocket scientist to figure out what Carrie Weston was doing. The girl had arranged this broken faucet just so he'd have a chance to see Charlotte. The kid seemed to think that once Jason got a good look at her mother, he'd change his mind about wanting to date her. Well, there wasn't much chance of that.

Apparently the girl thought he was something of a player. Jason might've gotten a kick out of that a few years ago, but not now. Not when he was nearing middle age. These days he was more concerned about his cholesterol level and his weight than with seducing a reluctant woman.

He probably would've ended up getting married if things had worked out between him and Julie, but they hadn't. She'd been with Charlie nearly seven years now, and the last he'd heard, she had three kids. He wished her and her husband well, and suffered no regrets. Sure, it had hurt when they'd broken off their relationship, but in the end it just wasn't meant to be. He was pragmatic enough to accept that and go on with his life.

Jason enjoyed the company of women as much as any man did, but he didn't like the fact that they all wanted to reform him. He was disorganized, slovenly and a sports nut. Women didn't appreciate those qualities in a man. They would smile sweetly, claim they loved him just the way he was and then try to change him. The problem was, Jason didn't want to be refined, reformed or domesticated.

Charlotte Weston was a prime example of the type of woman he particularly avoided. Haughty. Dignified. Proper. She actually washed lettuce. Furthermore, she made a point of letting him know it.

"Hi." Carrie opened the door for him, grinning from ear to ear.

"The faucet broke?" Jason didn't bother to keep the sarcasm out of his voice.

She nodded, her smile as sly as a wink. "Kind of accidentally on purpose," she explained under her breath.

Jason was surprised she'd admit as much. "I thought that might be the case."

She pulled a screw from the small front pocket of her jeans and handed it to him. "It was the only way I could think of to get you here to see my mother up close— only don't be obvious about it, all right?"

"Carrie, is it the apartment manager?" The subject of their discussion walked into the living room, drying her hands on a terry-cloth apron.

Not bad was Jason's first reaction. She'd changed her hair since the last time he'd seen her; it was a cloud of disarrayed brown curls instead of the chignon she'd worn a year earlier. The curls gave her a softer, more feminine appeal. She was good-looking, too, not trying-to-make-an-impression gorgeous, but attractive in a modest sort of way. Her eyes were a deep shade of blue, as blue as his own. They were also intense and…sad, as though she'd withstood more than her share of problems over the years. But then, who hadn't?

Her legs were attractive, too. Long and slender. She was tall—easily five-eight, maybe five-nine.

"She's not bad-looking, is she?" Carrie asked in a whisper.

"Shh." Jason slid back a warning.

"Mom, this is Dr. Jason Manning, remember? Our apartment manager," Carrie said, her arm making a sweeping gesture toward her mother.

"Hello." She stayed where she was, her fingers still clutching the apron.

"Hi. You called about the broken faucet?" He took a couple of steps into the room, carrying his tool kit. He'd have a talk with Carrie later. If this took more than a few minutes, he might be late for the Lakers play-off game. It was the fifth game in the series, and Jason had no intention of missing it.

"The broken faucet's in the kitchen," Charlotte said, leading the way.

"This shouldn't take long." Jason set his tools on the counter and reached for the disconnected faucet. "Looks like it might be missing a screw." He turned pointedly to Carrie, then made a show of sorting through his tool kit. "My guess is that I have an identical one in here." He pretended to find the screw Carrie had handed him, then held it up so they could all examine it. "Ah, here's one now."

"Don't be so obvious about it," Carrie warned in a heated whisper. "I don't want Mom to know."

Charlotte seemed oblivious to the undercurrents passing between him and Carrie, which was probably just as well. He'd let the kid get away with it this time, but he wasn't coming back for any repeat performances of this handyman routine.

"I should have this fixed in a couple of minutes," he said.

"Take your time," Carrie told him. "No need to rush." She walked up behind Jason and whispered, "Give her a chance, will you?"

True to his word, it took Jason all of thirty seconds to make the necessary repair.

"The bathroom faucet's been leaking, hasn't it, Mom? Don't you think we should have him look at that, too, while he's here?"

Jason glanced at his watch and frowned. If the kid kept this up, he'd miss the start of the basketball game. But he decided he had little choice: pay now or pay later. He gave Carrie the lead she was hoping for. "Or it'll need fixing tomorrow, right?"

"Probably." There was a clear glint of warning in the fifteen-year-old's eyes.

Charlotte turned around and glanced from one to the other. Crossing her arms, she studied her daughter, then looked at Jason as if seeing him for the first time. Really seeing him. Apparently she didn't like what she saw.

"Is something going on here I don't know about?" she asked.

"What makes you say that?" Carrie said with wide-eyed innocence.

Jason had to hand it to the girl; she had the look down to an art form.

"Just answer the question, Caroline Marie."

The mother wasn't a slacker in "the look" department, either. She had eyes that would flash freeze a pot of boiling water.

The girl held her own for an admirable length of time

before caving in to the icy glare. She lifted her shoulders with an expressive sigh and said, "If you must know, I took the screw out of the faucet so we'd have to call Jason over here."

Once again Jason glanced at his watch, hoping to extract himself from their discussion. This was between mother and daughter—not mother, daughter and innocent bystander. He hadn't meant to let Charlotte in on her daughter's scheme, but neither was he willing to become a full-time pawn in Carrie's little games. No telling how many other repair projects the girl might turn up for him.

"Why would you want Dr. Manning here?" Charlotte asked with a frown.

"Because he's a good-looking man and he seems nice and I thought it would be great if you got to know each other."

It was time to make his move, Jason decided. "If you'll excuse me, I'll be leaving now."

"You purposely broke the faucet so we could call him down here?" Charlotte gestured toward Jason.

Carrie sent him an irritated look as though to suggest this was all his fault. "I wanted him to see you. For being thirty-five, you aren't half bad. Once he saw your potential, I was sure he'd ask you out on a date. I tried to talk him into it earlier, but—"

"You *what?*" Charlotte exploded. Color flashed into her cheeks like bright neon lights. Her eyes narrowed. "Tell me you didn't! *Please* tell me you didn't!"

Carrie snapped her mouth shut, about ten seconds too late to suit Jason.

"This is all a big joke, isn't it?" Charlotte turned to Jason for reassurance, which was a mistake, since he was glaring at Carrie, irritated with her for saying far more than necessary.

"I had to do something," Carrie cried, defending herself. "You need a man. I saw the look on your face when you were holding Kathy Crenshaw's baby. You've never said anything, but you want more children. You never date... I don't know what my father did to you, but you've shut yourself off and—and...I was just trying to help."

Charlotte stalked to the far side of the small kitchen. "I can't *believe* this. You actually asked a man to take me out?"

"I did more than ask. I offered him money!"

Charlotte whirled on Jason. "Just what kind of man are you? Agreeing to my daughter's plans... Why... you're detestable!"

Despite himself, Jason smiled, which was no doubt the worst thing he could have done. "So I've been told. Now if you'll both excuse me, I'll leave you to your discussion."

"What kind of man are you?" Charlotte demanded a second time, following him to the door, blocking his exit.

"Mom..."

"Go to your room, young lady. I'll deal with you later." She pointed the way, as if Carrie needed directions.

Jason hadn't imagined things would go like this,

and he did feel badly about it, but that didn't help. Charlotte Weston could think harshly of him if she wanted, but now Carrie was in trouble and Jason felt halfway responsible.

"She was just trying to do you a good turn," he said matter-of-factly. "Think of it as an early Mother's Day gift."

Two

With her daughter out of the room, Charlotte scowled at Jason Manning, angrier than she could ever remember being.

"You're…" She couldn't think of anything bad enough to call him.

"*Detestable* is a good word." He was practically laughing at her!

"Detestable," she repeated, clenching her fists. "I'll have you know I'm reporting you to…" The name of the government agency, any government agency, was beyond her.

"Children Protective Services," he supplied.

"Them, too." She jerked the apron from her waist and threw it on the floor. Surprised by her own action, Charlotte tried to steady herself. "According to the terms of our rental agreement, I'm giving you our two-weeks' notice as of this minute. I refuse to live near a man as…"

"Heinous," he offered, looking bored.

"Heinous as you," she stated emphatically. Then with an indignant tilt of her chin, she said as undramatically as she could manage, "Now kindly leave my home."

"As you wish." He opened the door and without a backward glance walked out of her apartment. He'd worn a cocky grin throughout, as if he found her tirade thoroughly amusing.

His attitude infuriated Charlotte. She followed him to the door and loudly turned the lock, hoping the sound of it would echo in his ears for a good long time.

When he'd gone, Charlotte discovered she was shaking so badly she needed to sit down. She sank onto a chair, her knees trembling.

"Mom?" A small voice drifted down from the hallway. "You weren't serious about us moving, were you?"

"You're darn right I'm serious. I'm so serious I'd prefer to live in our car than have anything to do with that…that…apartment manager!"

"But why?" Carrie's voice gained strength as she wandered from her bedroom to the living room, where Charlotte was seated. "Why are we moving?"

Charlotte had clearly failed as a mother. One more layer of guilt to add to all the others. "You mean you honestly don't know?"

"To punish me?" Carrie asked, her eyes brimming with unshed tears. "I'm really sorry, Mom. I didn't mean to embarrass you."

What Carrie had done was bad enough, but Jason Manning was an adult. He should've known better. True, her daughter had played a major role in all this, but Carrie was a child and didn't fully understand what she was suggesting. Her daughter had Charlotte's best interests at heart, misguided though she was.

Jason Manning, on the other hand, had planned to take advantage of them both.

"It isn't you I'm furious with, it's him." Charlotte pointed after Jason. To think a professional man would actually agree to such an idiotic scheme.

"Dr. Manning?"

"The man's a sleaze! Imagine, taking money from you—"

"He didn't."

Charlotte hesitated, the sick feeling in her stomach intensifying. "Of course he did," she argued, "otherwise he wouldn't have played out this ridiculous game with you."

"I was the one who took the screw out of the faucet, Mom. Jason Manning didn't know anything about it. When I asked him if he'd agree to take you out on a date, he refused. He was really nice about it and everything, but he didn't seem to think it was a good idea. That's when I offered him the babysitting money I've been saving, but he wouldn't take it."

A dizziness replaced Charlotte's nausea. Several of Jason's comments suddenly made sense, especially the hint of sarcasm she'd detected when he'd held up the missing screw. Yet he'd allowed her to rant at him, not even bothering to defend himself.

"But…"

"You really aren't going to make us move, are you?"

Charlotte closed her eyes and groaned. She'd had a rotten day at the office, but misplacing a file and getting yelled at in front of an important client didn't compare with the humiliation that had been awaiting her at home.

"I wonder how many fat grams there are in crow," she muttered under her breath.

"Fat grams in crow? Are you all right, Mom?"

"I'm going to be eating a huge serving of it," Charlotte grumbled, and she had the distinct feeling she wasn't going to enjoy the experience.

She gave herself an hour. Sixty minutes to calm her nerves, have dinner and wipe down the counters while Carrie loaded the dishwasher. Sixty minutes to figure out how she was going to take back her two-weeks' notice.

"You're going to talk to him, aren't you?" Carrie prodded her. "Right away."

Charlotte didn't need Carrie to identify *him*. They both had only one *him* on their minds.

"I'll talk to him."

"Thank heaven." Carrie sighed with relief.

"But when I finish with Jason Manning, you and I are going to sit down and have a serious discussion, young lady."

Some of the enthusiasm left Carrie's pretty blue eyes as she nodded reluctantly.

Charlotte would've preferred to delay the apology, but the longer she put it off, the more difficult it would become.

Her steps were hesitant as she approached Jason's apartment. For some reason, she chose to knock instead of pressing the doorbell.

When he didn't answer right away, she assumed, gratefully, that she'd been given a reprieve. Yet, at the same time, she hated letting the situation fester overnight. With reinforced determination, she knocked again.

"Hold your horses," Jason shouted from the other side of the door.

Charlotte took one step in retreat, squared her shoulders and drew in a deep breath. He opened the door. He looked preoccupied and revealed no emotion when he saw her.

"Hello," she said, hating how shaky she sounded. She paused long enough to clear her throat. "Would it be okay if I came inside?"

"Sure." He stepped aside to let her into his apartment. One glance told her he wasn't much of a housekeeper. A week's worth of newspapers were scattered across the carpet. Dirty dishes, presumably from his dinner, sat on the coffee table, along with the remote control, which he picked up. The TV was instantly muted. He walked over to the recliner and removed a pile of clothes, probably things he'd recently taken from the dryer.

"You can sit here," he said, indicating the recliner, his arms full of clothes.

Charlotte smiled and sat down.

"You want a beer?"

"Ah…sure." She didn't normally drink much, but if there was ever a time she needed to fortify her courage, it was now.

Her response seemed to surprise him. It certainly surprised her. He went into the kitchen, returning a moment later with a bottle and a glass. Apparently he found something he didn't like in the glass because he grabbed a dish towel from the stack of clothes he'd dumped on the floor and used it to rub the inside. When he'd finished, he raised the glass to the light for inspection.

"Don't worry about it. I prefer to drink my beer from the bottle."

He nodded, then sat down across from her, leaning back and resting his ankle on his knee. He seemed completely relaxed, as well he should. *He* wasn't the one who'd have to plead temporary insanity.

"It's about what happened earlier," she began, gripping the beer bottle with both hands. "I talked to Carrie and discovered you hadn't exactly, uh, fallen in with her scheme. I'm afraid I assumed you had."

"Don't worry about it. It was a simple misunderstanding."

"I know. Nevertheless…"

"I'll place an ad in the paper for the apartment tomorrow. Would it be okay if I started showing it right away?"

So, he was going to make this difficult after all. "That's another reason I'm here."

"You've changed your mind about moving?" he asked conversationally, his gaze slipping from her to the television screen and back. Charlotte, however, wasn't fooled. Like any other man, he would enjoy watching her squirm.

His eyes wandered back to the silent TV. He made a fist, then jerked his elbow back in a gesture of satisfaction. Obviously things were going well for whichever team he was rooting for—much better than they were for her.

"I'd prefer not to move… Carrie and I like living where we do. The area suits us and, well…to be honest, I spoke in anger." This was all she was willing to give. If he was vindictive enough to demand she vacate the apartment, then so be it. She wasn't going to beg.

"Fine, then." He shrugged. "You're a good tenant and I'd hate to lose you." His gaze didn't waver from the television.

"Who's playing?"

He seemed surprised by her question, as though she should know something so elementary. "The Lakers and the Denver Nuggets."

"Go ahead and turn up the sound if you want."

He frowned. "You don't mind?"

"Of course not. I interrupted your game. If I'd known you were watching it, I would've waited until it was over." She took a swig of beer so he'd realize she intended to be on her way shortly.

He reached for the remote control with an eagerness he didn't bother to disguise. He pushed the volume button, dropped his leg and scooted forward, immediately absorbed in the game.

Charlotte didn't know that much about sports. Generally they bored her, but perhaps that was because she didn't understand the rules. No one had ever taken the time to explain them to her. Football seemed absolutely senseless, and basketball hardly less so.

As far as she could tell, basketball involved a herd of impossibly tall men racing up and down a polished wooden floor, passing a ball back and forth until one of them forged ahead to the basket to try to score. It seemed that whenever the contest became interesting, the referees would blow their whistles and everything would come to a grinding halt. She couldn't understand why the referees chose to wear zebra-striped shirts, either, since it wasn't likely anyone would confuse the short, balding men with the players.

"Who's winning?" That was innocuous enough, she decided. Such a simple question wouldn't reveal the extent of her ignorance.

"For now, the Lakers. They're up by four, but the lead's been changing the entire game."

"Oh." She watched for several minutes, then asked what she considered to be another harmless question. "Why do some throws count for three points and others only two?"

The thoroughness of his response astonished her, prompting several more questions. By the time he'd answered them all, he must've been aware that she barely knew one end of the court from the other. But if he was shocked by her lack of knowledge, he didn't let it show.

Soon Charlotte found herself actually enjoying the game. Now that it made a bit more sense, she began to understand why Jason liked it so much. The score was tied a minute before halftime and when the Lakers scored at the buzzer to take the lead, Charlotte leapt to her feet and cheered.

Jason raised his eyebrows at her display of enthusiasm, which made Charlotte all the more self-conscious. Slowly she lowered herself back into the chair. "Sorry," she mumbled.

"Don't be. I just didn't expect you'd be the type to appreciate sports."

"Generally I'm not. This is the first time I've had any idea what was going on."

A patronizing smile flashed in and out of his eyes. But that one instant was enough. Charlotte recognized the look; she'd seen other men wear the same expression. Men seemed to assume that because they could change their own oil and hook up a TV by themselves, they were naturally superior to women. Charlotte had run into that attitude most of her life.

Since it was her duty to defend womankind, and because she'd been fortified with a beer, Charlotte jumped to her feet. "Don't get haughty with me, Jason Manning!" she said.

Trying to recover her dignity, she sat back down, tucking one leg beneath her. "You think just because you happen to know a few sports rules, men are superior to women."

"We are," he returned wholeheartedly, without the least bit of reservation.

Charlotte laughed. "At least you're honest. I'm sick of men who pay lip service to women, then go into the men's room and snicker behind our backs."

"I'm honest to a fault," Jason agreed. "I'm willing to snicker right in front of you."

"Somehow I don't find that much of a compliment."

"Hey, admit it. Men *are* superior, and if you haven't owned up to it by now, you should. Don't forget, God created us first."

"Give me a break," Charlotte said, rolling her eyes.

"All right. If you can, name one thing a woman does better than a man, other than having babies, which is a given."

"I'll improve on that. I'll name…several."

"Several? You won't be able to come up with one."

"Okay, then," Charlotte said, accepting his challenge. "Women are more sensitive than men. Really," she added when he snorted in response.

"Sure, you cry in movies. That negates your whole argument."

"I'm not talking about crying." She frowned at him. "I'm referring to feelings! Women aren't afraid to face their feelings. Men are so terrified of emotion they hold it inside until they're totally bent out of shape."

Jason laughed, although grudgingly. "I suppose you think women are smarter than men, too."

"No," she said sincerely. "I'd say we're about even in that department."

"Go on," he urged, as though he suspected she'd depleted her list.

"Another thing. Women are better at multitasking than men. We're used to juggling all kinds of responsibilities."

Jason snickered.

"I'm serious," she returned. "If you think about it, you'll realize it's true. Women are expected to help support the family financially. Not only that, we're *also* expected to assume the role of emotional caretaker. Responsibility for the family falls on the woman's shoulders, not the man's. Have you ever noticed how rarely men put the needs of others before their own?"

"'Needs,'" Jason echoed. "Good grief, what's *that?* Some pop-psych buzzword."

Charlotte ignored him. "Frankly, I feel sorry for you guys. You've been allowed to remain children most of your lives. You've never been given the chance to grow up."

Jason looked as though he wanted to argue with her, but couldn't come up with an adequate rebuttal.

"Women handle pain better than men, too." Charlotte was on a roll. "I've never seen a bigger baby in my life than a man who's got a minor case of the flu. Most of them act as though we should call in the World Health Organization."

"I suppose you're going to drag the horrors of giving

birth into this now—which, I'll remind you, is completely unfair."

"I don't need to. Men have a hard time just dealing with a simple cold. If God had left procreation up to the male of the species, humanity would've died out with Adam."

"That's three," Jason muttered ungraciously. "Three is not several. Three is a *few*."

Charlotte shook her head. "It's enough. You don't have a leg to stand on, but you're too proud to admit it, which is something else a woman's more capable of doing."

"What? Standing on one leg?"

"No, admitting she's wrong. Don't get me started on that one. It happens to be a personal peeve of mine."

"You mean the others weren't?"

"Not particularly. I was just listing a few of the more obvious facts, waiting for you to come up with even one logical defense—which you failed to do."

He didn't seem willing to agree, but it was apparent from the smile he ineffectively struggled to hide that he was aware of his dilemma. He had no option, no argument.

"You realize you've backed me into a corner, don't you? I don't have any choice but to agree with you, otherwise you'll brand me as being smug and insensitive, unaware of my feelings and too childish to accept the truth."

"I suppose you're right." If anyone was wearing a smug look, it was Charlotte. She felt triumphant, better than she had all day. All week. Come to think of it, she couldn't remember when she'd enjoyed herself more.

Conceding defeat, Jason moved into the kitchen and returned with a second cold beer for each of them. Charlotte hesitated. She'd never intended to stay this long, and Carrie might be concerned. After all the lectures she'd delivered about being gone longer than expected, Charlotte felt she should go home now. But, to her amazement, she discovered she didn't want to leave. Watching the rest of the Lakers game with Jason appealed to her a lot more.

"Thanks, anyway, but I should get back to Carrie," she said.

Although she smiled brightly, some of her reluctance must have shown because Jason said, "So soon?"

"I stayed much longer than I'd planned to."

"But the game's only half over."

"I know, but…"

"Why don't you call her?" Jason suggested, pointing toward the counter where he kept his phone.

It seemed like a reasonable idea. Charlotte smiled and headed for the kitchen. She punched out her number and waited. Carrie answered on the third ring.

"Oh, hi, Mom," she said in an unconcerned voice.

"I'm watching the Lakers game with Jason."

"Okay. We're not going to move, are we?"

"No, Jason was kind enough to let me withdraw my two-weeks' notice."

"Oh, good. He's a great guy, isn't he?"

"Yeah." Charlotte was surprised by how much she

meant it. Jason *was* a great guy. She hadn't stumbled on many in the past few—or was that several?—years. It was a treat to encounter a man who was candid, sincere and fun. But Charlotte had been fooled by men before, so she wasn't taking anything for granted.

"Well?" Jason asked when she replaced the receiver.

If she needed an excuse, he was handing her one on a platter. All she needed to do was make some vague reply about Carrie and she'd be on her way.

"Carrie says she'll call if she needs me."

"Excellent."

His smile was definitely charming, Charlotte decided.

"How about some popcorn?" he asked.

Charlotte nodded eagerly. She hadn't eaten much dinner, unnerved as she was by her discovery, knowing she'd need to confront him. Jason's offhand acceptance of her apology endeared him to her even more. If Jason was like her boss, he'd have flayed her alive. Instead, he'd just shrugged it off and given her a beer.

"Let me help," she said, following him into the kitchen.

"There's not much to do," he said, opening his microwave and tossing a bag inside. He set the timer, pushed a button and within a minute the sound of popping kernels filled the kitchen. The smell was heavenly.

When it was ready, Jason poured the popcorn into a large bowl and carried it out to the living room. Charlotte brought paper towels, since she couldn't find any napkins.

He placed the bowl in the middle of the coffee table and Charlotte joined him on the sofa. The game was about to resume. She tucked her feet beneath her as she'd done earlier, leaning forward now and then to scoop up some popcorn. It tasted wonderful, but that might've been because of the company. Or the fact that for the first time all day, she was feeling relaxed.

The Lakers scored twelve straight points and Charlotte rose to her knees, cheering loudly. Normally she was far more reserved, more in control of her emotions. It was as if someone else had taken charge of her mind. Someone more free-spirited and uninhibited. Someone who'd downed two beers on a near-empty stomach. Apparently, hearing that her daughter was bribing men to date her had that kind of effect on her.

Jason cheered, too, and they turned to smile at each other. Their eyes met and held for the longest time. Flustered and unnerved, Charlotte was the first to glance away.

She hadn't shared such an intense look with a man since college. A look that said, I'm enjoying myself. I'm attracted to you. I'd like to get to know you better...a whole lot better.

Her heart was thumping as she forced her attention back to the TV. She took a deep swallow of beer to hide her discomfort.

Jason went strangely quiet afterward, too. They both made a pretense of being involved in the game. As time went on, however, it wasn't the Lakers who held their attention—it was each other.

"So," Jason said abruptly, "where do you work?"

"Downtown, for a large insurance agency. You might've heard of them. Davidson and Krier. They have a radio commercial that's played a lot." In an effort, weak though it was, to disguise her uneasiness, she sang the all-too-familiar jingle.

"I have heard of them," Jason said, nodding. His rich baritone concluded the song.

They laughed self-consciously. Charlotte wished she'd had the sense to leave at halftime. No, she amended silently, that wasn't true. She was glad she'd stayed. If she regretted anything, it was that she was so clumsy when it came to dealing with male-female relationships.

Maybe it wasn't so strange that Carrie had tried to bribe someone to ask her on a date. Charlotte hadn't been out with a man in three years. But she hadn't really missed the dating scene. How could she miss something she'd never actually experienced? She'd hardly dated at all since Tom left.

Tom. The accustomed pain she felt whenever she thought of her ex-husband followed on the heels of the unexpected attraction she felt toward Jason. The two didn't mix well. One brought back the pain of the past and reminded her that she had no future. The other tempted her to believe she did.

"I should be going," she announced suddenly, her decision made. She scurried to her feet as if she had a pressing appointment.

"The game's not over," Jason said, frowning. He didn't move for a moment. "Don't go yet."

"I'll watch the rest of it at my place. Thanks so much for the wonderful evening. I enjoyed myself. Really, I did." She picked up the empty popcorn bowl and the two beer bottles and took them into the kitchen.

Jason trailed her, his hands buried deep in his pockets. He nodded at his garbage can, which was over-flowing. There was a semicircle of half-filled bags stacked around it.

"I've been meaning to take this out to the Dumpster," he explained, removing the bottles from her hands and throwing them into a plastic recycling bin.

"I appreciate how understanding you've been," Charlotte said as she walked to the door.

"About what?" he asked.

"Carrie and me and…everything."

"No problem," he said a few steps behind. He slipped in front of her and stood by the door.

Charlotte knew she was running away like a frightened rabbit. The trapped feeling had returned and it terrified her as it always had. She'd thought it would be different this time, but that had been the beer. Her fears would never change, never go away. They'd always be there to remind her of her shortcomings, how inadequate she was, how no man could ever be trusted. Tom had proved that. She was anxious to be on her way now, but Jason was blocking her only means of escape.

When she glanced up, some of the fear must have shown in her eyes because he hesitated, studying her.

There was a short silence, too deep to last long, but

too intense to ignore. Charlotte held his gaze for as long as she dared before looking away. His eyes were so blue, so serious, so filled with questions. She'd perplexed him, she knew, but she couldn't explain. *Wouldn't* explain.

They'd laughed and teased and joked. But Jason was somber now. Funny, this mood was as appealing as the lightheartedness she'd sensed in him earlier. His mouth, even when he wasn't smiling, was perfectly shaped. Everything about him was perfect. His high cheekbones, his wide brow and straight nose. Too perfect for her.

The paralyzing regret threatened to explode within her, but Charlotte managed to keep it in check. How, she wasn't sure. It must've been her fear, she decided. Fear of what could happen, the happiness a relationship with him could bring—and the disappointment that would inevitably come afterward. The disappointment he'd feel in her. Then it would be over almost before it had begun.

She looked up one last time, to say goodbye, to thank him, to escape.

In that instant she knew Jason was going to kiss her. But one word, the least bit of resistance, and he wouldn't go through with it. Charlotte was completely confident of that.

Need and curiosity overcame the anxiety, and she watched, mesmerized, as his mouth descended toward her own. His lips, so warm and seductive, barely touched hers.

Charlotte closed her eyes, trembling and afraid. Her

body, seemingly of its own accord, moved toward him, turning into his, seeking the security and the strength she felt in him.

He moaned softly and Charlotte did, too, slanting her head to one side, inviting him to deepen the kiss.

Yet Jason held back. The kiss was light. Sweet. More seductive than anything she'd ever known. It felt wonderful. So wonderful…

Charlotte didn't understand why he resisted kissing her completely, the way her body was begging him to. Restraining himself demanded obvious effort. She could tell by the rigid way he held himself, the way his hands curved over her shoulders, keeping her at bay. Keeping himself at bay.

Her head was full of the promise his lips had made and hadn't kept. Full of the possibilities. Full of the surprise and the wonder. She'd never felt like this before.

Once again his mouth brushed over hers, warm and exciting. Moving slowly—so slowly—and so easy, as though he had all the time in the world.

"Jason." It was a battle for her to breathe. Her heart sounded like a frantic drumbeat in her ears, drowning out coherent thought.

He tensed, then kissed her, really kissed her, wrapping himself around her, absorbing her in his size, his strength, his need.

They remained entwined, arms around each other, until Charlotte could no longer stand. She broke away and buried her head in his shoulder, her breathing heavy.

"Charlotte, I didn't mean to frighten you."

"You didn't." It was the truth; any fear she felt had nothing to do with him. "I have to go… Thank you. For everything."

But most of all for that kiss, she added silently. It was unlikely he'd ever know how much that single kiss had meant to her.

Three

He'd kissed her. He'd actually kissed Charlotte. An hour later, Jason still had trouble taking it in.

Oh, he'd kissed plenty of women in his day. But this time, with this woman, it was different. He didn't know how he understood that, but he did. He'd realized it long before he'd touched her. Perhaps because she was so different from what he'd assumed. He'd figured she was dignified, straitlaced, unapproachable. Then, as soon as he'd told her about basketball rules, she'd kicked off her shoes and was cheering as enthusiastically as he was himself. What a contrast he found in her. Prim and proper on the outside, a hellion waiting to break loose on the inside.

She intrigued him. Beguiled him.

At some point during their evening together—exactly when, he couldn't be sure—he'd felt an unfamiliar tug, a stirring deep within. The feeling hadn't gone away. If anything, it had intensified.

What they'd shared wasn't any ordinary kiss, either. Perhaps that explained it. They'd communicated on an entirely different level, one he'd never known before. It seemed their spirits—the deepest, innermost part of themselves—had somehow touched. He shook his head. He was getting fanciful.

No, this wasn't the kind of kiss he'd had with any other woman. He'd never gone so slowly, been so careful. Although she'd acted blatantly provocative, urging him to deepen the contact, he'd resisted. That same inner voice that had said Charlotte was different had also warned him to proceed with caution. He'd sensed how fragile she was, and the urge to protect her, even from himself, had been overwhelming.

Jason wasn't generally so philosophical. He didn't waste time deliberating on relationships or motivations. He wasn't sure what he was thinking right now. His reaction to Charlotte was unwarranted—wasn't it? Although it'd been a nice kiss, it wasn't so spectacular that his whole world should be turned upside down.

Yet it was—flipped over completely.

Jason felt almost giddy with sensation. These feelings weren't logical. It was as if God had decided to play a world-class trick on him.

Jason considered himself too old for romance. He didn't even know what romance was. Pure foolishness, he thought sarcastically. It was one of the primary reasons he'd never married, and never intended to. He wasn't a romantic kind of guy. A pizza and cold beer while watching a football game interested him far more than staring across a candlelit table at some woman and pretending to be overwhelmed by her beauty. Flattery and small talk weren't for him.

And yet...he remembered how good Charlotte's arms had felt around his neck. She'd held her body so tightly against his that he could feel her heart beat. It was a closeness that had transcended the physical.

By the time she'd left, Jason felt heady, as if he'd had too much to drink. He didn't understand her rush, either. He hadn't wanted her to leave and had tried to come up with a reason for her to stay. Any reason. But she'd quietly slipped out of his arms and left before he could think of a way to keep her there. If he was witty and romantic he might've thought of something. But he wasn't, so he'd been forced to let her go.

Jason started pacing, the Lakers game forgotten. He needed to clear the cobwebs from his head. He wasn't any good at analyzing situations like this. All he knew was that he'd enjoyed holding Charlotte in his arms, enjoyed kissing her, and he looked forward to doing it again.

He sank down in front of the television, surprised to find the basketball game already over. Stunned, he stared at the credits rolling down the screen. He didn't even know who won. He waited, hoping the camera would scan the scoreboard, but it didn't happen.

He had a bet riding on the outcome of the game. Nothing major, just a friendly wager between brothers. Nevertheless, high stakes or low, it wasn't like Jason Manning to be caught without a final score.

The phone rang and Jason hurried to the kitchen to answer it.

"Hello," he said absently, keeping his eye on the television, still hoping to learn the final outcome.

"I knew I never should've picked the Nuggets," Rich muttered.

"You mean the Lakers won?"

"By eight points. Where have *you* been all evening?"

"Home," Jason returned defensively. "I had company. A tenant stopped in to chat."

"During a play-off game, and you didn't get rid of them?"

Actually Jason hadn't intended to tell his brother even that much, but Rich had a point. Jason wasn't one to sit around and shoot the breeze when he could be watching a game. Any kind of game.

"It was business," he explained, unnecessarily annoyed. He felt mildly guilty for stretching the truth. Charlotte's original intent had been to apologize and tell him she'd changed her mind about moving. That was business. Staying the better part of two hours wasn't.

Ignoring Jason's bad mood, Rich chatted on, replaying the last half of the fourth quarter in which the Lakers had made an "amazing" comeback. While his brother was speaking, Jason glanced at the list of his tenants' phone numbers, which he kept by the phone for easy reference. The way his eyes immediately latched on to Charlotte's name, anyone might think it had been circled in red. He was so distracted by reading her name over and over in his mind that he missed most of what Rich was telling him.

When the conversation with his brother ended, Jason couldn't recall more than a few words of what they'd said. Just enough to regret that he hadn't been watching the game. Just enough to wish he'd thought of something that would've prompted Charlotte to stay.

Without a second's deliberation, he reached for his phone and dialed her number. Carrie answered before the first ring had been completed. She must not have recognized his voice, because she got Charlotte without comment.

"Hello."

"Hi," he said, feeling gauche. "The Lakers won."

"I know."

Apparently their kiss hadn't deranged her the way it had him. She must have gone back to her apartment, plunked herself down and watched the rest of the game, while he'd been walking around in a stupor for the past hour.

"I was thinking," Jason began, "about dinner tomorrow night. That is, if you're free."

"Dinner," she repeated as if this was a foreign concept. "What time?" she asked a moment later.

"Six."

"Sure."

His mood lightened. "Great, I'll pick you up then." He replaced the receiver and glanced around his kitchen, frustrated by how messy it was. He hated housework, hated having to pick up after himself, hated the everyday chores that made life so mundane. Every dish he owned was dirty, except the ones in his dishwasher, which were clean. It didn't make sense to reload it while there were clean dishes he could use in there.

Needing something to occupy his mind, he tackled the task of cleaning up the kitchen with unprecedented enthusiasm.

Jason's eagerness to see Charlotte again had waned by the following afternoon. A good night's sleep and a day at the clinic had sufficiently straightened out his brain. He'd behaved in a manner that was completely out of character. He couldn't even begin to figure out why.

Charlotte was a woman. There wasn't anything special about her. No reason he should be falling all over himself for the opportunity to take her out. He'd missed the last half of an important basketball game because his thoughts had become so tangled up with her. That would've been devotion enough for any woman in his life—only she wasn't in his life, and he intended to keep it that way.

Furthermore, Jason wasn't that keen on Charlotte's teenage daughter thinking he'd fallen in with her scheme. He could see it now. Carrie would give him a brilliant smile and a high-five when he arrived. The girl was bound to believe she was responsible for Jason asking Charlotte out. She might even try to slip him some of the money she'd offered him earlier. The whole thing had the potential for disaster written all over it.

If a convenient excuse to cancel this date had presented itself, Jason would've grabbed it with both hands.

The way his luck was going, they'd probably run into his parents, and his mother would start hounding him again about getting married. He'd never understood why women considered marriage so important. Frustrated, he'd asked his mother once, and her answer had confused him even more. She'd looked at him serenely without interrupting the task that occupied her hands and had casually said, "It's good to have a partner."

A partner! She'd made it sound like he needed a wife in order to compete in a mixed bowling league.

His parents weren't exactly throwing potential mates his way, but they'd let it be known that they were hoping he'd get married sometime soon. Jason, however, was intelligent enough not to become involved in a lifetime relationship just to satisfy his parents' wishes.

Whatever craziness had prompted him to ask Charlotte out to dinner had passed during the night. He'd awakened sane and in command of his usual common sense.

As the day went on he found himself actually dreading the date. The two of them had absolutely nothing in common. He'd go through with this, Jason decided grimly, because he was a man of his word. Since he told her he'd be there by six, he would be, but snow would fall at the equator before he gave in to an impulse like this again.

* * *

She was dressed completely wrong, Charlotte realized as soon as Jason arrived. Not knowing what to wear, she'd chosen a navy blue suit, not unlike the one she'd worn to the office. She'd attempted to dress it up a bit with a bright turquoise-and-pink scarf and a quarter-size silver pin of a colorful toucan. Jason arrived in jeans, sweatshirt and a baseball cap with a University of Washington Huskies logo on it.

"Hello," she said, forcing herself to smile. A hundred times in the last hour she'd regretted ever agreeing to this date. Jason had caught her off guard when he'd phoned. She hadn't known what to say. Hadn't had time to think of an excuse.

Now she was stuck, but judging by his expression, Jason didn't seem any more pleased than she was. He frowned at her until she was so self-conscious, she suggested changing clothes.

"Don't worry about it," he muttered, tucking the tips of his fingers into his back pockets. They definitely made a pair. He'd dressed like someone visiting the amusement park, and she looked like a student of Emily Post.

Charlotte was grateful that Carrie had gone to the library with a friend. The other mom was picking them up, but it would give Charlotte a convenient excuse to hurry home.

"Where would you like to eat?" Jason asked once they were outside the apartment.

"Wherever you want."

"Mexican food?" He didn't sound enthusiastic.

"Fine." Especially since there was a restaurant close by. "How about Mr. Tamales on Old Military Road?"

"Sure," he agreed easily enough. He was probably thinking the same thing she was. The sooner they got there, the sooner they'd be finished and could go back to their respective lives instead of dabbling in this nonsense.

For the short time they were together, Charlotte figured she might as well enjoy herself. The restaurant was little more than a greasy spoon, but the food had earned its excellent reputation.

The place apparently did a brisk business on week-nights because there was only one spot available.

"I never would've thought we'd need reservations," Jason said, looking as surprised as Charlotte.

The hostess, wearing an off-the-shoulder peasant blouse and black skirt, smiled and escorted them to the booth. The waitress followed close behind. She handed them each a menu shaped like a cactus and then brought water, tortilla chips and salsa. Charlotte read over the choices, made her selection and scooped up a jalapeño pepper with a chip.

"You aren't going to eat that, are you?" Jason asked, staring at her as if she'd pulled the pin activating a grenade.

Charlotte grinned. "Oh, that's another thing I forgot to mention last night—women can eat chili peppers better than a man."

"Not this time, sweetheart. I was weaned on hot peppers." He took one, poising it in front of his mouth.

"Me, too," she challenged.

They bit into the peppers simultaneously. The seeds and juice dribbled down Charlotte's chin and she grabbed a paper napkin, dabbing it against her skin.

"You weren't kidding," Jason said, obviously impressed.

"I never kid." A five-alarm fire was blazing in her mouth, but she smiled and reached casually for another chip and some water. The water intensified the burning, but she smiled cheerfully as though nothing was wrong.

"Rich and I used to eat these peppers right out of Dad's garden."

"I take it Rich is your brother?"

"I'm one of five," Jason went on to explain, and she noted that his eyes brightened with pride. "Paul's the oldest, then there's me, followed by Rich. My sisters, Taylor and Christy, round out the family."

"Are any of them married?"

"Everyone but me. I'm beginning to lose track of how many nieces and nephews I've got now, and there doesn't seem to be a lull yet."

Charlotte had never had much of a family. Her father had deserted her and her mother when Charlotte was too young to remember him. Then her mother had died just about the time Charlotte graduated from high school. The insurance money was set up to cover her college expenses. Only the money hadn't been used for her. Instead, Tom had been educated on her inheritance; he'd robbed her of even that.

Charlotte lowered her gaze. It hurt too much to think

about Tom and that bleak period of her life when she'd been so lost and vulnerable. So alone, with no family. Her ex-husband had used her and when he'd finished, he'd thrown her aside.

All the time she was growing up, Charlotte had dreamed about being part of a large, loving family. How she envied Jason his brothers and sisters.

"The story of my family tree is less about the roots," he said, grinning as he spoke, "than the sap."

Charlotte's laugh was spontaneous. She picked up her water, warmed by his wit and his willingness to laugh at himself. "I was an only child. I promised myself I'd have a houseful of kids when I got married so my children wouldn't grow up lonely."

"Lonely," Jason echoed. "I would have given anything for some peace and quiet. The girls were the worst."

"Somehow I guessed you'd complain about the women in your family."

"You know," he said, "I never thought I'd say this, but I really miss Taylor and Christy. They're both living in Montana now, raising their families. We get together when we can, which isn't nearly often enough. It's been over a year since we saw each other."

The waitress came for their order. Charlotte asked for the specialty salad, which consisted of beans, rice, cheese, shredded chicken, lettuce and slices of tomato and jalapeño peppers. Jason chose the chicken enchiladas.

"Do your brothers live in the Seattle area?"

Jason nodded. "Paul's a journalist and Rich works as an engineer for Boeing. We see each other frequently."

Their orders arrived and they chatted amicably over their meal. Jason sampled her salad and fed her a bite of his enchiladas; both were delicious. Soon they'd asked the waitress for two additional plates and were unabashedly sharing their meals.

It was only seven-thirty when they'd finished, even though they lingered over coffee. Charlotte couldn't remember time passing more quickly.

All day she'd been worried about this dinner—and for nothing. She'd enjoyed herself even more than she'd hoped, but that was easy to do with Jason. He didn't put on airs or pretend to be something he wasn't. Nor did he feign agreement with her; their differing opinions meant a free and interesting exchange of ideas.

"I should be heading home," Charlotte said, although she could happily have sat there talking. They weren't at a loss for topics, but the restaurant was busy and Carrie would be home soon.

"Yeah, I suppose we should go," he said reluctantly, standing. He left a generous tip and took the tab up to the counter.

After talking nonstop for nearly an hour, both were strangely quiet on the drive home. Charlotte had been determined to enjoy herself from the start, but she'd expected to make the best of a bad situation. Instead she'd had a wonderful time.

She hadn't known how starved she was for adult companionship, hadn't realized how empty she'd felt inside, how deep the void had become.

As they neared the apartment complex, she realized one more thing. She didn't want this evening to end.

"Would you like to come in for coffee?" she asked as he parked his car. For half the ride home, Charlotte had been engaging in a silent debate. She was sure that if Carrie was home, she'd make a big deal about Jason's presence. But Charlotte would get the third degree from her daughter anyway, so she decided it didn't matter if Jason came in.

"I could use another cup of coffee," Jason told her, although they'd both had large mugs at the restaurant.

As luck would have it, Carrie wasn't home yet. Charlotte had been counting on her teenage daughter to act as a buffer between her and Jason. She half suspected Jason was thinking the same thing.

"Carrie's at the library with a friend," she explained. "But I'm sure she'll be back any minute."

"I wondered what she was up to tonight."

"I'll put on the coffee," she said self-consciously, going directly to the kitchen. "Make yourself at home."

While she scooped up the grounds and poured water into the pot, she saw that Jason had lowered himself onto her sofa. He reached for a magazine and flipped through the pages, then set it back and reached for another. Since it was upside down, his attention was clearly elsewhere. He noted his mistake, righted the magazine, then placed it with the others. Apparently *Seventeen* magazine didn't interest him after all.

There was no reason for him to be so nervous. It was funny; they'd chatted like old friends at the restaurant, but the instant they were alone, they became uncomfortable with each other.

"I thought you might like some cookies," she said, as she carried the tray into the living room. She'd baked chocolate chip cookies that weekend, and there were plenty left over.

Being a single mother left her vulnerable to attacks of guilt—guilt that often led to an abundance of homemade cookies. There were so many things she didn't know about family, so much she'd missed out on. It bothered her more than she wanted to admit. Whenever Charlotte was feeling anxious or contrite about something, she baked. And with the ninth-grade dance hanging over her head, she'd been doing a lot of baking lately. The cookie jar was full. The freezer was packed, too. Even Carrie was complaining about all the goodies around the house. Too tempting, she said. Her daughter claimed Charlotte was trying to raise her cholesterol and kill her off.

More guilt, more need to bake cookies. It was a vicious circle.

"Homemade cookies," Jason said, sliding forward, far more appreciative than her daughter. "I didn't know anyone but my mother baked these days." He took one and downed it in two bites, nodding vigorously even before he'd finished chewing.

Charlotte smiled at the unspoken compliment and

poured their coffee in plain white china cups. "There's plenty more where those came from."

Jason helped himself to a second and then a third.

Charlotte was pleased that he seemed to value her culinary skills. "I guess it's true, then."

He cocked one eyebrow. "What?"

"Never mind," she muttered, sorry she'd brought up the subject.

"If you're thinking the way to a man's heart is through his stomach, forget it. Others before you have tried that route."

"Several dozen, no doubt," she teased, amused by his complete lack of modesty. Not to mention his arrogance.

"I've suffered my share of feminine wiles."

"Feminine wiles," Charlotte repeated, trying hard not to laugh out loud. He acted as though she was setting a trap for him. She was about to reassure him that she had no intention of remarrying, then decided against it. She'd let him assume whatever he wanted. After all, he was helping her get rid of these cookies before they overran the apartment.

She did bring up another topic, though, one she couldn't help being curious about. "Why aren't you married?" She hoped he wouldn't be offended by her directness; based on their previous conversations she didn't expect him to be.

Jason shrugged and swallowed the last bite of the last cookie she'd set out. He seemed to be thinking over his response as he picked up his coffee and relaxed against the back of the sofa. "I learned something recently about the differences between a man and a woman. It's information that's served me well."

They certainly had a routine going with this subject. "Oh, what's that?"

"Tell me, all kidding aside," he said, his blue eyes serious, "what is it women want from a man?"

Charlotte thought about that for a moment. "To be loved."

He nodded approvingly.

"To be needed and respected."

"Exactly." He grinned, clearly pleased by her answer.

He was making this easy, and Charlotte warmed to her ideas. "A woman longs to be held, of course, but more than that, she wants to be treasured, appreciated."

"Perfect," Jason said, smiling benignly. "Now ask me what a man wants."

"All right," she said, crossing her legs, holding the saucer with one hand, her cup in the other. "What is it a man wants?"

"Tickets to the World Series," Jason returned without a pause.

Charlotte nearly choked on her laughter. Fortunately she wasn't swallowing a sip of coffee at the time. "I see what you mean," she said after she'd composed herself. "There does seem to be a basic, shall we say, disconnect here."

He nodded. "It was when Rich gave up two tickets for a Seahawks football game that I knew he'd fallen in love."

"That's sweet," Charlotte said with a sigh, enjoying the romance of it all.

"Don't go all soft on me. It wasn't like it sounds. He gave the tickets to a friend as a bribe. Rich didn't want to date Jamie himself, he wanted someone else to fall in love with her."

"He bribed another guy to take her out?"

"Yup. He was in love with her himself, but like the rest of us, he's useless when it comes to romance. I figured it out before he did, and I know next to nothing about that kind of stuff." Jason grinned. "From that point on, it was all downhill for Rich. He's married and has a couple of kids now. A girl and a boy."

"I don't care what you say. That's sweet."

"Perhaps."

Charlotte was relaxed now. She removed her shoes and propped her feet on the coffee table, crossing her legs at the ankles. "Have *you* ever been in love?" At Jason's hesitation, she hurried to add, "I shouldn't have asked that."

"I don't mind, if you won't take offense at my answer—which is, I don't know. I thought I was once, several years back, but in retrospect I'm not sure. It hurt when we broke up, and I was sorry we hadn't been able to work things out, but I don't have any real regrets."

"What was her name?"

"Julie. She's married now."

Charlotte didn't understand where she found the courage, but she reached forward and brushed her index finger down the side of Jason's face. She wanted to ease the pain she read in his expression, the pain he discounted so casually. A pain she recognized, since she'd walked through this valley herself, with the cold wind of despair howling at her back.

Jason's gaze met hers and she felt immersed in a look so warm, so intense, that her breath caught. She couldn't remember a man ever looking at her that way, as though he wasn't sure she was even real. As if he was afraid she'd vanish if he touched her.

Jason removed the cup and saucer from her hands and set them on the tray next to the empty plate.

He was going to kiss her; she realized it in the same moment she owned up to how much she wanted him to. All night she'd been looking forward to having him do exactly this, only she hadn't been willing to admit it.

His mouth was gentle and sweet with the taste of coffee and chocolate. He kissed her the way he had the night before, and Charlotte could barely take in the sensation that overwhelmed her. She'd never thought she'd feel anything so profound, so exciting, again. She hadn't believed she was capable of such a rush of feeling....

She whimpered and wrapped her arms around his neck, holding on to him in a world that had started to spin out of control. His hands framed her face and he slanted his mouth over hers, answering her need with his own.

Jason kissed her again and again.

The sound coming from the front door barely registered in her passion-drugged brain.

"Mom...Jason..." was followed by a shocked pause, then, "Wow, this is great."

Charlotte broke away from Jason and leapt to her feet.

"Gee, Mom, there's no need to get embarrassed. People kiss all the time." Carrie floated across the carpet, then threw herself into a chair. "So," she said, smiling broadly, "is there anything either of you want to tell me?"

"Like what?" Charlotte asked.

Carrie shrugged with utter nonchalance. "That you're getting married?"

Four

On his way back to his apartment, Jason had to admit that Charlotte's daughter possessed a knack for the unexpected. Arriving when she did was only the beginning; introducing the subject of marriage had nearly sent him into hysterics.

Him married? It was downright laughable.

Thinking about it, Jason realized Charlotte had brought up the subject herself, wanting to know why he hadn't married, asking him if he'd ever been in love. Typical women questions.

Perhaps mother and daughter were in cahoots, plotting his downfall. No, that was equally laughable.

Jason simply wasn't the marrying kind. Not because he was a womanizer or because he had anything against the opposite sex. He liked women…at times, enjoyed being with them…occasionally. Liked kissing them… definitely. But he relished his freedom too much to sacrifice it to commitment and responsibility.

No, he told himself resolutely, Charlotte wasn't involved in any scheme to drag him to the altar. She'd been so embarrassed and flustered by Carrie's suggestion, her face had gone bright red. The woman's face was too open to hide her feelings. She had chastised Carrie, asked for and received an apology, and looked genuinely grateful when Jason said it was time he left.

Despite the episode with Carrie, Jason had thoroughly enjoyed his evening with Charlotte. He hadn't expected to. In fact he'd originally regretted having asked her out, but in the end their date had been a pleasant success.

Once again he was bewildered by the strong desire he experienced when he kissed her. He had ordained a hands-off policy for the night, but had shelved that idea the minute she'd sat next to him, gazing up at him with those pretty eyes of hers.

Actually, he'd known he was in trouble when he accepted her invitation to come inside for coffee. He'd thought of it as a challenge; he'd wanted to see how far he could push his determination. Not far, he concluded. When she'd looked at him, her eyes soft and inviting, he was lost. His hands-off policy had quickly become a hands-on experiment.

There was something about Charlotte Weston that got to him. Really got to him.

All that outward confidence she worked so hard to display hadn't fooled him. Beneath a paper-thin veneer, she was vulnerable. Any fool with two functional brain cells would have figured that out on the first date.

Only she didn't date.

Carrie had told him it'd been years since her mother had even gone out with a man. Undoubtedly she'd been asked—and if she hadn't been, why not? She was attractive, intelligent and fun. Offhand, he knew a half-dozen men who'd jump at the chance to meet a woman like Charlotte.

If she'd turned down offers, and surely she had, then there must be a reason. The question that confused Jason was: If she didn't date, then why had she agreed to have dinner with him?

Probably the same reason that had goaded him to ask, Jason concluded. The kiss. That infamous first kiss. It had rocked them both. Taken them by surprise, leaving them excited—and unsure.

As for the other questions that hounded him, Jason didn't have any answers. Nor did he understand everything that was happening between him and Charlotte. One thing he did know—and it terrified him the most—was that they were, in effect, playing with lighted sticks of dynamite, tossing them back and forth. The attraction between them was that explosive. That dangerous.

Carrie's arrival had been more timely than she'd realized.

All right, Jason was willing to own up, albeit grudgingly, that he was fascinated with Charlotte. He suspected she'd confess to feeling the same thing. To his way of thinking, if they were so strongly attracted to each other, they should both be prepared to do something about it.

In other words, they should stop fighting the inevitable and make love. That would get it out of their system—he hoped.

Naw, Jason mused darkly. Charlotte wasn't the kind of woman who'd indulge in an affair. She might wear only straight, dark business suits to work, but deep down she was the romantic type, which made her impractical. Most women seemed to be. If they were going to make love, they wanted it prettied up with a bunch of flowery words, a declaration of undying love and promises of commitment.

Well, Charlotte, along with every other woman, could forget that, he told himself. As far as he was concerned, romance and commitment were out of the question.

What he wanted in this relationship was honesty. If it were up to him, he'd suggest they do away with the formalities, admit what they wanted and then scratch that itch.

He mulled that over for a few minutes, knowing it was unlikely that Charlotte would see the situation his way. He might not know her well, but Jason readily acknowledged that she wasn't going to be satisfied with so little. Women tended to see lovemaking as more than just the relief of a physical craving.

Well, he, for one, wasn't going to play that game. He liked Charlotte—how much he liked her surprised him—but he knew the rules. Either they dropped everything now, while they still could, or they continued driving each other insane. Sooner or later, one of them would have to give in.

Without a second's hesitation, Jason knew it would be him.

Charlotte affected him deep down. He couldn't bear the thought of hurting her or causing her one second of unhappiness. In the end he'd say all the words she wanted to hear, and he'd do the best job he could, because pleasing her would mean so much to him.

Then he'd get what he wanted; she'd make love to him willingly, with everything in her. He'd give her all he had, too. The problem was—and he knew it was inevitable—that before he'd quite figured out what was happening, they'd be talking about marriage, which was something he hadn't done since Julie.

Jason stopped right there. If he started thinking along those lines, everything would change. Soon Charlotte would be organizing his life, straightening up his apartment, making suggestions about little things he could do to improve his sorry lot. Women always saw his lot as sorry. He was happy living the way he was, but women couldn't accept that. They didn't believe a man could survive without them constantly fussing over him, dictating his life.

Bit by bit, Charlotte would dominate his world, eroding his independence until he was like every other married man he'd ever known—willing to change his ways for a wife. Picking up his socks, getting hassled about sports games on TV, the whole deal.

No, the domesticated life wasn't for him. Still, Charlotte tempted him more than anyone else had in ages, and he could *almost* imagine their lives together. Not quite, but almost.

He stared at his apartment door, wondering how long he'd been standing there mulling over his thoughts. He was light years ahead of himself, he realized. Good grief, he was already trying to finagle his way out of marrying her and they'd only gone out on one date. He'd only kissed her twice.

But, oh, those kisses…

Like he'd told himself before, they were playing with explosives, and the best way to avoid getting hurt was to get out now, before they became too involved. Before he lost the strength to walk away from her.

"Aren't you going to *do* something?" Carrie demanded.

"About what?" Charlotte returned calmly, feigning ignorance. She glanced up from her novel, looking over the rims of her reading glasses with practiced innocence.

"Jason!" Carrie cried. "You haven't heard from him in a whole week."

"Has it been that long?" Seven days, two hours and three minutes, but who was counting? Certainly not her.

"Mom," Carrie insisted, hands on her hips, "you know how long it's been. You jump every time the phone rings. You keep making excuses about checking the mail and getting the newspaper. We both know you're hoping to run into Jason."

It hurt Charlotte's pride to learn she'd been so obvious.

"You like him, don't you?" Carrie asked. Her expression said that if *she* were in charge, this romance would be making far greater progress. Charlotte, however, had no intention of letting her daughter take control of her relationship with Jason Manning.

"I think Jason's wonderful," Charlotte admitted softly. She did like her landlord. Yet, at the same time, she was grateful he hadn't taken the initiative and contacted her again. If he had, she wasn't sure how she would've responded.

"If you're so crazy about him, then do something about it," Carrie said again.

"Like what?" Even if Charlotte had a drawerful of ideas, she doubted she'd ever find the courage to use any of them. She didn't know how to chase after a man and had no interest in doing so.

"You're asking me?" Carrie asked. "C'mon, who's the kid here?" She launched herself onto the cushion beside Charlotte. "What went wrong?" she asked, looking up at her mother with mournful eyes. "The two of you seemed to be getting along really well when I walked in last week."

Charlotte slid her arm around Carrie's shoulders. Despite her efforts not to, she grinned, remembering when she, too, had been so wise and confident.

"It might've had something to do with the subject of marriage—which *you* brought up. He seemed to get a bit green around the gills at that point."

"You think it frightened him off?" Carrie asked anxiously.

Charlotte shrugged. She'd brought up the subject herself, not quite as directly, but she *had* mentioned it. If ever there was a born bachelor, she decided, it was Jason Manning. Together, mother and daughter had managed to terrify the man. He must think they were sitting in their apartment ready to ambush him, tie him up and drag him in front of the closest preacher.

Charlotte wasn't sure what she wanted anymore. Perhaps she was protecting her ego by convincing herself that she wouldn't have gone out with Jason if he'd asked again. Perhaps it was just her pride. Charlotte didn't know because the opportunity hadn't come up.

She was embarrassed to admit it, but what Carrie had said about her hanging around the mailbox hoping to *accidentally* run into Jason was true. But she wasn't looking for a way to get him to ask her out, she told herself. She only wanted to set things straight. Since they hadn't met, accidentally or otherwise, Charlotte was content to let it drop. He apparently was, too.

Jason Manning had been a brief but pleasant interlude in her—she had to acknowledge it—humdrum life.

She was grateful for their time together. He'd taught her everything she needed to know about basketball. He'd challenged her in a battle of wits about male and female roles in society. Convinced her never again to eat a jalapeño pepper to prove a point. And most important, he'd kissed her in a way that made her believe, for those few minutes, that she was whole and desirable. It'd felt so good to surrender her fears and her doubts. If nothing else, she'd always be grateful for that.

"Maybe he's waiting to hear from you," Carrie said next. "It's your turn to ask him out, isn't it?"

"It doesn't work that way with adults, sweetie." Although Charlotte had no idea if that was even true.

"Then it should. I'm not going to sit home and wait for a man to call me. If I like him, I'll phone him. It's ridiculous to be a slave to such an outdated tradition."

Charlotte agreed with her daughter, but in this instance she planned to do nothing at all. And that included hovering around the mailboxes.

It had been a long day, and Jason was tired when he pulled into the parking lot outside his apartment complex. He scanned the limited spaces, looking for Charlotte's car. The blue PT Cruiser was in the appropriate slot, so he knew she was home.

It wasn't that he was trying to run into her, but he wouldn't mind seeing her, finding out how she was doing—that sort of thing. He didn't intend anything more than a wave and maybe a friendly "I'm fine how are-you?" exchange. Then he'd go about his business and she could go about hers.

Not calling Charlotte was proving to be more difficult than he'd ever expected. He thought about her even more now. He dreamed about her. Just that morning, the alarm had gone off and he was lying there in bed, trying to force himself to get up, when Charlotte casually sauntered into his mind. He couldn't help thinking how good it would feel to have her there beside him, how soft her body would feel next to his. He'd banished the thought immediately, angry about indulging in such a fantasy.

It had started the night before. When he'd arrived home from work, he'd found himself checking out the rear tire of Charlotte's car. From a distance it looked like it might be low on air. On closer examination, he realized it wasn't. He felt almost disappointed not to have an excuse to speak to her.

This evening he could tell from a distance that there wasn't anything wrong with her tires. Once again he wished there was, so he could talk to her.

Inside his apartment, he reached for the remote control and automatically turned on the television. The six-thirty news crew made for excellent company.

As the forecaster gave dire warnings about the weather, Jason checked out the meager contents of his refrigerator. One of these days he'd have to break down and buy groceries.

As he suspected, nothing interesting presented itself, at least nothing he'd seriously consider eating. An empty cardboard carton from a six-pack of beer. A can of half-eaten pork and beans. A leftover taco, probably harder than cement, wrapped in a napkin, and a jar of green olives. He opened the jar, stuck his hand inside and fished out the last two, returning the container of liquid to the shelf. Chewing on the olives, he closed the door.

What he was really in the mood for was—he hated to admit it. What he'd really like was chocolate chip cookies. Well, he could forget that. The store-bought ones tasted like lumpy paste, and his mother would keep him on the phone with an endless list of questions if he were to call her and request a batch. Besides, it wasn't his mother's recipe he craved. It was Charlotte's.

Well, you can forget that, ol' boy.

A box of macaroni and cheese was the most interesting prospect his cupboard had to offer. He took it out and checked the freezer compartment of the refrigerator and brought out two frozen wieners wrapped in aluminum foil.

He was adding water to a pan when there was a frantic knocking on his door. Whoever it was pounded again before he had time to cross the apartment.

He saw Charlotte, pale and stricken, her lavender cardigan covered in blood. Her eyes were panicky. "A dog...someone ran over a dog...they didn't even stop. Please...can you come?"

"Of course." He kept a black bag at the house for just such emergencies. He grabbed that and hurried after her.

Charlotte was waiting for him, her eyes bright with tears. "He's unconscious."

"You moved him?"

"Only to get him out of the street."

"Did you see it happen?" he asked, trotting along behind her.

"No. I heard tires screech and a yelp, and that was

it. By the time I got outside, a few kids had gathered around, but no one knew what to do."

Her pace slowed as they approached the injured animal. A group of neighborhood children had gathered around. Jason knelt beside the small, black dog. He was a mixed breed, mostly spaniel, Jason guessed. He was badly hurt and in shock. Probably a stray, since he wasn't wearing a collar, and the poor thing looked mangy and thin.

"Does anyone know who he belongs to?" Jason asked.

"I don't think he belongs to anyone," a boy on a bicycle answered. "He's been around the last couple of days. I never saw him before that."

"I'm going to take him to my office," Jason said after a preliminary examination. He didn't feel too positive about the dog's chances.

"Is he going to live?" Charlotte alone voiced the question, but she seemed to be the spokesperson for the small gathering—each one wanted, indeed needed, to know. The children and Charlotte stared down at Jason, waiting for his response.

"I'm not sure," Jason answered honestly. "He's got a broken leg and internal injuries."

"I'll pay for his medical expenses," Charlotte offered, using her index finger to wipe a tear from her eye.

Jason wasn't even thinking about the expenses. Frankly, he didn't think the dog would last the night. "Give me your sweater," he told Charlotte. Since it was already stained with blood, he figured they'd save time by using it to transport the injured dog.

She did as he asked, and he spread it out on the pavement, then placed the wounded dog on it. Jason carefully lifted him, using the sweater sleeves, and walked toward his car.

"I'll go with you," Charlotte said, while Jason placed the now-unconscious dog in the backseat.

"You're sure?" he asked. "This could take some time."

"I'm sure." Carrie came running up to the car. The girl had tears in her eyes, too. Mother and daughter briefly hugged before Carrie stepped away. She looked so mournful it was all Jason could do not to stop and reassure her. But he had no reassurances to offer.

His veterinary clinic was only a few blocks from the apartment complex. Charlotte followed him in. He set the injured dog on the stainless-steel examination table and turned on the lights above it. Charlotte's sweater was soaked with blood beyond the point of salvaging it, but she didn't seem concerned.

Jason examined the dog's injuries and it was as he'd feared: surgery would be required.

He told Charlotte and she nodded bravely. "Can I do anything? I'm not a nurse, but I'd like to assist—that is, if you think I'd be any help?"

Jason hesitated, uncertain, then decided. "You can if you really want to."

She nodded. "Please."

"You don't have to," he said. This wasn't going to be pretty and if she was the least bit squeamish, it would be better to sit out in the waiting room. He told her as much.

"I want to," she said confidently. "I can handle it."

Jason didn't take long to set up everything he needed for the surgery. They both scrubbed down and he gave her a green surgical cap and gown. He smiled at her before administering the anesthesia, taking pains to explain what he was doing and why.

The procedure didn't last more than an hour. When he'd finished, he transferred the dog to the hospital portion of his facility. There was a night-time staff member who'd watch over the spaniel and the other pets who required continuous care.

"What do you think?" she asked hopefully when he returned.

"It doesn't look promising," Jason told her. He didn't want to give her any false hopes or mislead her. "But he might surprise us. He's only a couple of years old and he's got a strong heart. The next twenty-four hours will be critical. If he survives until tomorrow night, then he should do okay. But he's going to need a lot of attention and love afterward."

"Carrie and I will make sure he gets it. Can we come see him?" She paused. "Do veterinary hospitals have visiting hours?"

"You can come anytime you like." He sighed and rubbed his hand along the back of his neck. He was tired and hungry.

"You were wonderful…." She seemed to sense his worry and exhaustion.

"Let's decide that in the morning."

"If Higgins lives, we'll owe everything to you."

"Higgins?"

"I thought it was a good name. Do you like it?"

He shrugged. He was too tired and too hungry to have much of an opinion on anything at the moment.

"You haven't had dinner, have you?" she surprised him by asking.

"No. How'd you know that?"

"You look hungry."

"That's because I am. You want to grab something?" he asked as if it were the most natural thing in the world.

She smiled. "Only this time I'll treat."

"Charlotte…"

"I insist. Please don't argue."

He didn't have the energy to protest, so he simply agreed. Since she was buying, he let her choose the restaurant. She decided on a nearby sandwich shop. He breathed in the scent of freshly baked bread as soon as he walked in the door.

It was the type of place where customers seated themselves and the silverware was wrapped in a red checkered napkin. The waitress, who looked all of sixteen, took their order, and promptly brought coffee. She came back a few minutes later with six-inch-high sandwiches, layered with sliced turkey, ham, roast beef, lettuce, tomato slices and onion.

"How have you been?" he asked casually after wolfing down the first half of his sandwich.

"Until the accident tonight I was just fine," Charlotte

told him, her eyes flitting away from his. "I don't know what came over me. I'm usually not so emotional, but seeing that poor little dog on the road bleeding and hurt like that really got to me."

"It gets to me, too." The sight of an innocent animal suffering never failed to disturb Jason, although he saw it time and time again. The helplessness of the situation, the complete disregard for life that a hit-and-run accident revealed, angered him.

"I'm so glad you were home," Charlotte said, keeping her gaze lowered. "I don't know what I would have done otherwise."

"I'm glad I was there, too." He reached across the table, taking her hand, linking their fingers. Her skin was smooth and soft, just the way he remembered.

His eyes sought hers. He smiled and she smiled back. Jason felt ridiculously, unreasonably pleased that they were together. For days he'd been fighting it, and now that they were together, he felt foolish for having put up such a struggle. He should quit worrying about the future, he told himself. Live for the moment. Wasn't that what all the self-help books said? One day at a time. One kiss at a time.

After what seemed like an eternity, Charlotte dragged her eyes from his.

"How about dessert?" he asked.

Charlotte picked up the menu and read over the limited selection.

"I was thinking more along the lines of homemade chocolate chip cookies," Jason said.

"They don't seem to have… Oh, you mean *mine?*" She raised eyes as blue as a summer sky.

He nodded enthusiastically. "I've reconsidered. It's true." His voice sounded slightly hoarse and, if he didn't know better, seductive.

"What is?"

"The way to my heart takes a direct route through my stomach."

"Oh." She blinked as if he'd caught her off guard. She was beautiful, he realized all over again. So gentle and caring. He'd missed her, yet he'd tried to convince himself otherwise, and had been doing a good job of it, too—too good, in fact.

The world seemed to stop. Jason knew his breathing did. He felt as if he were drowning in her eyes. He would've liked to blame it on how tired he was, but he'd only be lying to himself.

"You like softball?" he found himself asking next.

She nodded, obviously trying to keep her eyes averted from his. Apparently she was having a difficult time of it, because whenever their eyes met, it would be several moments before she looked away.

"I understand softball, more than basketball at any rate," she said, sounding slightly breathless.

"My brothers and I play on a team Saturday mornings. Do you and Carrie want to come and watch this weekend?"

Charlotte nodded.

"Good."

* * *

They were both silent on the way home. Jason knew he was going to kiss her again. He couldn't imagine *not* kissing her again.

Charlotte must have read his intentions, because her hand was on the car door the minute he shut off the engine. She reminded him of a trapped bird, eager to escape, and yet she didn't move.

His hand on her shoulder turned her toward him. His heart tripped wildly as she leaned toward him. He felt sure her heart was pounding as furiously as his.

Slowly, so slowly he wondered if he was dreaming it, Charlotte swayed closer. He lowered his mouth to hers. Jason wanted this kiss, wanted it more than he could remember wanting anything. It'd been over a week since he'd seen her and it felt like a lifetime. A thousand lifetimes.

Charlotte's hands were braced against his chest as he kissed her again, deeper, more fully. Again he kissed her, and again. Finally she broke away.

"Stop," she pleaded. The words were breathless and he could feel her shudder.

Reluctantly, Jason pulled back. Their eyes met again, and for the second time that night, Jason had the feeling she was frightened, although he didn't understand why. Wanting to comfort her, he traced a knuckle down the curve of her cheek.

"Carrie will be worried," she said.

He said nothing.

"I can't thank you enough. For saving Higgins. The dog."

Again Jason said nothing.

"Jason," she whispered. "Don't look at me like that."

"Like what?"

"Like you want to kiss me again."

"I do." He wasn't going to lie about it.

He saw that her hand was shaking as she opened the car door and climbed out. She seemed eager to make her escape now.

"Good night," she said with obvious false cheer.

"Little coward," Jason muttered under his breath, amused. "Saturday morning!" he shouted after her.

"What time?" She turned to face him again.

"Nine-thirty. Is that too early?"

"I'll be ready."

"I'll call you in the morning about Higgins."

"Please," she said, her eyes widening as though she'd momentarily forgotten the dog. "Oh, please do." She snapped open her purse and withdrew a business card, walking toward him now. "This is my number at the office. I'll be there after nine."

"Then I'll phone at nine."

"'Night."

"'Night," he echoed, returning to his apartment.

He wasn't there more than five minutes when his doorbell chimed. He certainly wasn't in the mood for company, but as the building owner and manager, he couldn't very well ignore a visitor.

He opened his door to discover Carrie standing on

the other side, a covered plastic bowl in her hand. "These are for you."

He accepted the container with a puzzled frown.

"Mom asked me to bring you some chocolate chip cookies," she said, grinning broadly.

Five

"Mom, you look fine."

"I don't look fine...I look wretched," Charlotte insisted, viewing her backside in the hallway mirror. She must've been mad to let Carrie talk her into buying jeans. Fashionably faded jeans, no less. Not only had she plunked down ninety bucks for the pair, they looked as if they'd spent the past ten years in someone's attic.

"You're acting like a little kid," Carrie said, slapping her hands against her sides in disgust. "We're going to a softball game, not the senior prom."

"Why didn't you tell me my thighs are so...round?" Charlotte cried in despair. "No woman wants to be seen in pants that make her legs look like hot dogs. I'm not going anywhere."

Carrie just rolled her eyes.

"Call Jason," Charlotte told her daughter. "Tell him...anything. Make up some excuse."

"You can't be serious."

"Please do as I say."

"Mom?"

"We're meeting his *family*," Charlotte cried. "I can't meet his brothers and sisters-in-law looking like this."

"Change clothes, then, if you're so self-conscious."

As though she had anything to change into. Charlotte's wardrobe was limited to business suits and sweatpants. There was no in-between. She couldn't afford to clothe both of them in expensive jeans. But after Jason had invited her out for today, she'd allowed Carrie to talk her into a shopping spree. Thank heaven for Visa. And thank heaven for Jason's generosity; he'd refused to accept any payment for the dog's care.

"I'm not calling Jason!" Carrie crossed her arms righteously. The girl had a streak of stubbornness a mile wide, and Charlotte had collided with it more than once.

Defeated, Charlotte muttered under her breath and fled to her room, sitting on the end of her bed. Before the shopping trip, she'd managed to put today's plans out of her mind and focus her attention on Higgins. Then the softball game had turned into the better part of a day, including a picnic, involving most of his family.

"Mom," Carrie said, approaching her carefully. "What's wrong?"

Charlotte shrugged, not sure how to explain her nervousness. "I wish I'd never agreed to this."

"But why?" Carrie wanted to know. "I've been looking forward to it all week. Just think of all the babysitting prospects. Jason's family is a potential gold mine for me." Carrie sat on the bed beside Charlotte. "We're going, aren't we?"

Charlotte nodded. She was overreacting, and she knew it. After shelling out ninety bucks she was wearing those jeans, no matter how they made her look.

"Good," Carrie said, leaping excitedly to her feet. "I've got the picnic basket packed. Honestly, Mom, we're bringing so much food, we could open a concession stand."

"I didn't want to run short." Charlotte didn't bother denying that she'd packed enough to feed Jason's entire family. A fruit-and-cheese plate, sandwiches, potato salad, a batch of chocolate chip cookies and a variety of other goodies she'd thrown in at the last minute.

Jason had casually mentioned the picnic the day before, when she'd gone to the hospital to visit Higgins. The dog was just beginning to respond to them. He was recovering slowly, but according to Jason, they'd be able to bring him home within a week. Charlotte soon discovered that visiting her new dog was a dual-edged sword. Every time she was at the veterinary hospital, she ran into Jason. Usually they had a cup of coffee together and talked; once he'd suggested dinner and Charlotte hadn't been able to dredge up a single excuse not to join him. He'd even taken her and Carrie to a movie. Now she was meeting his family, and it terrified her.

Ten minutes later, as Charlotte was rearranging their picnic basket to find room for a tablecloth and paper napkins, Jason arrived.

Carrie answered the door and directed him to the kitchen.

"Jason's here," she said unnecessarily.

"Hi." Charlotte greeted him nervously, turning around, a tense smile on her face. She was watching him carefully, wanting to read his expression when he saw her in the tight jeans.

"Hi, I was just—" He stopped abruptly, letting whatever he meant to say fade into nothingness. He stood before her, his mouth dangling open. Slowly his eyes widened.

With appreciation.

At least she thought it was appreciation. She prayed that was what it was, and not disgust or shock or any of the emotions she'd endured that morning.

"I…I've got everything ready." She rubbed her suddenly damp hands down her thighs. "Carrie says I've packed too much food, but I don't think so. I hope you like cantaloupe, because I just added one." She knew she was chattering aimlessly, but couldn't seem to stop.

"You look…fabulous."

"I do?" Charlotte hated how uncertain she sounded.

Jason nodded as though he wouldn't be able to take his eyes off her long enough to play ball, which had to be the nicest compliment he'd ever paid her.

"Carrie talked me into buying the jeans," she mumbled, tossing the napkins on top of the heap and closing the lid as far as it would go.

"Remind me to thank her."

He didn't say any more, just reached for the basket and brought it out to the car. Charlotte was so relieved, she wanted to weep with gratitude. Her spirits lifted— more than lifted—they soared as she and Carrie followed him. Carrie climbed in the backseat as Charlotte got in the front, hoping her jeans wouldn't split.

The ball field was several miles away, near the Southcenter shopping mall. Charlotte was grateful to Carrie for carrying the conversation. Thrilled with the outing, the girl had plenty to say.

Charlotte had never been to this park before, and when she saw it she was astonished she hadn't heard of it. It had several baseball diamonds, and an equal number of soccer fields. The Green River intersected the park, with several footbridges spanning its banks.

"I didn't mention I was bringing anyone," Jason told her after he'd parked the car. "Everyone's going to ask you a bunch of embarrassing questions. Do you mind?"

"No," she answered, having trouble meeting his eyes. "Don't worry about it." She was a big girl—she could deal with a bit of curiosity.

"I don't usually bring someone."

Charlotte stiffened, not because she was timid or dreaded the questions, but because it confirmed something she'd rather not deal with right then. Jason was attracted to her. As attracted as she was to him.

What did bring fear to her heart was that he might be taking their time together seriously—that he might really start to care for her. That would be disastrous.

You care for him, her heart reminded her. Yes, but that was different.

Kissing was all they'd done; it was all Charlotte had allowed. A few innocent kisses didn't amount to much. Or did they?

"Uncle Jase!" Two boys—Charlotte guessed they were seven or eight—raced across the green lawn toward Jason. One glance told her the pair were identical twins.

"Hello, boys," Jason said with a wide smile.

They stopped abruptly when they noticed Charlotte and Carrie, their eyes huge and questioning. Suspicious.

"These are my friends, Charlotte and Carrie," Jason said, motioning toward them.

"They're *girls,*" one of the pair muttered.

"I noticed that myself," a tall, athletic man said as he strode toward them. He was wearing the same uniform as Jason. Charlotte didn't need an introduction to know this was his brother.

"This is Paul, my oldest brother," Jason said, tucking a couple of baseball bats under his arm, along with his mitt. The task appeared to demand a great deal of attention.

In the next five minutes, Charlotte was introduced to Leah, Paul's wife, who was five months pregnant and chasing after a toddler named Kelsey. Jason's younger brother, Rich, his wife, Jamie, and their two children, Bethany and Jeremy, arrived shortly afterward, and there was another series of introductions.

Charlotte's head was spinning with all the names and faces. Everyone was friendly and helpful. Openly curious, too. Carrie, who loved children, was delighted when Rich's daughter wanted to sit in the bleachers with her.

The men were on the diamond warming up when Jamie sat next to Charlotte. Leah joined them, sitting on her other side. Charlotte smiled from one to the other. Their curiosity was almost visible. As the silence lengthened Charlotte frantically sorted through a number of possible topics, but try as she might, the most inventive thing she could think of was the weather.

Oh, what the heck, she decided. "I imagine you're curious about me," she said. After the morning she'd had, she wasn't up to a game of Twenty Questions.

"We didn't mean to be so blatant about it," Leah, the shorter of the two, murmured. She had one of the nicest smiles Charlotte had ever seen.

"You weren't," Charlotte lied.

"Yes, we were," Jamie said with a laugh. "We can't help it."

"Ask away," Charlotte invited.

"How long have you known Jason?" Rich's wife asked without hesitation.

Charlotte found Jamie Manning to be a study in contrasts. Rich, Jamie's husband, was probably one of the best-looking men she'd ever seen. Definitely *GQ* material. Yet, at first glance, his wife seemed rather plain. Charlotte soon learned how misleading first impressions could be. Five minutes with Jamie, and Charlotte was awed by her radiance. She had an inner glow that touched those around her.

"I met Jason about a year ago," Charlotte answered, when she realized both women were staring at her, waiting for her response. "My daughter and I live in one of his apartments."

"A year," Jamie repeated, leaning forward so she could exchange a wide-eyed look with Leah. "Did you hear that? He's known her a whole year."

Charlotte felt she should explain further. "Actually, I met him a year ago, but we've only recently started to, uh, know each other."

"I see." Once again it was Leah who spoke, wearing a subtle smile as though she was amused and trying to disguise it.

"You'll have to forgive us for acting so surprised, but Jason doesn't usually bring anyone with him on Saturdays," Leah elaborated.

"Or any other day for that matter," Jamie added.

"So I understand. I...I take it he doesn't date often?" Charlotte asked. In some ways she was hoping they'd tell her he went through women like water. But in her heart she knew it wasn't true. If anything, it was just the opposite. Charlotte didn't want to hear that, either, didn't want to know she was special, because it made everything so much more difficult.

"Let's put it this way," Jamie answered, crossing her legs and resting her elbows on her knees. "We've been coming out here for what, two, three summers now, and this is the first time Jason's ever brought a woman."

Charlotte drew in a slow, deep breath.

"I don't remember Jason bringing a woman to any family function, ever," Leah said, looking positively delighted. Her eyes sparkled. "I'd say it was about time, wouldn't you, Jamie?"

"About time, indeed," Leah's sister-in-law said with a grin.

From his position on the diamond, Jason could see his two sisters-in-law on either side of Charlotte. No doubt they were pumping her for information, wanting to know every minute detail of their relationship. The distance was too great for him to be able to read Charlotte's expression.

If he had half a brain, he would've realized what he was doing before he invited her to join him. Why had he asked Charlotte to this game? Clearly he needed his head examined. Only an idiot would thrust a lamb like Charlotte into a pack of hounds without warning.

He'd told her his family would probably be curious about her, but he'd said it casually in the parking lot after they'd arrived. It wasn't like he'd given her much advance warning.

His family was far too nosy. By the end of the afternoon, Charlotte would be so sick of answering questions, she'd never want to go out with him again.

He pitched the ball to Paul with enough force to make his oldest brother remove his mitt, shake his hand and cast Jason an odd look.

Jason was angry. But it wasn't the way Leah and

Jamie had surrounded Charlotte that had set him off. He'd had no business inviting Charlotte and Carrie to this game. For one thing, they were playing the league leaders and likely to be soundly defeated. If he was going to ask someone to come and watch him play ball, it should be against a team that'd make him look good, not like a bunch of fools. The outcome could prove to be downright embarrassing.

Not only were they likely to get their butts kicked, but Charlotte was going to spend the entire time being interrogated. First by Jamie and Leah, and then, when the game was over, by his brothers. They wouldn't be subtle about it, either. The first woman he'd cared about in years was going to come away thinking his family had been trained by the CIA.

Even now, Jason wasn't sure what had prompted him to ask Charlotte to come. But he certainly remembered the night he'd done it....

They'd been sitting in the car outside the apartment the night of Higgins's surgery. She'd been shaken by the accident, struggling to hide how much. He had known when he dropped her off that he was going to kiss her again. She'd known it, too. His lips had brushed hers. Lightly. Briefly. He had sensed she was still frightened—of him? Of their mutual passion? Of her own desires? Until she was at ease with him, he was content to proceed slowly. He'd never indulged in any kisses more sensual or seductive than those he'd shared with Charlotte.

He could tell she was a novice when it came to lovemaking. That surprised him because she'd been married. He'd never asked about her ex-husband, preferring to wait until she was comfortable enough to talk about it on her own. But from what Carrie had told him the day she'd come to his office, the marriage had been short and disastrous.

Jason was convinced Charlotte hadn't realized how much he enjoyed their kissing sessions. How much holding her satisfied him. How she left him feeling dizzy with need.

The same magic that had made him kiss her that night had encouraged him to risk inviting her to the ball game. Only now did he understand what he'd done. He'd dragged Charlotte into an impossible situation. Carrie, too. He was glad they were with him, but he wished he'd thought of some other way of introducing Charlotte and her daughter to his family. Some other time, when he'd be at her side to ward off their curiosity.

"Jase!" Rich's voice shot past his ear two seconds after a ball nearly creamed the side of his head.

Stunned, Jason took two steps backward.

"What's wrong with you?" Rich demanded furiously.

"You mean you don't know?" Paul shouted from the shortstop position. He looked pointedly toward the stands. "It seems to me that he's met his Waterloo."

After nearly getting his head knocked off by a fly ball, Jason focused his concentration on the game, which to his surprise wasn't going badly. Every now and then he could hear a high-pitched shout, which

---

100   *Debbie Macomber*

he'd like to think came from Charlotte. By the end of the seventh inning the score was tied.

Jason came to bat at the bottom of the ninth. The all-important ninth inning. The score remained tied and there were already two outs. Either he pulled off a hit or they were going into extra innings.

Charlotte was sitting in the stands almost directly behind him. He set the bat over his shoulder and eyed the pitcher. The first pitch was a fast ball and Jason swung, determined to hit it out of the field. More to the point, he was hoping not to be embarrassed in front of Charlotte.

He heard the cracking of the wood against the ball and he dropped the bat, then started running as though his life depended on making it to first base. It wasn't until he got there that he realized he'd hit a home run. He felt jubilant as he rounded the bases.

He cast his eyes toward the bleachers to find Charlotte on her feet, cheering and clapping. Her face was bright with excitement. In all his life, Jason had never felt such elation.

He crossed home plate and didn't stop. His brothers, his whole team, stared at him as he trotted behind the protective barrier between home plate and the viewing stands and headed straight for Charlotte. Excitedly, she launched herself into his arms.

Jason grabbed her around her waist, lifted her from the bleachers and swung her down. Her eyes shone with happiness and Jason thought he'd never seen a more beautiful woman.

Charlotte threw back her head and laughed. It wasn't for several minutes that Jason was even aware of the crowd that had gathered around them.

A bit self-conscious now, he lowered Charlotte to the ground, but kept his arm around her. Paul and Rich were the first to congratulate him, followed by several other teammates, who slapped him heartily on the back. One suggested Jason bring Charlotte again, since she was definitely his good-luck charm.

"You were wonderful," Charlotte said, smiling at him proudly. Jason found it difficult to pull his gaze away. The urge to kiss her was so strong, he had to fight to restrain himself. He would've done it, too, would've kissed her in front of everyone and ignored the consequences, if only his brothers hadn't been present. He held back more to protect Charlotte from embarrassment than to ward off any razzing he'd get from his family.

"I'm hungry," Ryan, one of the twins, announced once the excitement had died down. "When are we gonna eat?"

"Soon," Leah promised. Paul headed toward the parking lot.

"I'll be right back," Jason said and, without thinking, did the very thing he'd decided against. He kissed Charlotte briefly, before trailing after his brother to get the picnic basket in the trunk of his car.

Jason couldn't believe he'd done that. Neither could Charlotte, judging by the look of surprise that flashed in her blue eyes.

"Are you going to fess up?" Paul asked, holding a heavy cooler with both hands, studying Jason.

"To what?" he demanded, narrowing his eyes, hoping his brother would take the hint.

"Charlotte."

"What about her?"

"Don't go all defensive on me. I was just wondering how you met."

Jason relaxed a little. He was being too touchy. "She lives in the complex." He didn't think it would sound good if he admitted Carrie had offered him money to take her mother out.

"She seems nice."

"She is. Lay off her, though, will you?"

Paul's eyes went solemn, as if he was offended by Jason's remark. Then he nodded. "Whatever you want."

Paul must've said something to Rich, too, because when they sat down to eat, after pushing three picnic tables together, no one gave Charlotte more than a glance. It was as though she'd been part of the family for years. Which was just the way Jason wanted everyone to treat her. Heaven forbid she figure out how special she was to him. He'd already made a big enough fool of himself, simply by inviting her and Carrie to this outing.

Charlotte's daughter had won a few hearts all on her own, Jason saw, secretly pleased. Ryan and Ronnie had clamored to sit next to her at lunch, beating out Bethany, who cried with disappointment until Carrie agreed to hold the little girl on her lap.

"I think Carrie's made a conquest," Jason said to

Charlotte, munching on a chocolate chip cookie. His fourth, and he was ready for another.

"She loves children. She's the type of kid who'd prefer to be the oldest of ten."

Jason watched as a sadness, however brief, flashed in Charlotte's eyes. It told him she wasn't speaking only for Carrie, but herself, as well. She must've wanted so much more from her marriage than she'd gotten. He remembered something else then, something Carrie had told him about Charlotte wanting more children. At the time he'd decided to stay away. A woman with marriage and children on her mind was someone he planned to avoid. Strangely, the thought didn't terrify him nearly as much now.

Still, he had to admit that the fleeting look of pain got to him. He'd experienced the desire to protect her in the past, to guard her from hurt, but only when she was in his arms. Only when he feared *he* might hurt her. Now, the need to keep her safe burned in his chest. He wanted to block out anything that would cause her pain. Most of all, he wanted to meet the ex-husband who'd walked away from his family, and he'd prefer it be in a dark alley some night.

Although he didn't know any details of the divorce, Carrie had told him she never heard from her father. What kind of man would desert his family? What kind of man would turn a warm, vivacious woman like Charlotte into a near-recluse?

"I like your family," Charlotte said, smiling up at him, distracting him from his thoughts.

"Did Leah and Jamie bombard you with questions?"

"A few, but they're so nice, I didn't mind."

"What did you tell them?" Jason was eager to know, partially because it might clear up a few questions he had himself. Maybe Charlotte could put into perspective what he was feeling and was unable to define.

She laughed, causing the others to momentarily look their way. "Are you worried?"

"No." The question surprised him.

"For a moment there, you looked as if you were afraid I might've told them something you'd rather I didn't."

"You can tell them anything you want," he said decisively, meaning it. If she chose to imply that they were madly in love, then fine, he'd deal with it. On the other hand, if she'd chosen to let his family believe they'd only just met, which wasn't so far from the truth, then he'd live with that, too.

"I told them we're friends…special friends."

Jason approved. He couldn't have said it better.

"Uncle Jase," Ronnie shouted, clutching a Frisbee. "Are we ready to play?"

"Play?" Jason didn't need to be invited twice. His favorite part of these family get-togethers was the time after lunch that he spent with his nieces and nephews. Chasing after Ronnie and Ryan and a Frisbee kept him young at heart, he told himself. Though he didn't care to admit out loud just how much he liked running around with a pair of eight-year-olds. The boys enjoyed it, too, and before the afternoon was over Rich and Paul invariably joined in.

As they did now. The two brothers against Jason and a handful of youngsters in a game of Frisbee football. A few minutes into the competition, Jason dived to catch a wild throw, catapulting himself into the air and latching triumphantly on to the disk.

Ronnie and Ryan cheered, and Jason felt as pleased with his small feat as he'd been with the home run. After an hour, the two teams took a break. Breathless, he reached for a cold soda, pulled back the tab and guzzled it down.

He turned, looking for Charlotte. The last time he'd seen her she was with Leah and Jamie cleaning up the remains of their picnic. He saw her sitting on a blanket under a madrona tree, bouncing Jeremy on her knee. Bethany and Kelsey were sprawled out, napping, beside her. She was playing a game with the baby, nuzzling his neck and making cooing sounds. Her eyes radiated a happiness he'd never seen. A joy that transfixed him.

"Jason, are you in or out?"

Jason barely heard the words, his gaze on Charlotte.

"In," he decided, tossing the empty can in the garbage and heading back to the field. A couple of minutes later he was completely engrossed in the game. Carrie had sided with his brothers against him and was proving to be a worthy opponent. Ronnie caught the Frisbee and lobbed it to his twin. Jason glanced toward Charlotte again and saw her lift Jeremy above her head and laugh up at him.

Jason's heart constricted. Watching Charlotte with his brother's child did funny things to his chest. She was smiling, happy. A powerful emotion seized his heart in a way that was almost painful.

One pain was followed almost immediately by another as the Frisbee hit him hard. The wind momentarily knocked out of him, he doubled over.

"Uncle Jase!"

"Jason!"

Paul and Ronnie were the first to reach him.

"You all right?" Paul asked.

Jason's eyes moved toward Charlotte and he shook his head. "No," he muttered, "I don't think I am."

Six

So this was what it meant to be part of a family, Charlotte mused, as Jason drove her and Carrie home from the ball field. This profound sense of belonging, of acceptance. She'd never experienced anything like it before. It was as though Jason's family had known and loved her for years. As though they genuinely cared for her. Charlotte couldn't recall a time when she'd felt anything as uplifting as she had that afternoon.

After the game they'd gathered together for a picnic. Charlotte didn't think she'd ever laughed more. There'd been good-natured teasing, jokes, games. Even now, driving home, laughter echoed in her ears. The cousins were as close as brothers and sisters, the older ones watching out for the smaller children. They fought like brothers and sisters, too, mostly over Carrie, each wanting her attention.

Carrie had beamed, loving every minute of it.

After the initial round of questions, Leah and Jamie

had treated Charlotte like…well, like family. The women were obviously good friends, yet included Charlotte in all their conversations. Jason's brothers, too, had tried to make her feel comfortable. Neither Paul nor Rich had asked a single question about her relationship with Jason, probably content to have their wives fill in the gaps later.

"You're very quiet," Jason said, taking his eyes off the road for a second. "Anything wrong? My brothers didn't—"

"No," she assured him with a smile.

The only sound was the hum of the road. Carrie, usually filled with boundless energy, was exhausted after chasing the children around for most of the afternoon. She'd enjoyed herself as much as Charlotte had.

And perhaps her daughter was thinking the same thing Charlotte was—that she'd missed out on something important because they only had each other.

Jason parked the car, then carried the near-empty picnic basket into her kitchen. He hesitated after setting it on the counter. "You're *sure* nothing's wrong?"

Charlotte nodded. "Positive. I had a wonderful time. A fabulous time. Thank you for asking Carrie and me."

He didn't seem to believe her. "Did Leah and Jamie hound you with questions?" he asked for the second time that day, a pensive frown on his face.

"Jason," she murmured, resting her hands on his forearms and gazing up at him. "I meant it. Every word. This day with you and your brothers and their families was one of the happiest of my life. If I'm being introspective it's because...well, because I've never realized until now how much I've missed in life." Jason's questioning eyes sought hers, as if he wasn't sure he understood.

She managed to meet his eyes. She felt close to Jason just then, closer than she had to anyone, and that confused her. She was falling in love with this man and that was something she couldn't allow. Was it Jason she loved, or his family?

"Charlotte, look at me."

She ignored the request. "I was an only child, too," she told him, "like Carrie." She wanted to explain. "There were never outings that included aunts and uncles or cousins. This is a new experience for Carrie *and* me."

"Look at me," he said again, his voice low and commanding.

Slowly her gaze traveled the length of him, up his chest, over the width of his shoulders, to his eyes. She stared into them and felt a sudden sense of connection. It was a powerful sensation, powerful and exciting.

"Where's Carrie?" Jason asked, glancing over his shoulder.

"She's on the phone in her room. Why?"

"Because I'm going to kiss you."

Charlotte's heart tripped into double time. She was tempted to make some excuse, anything that would put an end to the craziness that overcame her with Jason, but she didn't trust her voice, let alone her heart.

Whatever she might've said was never meant to be.

Jason's kiss saw to that. He gathered her in his arms, and lowered his mouth to hers. His lips were there, warm and moist, reminding her of sunshine. The kiss was chaste, yet curiously sensual.

Of her own accord she deepened their kiss. Jason responded quickly.

He moaned, or perhaps it was her own voice making those soft sounds. She melted into him, her body responding instinctively, naturally, to his.

"Charlotte." He brought her even closer, and their kiss went on and on. She grew hot, and hotter, then hotter still…until…

"No more…" she cried, breaking away, panting. "Please…no more."

Jason trembled with restraint, closing his eyes. "You're right," he murmured. "Carrie's in the other room."

"Carrie," Charlotte repeated, grateful for the excuse.

Jason drew in several deep breaths, then said, "I should be leaving."

Charlotte nodded, but she didn't want him to go. Her body was on fire. She wondered if he was experiencing the same kind of torment himself—and if he was angry with her for sending him away.

"Would you like to come with me again next Saturday?" The question was offhanded, as though he'd just thought of it.

Charlotte's heart soared at the prospect. "If you're sure you want me."

Laughter leapt into his eyes, melding with the fire that was already there. "Trust me, Charlotte, I want you."

With that, he was out the door.

No sooner had Jason left than Carrie appeared in the kitchen. "Did Jason leave?"

Charlotte nodded, too preoccupied to answer outright. She was trembling, and all because of a few words. *He wanted her.* He'd been honest and forthright as she'd come to expect.

"Mom, we need to talk."

"Go ahead," Charlotte said, as she unloaded the picnic basket. There was surprisingly little food left over. Ryan and Ronnie had discovered her chocolate chip cookies, thanks to Jason, and the three dozen she'd brought had disappeared in no time. She'd set out the fresh fruit-and-cheese platter and that had disappeared, too. There were a couple of sandwiches still wrapped, but they'd keep for her and Carrie to eat the following day.

"It's about the ninth-grade dance," Carrie said stiffly from behind her.

Charlotte froze. This wasn't a subject she wanted to discuss, not again. "I've said everything I'm going to say about it, Carrie. The subject is closed."

"I hope you realize you're ruining my entire life," Carrie announced theatrically.

"Dropping you off at the dance and picking you up myself is a reasonable compromise, I think."

"Then you think wrong. I'd…rather walk to school

naked than have you drive me to the dance as if…as if there wasn't a single boy in the entire class who wanted to be seen with me."

She sighed. "I'll be happy to pick up Brad, too, if that'll help." That was more than she was really in favor of, but she supposed she could live with it.

"Then everyone will think I asked Brad to the dance. I mean, I know girls do that, but it's important to me that a certain girl find out that Brad asked *me*. How can you do this, Mom? Can't you see how important this is?" Her eyes were imploring, a look designed to melt any mother's heart.

Charlotte steeled herself. "You're too young, Carrie, and that's the end of it."

"You don't understand what you're doing to me!" Carried wailed.

"The subject is closed."

"Fine, ruin my life. See if I care." She stalked out of the kitchen, arms swinging.

With a heavy sigh, Charlotte watched her go. This argument was getting old. She'd been under the impression that her daughter had accepted her decision. But now it was apparent Carrie had only been regrouping, altering her tactics. Cool reason had evolved into implied guilt. Her fifteen-year-old made it sound as though Charlotte had done untold psychological damage by not letting her go on an actual date. Well, so be it, Charlotte decided. This issue was one she didn't intend to back down on any more than she already had.

Pulling out a kitchen chair, Charlotte sank tiredly into it, resting her face in her hands. She sighed again. She had trouble enough raising one child; she was insane to even contemplate having another.

A baby.

But she *did* want another child, so badly she ached with it. Holding Jeremy, Jamie and Rich's little boy, had stirred to life a craving buried deep within her heart. She attempted to push the desire away, rebury it, anything but acknowledge it. She'd had to repress this desire several times over the years.

A baby now was out of the question, she stubbornly reminded herself. She was too old; there were dangers for a woman on the other side of thirty-five. But age was the least of her concerns.

Getting pregnant required a man. Even more problematic, it required making love.

The sadness that weighed down Charlotte's heart felt impossible to carry alone. Tears blurred her eyes. If ever there was a man she could love, it was Jason Manning. But the thought of falling in love again terrified her. Charlotte was afraid of love. Afraid of all the feelings and desires Jason had stirred to life. He was wonderful. His family was wonderful. But it was a painful kind of wonderful, taunting her with all that was never meant to be in her life.

Charlotte had dealt with her share of problems. Finances. Isolation. Low self-esteem. Everything had been a struggle for her. She didn't know how to react to *wonderful*.

For the first time since her divorce, Charlotte felt the protective walls she'd erected around her heart being threatened. Those barriers were fortified by years of disappointment, years of resentment and pain. Now they seemed to be crumbling and all because of a man she'd never even seen without a baseball cap.

For now, Jason was attracted to her, but in her heart she believed his interest in her wouldn't last. It couldn't. The time was fast approaching when she wouldn't be able to put him off, and he'd know. That very afternoon, she'd seen the way he'd trembled in an effort to restrain himself. She'd watched as he'd closed his eyes and drawn in several deep breaths.

Soon kissing wouldn't be enough for him. Soon he'd discover how inadequate she was when it came to making love. She had never satisfied Tom, no matter how hard she'd tried. In the end he'd taunted her, claiming the day would come when she'd realize all the ugly things he'd said about her were true. She didn't have what it took to satisfy a man.

When Jason learned that, he'd start to make excuses not to see her again. He'd regret ever having met her, and worse, he'd regret having introduced her to his family.

She never should've accepted his invitation. It would make everything so much more awkward later....

The tears slipped from her eyes before she was aware she was crying. The soul-deep insecurity, awakened by the memories of her marriage, returned to haunt her.

The doubts, the fear and dread, were back, taking up residence in her mind.

Covering her face with her hands, Charlotte swallowed the sobs beginning to spill out in huge swells of emotion. In an effort to gain control, she held her breath so long her lungs ached.

She heard her ex-husband's words—*you aren't woman enough*—inflicting injury all over again until she covered her ears and closed her eyes, wanting to blot them out forever.

Why should Jason fall in love with her when the world was full of whole, sexual women who'd gladly satisfy his needs? Passionate women who'd blossom in his arms and sigh with pleasure and fulfillment. She was incapable of giving a man what he needed. Tom had repeatedly told her so. She was inept as a woman, inept at lovemaking.

"Mom," Carrie said coolly from behind her. "I'm going to Amanda's house." She waited as though she expected Charlotte to object.

Charlotte nodded, then stood and resumed unpacking the picnic basket, not wanting Carrie to see her tears. "Okay, honey. Just don't be late."

"I may never come home again," Carrie said dramatically.

"Dinner's at six."

"All right," Carrie muttered and walked out the door.

It wasn't until later, much later, while she was in bed finding it impossible to sleep, that Charlotte's thoughts returned to Jason. She'd allowed things to go further than she should have. It was a mistake. One she had to correct at the earliest possible moment. She must've been crazy to let their relationship reach this point.

Crazy or desperate? Charlotte didn't know which. It had all started weeks earlier when she'd held a friend's baby. Funny how she could remember the precise moment with such accuracy. The longing for a child had escalated within her, gaining momentum, refusing to be ignored. She'd gone home and wept and although the tears had finally dried, inside she hadn't stopped weeping.

Shortly after the incident with Kathy Crenshaw and her baby, Charlotte had met Jason. He'd kissed her that first night and it had been… She hadn't tensed or frozen up and that had given her hope. Her confidence continued to grow when he kissed her again and again; he'd always been gentle and undemanding. He was special that way, and she'd be forever grateful for the uncanny gift he had of understanding her needs.

But Jason was a man of raw sensuality. He wouldn't be satisfied with a few chaste kisses for much longer. He had no idea how terrified she was of him, of any man.

No, it was only a matter of time before the best thing that had happened to her in years came abruptly to an end.

On Sunday, Jason wasn't in the mood to cook. Microwave popcorn for dinner suited him better than a frozen entrée. He popped a batch and sat down in front of the television to watch a bowling tournament. Not his favorite sport, but there wasn't much to choose from.

When his phone rang, he stood on the sofa and reached across to grab it from the kitchen counter. He was half hoping it was Charlotte.

It wasn't.

"Jase, I don't suppose you've got Charlotte's phone number, do you?" Paul asked cordially enough, only Jason wasn't fooled. As the oldest, his brother sometimes got the notion that he needed to oversee family matters. That didn't include Charlotte, and Jason intended to make sure Paul understood that.

"Jase?"

Of course he had Charlotte's number. "Yeah. What do you want it for?" Suspicions multiplied in his brain. Being a newspaper reporter, Paul was used to getting information out of people.

"Don't get all bent out of shape, little brother. Leah and I want to go to a movie."

"So?"

"So, we'd like Carrie to babysit. She was a real hit with the boys yesterday. You don't mind, do you? The girl's a natural with kids."

"Of course I don't mind." The fact was, Jason felt downright pleased. If Paul and Leah wanted Carrie to babysit, then Charlotte would be at home alone. He could come up with an excuse—Higgins would do—and casually drop in on her.

They needed to talk, and the sooner the better, although it wasn't talking that interested him.

He tossed what remained of his popcorn in the garbage, brushed his teeth and shaved. He even slapped on some cologne. He wasn't accustomed to using anything more than aftershave, but this evening was an exception.

He was whistling when he'd finished, his spirits high.

On the pretense of asking about next Saturday's ball game, he phoned his brother to be certain Paul had managed to get hold of Carrie. He had. In fact, he'd be picking her up in the next half hour. Allowing ten minutes for Paul to whisk Carrie out of the apartment, that left him with forty minutes to kill.

Forty minutes would go fast, Jason mused, as he sat back down and turned on the TV. But his mind wasn't on the bowling match. A far more intriguing match was playing in his mind. One between Charlotte and him.

Tonight was the night, he decided, determined to take Charlotte beyond the kissing stage. He didn't mean to be calculating and devious about it… Well, yes, he did, Jason thought with a grin.

He'd be gentle with her, he promised himself. Patient and reassuring. For years he'd been treating terrified animals. One stubborn woman shouldn't be any more difficult. He had no intention of pressuring her into anything. Nor would he coerce her if she was at all uncomfortable. He'd lead into lovemaking naturally, spontaneously.

He glanced at his watch, eager now, and was disappointed to see that only ten minutes had passed. Half an hour wasn't *really* very long, but it seemed to feel that way to Jason.

"I'm leaving now, Mom," Carrie called out.

Charlotte walked out of the kitchen, drying her hands on a terry-cloth towel. She smiled at Paul, then looked at her daughter. "Do you know what time you'll be home?"

"Before ten. Don't worry, I know it's a school night."

"I'll have her back closer to nine," Paul assured Charlotte.

"Okay." She nodded. "Have fun."

"I will," Carrie said as they left, offering her first smile of the day. Actually, Charlotte had been talking to Paul, but she let it pass. Carrie was still upset about the school dance and had been cool toward Charlotte all afternoon.

Charlotte had just settled down with a book when there was a knock at the door. *Please, God, don't let it be Jason,* she prayed, but apparently God was occupied elsewhere. Just as she'd feared, she opened the door and came face to face with Jason, boyishly handsome in his baseball cap.

"Hi," he said, charming her with his smile. It wasn't fair that a man should be able to wreak such havoc on a woman's heart with a mere movement of the lips.

"Hello." She'd been dreading this moment all day. "I was going to phone you later." A slight exaggeration;

she'd been planning to delay calling for as long as possible.

"Oh?"

"Yes…I won't be able to go to the ball game with you next Saturday after all."

"Don't worry about it," he said, making himself comfortable on her sofa. He anchored his ankle on the opposite knee and grinned up at her. "There'll be plenty of other Saturdays. The summer is filled with Saturdays."

It was awkward for her to be standing, while he seemed completely at home. So Charlotte sat, too—as far away from him as she could while still being on the same sofa. She angled her legs sideways, her hands clasped. "I'm afraid I won't be able to make it any other Saturday, either."

A pause followed her announcement. "Why not?"

"I…I…" She couldn't look at him. "I don't think it's a good idea for us to see each other anymore."

"Uh-huh." He didn't reveal his reactions one way or another.

Emotion seemed to thicken the air. He might not be *saying* anything, but he was feeling it. Charlotte was, too.

"Is it something I said?"

She lowered her eyes farther and shook her head.

"Something I did?"

"No… Oh, please, Jason, just accept this. Don't make it any more difficult than it already is." Her voice, which had remained steady until then, cracked.

"Charlotte," Jason said, moving next to her with startling agility. "For heaven's sake, what's wrong?"

She covered her mouth with one hand and closed her eyes.

"I'm not leaving until you tell me," he said.

"I can't."

"Why can't you?"

"Because!" she cried, leaping to her feet. "Everything would've been all right if you hadn't been so...so nice." She was angry now, unreasonably angry, and not quite sure why.

Jason stood, too, his gaze holding hers. "I'm not sorry I kissed you. Nothing would make me regret that."

His words made it all so difficult. She wasn't sorry, either.

Her expression must have told him as much. He relaxed visibly and reached for her, gently holding her shoulders. Slowly, he drew her forward. Charlotte had no resistance left, and walked right into his embrace.

She sobbed once, then hid her face in his chest and wept openly.

Jason stroked her hair and whispered reassurances in her ear, as if she were a small child needing comforting. In some ways, she was exactly that.

After several minutes he lifted her face upward to meet his mouth. Over and over again he kissed her, lightly, softly, gently. Her breathing grew shallow.

"Jason..."

"Yes?" He raised his head, his eyes meeting hers.

"You're doing it again."

His mouth curved into a deliberate smile. "I know."

Her hands were against his chest when he sought her mouth again. He was still gentle, but the kisses changed in texture and intensity. Their lips were fused together, the heat between them burning so fierce, she thought it might scorch her. Charlotte found it difficult to breathe, but she didn't care. Breathing wasn't important. She held on, her hands clutching his upper arms.

Jason led her back to the sofa, and without protest, Charlotte followed. He sat down and brought her into his lap. He didn't give her the opportunity to protest before he directed her lips back to his. When her mouth opened in exultant welcome, he moaned. He kissed her again and again, until she was panting. Until her heart seemed to stop beating. Until there was nothing in her world but him.

His hands were opening the front of her blouse even before she realized his intent.

"Jason, no," she said in a panic. "Please, no."

"All right." Jason twisted around and turned off the light. The room dimmed and shadows danced across the walls. "Is this better?" he asked.

Charlotte clamped her eyes shut. "I...I'm not very good at this," she whispered, close to tears. "I'm not...sexy enough." The only thing that kept her from springing free of his hold was fear. It held her immobile.

"You're beautiful," he whispered. "Charlotte, do you hear me? You're perfect."

She buried her hands in his hair. His cap was gone,

but she didn't remember when he'd removed it. Or if he had. She sighed.

He kissed her again, his mouth hard and hungry. Charlotte understood his hunger, but she wasn't capable of satisfying it. "No," she whispered when she could.

"No?" How disappointed he sounded.

"No," she said a second time.

"You're sure of that?" he asked, sounding regretful.

"Y-yes."

He nodded, kissed her once more, then inhaled sharply. "I just wanted to check."

Seven

"Who told you that you aren't sexy?" Jason asked, relaxing on her sofa.

Charlotte's hands stilled as she poured coffee into two mugs.

How do you expect a man to get excited when his wife's such a cold fish? No wonder you're a failure at lovemaking. Are you sure you're even a woman?

Charlotte's heart reeled as Tom's words returned to haunt her. She'd laid to rest as much of his vindictiveness as she could, bound her wounds and gone on with her life. Pulling away the bandage, examining the damage now, just seemed pointless.

"Charlotte?" he probed gently.

"My ex-husband," she muttered.

"He's wrong, you know."

She nodded, rather than argue with Jason. For the moment he was infatuated with her, but his fascination wouldn't last, and eventually he'd feel the same way as Tom.

"You never mention your ex-husband."

"There's not much to say." She carried the two mugs into the living room. "Carrie was excited about baby-sitting Paul and Leah's children," she said, pointedly changing the subject.

Jason stood and took a cup from her hands, then sat next to her on the sofa, sliding his arm around her shoulders. His touch was warm against her chilled skin.

"You're perfect," he whispered and kissed her cheek. "You're lovely and sensuous and beautiful. Don't ever let anyone tell you differently. I'm not going to force you to discuss your marriage. Not now, but I want you to know I'll be ready to listen whenever you're ready to talk."

She smiled wanly, determined to steer the conversation away from the past.

Jason drank his coffee and left soon afterward, when it was apparent Charlotte wasn't in the mood to talk. She wasn't sure *what* her mood was, but she lacked the strength to analyze it.

Before leaving, Jason asked if she'd changed her mind again about the ball game on Saturday, and after a short hesitation, she nodded. Yes, she'd go, she told him. Jason smiled, obviously pleased, and headed out the door.

Something was happening to her, Charlotte thought, trembling. And it was happening against her will.

She'd made the decision earlier—she wasn't going to see him again. After careful deliberation she'd decided it was best to end everything now before one or both of them ended up hurt. It was a simple, cut-and-dried conclusion.

Yet…yet when she'd tried to talk to him about it,

regret and doubt had consumed her until she'd dissolved in tears and pain.

Heaven help her, she didn't want it to end! Jason must've sensed that because he hadn't appeared too concerned when she'd told him.

His confidence was well-founded. Within minutes, he'd broken through her resolve and was kissing her senseless. And Charlotte hadn't raised a single objection.

It was too late. Too late to walk away from him. Too late to go back to the way her life had been before Jason. She was trapped by her own weakness and would continue to be until Jason discovered the truth for himself.

Carrie arrived home soon afterward, full of tales about the twins and Kelsey. Seconds later, it seemed, she was in her room and on the phone. Her thoughts heavy, Charlotte appreciated the privacy.

It wasn't as though this was the first time Jason had kissed her. The impact he had on her senses wasn't startling or new. The man had the uncanny knack of stirring awake the part of her she'd thought had died the day Tom asked for a divorce.

She felt reborn, alive with hope. And yet she was more frightened than she'd ever been before. Everything was different with Jason. In his arms she experienced an excitement she'd never even known was possible. His tenderness, the loving gentle way in which he touched her, had given her cause to wonder, for the first time, if what Tom had said was true.

What if it wasn't? Could that be possible? With Jason she felt none of the dread she'd felt when Tom had kissed her. His lovemaking had always been so hurried, so raw, as if he were in a rush to complete the act so he could turn away from her. She couldn't imagine Jason being anything but compassionate and tender.

But what if all the things Tom had said *were* true? Her heart slowed with uneasiness. Jason Manning was an attractive, sensual man. A passionate man. And he'd expect—no, he'd need—a passionate woman.

Thinking of her years with Tom conjured up such ugly images in her mind. His taunts echoed like the constant sound of waves in a seashell, never stopping, never fading, always there to remind her of what a failure she was.

At ten, Charlotte turned out the lights, made sure Carrie was off the phone and went to bed. She should've guessed that sleep would escape her that night.

You're perfect, Jason had said.

Only she wasn't—Tom had made certain she knew as much. The need to weep welled up within her, tightening her throat.

She had loved Tom. She'd hated him.

He had stripped her of her pride when he left.

Her life had ended that day. Yet, in other ways, her life had begun.

She'd known for weeks, months, that Tom was involved with another woman, and she'd said nothing because she was afraid. Because she feared life alone.

Because she was willing to do whatever she could to save her marriage, even if that meant denying the truth. So she'd chosen to believe his lies.

When he'd forced her to face reality, he'd come at her in anger and guilt...and hate. She hadn't cried. Not a single tear, not even when the divorce was decreed final. It wasn't until years later that she gave herself permission to grieve for the marriage, the fantasy she'd built in her mind of what might have been.

In the beginning she'd been too numb with shock, too dazed by that last horrible scene, to experience any emotion. Gradually, as time passed, Charlotte began to feel again, a little at a time. It was like an anesthetic wearing off. As the years went by, as the numbness faded, she had to deal with the pain. A throbbing, savage pain.

Her grief came in waves. Regret struck first, reminding her of all the might-have-beens; one fantasy led to another. By now they would've had more children, she'd told herself. Tom would be established in his career and she'd be living the life she'd been cheated of as a child.

Anger followed regret. How could she have given her heart to a man who'd ravaged her self-respect? How could she have loved him when he'd treated her so poorly? But love him she had, so much that she still ached at losing the life she'd dreamed they'd share.

But mostly, as the years went on, Charlotte felt an overwhelming sense of guilt. She knew it was unreasonable. After all, it was Tom who'd cheated on her,

Tom who'd walked out on his family, abandoned his wife and child. It was Tom who'd forsaken their vows. Yet *she* was the one who accepted responsibility.

Sometimes the guilt was so overpowering, Charlotte found it intolerable. If she'd been a better wife, Tom wouldn't have sought another woman. He'd said so himself. If she'd been more enticing, more sexual, more attractive, more satisfying, he wouldn't have done it. She was too thin, too flat, too cold. The list was endless.

After years of telling herself that Tom had used her inadequacies as an excuse for adultery, years of struggling to repair her self-esteem, Charlotte gave up. Surrendered. She bought it all. The reassurances she tried to offer herself were empty. Null and void.

Everything Tom had said was true. She was a failure as a woman. A failure as a wife. No man would ever be satisfied with her. Not for long. Tom hadn't been and Jason wouldn't be, either. She might as well accept that now and stop fighting the inevitable.

The doorbell chimed just as Jason finished reading the latest issue of one of the veterinary periodicals he subscribed to.

"Yeah?" he said, opening the door, half expecting one of his tenants.

"Hi," Carrie said, striding purposefully into his apartment. "Have you got a minute to talk?"

"Sure." Jason led the way into the living room and sat down. Carrie started to pace in front of his television, hands behind her back. Walking in his apartment was dangerous with the week's worth of newspapers spread across the carpet.

"Is it Higgins?" he prompted, when she didn't speak right away.

She shook her head, eyes lighting up. "Higgins is doing great. He's eating and everything. I think he likes it with Mom and me."

"I'm sure he does." They'd lavished the dog with love and attention from the moment Jason had carried him into their apartment on Monday afternoon. One would've thought the mutt was some kind of hero. In a way he was, Jason decided. If it hadn't been for the dog, Jason didn't know how long it would have taken him and Charlotte to connect.

"What can I do for you?"

"It's Mom," Carrie said.

"What about your mother?" He saw that tears had pooled in Carrie's eyes, and she wasn't trying to hide the fact. Like most men, Jason was uncomfortable when a woman started to cry. No matter what the cause, he felt personally responsible. And he felt an overpowering urge to do whatever he could to rectify the problem.

He certainly felt that way with Charlotte—even more so. She'd look at him with her beautiful blue eyes and the instant he saw the slightest hint of tears, he'd be putty in her hands. He was putty in her hands, anyway, tears or not, but that was because it was Charlotte.

"My mother's ruining my life," Carrie was saying.

Jason was no psychiatrist, but he wasn't completely

obtuse. "Does this have something to do with that dance?"

Carrie nodded. "There's this boy…his name's Brad. He's the cutest boy in class and the star of the track team. Every girl in school's crazy about him and he asked *me*. Me," she emphasized again, bringing her hand to her heart. "He asked me to the ninth-grade dance. When I talked to Mom, she said I could go, but when I said Brad's father was picking us up and…and driving us there, she went totally weird on me."

"I'm sure your mother has a good reason for feeling the way she does."

"She won't even talk about it."

"Carrie, listen. I'd like to help, but this is between you and your mother. I can't interfere with a parenting decision."

Carrie nodded, her throat working as she struggled not to cry. "I don't expect you to interfere… I was hoping that you'd help me—tell me what to say to make Mom understand how old-fashioned she's being. I haven't said anything to Brad about my mom not wanting me to be in the same car as him and his dad and…and the dance is next Friday night. There isn't much time left."

Jason rubbed the side of his face. "What's your mother's primary objection?"

"She thinks driving with him makes it a real date. And I'm not allowed to *date* until next year."

"I see. What if she drove you and Brad to the dance?"

"That won't work, either…. Everyone will think I asked him and…it might be silly, but I want Suzie Jennings to know otherwise." She wiped her eyes and took a moment to regain her composure.

"How about if Brad's dad drops you off and your mother picks the two of you up after the dance?"

Carrie dropped her hands to her side. "Picks us up?" she repeated thoughtfully.

"It wouldn't be considered a date then, would it? The two of you obviously need to be driven to and from the dance and this would simply be a means of transporting you."

"There's a party at Amanda Emerich's house right afterward, but it's directly across the street from the school and everyone's invited."

"I have an even better idea," Jason said enthusiastically. At Carrie's blank stare, he explained. "How about if your mother offered to chaperone the dance?"

Judging by the look Carrie gave him, she didn't share his enthusiasm. "That wouldn't work because she'd need a date. Chaperones at our school dances are always couples."

"I'll go with her," Jason said casually. As soon as he made the suggestion, he wanted to jerk it back. Him dancing? The last dance he'd attended had been his sister's engagement party. He'd rented a tuxedo and been miserable most of the night. Before then, his only other experience on the dance floor had been as a high-school junior. He didn't know how to dance then and he hadn't learned since.

"You'd do that?" Carrie asked, her voice rising. For the first time since she'd entered his home, her eyes sparkled with hope.

"Ah..." Oh, what the heck, he'd do it if it would help the kid. "Sure," he answered. "I'd volunteer to be a chaperone."

Carrie let out a cry of glee and raced across the room to throw her arms around his neck.

"Your mother might not be willing—"

"She will," Carrie said confidently. "Mom's crazy about you."

"Yes, but will she be crazy about the idea of Brad's dad driving you there and the two of us taking you home?"

Carrie mulled that over for a moment. "Of course she will," she said, revealing no doubt. "Why shouldn't she be? It's a wonderful compromise. We'll both be satisfied.... I mean, this plan isn't perfect—no one wants their mother chaperoning a school dance—but it'll work because Mom's going to agree when she knows you suggested it."

Jason was suffering from second thoughts when he rang Charlotte's doorbell an hour later. Carrie had devised a plan for approaching Charlotte with his idea. At the appropriate point, he was to suggest the two of them chaperone the dance and make it sound like a spur-of-the-moment idea.

He was rather proud of his compromise—not the part about chaperoning the dance, but the shared-driving idea. By the time Carrie had left his apartment, he felt like an expert. Raising children wasn't so difficult if you applied a bit of common sense.

Now, though, he wasn't entirely sure he should get involved. The dance was an issue between Charlotte and Carrie, and his instincts told him he was trespassing.

It would've been different if Charlotte had come to him for advice, but she hadn't and he doubted she would. There wasn't any reason for her to, at least not with regard to Carrie. Charlotte was the one with parenting experience, not him.

Despite his second thoughts over his role in this drama, he'd agreed to help Carrie—even though his instincts now told him he was going to regret this.

Carrie answered the doorbell and smiled brightly when she saw him.

Charlotte looked pleased to see him, too, but she also looked like she'd rather not be. Jason was learning to read her quite well, and that skill was coming in handy.

"Hello, Jason," she said softly.

"Hi. I stopped by to see how Higgins is doing." A weak excuse, and one she was bound to see through in the next couple of minutes.

The black dog trotted toward him, his tail wagging slowly. Jason squatted beside him and affectionately rubbed his ears. "How do you like your new home, fellow?" he asked.

"Do you want a cup of coffee?" Carrie called out from the kitchen. Her voice was enthusiastic. The kid wasn't any better at disguising her emotions than her mother was.

"Please." Jason glanced up at Charlotte. He didn't know what was going on with her lately. She'd been avoiding him—that much he understood—but he was willing to give her the space she needed. For now. He was a patient man. She was attracted to him, fighting it as hard as she could, but her resistance wasn't strong enough to defeat him.

For the first time in his life, Jason had met a woman who needed him. Unfortunately she was too self-sufficient and proud to admit it. Charlotte Weston brought out all his protective urges. And his intuition told him he'd begun to bring out qualities in her—a sensual confidence and an ability to laugh, have fun—that she'd been repressing for years.

The woman was a puzzle, but slowly, surely, he was putting together the various pieces she revealed. Once he had the whole picture, he'd be able to scale those defensive walls of hers.

He strongly suspected Charlotte's problems revolved around her ex-husband and her marriage. She'd been badly hurt, and gaining her trust and her love would require time and patience. Where Charlotte was concerned, Jason had an abundant supply of both. Carrie brought him a cup of coffee, and Jason pulled out a kitchen chair, then nonchalantly sat down. Carrie did the same. Higgins ambled over and settled at his feet.

Charlotte glanced at the two of them and frowned. "Is something going on here that I should know about?"

The kid couldn't have been more obvious, Jason mused again. "Carrie came to me earlier this afternoon," he announced, deciding honesty was the best policy, after all. The way he figured, if they were forthright about *what* they'd discussed, then Charlotte might be willing to forgive them for discussing it behind her back.

"Jason," Carrie muttered a warning under her breath.

"Carrie came to you?" Charlotte demanded. "About what?"

"The dance," Carrie admitted sheepishly.

"You went to Jason about an issue that's strictly between you and me?"

"I needed to talk to someone," Carrie cried, pushing back the chair when she stood. She faced her mother, feet braced apart, hands on her hips. "You're being completely unreasonable and Jason agrees with me. He came up with—"

"Carrie." Jason could see he'd been wrong. In this case, honesty might not have been the best policy. "I didn't ever say I thought your mother was unreasonable."

His defense came too late. Charlotte whirled on him, her face red and growing redder. Her eyes, the eyes he'd always found so intriguing, were filled with disdain.

"Who gave you the right to intrude in my life?" she flared.

"Charlotte, it's not what you think." Jason could feel himself sinking waist-deep in the quicksand of regret.

"You're undermining my authority."

"Mom…please, hear me out."

"Charlotte, give me a chance to explain." Jason didn't have much of an argument; he should've listened to his instincts and stayed out of this.

"You may think because…because I've let you get close to Carrie and me that you have the right to express your opinion on how she should be raised, but you're wrong. What goes on between my daughter and me is none of your business. Do I make myself clear?"

Feeling all the more chagrined, Jason nodded. The best thing to do now was make a hasty retreat. "I can see I've—"

"Just go." Charlotte's voice trembled as she pointed to her door.

"Mom," Carrie shouted. "The least you can do is listen to him."

Charlotte ignored her daughter while Jason, calling himself every kind of fool, made his way out of the apartment. He paused long enough to cast an apologetic glance at Carrie, but he agreed with Charlotte. He'd butted in where he didn't belong.

After Jason's departure, Carrie went to her room, slamming her door with such force Higgins scrambled across the living room, frantically looking for a place to hide.

Charlotte was so angry, it was all she could do not to follow Jason and tell him she never wanted to see him again. She would have done it, too, if she didn't know she'd regret it later. And if she didn't need to coax Higgins out from behind the couch and comfort him.

The man had some nerve! If Carrie thought she was going to manipulate her into giving in by getting Jason to side with her, then her daughter was wrong.

"I hope you realize what you've just done!" Carrie shouted as she opened her door.

Still stroking Higgins, Charlotte ignored her.

"You've insulted Jason."

"He deserved it."

"Like hell."

"Watch your language, young lady."

Thirty silent minutes passed while Charlotte cooled her temper. Carrie was apparently doing the same thing. A short while later, her bedroom door opened again and she walked out. She was pale and her eyes showed evidence of crying, but she appeared to have composed herself.

The same didn't hold true for Charlotte. She was still furious. How dare Jason involve himself in her affairs!

"I've called Brad," Carrie announced, opening the refrigerator. She stared at the contents, took out a cold pop and pulled back the tab. After taking one long drink, she turned to face Charlotte. "Brad said he'd tell his dad you'd be driving us to and from the dance."

Of all the things Charlotte might have expected, this wasn't one. "Good," she said, feeling only a little better.

"I...was hoping you'd be willing to split the duties. Let Brad's father drive us there and you pick us up."

Charlotte mulled it over. That didn't sound so unreasonable. She'd have a chance to meet the boy's father when he came to get Carrie, and it wasn't as if the two kids would be alone in the car—or at the dance.

"I...I'd be willing to agree to that."

Charlotte thought Carrie would be grateful or relieved; instead she broke into giant hiccuping sobs. Her daughter slumped in a kitchen chair and buried her face in her arms and wept as if she'd lost her best friend.

"Carrie." Charlotte placed her hand on Carrie's shoulder. "What's wrong?"

She raised her head and brushed the tears from her face, her shoulders heaving with the effort to stop crying. "You should never have said those things to Jason."

"Carrie, he intruded in my affairs."

"But I was the one who asked him to talk to you. If you're going to be angry with anyone, it should be me, not him."

Charlotte realized Carrie didn't understand the nuances of a male-female relationship. Frankly, she wasn't that well acquainted with them herself. She'd admit that she'd reacted in anger, but it was justified. Jason had simply assumed too much.

"But Jason didn't want to interfere," Carrie sobbed. "It took me forever to get him to agree and...and he only did it because I was desperate."

"He overstepped the bounds." Charlotte tried to remain adamant.

"You made him leave without even bothering to listen."

Charlotte said nothing.

"I like Jason—and you do, too," Carrie added unnecessarily. "He's the best thing that's ever happened to us. Higgins is alive because of him and...and he took us to meet his family. Saturday was the most fun day I've ever had. It...it was like we belonged with Jason and his brothers."

Charlotte had felt the same way.

"Jason wasn't minding your business, Mom, at least not the way you think. He...he was helping a friend. Me. And you hated him for that."

"I don't hate Jason." Far from it. She was falling in love with him.

"He's the one who came up with the idea of Brad's father driving one way and you driving the other. He...he suggested you chaperone the dance just so you'd feel comfortable about everything." She drew in a shaky breath. "When I told him you'd need a date for the dance if you were going to be a chaperone, he said *he'd* take you. I mean, Jason isn't the kind of man who dances...but he'd be willing to do it, for me, because he's my friend. And for you, too, so you'd be comfortable at the dance. And what did he get for being so nice?"

"My anger," Charlotte whispered, feeling wretched.

"You kicked him out of the house, and I don't think he'll ever want to come back. I know I wouldn't."

Charlotte sat down next to her daughter, feeling strangely like weeping herself.

"I wanted to go to the dance with Brad more than anything," Carrie admitted, "but now I don't care if I do or not."

"Carrie, this isn't the end of the world."

"I *really* like Jason," she said emphatically. "When I asked him if he'd ask you out, I did it for selfish reasons, and I apologize for that…but I'm glad I did it. You're happier when you're with him, Mom. You don't think I notice, but I do. Jason makes you smile and laugh and forget how much you don't like your job."

Charlotte folded her arms around her middle. What Carrie said was true. It was as if her life had started all over again when Jason first kissed her.

"I don't care about the dance anymore," Carrie murmured. "But I care what happens with you and Jason. Go to him, Mom. Tell him you're sorry. Please."

Her daughter's entreaty affected Charlotte more than any regrets she might feel about what she'd said and done. For one thing, she hadn't realized how fond Carrie was of Jason.

"Will you do it, Mom?"

It didn't take Charlotte long to decide. "Yes," she said. She would apologize, for not giving him the benefit of the doubt, for not being willing to listen to him and Carrie, but mostly for the rude way in which she'd told him to leave her apartment.

It was the second time she'd had to apologize to this man.

"When?" Carrie asked.

"Soon," Charlotte promised.

The opportunity came the following morning. After walking Higgins, Charlotte was on her way to the office, crossing the parking lot. She'd spent a sleepless night composing what she intended to say to Jason. She'd wait until that evening, go to his apartment and say what needed to be said.

She was halfway to her car when she heard her name. Her heart filled with dread when she saw Jason jogging toward her.

"Hello," she said, feeling wretched.

"I won't keep you." His eyes bore into hers. "I want you to know I'm sorry for what happened yesterday. I should never have gotten involved. This is between you and Carrie, and I was out of line."

"I should never have spoken to you the way I did."

"You were angry and you had every right to be."

"But you… Oh, Jason, I feel terrible."

He frowned. "Why should you?"

"Carrie told me how you were willing to help chaperone the dance and…and I didn't have the common decency to hear you out."

"It's probably for the best. I'm not much of a dancer."

Charlotte smiled up at him, knowing her heart shone in her eyes, and not caring. "Why don't you let me find that out for myself Friday night?"

Eight

"You need to borrow a suit?" Rich asked, looking smugly amused as he led Jason to the walk-in closet in the huge master bedroom. The home had been built several years earlier, when Jamie was pregnant with Bethany. Rich himself had designed the sprawling L-shaped rambler that overlooked Puget Sound, and he was justifiably proud.

"Yes, I need to borrow a suit," Jason muttered, not giving his brother the satisfaction of explaining. Already he regretted having volunteered to be a chaperone for this dance. No matter how hard he tried, he wasn't going to be whirling around a dance floor as if he knew what he was doing. He'd probably make a fool of himself in front of Charlotte and a bunch of smart-aleck ninth-graders.

As an engineer, Rich was required to dress more formally on the job than Jason was. Jason owned a suit, but it was outdated. Maybe if he waited a few more years it would become fashionable again.

If the truth be known, he wasn't even sure when he'd last worn it. Sometime in college, he guessed. He'd buy another one if he thought he'd get any use out of it, but that didn't seem likely.

"What do you need a suit for?" Rich asked outright.

"I wouldn't be borrowing one if I'd known I was going to face an inquisition."

Rich chuckled, clearly enjoying Jason's discomfort. "I just want to be sure you aren't going to run off and marry Charlotte. Mom would kill you if you pulled a stunt like that."

Jason snickered, hoping to give the impression that marriage was the farthest thing from his mind, which it was. Wasn't it?

"Hey, don't act like it couldn't happen," Rich said, pushing hangers aside as he sorted through several tailored jackets. "With our family's history, it wouldn't be unheard-of for you to elope."

Jason couldn't argue with that. It had all started with Taylor. A few years back, his sister had moved to Montana and within three months had married Russ Palmer. The decision to marry had apparently been impulsive—and it happened while they were chaperoning the high-school drill team in Reno. The deed was done by the time they bothered to contact any family.

Jason frowned. Taylor had been a chaperone, too, and look where it had led. This high-school dance was beginning to sound more and more dangerous.

Christy had married on the sly, too, again without

telling anyone in the family. There were extenuating circumstances in her case, however. Well, sort of. His youngest sister had actually been engaged—to a lawyer, James Wilkens—when she'd gone to Idaho with Cody Franklin and married him. Their marriage had caused quite a ruckus in the family, but eventually everything had been smoothed over. Anyway, Christy was much better suited to Cody than to James, although the attorney had remained a good family friend.

Rich had followed suit, marrying Jamie with some idiotic idea of being a sperm donor for her baby. Jason had stood up for his brother, but he'd known from the beginning that the two of them were in love. He'd predicted that this sperm donor business wouldn't pan out, and he'd been right. Jamie had gotten pregnant, sooner than either of them had expected, and the process hadn't involved any artificial insemination, either.

Paul had been next. Diane, Paul's first wife, had died tragically, shortly after giving birth to Kelsey. Her loss had sent the family reeling. For six months, Paul had shunned his family's offers of help, attempting to balance his duties at home with his job and at the same time comfort his grieving children, all preschoolers. He'd been proud and angry. Leah, Diane's sister, had convinced him he couldn't continue alone. She'd given up her teaching position at the college and moved in with Paul and the children. Shortly afterward, they were married. But once again, no one in the family was informed of the ceremony.

The only single Manning left was Jason, and he

didn't plan to get married. He'd decided that years before. It was unfortunate that his parents had been cheated out of putting on a large wedding, but those were the breaks. He wasn't marching down any aisle just to satisfy his mother's need to work with caterers and some florist friend she'd known for years.

"So, Jase," Rich said casually, breaking into his thoughts. "How are things with you and Charlotte?"

"Fine."

"Fine?" Rich repeated, with that smug look Jason found so irritating.

"You don't need to concern yourself with my affairs," Jason said, resenting the way Rich and Paul made his love life their business.

"Are you going to ask her to marry you?" Almost in afterthought, Rich held up a well-cut gray suit coat. The tailoring was excellent and the material was top of the line.

Jason ignored the question and reached for the jacket, trying it on over his black T-shirt with *Seattle at Night* silk-screened across the front.

"What are your intentions toward Charlotte?" Rich asked with a pensive frown. He sounded oddly formal—and unusually serious.

"My intentions are my own, but since you asked," Jason said, turning around to admire his profile in the full-length mirror, "I'll tell you…. They're dishonorable, as always." He tried to make a joke of it, laugh off the attraction he'd been battling from the moment he'd met Charlotte Weston over a leaky faucet.

His joke, however, fell decidedly flat.

"Not this time, big brother."

"What do you mean by that?" Jason demanded. He didn't like his brother sticking his nose where it didn't belong, but he couldn't help being curious about Rich's remark.

"You're in love with her."

"Is that right?" Jason returned flippantly.

"It's the first time you've ever invited a woman to watch you play softball."

Rich made it sound as if that alone was enough to force him into a shotgun wedding. Jason refused to get into an argument with his younger brother. It wouldn't do him any good. Just because Rich and Jamie were so happy together, his brother seemed to think he was an expert on the subject of love and marriage. Jason didn't want to be the one to disillusion him.

Perhaps he did have some deep affection for Charlotte, Jason told himself. He'd be the first to admit he was strongly attracted to her, but marriage? Out of the question.

This was a familiar argument, one he'd worked through early in their relationship. It had worried him then, but he'd been so fascinated with her that he'd pushed his apprehensions to the back of his mind, deciding to take one day at a time.

He'd face one hurdle, he decided, before he confronted another. For now, the obstacle was their physical relationship. When she trusted him enough to put aside her fears and allow him to make love to her, it would be time to reevaluate what was happening between them. But not yet.

"Are you going to let me borrow the suit or not?" Jason asked stiffly. "If I have to stand here and listen to a lecture, too, I'd rather go to the rental shop."

He half expected Rich to jerk the coat off his shoulders and send him on his way. Instead, his youngest brother grinned, as if he knew something Jason didn't. It was another irritating habit of his.

"You're welcome to keep the suit as long as you like," Rich assured him. "You never know when you're suddenly going to need one."

Friday evening came, and it took Jason a full half hour to knot his tie correctly. He was out of practice, and getting it just right frustrated him. He should've borrowed the clip-on variety, but he hadn't thought of asking for one. No doubt Rich had plenty of each type.

Surveying his reflection in the mirror, he barely recognized himself. He was tall, besting his brothers by an inch or more, his shoulders were wide and, if he had anything to be proud of physically, it was that his stomach had remained flat. Haphazard meals and baseball did that for a man.

Charlotte probably wouldn't recognize him, either. If memory served, it was the first time she'd gone anywhere with him when he wasn't wearing a baseball cap. He brushed his hand along the side of his head, making sure his hair stayed flat. He carefully examined himself to see if he could find any gray hairs for a more distinguished look. When he didn't, he was actually disappointed.

He checked his watch. If everything had gone according to schedule, Carrie would have been picked up fifteen minutes ago for a pre-dance buffet. Since the dance didn't start for another two hours, Jason had suggested taking Charlotte out to dinner.

He didn't know what had gotten into him lately. He'd made reservations at an expensive restaurant, and ordered a fancy corsage to give her when they arrived.

Normally, his idea of a night on the town included pizza, beer and a Mariners' game. Drag an irresistible woman into his life, and before he knew it, he was forking out major bucks for dinner and flowers. The thing was, he'd come up with the idea on his own and was even excited about it, knowing how pleased Charlotte would be.

He'd seen this happen with his friends—his brothers, too—but he would never have believed *he'd* fall such willing prey to a woman's charms. It wouldn't have happened with anyone but Charlotte. Of that, he was certain.

At exactly seven, he walked over to Charlotte's apartment and rang the bell. She kept him waiting for several minutes before she opened the door—not a promising sign.

When she finally did come, Jason was about to complain. He was going to a lot of trouble for this blasted dance; the least she could do was be ready on time.

Whatever he'd intended to say, however, flew out of

his mind when he saw Charlotte. For the longest moment of his life, he stood there immobile.

This was Charlotte! She was…stunning.

"I'm…sorry," she said, sounding flustered. "I didn't mean to keep you standing out here, but I'm having a problem with this dress."

She was beautiful.

The word didn't begin to describe how breathtaking she looked. Her hair was done in a way he'd never seen before, swirled to one side, exposing the smooth skin of her cheek and her long, slender neck. Dangling gold earrings swung from her ears. Her eyes were a brighter blue than ever before, the color of the sky washed clean by a summer squall. Her dress was a paler shade of blue… Her dress… Jason's gaze slid over the sleeveless dress with its tight bodice and flared skirt, and an invisible hand seemed to appear out of thin air and knock him senseless.

"Jason." Her eyes implored him as she held one hand behind her back. "Is something wrong? I look terrible, don't I? Don't worry about hurting my feelings… This dress is too fancy, isn't it?"

It was all he could do to close his mouth. "You look…fabulous." Which was the understatement of the century. Jason felt sorry that he wasn't more sophisticated and urbane.

If he had been, he might have told her how exquisite she was. He might have found the words to say he'd gladly rework the knot in his tie for another hour if it meant he could spend the evening with her. For the first time since he'd donned the suit jacket, he felt no remorse for volunteering to escort Charlotte to her daughter's dance.

"I can't get the zipper all the way up," Charlotte explained. "I was so busy helping Carrie get ready before Brad and his father arrived that I...I didn't get dressed myself, and now I can't reach the zipper. Would you mind?"

She presented him with her back and it was all Jason could do to pull the tab up instead of down. If he went on instinct he'd have had her out of that dress, in his arms and on the way to the bedroom. He couldn't recall a time he'd wanted a woman more than he did Charlotte Weston right then and there.

"Jason?" She glanced over her shoulder when he delayed.

His hand felt clammy, and at first his fingers refused to cooperate, but with some effort he managed to do as she asked, sliding the zipper up her back.

"Thank you," she said. "You can't imagine what a madhouse it's been around here," she went on. "Carrie was so nervous. She looked so grown-up. I can't believe my baby isn't a baby anymore."

Jason returned her smile. "My mother felt the same way when Christy—my sister—attended her first big dance."

Even now, Jason was having trouble forming coherent sentences.

"The dress isn't mine," she told him as she searched for her evening bag, wandering from one room to the next until she located it. "I borrowed it from one of my friends at the office… It's too close to the end of the month to go out and buy one." She sighed, sounding breathless. "Even if I'd had the extra money, I doubt I would've been able to find one at the last minute. I'd feel dreadful if something happened to Cheryl's dress."

"I borrowed the suit from my brother." Maintaining an intelligible conversation, he discovered, wasn't as much of a problem as keeping his eyes off her.

Charlotte drew in a deep, steadying breath. "I know it's silly, but I'm as nervous as Carrie."

He smiled, trying to reassure her.

"The last dance I attended was in college," she said. "I…I don't know if I can dance anymore."

"I'm not exactly light on my feet, Charlotte," Jason felt obliged to remind her. He'd warned her earlier, but he doubted she'd taken him seriously.

"Do you think we should practice?" she asked.

She was gazing up at him with wide eyes. Jason would've given everything he owned to find out if she was feeling anything close to the emotional havoc he was.

"Practice?" he echoed. "That's an idea." He swallowed, wondering exactly what he was inviting. Trouble with a capital *T,* considering the way his body was reacting.

Charlotte set aside her evening bag and walked into his embrace. "I'm afraid I'm not going to be very good at this," she murmured.

"Don't worry. Hey, as far as I'm concerned, those

ninth-graders are going to dance circles around us anyway."

Charlotte's laugh sounded sweet and soft, and Jason's heart constricted. Could this be love? This pleasure he felt in doing small things for her—like the dinner and flowers? This need to hold her in his arms? This desire to be with her and her alone?

The feel of Charlotte's body against his was the purest form of torture he'd ever experienced. She fit in his arms as though she belonged there. Had always belonged there. He tried to ignore how right it felt.

And couldn't.

He tried to ignore the fragrance of wildflowers that whispered through her hair whenever she moved her head.

And didn't.

He tried, but failed.

Everything went fairly well for the first few minutes. At least he wasn't stepping on her feet. Then Jason realized their feet weren't moving and they were staring at each other more than they were dancing. Gazing at each other with starry-eyed wonder.

He shifted his hand upward, wanting to lessen the feeling of intimacy, but his fingers inadvertently grazed the skin of her upper back.

Either he kissed her now or he'd regret it the rest of the night. Either he continued the pretense or confessed openly to how vulnerable she made him feel.

He brought her closer to him. He could feel her heart

racing, echoing his own. Once he kissed her, he knew there'd be no stopping. Not this time.

He lowered his head ever so slightly and waited.

Charlotte sighed, closed her eyes and lifted her mouth enticingly to his. He suspected she was unconscious of what she was doing, what she was seeking.

Frankly, Jason didn't care. He was so hungry for the taste of her, nothing mattered. His mouth found hers and he groaned. Charlotte did, too.

He hadn't touched her in days, wanting to give her time, give himself time to define the boundaries of their relationship. It had been too long. He felt so needy he trembled.

The kiss was long, slow, deliberate.

Slowly, reluctantly dragging his mouth from hers, he created a small distance between them. Her eyes slowly fluttered open and met his.

"Jason?"

"I want you, Charlotte." He couldn't be any plainer than that. "I need you."

Emotion flickered in her gaze. Was it fear? Pain? Jason found it impossible to tell.

"Do you want to stop?" His hands were in her hair. By the time she lifted her mouth from his, Jason was melting with a need so powerful it throbbed within him.

Charlotte sighed into the hollow of his throat. "Jason, will you be angry with me?"

He saw the emotions assailing her, but noted the

dignified way in which she tilted her chin and the proud squaring of her shoulders.

"No, I won't be angry."

She relaxed. Visibly. "Didn't you tell me you made dinner reservations for seven-thirty?"

"Yes." He recognized her fear and tried to ignore his own disappointment.

Self-conscious now, Charlotte broke away, quietly adjusting her clothes, then retrieved her evening bag. It wasn't until she looked up at him that he saw the anguish in her eyes.

He didn't know what her ex-husband—he assumed it was her ex-husband—had done. Her gaze linked with his, regret and misery so evident it was all he could do not to reach for her again. To comfort, not to kiss. To offer her solace, not passion.

Now, more than ever, Jason was determined to discover how her ex-husband had hurt her so badly. Determined to help her recover and teach her how beautiful love could be.

Charlotte was shaken to her very core. The intensity of their kisses had grown fervent and passionate, near the point of no return. If she'd given him the least bit of encouragement, he would have carried her into the bedroom.

For one wild moment, she'd been tempted to let him. Then the haze of desire had faded enough for sanity to return.

She felt grateful that Jason had allowed her to regain

her senses, had given her the option to stop or proceed. Not like Tom...

Charlotte was jarred by this latest exchange even more than the other times Jason had held her and kissed her.

He'd almost made her forget.

Since her divorce, Charlotte had been content in her own small, secure world. The world she'd so carefully constructed for herself and Carrie. It had been the two of them, prevailing against all odds, forging a life together. The borders of her world had been narrow and confining, but Charlotte had made peace with that, had accepted its limitations.

Then a series of events had thrown her into confusion. It had all started at the baby shower for her friend Kathy Crenshaw. Charlotte had held the newborn in her arms and the longing she'd managed to ignore all these years had struck her full-force.

Shortly afterward she'd met Jason, and her life hadn't been the same since.

Because of Jason, she'd recognized how restricted her world had become. How limited. If that wasn't enough, he'd shown her glimpses of a life she'd never dared hope existed. He'd taught her to dream, to believe in the impossible.

Almost.

After a protracted farewell to Higgins, they went out to the parking lot. Jason opened the car door and helped her inside, then stood in the fresh air for several minutes, hands in his coat pockets. He closed his eyes and turned his face toward the night sky.

Charlotte knew it was difficult for a man to cut the lovemaking off as abruptly as they'd done. He needed a few minutes to compose himself.

She watched him as he climbed into the car. He hesitated after inserting the key into the ignition and smiled over at her. "Ready?"

Charlotte nodded. "Are you…all right?"

"Never finer," he assured her, then clasped her hand to kiss her knuckles.

Nine

Jason Manning was a romantic. Beneath that I-don't-give-a-damn attitude was a tenderness and warmth that left Charlotte feeling like a starry-eyed adolescent. The candlelight dinner at an elegant cliffside restaurant had been wonderful. There he'd given her a fragrant rosebud corsage that was so lovely, it had brought tears to her eyes.

The dance had been the best part of their evening. They'd had a delightful time, despite being surrounded by ninth-graders and forced to endure an earsplitting mixture of songs.

Jason and Charlotte had discovered early on that they weren't going to be able to dance to rap music. After a number of hilarious attempts, they'd given up. Several of their efforts had left Charlotte laughing so hard, her ribs ached.

Jason had been equally amused, and after their unsuccessful attempts to blend in with the kids, he'd reached for Charlotte, guiding her into his arms. She'd draped her wrists loosely around his neck and he placed his hands on her hips. Then they'd invented their own dance....

Although Charlotte knew Carrie had risked her "cool" status, her daughter had come to her, eyes bright with excitement, to confess it wasn't so bad having her mother chaperone a dance, after all.

After the dance, while Carrie and Brad attended the nearby party, Charlotte and Jason sat outside in the schoolyard, gazing at the stars, laughing and kissing. Not the passionate, soul-deep kisses of earlier, but tender, sweet ones. By the end of the evening the barriers surrounding her heart had started to crumble.

Charlotte and Carrie came home at a respectable hour, their heads filled with romance. With barely a word, they wandered off to bed, passing each other like sleepwalkers in the hall.

Several hours later, Charlotte, unable to sleep, wrapped her memories around her like a cloak. Not since her own schooldays had she been more at ease with a man. In the space of one evening, she'd come to realize—without doubt, fear or regret—that she was deeply in love with Jason Manning.

After an hour of savoring every moment, she found she could finally sleep, knowing she'd be with him the next morning when he picked her up for the game.

"You ready, Mom?" Carrie called happily from the kitchen. It was shortly after ten. "Jason'll be here any minute."

Charlotte sucked in her stomach and zipped up her skinny jeans. Then she reached for a clean sweatshirt and tossed it over her head. Jason was already in the kitchen, checking the contents of the picnic basket, when she sauntered in from her bedroom. Her heart did a little dance when she saw him.

"Good morning." She felt shy, and couldn't explain it.

He turned around and their eyes met before he sent her a wide smile. "'Morning."

Charlotte opened the refrigerator and withdrew a six-pack of diet soda to add to the cooler.

"Is that all I get—just a friendly 'good morning'?" he asked, keeping his voice low so Carrie wouldn't hear.

"What else do you want?"

"You should know the answer to that. I swear, Charlotte, leaving you last night was one of the hardest things I've ever done." He slipped his arms around her waist and nuzzled his face in the slope of her neck.

Charlotte twisted around and stared up at him. "It was?"

"The only thing that got me through it was knowing I'd be with you again this morning." He lowered his mouth to hers, and she parted her lips. The kiss was slow and deep and hot.

"Honestly, you two are getting ridiculous," Carrie said from behind Charlotte. "Even Higgins thinks so." At the last minute, Carrie had convinced her they should bring the dog. Charlotte wasn't sure he was healed enough to run around the park, but Carrie had phoned Jason and he'd felt it would be all right.

"You ready?" Jason asked, picking up the wicker basket, his hand around Charlotte's waist as though, even now, it was difficult to let her go.

"*I've* been ready for the last ten minutes," Carrie said pointedly, holding Higgins's leash and leading him to Jason's car.

On the ride across town, Jason put on a CD and the three of them sang along with Bon Jovi. But as they pulled into the massive parking lot, Jason's voice stopped abruptly.

"What's wrong?" Charlotte asked.

"Nothing for you to worry about." He tried to reassure her with a smile, but she wasn't so easily fooled. She glanced around, wondering what could possibly be amiss. She couldn't imagine, unless it was a vehicle he happened to recognize.

"I'm going to take Higgins for a walk," Carrie announced as soon as she'd climbed out of the backseat. Charlotte knew her daughter was eager to show off the dog to Ryan, Ronnie and the other children.

When Jason was opening the trunk of his car and removing his softball equipment, Charlotte spoke.

"Is there someone here you'd rather I not meet? An old girlfriend, a former lover?"

He turned and his gaze met hers. He smiled, a smile that started with his eyes and worked its way down to his mouth. "Nothing quite so dramatic. My parents are here."

"I see," she said. "You'd rather I wasn't with you."

"No," he said vehemently, and she realized he wanted her with him as much as she wanted to be. A rugged sigh followed his response. "I don't like the idea of you having to endure another inquisition."

"I'm a big girl."

"You don't know my mother."

"I'd like to, though," Charlotte assured him. She couldn't help thinking Jason's parents must be exceptional people, to have raised such a wonderful family. Before meeting the Manning clan, she'd known so little of what it meant to be part of a family, one in which everyone supported and encouraged one another. Where joys were shared and grief divided. All her life, Charlotte had been on the outside looking in, yearning for that special bond.

"They're going to drive you crazy with questions," he said grimly.

"Don't worry about it. I know how to be evasive. You forget, I'm the mother of a teenage daughter."

Jason's laugh was automatic. He grinned over at her, tossed a baseball bat over one shoulder and reached for her hand, linking their fingers. Linking them in a way that would dissolve any doubts.

Charlotte's heart sang with a joy that radiated from her heart.

They strolled casually, hand in hand, across the freshly mowed lawn. Jason's steps slowed as they approached the playing field.

Charlotte glanced up to find his eyes on her. "I just pray I can keep from hitting a home run," he whispered.

Charlotte laughed as they walked toward the older

couple talking with Paul and Rich. Jason made the introductions and Charlotte smiled warmly and held her hand out to his parents.

"I've been looking forward to meeting you," she said confidently. "After getting to know Jason and his brothers, I can't help thinking you two must be very special people."

Jason waited a restless twenty-four hours for the summons. It arrived Sunday morning, disguised as an invitation to dinner at his parents' house that same evening. Jason, however, wasn't fooled. His mother intended to feed him, but he knew he'd be obliged to sing for his supper.

He showed up promptly at six and was pleased to see that his mother had gone to the trouble of preparing all his favorites. Homemade rolls hot from the oven. Crispy fried chicken, mashed potatoes and gravy, fresh-picked peas. A molded gelatin salad rested in the center of the dining-room table.

Jason had always been a meat-and-potatoes man, unless he had to cook for himself, which unfortunately he did most evenings. His eating habits were atrocious and he knew it. A homemade dinner like this was a rare treat.

"We don't see nearly enough of you," his mother said, as the three of them sat down at the table.

Jason noted that she'd set out her best china and silverware, as well as linen napkins and a matching tablecloth. This was going to be a heavy-duty interrogation.

And it didn't look as if he had much chance of escaping before his mother ferreted out the information she wanted.

His father handed him the platter of chicken and Jason thought he might have read sympathy in his eyes.

"Generally, when your brothers are here for dinner, I get so involved with the grandchildren," his mother said conversationally. "You and I don't have much of a chance to talk."

"We talk," Jason said, reaching for the rolls and adding three to his plate, along with a thick slab of butter and a spoonful of strawberry preserves. His mother would have to wait for her information while he enjoyed his dinner.

"Gravy, son?"

"Thanks, Dad." A look of understanding passed between them.

"I hardly know what's going on in your life these days," his mother continued, undaunted. "I haven't seen you in a month of Sundays."

"That's not true, Elizabeth. Jason was over two weeks ago. Now, let the boy eat. You can drill him about Charlotte later."

His father was nothing if not direct. His mother didn't even pretend to be affronted; she simply sighed and nodded. "If you insist."

"I do," his father muttered, ladling gravy over a modest pile of mashed potatoes. He set the gravy boat aside and shook his head. "I don't understand you, Elizabeth. You've been half starving me for months, claiming we've got to start eating healthier. I've been eating salads and fish and broiled chicken. Now *this*. I'm beginning to feel like it's my last dinner before facing the executioner."

"This is Jason's favorite dinner!" Elizabeth declared righteously.

"Don't be fooled, son," Eric Manning said, his elbows on the table. "Your mother's after something big this time."

"Eric!"

"Sorry, dear," Jason's father said contritely, then winked at him.

If his mouth hadn't been full of homemade bread, Jason would have laughed. His mother was in quite a mood. His father, too, but he was well aware of the love they shared. They had the kind of relationship he'd always hoped to have with a woman himself. For the first time in his life, he felt that might be possible.

They ate in relative silence with short discourses from Jason as he answered their questions about the veterinary hospital and his practice. He noticed how carefully his mother steered away from the subject of Charlotte and his social life.

No sooner had Jason and his father cleared the table than his mother brought out a deep-dish apple pie. Even the dessert was Jason's favorite.

While she dished up heaping bowlfuls and added ice cream, his father poured coffee.

"Now, Eric?" she asked, looking expectantly toward her husband.

"If you insist."

Jason glanced from his mother to his father, realizing his reprieve was about to end.

"I most certainly do. Jason," she said, shifting her attention to him, "as you probably know, your father and I are curious about you and Charlotte. *Very* curious."

"Yeah, I had that impression."

"We both liked her very much."

"She's a likable person," Jason said.

"How'd you meet her?"

He finished his pie, tipping the bowl on its side and spooning up the last of the melted ice cream. When he was convinced he'd gotten every drop, he wiped his mouth with the napkin, set it aside and reached for his coffee.

"She lives in the apartment complex."

"Widowed?"

"Divorced." He wasn't going to volunteer any more information than necessary.

"Are you in love with her?"

His mother was going for the jugular. Jason supposed she was entitled to the truth, since she'd gone to so much trouble with this dinner.

"Yes." The reaction he received was definitely satisfying. His mother's eyes grew huge, and she glanced excitedly at his father.

"I thought as much," she murmured.

"It's obvious the boy's in love, Elizabeth. I told you so, didn't I?"

"But it makes all the difference in the world that he's willing to admit it himself."

"Charlotte means a lot to me," Jason added without hesitation.

"Are you going to marry her?" His mother's voice had a breathless, hopeful quality.

Jason sipped his coffee. He was in love with Charlotte, no question. He woke in the morning and his first thoughts were of her. When he went to bed at night, she was there in his mind, following him into sleep. His whole day was focused on when he'd see her again. Kiss her again.

"Jason?" his mother urged.

"Yes, I'm sure I'll eventually marry Charlotte."

"Hot damn." His father slapped the table.

"Oh, Jason, I couldn't be happier." His mother dabbed the corners of her eyes with a napkin. "I'm so pleased," she said with a sniffle, reaching for her husband's hand.

"I'm happy you two are so happy." Jason hadn't talked about marriage with Charlotte yet, but he'd do that in due course. They were still beginning to know each other, feel comfortable together. By next summer at just about this time, they'd be ready to take such a monumental step.

"Now this is important, son," his father said, his eyes serious. "Your mother and I want your word that you're not going to do what your sisters and Rich and Paul did. In other words, don't marry Charlotte without the family being there."

Elizabeth backed her husband up. "I've waited all

these years for a family wedding and I refuse to be cheated out of my last chance. Do you understand me, Jason?"

"Don't worry," Jason said calmly. "When Charlotte and I get married, we'll do it up big, just for you. The whole nine yards."

"A reception, with a dinner and dance?" His mother's eyes implored him.

"As long as Charlotte agrees, and I'm sure she will. She enjoys that sort of thing."

"But will she mind…my helping with the arrangements?"

Jason shrugged. "My guess is she'd welcome it. She doesn't have any family of her own, you know."

"Personally, I don't care if your mother has her hand in the arrangements or not," his father muttered. "I just want to be sure you aren't going to marry Charlotte behind our backs."

"I already promised I wouldn't." Still, given their family's history, Jason could understand his parents' skepticism.

"So I have your word on this?" his mother asked anxiously.

"My word of honor. Only…"

"Only what?" His mother looked concerned.

"Nothing, Mom. Don't worry about it."

"What is it?" she demanded.

"Well, I was wondering… Once Charlotte and I decide to marry, would you show her how to make fried chicken like yours?"

* * *

It wasn't fair to bother Jason with her problems, but there wasn't anyone she trusted more, anyone's opinion she valued as much. Her day at the office had been one of the worst ever. Her boss, Mr. Ward, had been unreasonable and demanding in the past, but his abuse that afternoon had reached an all-time high. He'd shouted at her, called her incompetent, belittled her. And it had been over something that was completely out of her control. A client had left the agency due to a problem with accounting, not anything Charlotte had done, yet she'd taken the brunt of Mr. Ward's anger. Unfortunately the insurance agency wasn't large enough to have a Human Resources department, so there was no one to complain to, no recourse to speak of.

It wasn't the first time and it wouldn't be the last. For three years she'd been employed as an executive assistant at the insurance agency. In the beginning she'd enjoyed her job and thrived on the challenge. Then, six months ago, Mr. Beatty, her original boss, had retired, and she'd found his replacement to be the worst kind of supervisor.

She'd made her decision earlier that afternoon, prepared her letter of resignation and placed it on Mr. Ward's desk before leaving the office. Although she'd felt confident when she left work, she was vacillating now, uncertain that she'd made the right decision.

It always seemed to be like this. She'd become indignant, decide to leave, and later, after her anger had cooled, she'd change her mind. Mr. Ward would seem repentant, try to convince her that his outbursts weren't personal; they were just his way. She'd start to believe him, at least until the next time.

Then it occurred to her.

What kind of woman would allow a man to verbally abuse her like that? What kind of woman allowed herself to be swayed by cheap talk and empty promises? The kind of woman who'd stayed married to Tom Weston for as long as she had, that was who.

She needed a sounding board, someone who'd listen to her frustration and doubts without casting judgment, without anger. Someone whose self-esteem was strong enough to accept her decisions whether she took his advice or not. Someone like Jason Manning.

Jason answered the phone immediately, sounding delighted to hear from her.

"I...I had a crummy day," she said when he asked. "Do you...would you go for a walk with me?" She considered bringing Higgins, but he was curled up with Carrie on the sofa.

"I'll be right over."

As Charlotte left, Carrie was talking on the phone with Brad. She hadn't told her daughter about quitting her job, although she was sure Carrie would cheer her decision.

"Hello," Jason said, kissing her lightly on the lips when she stepped out the door.

Charlotte closed her eyes. They joined hands and walked in the direction of the community park several blocks over.

The evening was beautiful. The fragrance of rhododendrons filled the evening air, mingling with the scent of blooming azaleas. Birds chirped and several people were getting a start on their yard work.

"I…did something I'm not positive I should have done," she said, keeping her eyes lowered.

"Was it illegal?"

The question made her smile. "No."

"Then why look so grave?"

"Well…"

"Do you want to tell me about it?"

She nodded, grateful they'd arrived at the park. Jason steered her toward an unoccupied bench and they sat down, his hand still holding hers.

"I…I don't get along with my boss. I'm good at my job—at least I used to be. But now… Mr. Ward makes unreasonable demands and takes out his frustration on whoever's close at hand. Unfortunately most of the time that's me."

"It doesn't seem like a healthy atmosphere to be working in."

"It isn't." Charlotte wasn't the only employee who felt unhappy. Cheryl was on the verge of giving her notice, too, and so were a couple of the others. It wouldn't surprise Charlotte if half the office staff left with her.

"Then you should quit."

He made it sound so straightforward.

"I've never been a quitter. It's one of the reasons the divorce was so difficult for me. I—" She stopped abruptly. She hadn't meant to drag her marriage into this, lay it out for Jason to examine…yet, perhaps it was time.

"Go on," he urged.

Charlotte inhaled deeply, gathering her resolve. "I wrote my two-weeks' notice this afternoon and left it on Mr. Ward's desk and now…now I'm having second thoughts."

"Why? Do you want to continue working at the agency?"

"No."

"Are you afraid you won't be able to find another job?"

"Not particularly—there's always a high demand for executive assistants. It's just…I know what's going to happen in the morning. Mr. Ward will arrive and read my letter and call me into his office. He'll apologize the way he always does. He seems to know exactly what to say, and when he's through with the apology, he'll offer me a token raise."

"It'd be nice if he threw in a bouquet of flowers."

"He might. He has before."

"Are you going to be swayed by that?"

"No-o." Her voice trembled and she shut her eyes to hold back the tears that burned. "It's so much like my marriage."

"Having to deal with an angry unreasonable man?"

"Yes…but more than that. Mr. Ward treats me the same way Tom did, and I swore…I promised myself I'd never allow another human being to do the things he did to me. And yet I take it, day after day, and I hate myself for it."

Jason's arm was around her now, hugging her close as if he wanted to absorb her pain. She was thankful he wasn't kissing her; she couldn't have endured that just then.

"I feel so angry when I let someone manipulate me. I want so badly to believe that things will change…that they'll get better. But they never do. Sooner or later Mr. Ward will go back to doing exactly what he's always done…and I'll realize I've let myself be controlled again. I can't seem to deal with the truth…. I guess it's easier to deny everything than face the reality. Why is truth so painful?"

Jason waited a few minutes, his arm about her calm and comforting. "Is it your boss you're talking about or your ex-husband?"

"Both." Charlotte raised her head and wiped the tears from her eyes before they had a chance to fall. "Tom…had an affair. I knew it for months but…I pretended I didn't. I made believe we were happy and in love, while doing everything I could to win him back. But it wasn't enough… Now I know nothing would have been enough."

Jason didn't interrupt her with questions; once again she was grateful. The effort not to weep had produced a lump in her throat, and talking was almost painful. She hesitated, head still lowered.

Jason's mouth brushed her hair. "Your husband was a fool, Charlotte."

She didn't respond; she couldn't. Jason didn't know the full story, didn't understand that there'd been a reason Tom had turned to another woman. Any healthy male would have, or so her ex-husband had vehemently assured her time and again.

"I'm stubborn and hardheaded," she said, her voice cracking. "I don't know when to let go and…so I hold on, no matter how painful…or damaging."

"I can't tell you what to do," Jason said after a thoughtful moment, "but don't judge yourself so harshly. Some people know exactly what to say to get what they want. Everyone needs to hear they're important, that they're loved and appreciated. But those are only words, and talk is cheap. You got out of your marriage at the right time and—"

"No," she sobbed, "I didn't…. I didn't *want* out of the marriage, don't you see? It was Tom who asked for the divorce, Tom who forced everything into the open. I would've gone on pretending forever if he hadn't. I won't do it again. I won't! I'm quitting my job, Jason. I'm walking out two weeks from now and I won't look back. I swear to you, I won't look back."

There was a message from his mother when he returned to his apartment. His mind was heavy with everything he'd learned about Charlotte's marriage and he contemplated waiting to return his mother's call, but she'd sounded so excited.

Sighing, he reached for the phone. His mother answered on the first ring.

"Jason, I'm so glad you called! I have so much to tell you. I talked to Taylor and Christy and they've both agreed to come."

"Come?"

"You can't imagine what a day I've had," his mother continued, her voice animated. "I called Barbara Johnson, you remember Barbara, my friend who owns the floral shop, don't you? We went to high school together a thousand years ago."

"Mom…"

"Let me finish." With barely a pause to breathe, she went on, "Barbara was the one who got things started. She suggested we contact the yacht club right away and book a date for the reception. They're booked at least a year in advance. A year, I told myself. I know you, Jason, and when you're ready to do something, you don't want to wait an entire year. Barbara was right. The earliest date was August the year after next. I can tell you, I was shocked. I had no idea we'd need to book the reception so early."

"Reception? What reception?" Jason was starting to get a frightening premonition.

His mother ignored his question. "That's when I learned there'd been a cancellation in July. This July! I couldn't believe our luck. Naturally I booked it that very instant. Then I contacted the caterers and, as luck would have it, they agreed to do the dinner, although it's only three weeks' notice. *Three weeks,* Jason. Three weeks. It sounds crazy to even attempt something of this magnitude, but we're going to pull it off without a hitch."

Jason's vague premonition was beginning to solidify. "Mom, what are you talking about?" he asked with growing anxiety.

Once again his mother disregarded his question. "That's when I phoned Taylor and Christy. They both called back to say they're coming. They've already made their plane reservations. Russ is coming, and Mandy, too. Remember Mandy, Russ's sister? She's in college now, you know."

"Coming? To *what*, Mother?" Jason demanded.

"Why, Jason, I've spent the day making the arrangements for your wedding to Charlotte. What else would I be talking about, for heaven's sake?"

Ten

"Mother, have you gone stark, raving mad?" Jason had difficulty keeping a rein on his anger. "How can you set a wedding date and hire caterers when I haven't even *mentioned* it to Charlotte? This is insane." He rubbed his face, wondering if he'd imagined this entire fiasco.

"Your father warned me you'd be angry, but, Jason, I know you. Once you and Charlotte decide to marry, you won't want to wait two years."

"Mom, I don't suppose it dawned on you that there are other places we could have a wedding reception— *if* we were actually having one. The yacht club isn't the only venue in this town."

"Frankly, no, it didn't occur to me," his mother returned calmly. "Since we're just going to have one formal wedding in this family, we're doing it up big, and the yacht club's the best alternative."

Jason could see he was losing ground. "Let me talk to Dad."

"But, Jason—"

"Mother!"

"All right, just a minute."

That minute seemed to take an hour. By the time he had his father on the line, Jason was as angry as he'd ever been. The instant he heard Eric pick up the receiver, he shouted, "Has Mother gone crazy? Have you? How could you let things go this far?"

His father chuckled, apparently amused, something Jason most definitely wasn't. "I agree with you," his father said breezily, "your mother has gone a little crazy."

"Dad, listen, I know you and Mom mean well, but I refuse to let you run my life. Scheduling the reception, talking to florists, I can't believe you'd allow Mom to do all this without talking to me first."

"Don't forget, she's involved Taylor and Christy, as well. That's when I thought she'd stepped over the line. You haven't even asked Charlotte to marry you, and Elizabeth's got your sisters choosing bridesmaids' dresses. By the way, I don't suppose she told you about the honeymoon? Two weeks in Hawaii—it's our wedding gift to you."

Jason clenched his fist at his side and closed his eyes, trying to calm himself. It didn't work. The situation was absurd. And he was beginning to see that his father was in on this nonsense. "Two weeks in Hawaii…Taylor and Christy choosing bridesmaids' dresses. You've both gone off the deep end."

"To your mother's credit, she didn't intend for this

to happen. It just did. I know you're upset now, and to be honest, I don't blame you, but once you get used to the idea, it doesn't sound so ludicrous."

Get used to the idea, Jason mused. He felt like he was in the middle of a nightmare. "You honestly think I should agree to this…this outrageousness?" He could barely speak.

"Answer me this. Are you in love with Charlotte?"

"Yes." That much was a given—he'd already told his parents so.

"Do you intend to ask her to marry you?"

His dad knew the answer to that, too. "Yes…eventually, in my own time and my own way."

"If you're planning to marry the girl anyway, then what's the problem?"

"I wasn't going to do it in three weeks!"

"Three weeks, three months, what's the difference?"

Jason couldn't believe it. His father was talking pure craziness.

"I realize your mother and I went about this wrong, but after what happened with your brothers and sisters, all I ask is that you cut us a little slack."

"A little slack," he snorted. "Marriage is a serious step. A man doesn't make that kind of decision one minute and march up the aisle the next."

"I used to feel that way myself, but it's pretty much what happened with Taylor and Russ, as well as Christy and Cody. They made up their minds, then went right ahead and did it."

"All right, all right," Jason muttered, willing to

concede the point. Their weddings were spontaneous, to say the least. Same for Rich and Paul.

"I agree, marriage is a serious step," his father went on calmly, "but if you're in love with Charlotte and intend to marry her anyway, I don't see the harm in your mother getting the ball rolling."

The ball rolling. She'd started an avalanche. "Don't you think Mom's just a tad premature?"

"Perhaps," his father agreed amicably enough. "But you can't really blame her for that. She got caught up in the excitement of the moment. Once she talked to the yacht club, everything sort of fell into place. It makes sense once you analyze it. You've been a bachelor a long time, Jason. If you're as serious about marrying Charlotte as you claim, my advice is, just do it. If you wait, you might talk yourself out of it."

"Do it," Jason echoed. "You make marriage sound like taking up an exercise program." He could see he wasn't going to make any more headway with his father than he had his mother.

"Think about it, all right? That's all I ask."

"Aren't you forgetting something?"

"What?"

"Charlotte might say no."

His father laughed. "Charlotte's as much in love with you as you are with her. She'll marry you in a New York minute and we both know it."

"But, Dad…"

"Just think about it overnight. That's all your mother and I are asking. If you decide you'd rather not go through with this, then phone us in the morning and we'll put a stop to everything."

"I don't need to sleep on this," Jason argued. "I can tell you right now that I'm not going to agree. I've never heard anything more absurd in my life. A wedding in a few weeks! I was thinking more along the lines of two or three years!"

A heavy silence followed his words. "Then you must not be as much in love as your mother and I assumed. Give us a call in the morning," his father said and hung up the phone.

Jason was too furious to stand still. He paced his living room, jerked his baseball cap off his head and slapped it against his thigh. He tried to smooth out the crease in the bill, realized he couldn't and tossed the hat on top of the television.

Earlier that evening, he'd been talking to Charlotte about this very thing—people manipulating and controlling others. Well, he wasn't about to fall prey to it now. Especially not with his parents.

If he allowed his mother to schedule his wedding, there was no telling where she'd stop. The next thing he knew she'd be meddling in *all* his personal affairs. She'd be deciding when it was time for him and Charlotte to have a family.

He drew in a deep, calming breath to clear his head.

His assessment of his mother was unfair, he told himself a few minutes later. His parents hadn't interfered in his brothers' or sisters' marriages. From what he understood, they'd suggested Leah and Paul get married, but that was common sense. Leah and Paul should have seen it themselves. He knew his parents had debated long and hard about confronting them and had done so reluctantly, after much soul-searching.

But arranging his marriage to Charlotte was an entirely different matter. They'd stepped over the boundary there—although…although he did understand how easy it must have been to get caught up in the heat of the moment. Getting the date at the yacht club had set everything in motion, and before either of his parents were aware of it, they'd planned the whole wedding.

As he recalled from his dinner conversation the day before, Jason had told his mother that Charlotte would welcome her assistance in planning the wedding. She'd done a bit more than suggest what type of flowers to use in the bridal bouquet, however.

No, it was out of the question.

Jason flatly refused to be a pawn. When he was ready to marry Charlotte he'd…

Married. He and Charlotte.

He needed at least a year just to get used to the idea. A man his age didn't surrender his freedom without plenty of serious thought.

Then he remembered the phenomenon of holding Charlotte in his arms, of loving her, and the simple pleasure he found in spending time with her. He tried to imagine what his life would be like without her and discovered he couldn't. So his belief that he wasn't ready flew out the window.

But marriage, he told himself, would take away his freedom. He'd never watch another game on TV again without feeling guilty—a wife would make sure of that. Women nagged and controlled, didn't they?

Charlotte was a woman, but she wasn't like the others he'd known. She'd been controlled and manipulated herself; she'd fought against it. Jason couldn't in all honesty believe she'd try the same tactics on him.

Once again his argument wouldn't hold.

All right, maybe there were more things to consider besides his freedom. But here, too, he was losing ground. He'd found freedom in Charlotte, freedom to be himself, freedom to look toward the future.

Charlotte wanted children.

Another contentious issue. Children. Carrie had said as much the day she'd stopped by his office to bribe him to take out her mother. If he married Charlotte, he might as well accept that a year or so down the road they'd have a baby.

So? Wasn't that what he wanted?

He hadn't thought much about a family until recently. He vividly remembered the sensations that had overwhelmed him the first time he'd seen Charlotte holding Jeremy. Watching her play with his brother's son had left him breathless. Of course, being hit by a fast-moving Frisbee might have contributed to that.

Okay, so he wanted children. A man didn't marry a woman without giving the prospect some consideration. Since he was well past thirty, and fast approaching forty, he should start thinking along those lines soon. Charlotte was nearly thirty-six herself, and he knew it was safer for a woman to give birth before the age of forty.

Which meant he had to throw out his idea of waiting two or three years to get married. If he was serious, and he was, they should do it soon.

But three weeks was *too* soon....

He'd sleep on it, Jason decided, take his father's advice and give this whole wedding business some thought. But he could say right now, that on general principles alone, he was against it.

An hour later, after tossing and turning and wreaking havoc with his bedsheets, Jason knew. Knew it from the way he couldn't keep his hands from clenching. Knew it from the way his stomach tensed.

He was going to marry Charlotte Weston. The wedding was already scheduled.

Charlotte didn't know what was wrong with him. Jason had fidgeted all through dinner, although dinner had been his idea. He'd called her early that morning, before she'd left for work, and invited her out.

The invitation had sounded offhand, spur of the moment. Or that was how he'd apparently intended it to sound. But Charlotte wasn't fooled. His voice had tensed as though he wasn't sure she'd say yes—which was ridiculous. Surely he knew how crazy she was about him. Yet, when she assured him she'd be happy to join him for dinner, he hadn't seemed the least bit relieved.

She'd suggested Mr. Tamales, but he'd disagreed.

Instead he'd chosen a fancy seafood restaurant near the harbor. She'd been looking forward to chicken enchiladas, but certainly wasn't disappointed with her shrimp Louis.

Charlotte could have sworn, however, that Jason hadn't eaten more than three bites of his wine-sautéed scallops. "Jason," she said after a long silence. "Is something bothering you?"

"No," he replied abruptly.

"You haven't said a word in the last five minutes. Aren't you feeling well?"

"My stomach's in knots." His reply was quick and short-tempered. He reached for his water glass, emptying ice chips into his mouth, then chewed on them fiercely.

"Do you want to leave?"

His eyes met hers and for an all-too-brief moment the tension eased from around his mouth. "Not yet."

"Okay," she said, wondering at his strange mood.

"How did everything go with your boss?" he asked, seeming to want to change the subject.

She'd already told him, but apparently he hadn't been paying attention. "He's angry, especially since two other people also gave their notice when they learned I wasn't changing my mind."

"Did he try to make staying worth your while?"

Charlotte nodded. "He offered me and the others a raise." Mr. Ward had called all three of them into his office, smugly claimed he was willing to overlook this small mutiny and offered them each a raise if they'd withdraw their resignations.

"You didn't take his bride—I mean bribe—did you?"

"No." Charlotte was still basking in the satisfaction she'd felt when she told Mr. Ward she wasn't interested in withdrawing her notice. Cheryl and Janice hadn't changed their minds, either. Mr. Ward had been stunned, but she knew that would soon pass.

Before the end of the two weeks, he'd try every manipulative tactic in the book. When she didn't give in, he'd try anger, his least effective tool.

She was through with a boss who was so angry and unreasonable. Through with guilt and regret and abuse. She already had a line on another job, although she would've enjoyed taking the summer off.

Unfortunately, she couldn't afford it. As it was, she only had two months' budget in her savings account, and it had taken her a year to accumulate that much. She called it her "attitude money." It was a whole lot easier to walk away from her position at the agency, knowing she had some cash to fall back on if she didn't get a job right away.

"How about dessert?" Jason suggested after the waitress had taken their dinner dishes away.

She shook her head. "No, thanks. I'm stuffed."

He looked disappointed at her response.

"You go ahead, though," she urged.

Jason immediately rejected the idea, proving her initial impression wrong. But if he *wasn't* craving dessert, what did he want? He seemed restless, yet obviously wasn't inclined to leave.

Whatever was bothering Jason wasn't trivial, Charlotte realized. Jason Manning wasn't a man easily unnerved. She wondered if it was something she'd done, something she'd said. She didn't know what to make of his behavior. Throughout dinner, she'd considered various explanations, none of which seemed all that logical.

The silence between them lingered as they sipped their after-dinner coffee. From the moment he'd picked her up, she'd been surprised that Jason was wearing a suit, the same attractive gray one he'd had on the night of the dance. His brother's suit. She knew very well that he didn't dress formally unless it was some important occasion. His entire wardrobe consisted of jeans and T-shirts.

He hated wearing a suit. Five minutes after they'd arrived at the dance, he'd loosened his tie, and had completely discarded it by the end of the evening. Why he'd worn one this evening remained a mystery.

Charlotte frowned, trying to analyze what was wrong. Waiting for Jason to tell her was making her nervous. He looked miserable, which made *her* increasingly miserable.

She felt close to Jason, closer than she'd felt to any man since Tom. She hadn't meant that to happen, and she didn't think Jason had, either. Their relationship had grown steadily more intense in the past weeks. She'd fallen in love—it was that simple—and thought he had, too.

But perhaps falling in love wasn't what Jason

wanted. Perhaps he was trying to find a way to tell her they were in too deep, that he wanted out.

It made sense.

The fancy dinner, the hesitation and even regret. The fact that his eyes kept avoiding hers. The silence. That was the worst. The awkward silence, as though he couldn't bear to speak those final words.

"I'm ready to leave, if you are," she said with false enthusiasm.

He looked over at her, his expression uncertain. Perhaps he planned to tell her in the restaurant, in order to avoid a scene. She'd heard that was a popular tactic. All Charlotte wanted to do was leave, before she made a fool of herself by breaking into tears.

He was going to break up with her; she was sure of it. A hundred explanations crowded her mind. They'd gotten too close, too fast. It wasn't as if she was…unencumbered. True, she was single, but she had a child, and if a man was going to get serious with a woman, he'd prefer that she didn't bring along excess baggage. That was common knowledge. She'd heard it often enough from friends and acquaintances.

Jason's parents might have disapproved of her, too. It wasn't as if she came from a fine, upstanding family. His mother had asked her a number of questions Saturday morning about her parents and grandparents. Charlotte had found it difficult to explain that she had no idea where her father was, or even if he was still alive. Neither of the elder Mannings had seemed to disapprove of her openly. If anything, they'd been warm and gracious. But although they might have accepted her, even liked her, they might also think she was the wrong kind of woman for their son.

Jason paid the bill while Charlotte excused herself for a visit to the ladies' room, hoping to regain her composure.

He was waiting for her by the door when she returned. Silence accompanied them into the parking lot.

Jason opened her door. By the time he'd walked around the front of his car, Charlotte's hold on her poise was tenuous. When he glanced in her direction, though, she managed a smile. Her pride demanded it.

Charlotte expected Jason to drive her directly to the apartment, since he hadn't been able to break the news to her at the restaurant. At least when he delivered the blow, it would be in the comfort of familiar surroundings.

But he drove to a deserted stretch of beach, then pulled off the road, climbed out of the car and came around to her side.

"It's late," she said, frowning at her watch. "I should be getting home. Carrie's by herself."

"In a minute." He wore a pensive frown, the same expression she'd seen all evening.

She gazed past him to the shoreline. Small breakers rolled onto the sand, their motion soothing. Charlotte wasn't soothed, however, and she looked away to the wide expanse of darkening sky. The scent of the sea hung in the air.

"Just say it," she muttered. Her patience had evaporated and she couldn't bear the painful silence anymore.

"You know?"

"Of course I know." She walked onto the sand, removed her shoes and purposefully forged ahead, stopping at a thick log that was charred at one end.

Swallowing a mouthful of self-pity, she looked over her shoulder to discover that Jason had followed her onto the beach. She almost wished he'd driven away, left her behind. It would've been easier that way.

Her legs didn't feel as if they'd support her much longer, so she sat on the log and stared sightlessly out at the horizon, waiting for him to begin his litany of excuses and stumbling explanations.

"Charlotte…I'm not very good at this sort of thing."

"Who is? Listen, it's been great." She strove to sound flippant and knew she'd failed. She lowered her gaze to her hands, forcing herself to continue. "I'll always be grateful for this time with you." Tears rolled down her cheeks and she brushed them aside, not daring to look at Jason. "But as we both know, all good things must come to an end…."

Jason said nothing. Not one word, and that made everything even more difficult.

His hands were buried in his pants pockets and when she glanced up at his face, she saw that his jaw was tightly clenched. She didn't understand his anger, not when she'd made it so easy for him.

"So you had me sit through that whole miserable dinner," he said with barely controlled antagonism. "Did you enjoy watching me squirm?"

"No."

"You know, Charlotte, if you weren't interested in marrying me in the first place you could have—"

"Marrying you!" Charlotte's head snapped up. "You planned on asking me to *marry* you?" For one wild second she was paralyzed with shock, unable to move or think. There must've been a mistake. It was a joke. Jason Manning was a confirmed bachelor, wasn't he? Despite her feelings for him, Charlotte had accepted that.

"Don't pretend you didn't know," he said.

"But I thought...I thought you wanted to stop seeing me."

He snickered as though he didn't believe her and turned away. "Why would I take you to a fancy restaurant if I wanted to say something as ridiculous as that?" He turned back, glaring at her.

"To let me down easy. What did you expect me to think, when you were in such a bad mood?"

"I already told you I'm no good at this sort of thing. If you want romance and a bunch of pretty words, you're going to have to marry someone else."

She was on her feet and not quite sure how she got there. "You honestly want to marry me?" she repeated as her eyes brimmed with tears. They were tears of relief. Tears of joy.

"Sit down," he said gruffly. "If I'm going to do this, I want to do it right."

Charlotte complied and was shocked when Jason got down on one knee directly in front of her. He cleared his throat. "I love you, Charlotte. I wasn't planning to fall in love with you, but I knew it was happening, and I let it happen because—well, I don't really know. It happened and I'm glad it did. I can't think of spending a day without you at my side. I can't imagine playing softball without you there. I love you. I love the chocolate chip cookies you bake. I admire you for the wonderful job you've done raising Carrie. I'm deeply impressed by your wisdom and courage."

"Oh, Jase." She blinked back her tears and brought her fingertips to her lips.

"You're the first woman I ever dated who let me be myself. You didn't feel obligated to clean up after me. You don't act as if my refrigerator's some kind of scary science experiment." He grinned, apparently pleased with his own wit. "You even like sports."

The lump in her throat made it impossible to speak. Tears ran unrestrained down her face. With all her heart she wanted to shout, "Yes, I'll marry you," and throw her arms around him. But she was afraid to believe Jason would continue to love her once he learned how inadequate she was, how worthless she was as a lover. She didn't know if she could bear to disappoint him.

"If it helps," he said in a low voice, "I talked to Carrie, and she's all for us getting married."

Charlotte sniffed tearfully. "You mean my daughter's given you her seal of approval?"

"Yup."

There was another silence. Then he said, "I don't mean to rush you, but I have this sore knee. I slid into first base last week and I've been in pain ever since. So, if you don't mind, I'd prefer a quick answer."

Before she could stop herself, before she could listen to her head instead of her heart, she nodded. It wasn't a very enthusiastic nod, perhaps, but Jason didn't seem to have any objections.

"Thank God," he murmured, awkwardly rising to his feet.

"You idiot. You didn't have to get down on your knee," she whispered through her tears.

"Yes, I did," he said, but he sounded grateful to be off it as he sat down on the log beside her. A deep sigh rumbled through his chest. "It wasn't the most romantic proposal, was it?"

"Oh, Jase, it was perfect," she said, touching the side of his face and gazing into his eyes. Her throat was tight and constricted. "What you said about not being able to live without me…that's how I feel about you. Sharing cookies, going to ball games, walking the dog together—it all sounds wonderful. I guess I'm not much of a romantic, either," she said with a shy laugh.

"I didn't buy a diamond ring. I figured you'd want to pick a setting yourself."

A ring. Charlotte froze. Soon he'd want to discuss a wedding date. A chill worked its way through her, the same cold feeling she'd experienced whenever Tom wanted to make love. A sick sensation would build in the pit of her stomach and by the time they went to bed she'd feel encased in ice. All Tom had to do was kiss her and he'd know. Then the tirades would begin, the accusations, the ugliness.

Jason was going to kiss her, too. Now. His lips

grazed hers. Briefly. Lightly. The cold fear melted as if it had never been. Charlotte groaned and slipped her arms around his neck.

He kissed her again, but this time the kiss blossomed into something wild and erotic that left Charlotte panting, seeking more.

They drew apart, and she rested her forehead against his. When he spoke, his voice was husky and warm, as warm as heated brandy and just as intoxicating.

"We're going to be very good in bed," he whispered.

Charlotte tensed, panic a heartbeat away, but she forced it down, focusing instead on how gentle he'd always been with her. How patient. With Jason, she'd felt a level of pleasure she'd never realized she was capable of reaching. When he kissed her she felt hot and quivery from the inside out. Maybe it would be different this time, with this man. Maybe. She prayed that was true.

"You're worried about making love, aren't you?"

She nodded.

"I'd never hurt you, Charlotte. I hope you understand that. Whatever the problem is, we'll work it out together."

"I'm grateful…for that." Despite the excitement she felt at his kisses, she had to fight back the fear that threatened to choke her every time he mentioned the physical aspects of their relationship.

Her only recourse was to insist on a long engagement. That way she could slowly, gradually, feel comfortable with their sexual relationship. After they made love… She hesitated. There'd been a time she wouldn't have thought that was possible, but Jason had given her hope.

"Do you want to set the wedding date?" she asked, deciding to broach the subject now.

"Yes, but…" He shrugged. "There's one small problem."

"What's that?"

"I'm going to let my parents tell you. It's only fair. They're at home, waiting for us now."

Eleven

"I don't believe this!" Jason muttered under his breath as they pulled into his parents' driveway.

"What are all these cars doing here?" Carrie asked from the backseat. Jason had insisted on going back to the apartment to pick her up.

"You'll see," he said grimly.

Either his parents owned a car dealership or they were entertaining a houseful of company.

"This is going to be a real circus." He sighed as he helped Charlotte out of the front seat. Carrie bounded out from the back.

Charlotte's nervousness, already heightened by the prospect of an audience, grew exponentially.

The door opened and Elizabeth Manning stepped out of the house. Jason's father and brothers, sisters-in-law and several children all crowded on the front porch behind her. The porch light revealed a variety of expressions, from amusement to elation.

"Well?" his mother asked as she walked toward them.

Jason slid his arm around Charlotte's waist and slowly, sweetly smiled down at her. In those brief seconds, Charlotte was comforted and reassured by his love. Her senses sang and her heart fluttered wildly.

Jason lowered his head. Charlotte wasn't sure that kissing in front of his parents, his whole family, was the best thing to do. Oh, what the heck. She was marrying Jason. They were in love, so a simple kiss shouldn't offend anyone.

Their lips met and she moaned a little with surprise and wonder at the ready response he never failed to evoke from her. Her hand crept up his chest and gripped the lapel of his suit jacket as his mouth made love to hers.

When he broke away, he was breathless. For that matter, so was Charlotte. She marveled that he was able to speak at all. "Does that answer your question, Mother?"

"Charlotte's agreed to marry you?"

"In a heartbeat," she answered for herself.

"Isn't it great!" Carrie shouted.

Spontaneous applause broke out from the porch, followed by several earsplitting whistles. Ryan and Ronnie were pounding their feet but she doubted the little boys understood exactly what the family was celebrating.

The evening was lovely; honeysuckle and roses scented the air. The sun had almost set, casting— literally—a rosy glow over the scene.

Jason bowed as though he were a knight and she his lady, accepting his family's enthusiasm.

"I hope you realize you're getting the runt of the litter," Paul told her, laughing.

"Hey," Rich put in. "Just be grateful that Charlotte's willing to put Jason out of his misery. He's been walking around like a lovesick puppy for weeks."

Jason glowered at his brothers, but she could tell he wasn't angry. He took their teasing in stride. From the time he'd brought her to that first softball game, Charlotte had envied him his family, especially the close relationship he shared with his brothers. The three were more than brothers; they were best friends. They looked out for one another and, just as important, they laughed together.

Leah and Jamie were best friends, too. Yet they seemed eager to extend that camaraderie to Charlotte. They'd gone out of their way to include her, to make her feel welcome, a part of the family. One of them.

Jason's mother came forward, tears in her eyes as she hugged Charlotte. "I couldn't be more pleased. Jason couldn't have chosen better."

"Thank you," Charlotte said, blushing. Doubt bobbed like a cork to the surface of her mind. Not that she didn't love Jason. She did, with all her heart, but she still wasn't sure whether she was the right woman for him.

"I'm so happy for you—and for us," Jamie said, hugging her next. "The two of you are perfect for each other. Leah and I agreed on that the minute we saw you together."

A warmth permeated Charlotte's heart. She wanted so badly to believe it was true.

"We'll be sisters now," Leah whispered, taking Charlotte's hands and lightly squeezing her fingers.

"I couldn't be marrying into a more wonderful family," Charlotte said to Jason as they made their way into the house. Carrie followed, carrying Jeremy, while the other children raced excitedly ahead.

His brothers congratulated Jason, slapping him on the back.

Once inside, Jason and Charlotte sat on the couch and the family gathered around them, making them the center of attention. Every eye was on Charlotte, smiling and happy, yet expectant. Puzzled, she glanced up at Jason, wondering if they wanted her to say something, to make some speech or pronouncement.

"Does she know yet?" Paul asked.

"No," Jason murmured. "I'm leaving the explanation up to Mom and Dad."

"Smart boy," Rich said, sitting on the armrest of the couch. He leaned forward eagerly, as though waiting for the opening act of an award-winning play.

"What's everyone talking about?" she asked.

"Mom?" Jason gestured eloquently toward his mother.

Elizabeth hesitated and turned to her husband. Eric Manning grinned and gave his wife a reassuring nod, which only compounded Charlotte's curiosity.

"As I said, I'm delighted that you've agreed to marry

Jason," Elizabeth began. "He's waited all this time to meet the right woman and, frankly, Eric and I were beginning to wonder if that was ever going to happen. Now that we've met you, Charlotte, we're glad he waited so long. We understood the moment we saw you together how special you were to him."

A low murmuring chorus of assent brought a sheen of tears to Charlotte's eyes. If anyone should be grateful, it was her. Jason had changed her world, opened her mind to everything she'd believed was closed off to her. Love. Family. Joy. Partnership.

The room went strangely quiet. Charlotte looked around and, although everyone seemed genuinely pleased, there was a tension here, too.

"Just tell her, Mother," Jason advised. "No need to drag this out."

By now, Charlotte was more than curious. "Tell me what?"

"Don't rush me," Elizabeth said, chiding her son. "Charlotte," she began, "when Jason told us he'd fallen in love with you, his father and I naturally wondered about his intentions. Then he told us he intended to ask you to marry him, so we decided to do a bit of checking in regard to the arrangements. Weddings need to be planned."

Jason's fingers entwined with hers, his hold on her hand tightening.

Elizabeth paused as though she expected a response. "Well, yes," Charlotte said, since everyone was staring at her. "That's a practical thing to do."

"I learned some distressing news," his mother continued. "The yacht club, which we feel is the best place for the reception, is booked solid for the next twenty-three months."

Once again, like clockwork, all eyes in the room swiveled to Charlotte, awaiting her response. "I hope you put our name on a waiting list, then," she murmured.

Elizabeth brightened, and some of the tension lines on her forehead seemed to relax. "I did better than that. You see," she went on, her voice growing more confident, "there happened to be a cancellation, and so I asked they reserve that day for you and Jason."

"Wonderful."

"You're leaving out the most important part," Jason said, his lips barely moving.

"The date is July fourteenth," Elizabeth announced, folding her hands and nodding sagely. "Don't you think that's excellent timing?"

"That sounds fine," Charlotte agreed, when it was apparent once again that everyone was waiting for her to respond. A little more than a year would give her and Jason ample time to discover if a marriage between them was viable. By then, they'd certainly know if a sexual relationship was possible. A year gave them both an opportunity to adjust.

"It's not July fourteenth of *next* year," Jason filled in, his gaze locking with hers. "Mother meant July fourteenth of *this* year."

Charlotte was too stunned to respond, other than with a gasp. Her mouth fell open in shock.

"What's the problem, Mom?" Carrie asked, looking surprised.

"But…but no one can plan a wedding of any size in that length of time," Charlotte managed after a moment. "It's…impossible."

"Not for Elizabeth," Leah said, her eyes sparkling with excitement. "Mom's been working on this since Jason mentioned the word *marriage*."

"But…"

"I've seen to everything," Elizabeth said confidently. "And it *is* possible, very possible—if you'll agree to such a quick wedding. I realize we're being unfair to you, and I do hope you'll find it in your heart to forgive me for taking over like this. The thing is, I know my son, and once he makes up his mind, that's the end of it. Jason wouldn't have been willing to wait almost two years."

"But…there are other places. Besides the yacht club, I mean."

"Yes, but none of them are as special."

"Charlotte," Jason said, raising her hand to his lips and kissing it. "I know it sounds crazy, but Mom's right. I wouldn't have wanted to wait just so my mother could put on a fancy wedding. At first I thought she'd gone berserk. The idea's preposterous, but the more I thought about it, the more I liked it."

"Leah and I will do anything we can to help," Jamie inserted. "If you want the truth, we're both thrilled."

"Taylor and Christy and their families are flying out.

They've already made their reservations," Elizabeth added.

"But they can change them," Jason told her, frowning at his mother as if to say Charlotte was under enough pressure as it was.

And he was right. She felt as if a giant hammer was poised above her head, ready to smash down on her at any second. The entire family was waiting. Happy. Excited. Thrilled. Carrie's eyes begged her to say yes.

"Of course, Taylor and Christy can change their reservations, if necessary," someone said. That was Paul, and Charlotte wanted to thank him.

"Personally, I think it's wildly romantic," Leah added. She was sitting in the recliner, her hand resting on her swollen abdomen. Paul was sitting on the armrest, his arm wrapped around his wife's shoulders, his eyes filled with love as he gazed down on her.

"Naturally I haven't made any final decisions—that would be up to you," Elizabeth said.

"I...don't know what to say."

"You must think I'm a domineering old woman, and I suppose I am, but nothing's been finalized. I don't generally meddle in my children's lives, but—"

"Actually, if you want to be angry with anyone, it should be with the rest of us," Jamie told her. "Jason is the family's last chance for Mom to put on a big wedding. She'd been looking forward to it for years and we all disappointed her. She's always done a fabulous job with the receptions, though."

"We've had our hearts set on a formal wedding for so long," Eric said.

"But in three weeks?" Charlotte murmured.

"We'll all need to work together, of course, but we can do it." Jason's mother sounded utterly convinced of that. Her eyes sought out Charlotte's and, in their beautiful blue depths, Charlotte saw how much Elizabeth wanted this. How much the entire family did. They all looked forward to contributing.

"Charlotte," Jason said softly, "would you like more time to decide?"

She glanced around; everyone was waiting. The room had gone completely silent; even the children were quiet. Charlotte didn't know how she could refuse. She closed her eyes and tried to think. If she postponed the wedding, the elder Mannings might hold it against her. It could taint their future relationship. The others were just as eager for this to happen. Each one felt guilty for cheating Eric and Elizabeth out of the family wedding they wanted.

Her whole future with the Manning family could be at stake, Charlotte thought.

"Do I...need to decide now?" she asked after an awkward moment.

"There's so little time," Elizabeth warned.

Charlotte glanced from one to the other and knew she couldn't refuse. She loved Jason and wanted to marry him more than she'd wanted anything in her life. She could be happy with him, happy in ways she'd hardly imagined before. And for the first time she and Carrie had the chance to be part of a real family.

If she were to marry Jason there was the possibility of her having another child. *If* she conquered her fear of sex. The hollow ache inside her intensified as she studied the soft swell of Leah's abdomen.

She turned to Jason, needing some kind of confirmation, some indication of what he was thinking. His eyes, so like his mother's, blue and intense, reflected his love for her. His faith in her. The desire to be part of *her* life. He believed their love was enough to overcome any obstacle. Their love was all that was necessary.

For now, because she wanted to believe it, too, that was enough for her, too.

"We have a lot to do, then, don't we?" she said, reluctantly dragging her gaze away from Jason and back to his mother.

"Does that mean you agree?"

She nodded and the entire family broke into cheers.

The excitement and the enthusiasm carried Charlotte for a full two weeks. Two of the busiest weeks of her life. When she wasn't putting in her final days at work, she was with Jason's mother.

During their first afternoon together, it became apparent that Elizabeth was a gifted organizer. She'd have to be in order to pull off a full-scale wedding in less than a month.

Ignorance had been bliss. Had Charlotte realized the sheer magnitude of what they needed to accomplish in such a short time, she would have refused.

Not a day passed that she didn't have some kind of appointment, some place to be, someone to meet, some decision to make. There were dressmakers, florists, photographers, caterers and printers. And countless decisions, all of which had to be dealt with right that minute. There wasn't time to ponder or reflect. As soon as one task was completed, Elizabeth steered her toward the next.

Carrie was delighted to be her mother's maid of honor. Charlotte's four soon-to-be sisters-in-law were to be her bridesmaids, and that meant frequent conference calls between Montana and Seattle.

When Charlotte somehow found time to see Jason, it was for a few moments, and then only in passing. He, too, was exceptionally busy.

Just when it looked like everything was falling neatly into place, and Charlotte would finally be able to return to a life of her own, a series of showers and parties began. Every night was busy with one event or another. Even the women in the office held a bridal shower for her on her last day with the agency.

The Mannings were a well-established, well-liked family. Three of Elizabeth's closest friends decided to honor Charlotte with a shower the Monday before the wedding.

"I can't believe how generous everyone is," Charlotte said to Carrie, who had just attended the shower with her. They were carrying the wide array of gifts from the car into the apartment.

"Those old ladies don't even know you," Carrie remarked, her voice filled with astonishment. "All these gifts! You don't suppose they'd throw a birthday party for me sometime, do you?"

"Carrie!"

"Just joking, Mom." She hurried past Charlotte and brought in a gaily decorated box that was still unopened. Charlotte had been told the gift was for Jason, therefore he should be the one to open it. The giver was his godmother, a spry older woman named Donna Bondi.

"You want me to see if Jason's home?" Carrie asked eagerly.

Charlotte, too, was curious to see what was inside. "Go ahead." It was almost ten, and under normal circumstances Charlotte would've been more concerned about getting to bed so she'd be ready for work in the morning, but her two-weeks' notice was up and she was officially among the unemployed.

She had the entire week free, or as free as any bride's time could be five days before her wedding.

Carrie returned a few minutes later with Jason in tow. He smiled when he saw her and kissed her lightly on the lips, then bent to stroke an ecstatic Higgins. "What's this I hear about Mrs. Bondi sending me a gift?"

"She insisted you open it yourself."

Jason's look was skeptical. "Is it a gag gift?"

"I don't know. Why don't you find out?" Charlotte leaned against the kitchen counter and crossed her arms. "When you're finished, I'll show you all the loot we collected. I had no idea everyone would be so extravagant."

"Don't get any ideas about spending our honeymoon writing thank-you notes," he warned. He was grinning but she caught a serious undertone.

The honeymoon.

She wanted to talk to Jason about that, *needed* to talk to him about it, but there'd been so little time. They'd each been caught up in a whirlwind of activity. Since the evening he'd taken her to dinner and proposed, she hadn't spent any uninterrupted time with him. Now wasn't good, either. He was tired and so was she. Perhaps they could arrange to have lunch one day later this week.

Jason tore at the paper.

"You wouldn't believe Mom," Carrie said, her hands on the back of a kitchen chair as she looked on excitedly. "She doesn't tear a single piece of wrapping paper."

"It's all so pretty," Charlotte defended herself. "And I can use it again."

"It takes her forever to unwrap anything. I had to help her tonight, or we'd still be there."

Jason paused when he uncovered a plain white box. He raised his eyes to Charlotte.

"Don't look at me. I have no idea what Mrs. Bondi sent you."

Carefully he raised the lid and folded back the white tissue paper, but Charlotte couldn't see what was inside with Carrie bending over the table.

"All right, Mrs. Bondi," Jason said, emitting a low whistle.

Carrie covered her mouth and giggled before glancing at her mother.

"What is it?" Charlotte asked.

"Wait until you see this, Mom."

Using both hands, holding on to the thin straps, Jason lifted the sheerest, slinkiest, blackest nightie Charlotte had ever seen.

Charlotte forced a smile but she felt as though the older woman had slapped her in the face.

Charlotte knew better than to even try to sleep.

The next morning she'd walk down the church aisle and pledge her life to Jason Manning. She would vow to love and honor this man who'd come to mean so much to her.

To love him....

What would happen if she couldn't love him properly? What would happen when he realized she was incapable of satisfying him sexually? Would he claim he'd been cheated the way Tom had? Would he seek out another woman who'd give him the gratification she couldn't?

Oh, please, not that, not again—she couldn't bear it.

Charlotte didn't know how Jason would react, but she knew she'd find out soon.

She stared at the bright green numbers on her clock radio as one in the morning became two and then three.

The alarm was set for six. Charlotte's stomach tightened and a cold sweat broke out on her forehead. Her happiness had been supplanted by her fears, her anxieties and the certainty that her heart would be broken once again.

She'd made an effort to talk to Jason several times, she reasoned. It wasn't like she'd *planned* it this way. In the past week alone she'd called him three times, but he'd been so busy with his practice, tying up the loose ends so he'd have two uninterrupted weeks for their honeymoon in Hawaii.

The honeymoon terrified her even more than the wedding.

What was she supposed to do? Wait for Jason to say "I do," before she whispered in his ear that she wasn't sure she could satisfy him? Or should she say something before he slipped the ring on her finger?

It seemed cruel to wait until they got to their honeymoon suite. How could she possibly tell him something like that wearing the sheer black nightie Mrs. Bondi had sent?

The tightening in her stomach grew worse, until she thought she might actually throw up.

She shouldn't have left it to the last minute like this, but she'd had no other options.

She'd tried to spend time alone with Jason, to talk to him, but they hadn't connected all week. Whenever she saw him, there were other people around. She'd decided to demand time with him after the wedding rehearsal. They had to talk.

Only that hadn't worked, either.

They'd sat next to each other at the rehearsal dinner, but before she could say more than a few words, his brothers had spirited him away for a bachelor party.

Although she hadn't been in any mood to socialize, Charlotte had pretended to have a good time with Leah, Jamie, Jason's two sisters from Montana and her future mother-in-law. If any of them noticed how distracted she was, they must have attributed it to nerves.

By now the bachelor party would be over, probably had been for hours.

What was she going to do?

Her dinner, what little she'd eaten, soured in her stomach and she thought she might be sick. Tossing back the sheets, she climbed out of bed, waiting for the nausea to subside, then wandered aimlessly into the living room.

Dragging the afghan from the back of the sofa, she wrapped it around her shoulders and huddled in the recliner, the dog at her feet. Carrie and Mandy, Russ Palmer's half sister, were in the bedroom down the hall sleeping soundly, unaware of her torment.

Jason knew so little about her first marriage. He hadn't asked for information, and she'd volunteered even less.

Instead, he'd cautiously tried to learn the details, but she'd put off explaining, afraid she'd lose him.

Soon, within less than twenty-four hours, Jason would know for himself why Tom had gone to another woman. Charlotte would have to face her inadequacies all over again.

As she sat in the dark, the shadows from the street danced against the walls, taunting her, jeering, shouting that she was a fool to believe she could ever satisfy a man.

Another hour passed and still the trapped, restless feeling refused to leave her; if anything, it became more intense. If only she could sleep. If only she could disappear. Vanish. Go someplace where no one would find her.

Squeezing her eyes shut, she tried to force her body to relax, but closing her eyes was just one more mistake. In her mind, Tom rose, scorn engraved on his handsome features. A cocky smile lifted the edges of his mouth, as if to tell her this was exactly what he'd been waiting for. As soon as she tried to make love with another man, she'd know everything he'd told her was true. *He* wasn't the one to blame for the failure of their marriage; she was. Charlotte—a woman too cold, too stiff, too lacking in sensuality.

Her eyes shot open and hot tears dripped down her face. A series of sobs racked her shoulders and took control of her body until she was trembling from head to foot.

She couldn't bear it, couldn't deal with it. Tom was

right, he'd always been right. She was a fool to believe that a sexual relationship between her and Jason would be any different, any better. They could kiss without a problem, but after the wedding, he was going to expect a lot more than a few kisses.

Panic filled her lungs, and it was all she could do not to scream in sheer terror.

Jason was wrapped in a warm cocoon of blankets, but the irritating noise refused to go away. He reached out his hand to turn off the alarm, fumbling with the dials before he realized it wasn't his alarm.

Opening one eye, he read the digital readout and discovered it was only four. He was entitled to another couple of hours' sleep. His head throbbed. Who'd come up with the bright idea of a morning wedding, anyway? No one had asked *him* about it.

The noise increased. It was now a steady pounding.

Someone was at his door. If this was one of his brothers' idea of a joke, he wasn't amused. He'd only gotten a few hours' sleep so far. If anyone in his family was involved in this, he'd make his displeasure clear in no uncertain terms.

Apparently whoever was at his door wasn't leaving. Jason struggled out of bed, pulled on a pair of pants and walked blindly through his apartment.

"Who is it?" he demanded irritably, wiping a hand down his face.

"Carrie."

"And Mandy."

The two vaulted into the room as he opened the door.

"You've got to do something!" Carrie cried.

Although his vision was a bit fuzzy, he could tell that she'd been crying.

"We didn't know what to do," Mandy wailed.

"About what?"

"This." Carrie handed him an envelope with his name written across the front. He recognized the handwriting as Charlotte's, but her usually smooth script was jerky and uneven.

Puzzled that she'd resort to writing a letter and having it delivered in the wee hours of the morning by two worried teenagers, he removed the single piece of paper.

He read it quickly.

Jason,
I'm sorry seems so inadequate, but I can't go
through with the wedding. Please, if you can, find
it in your heart to forgive me.

She'd signed it with her name.

It was a joke. Not a very good one, but he'd laugh over it in a few minutes.

"Who put you two up to this?" he asked, using his sternest voice.

"No one!" Carrie sobbed. "It's true. I got up to go to the bathroom and Mom's bedroom light was on, so I went in to see what was wrong and she wasn't there. She wasn't anywhere."

"The car's gone, too," Mandy added.

The words galvanized Jason into action. He shook the hair out of his face.

"What are we going to do?" Carrie asked, still crying softly.

"*We* aren't doing anything," Jason answered firmly.

"But someone has to do something!"

"I'll take care of it," he assured them. "Don't breathe a word of this to anyone, understand?"

"But..."

"Just do as I say. There isn't time to argue. If I'm not back with Charlotte before the car comes to take her to the church, tell everyone she's with me."

"What are you going to do?" Mandy asked, her eyes following him as he trotted back to his bedroom. He turned back and grinned. "Do?" he repeated. "Find her, of course. She's got a wedding to attend."

Twelve

Jason couldn't even guess where Charlotte was. He finished dressing, grabbed his car keys and took off, determined to find her.

He drove around for an hour, considering various possibilities. He tried to think like she would. If he were a bride running away from a wedding, where would he go? But that didn't work; he'd never run away from anything in his life, certainly not a wedding.

Darned if he knew what Charlotte was thinking. He had difficulty enough understanding women under normal circumstances. Still, he'd thought Charlotte was different. He'd thought—he'd assumed, erroneously it seemed—that Charlotte was as eager for their wedding as he was. He was shocked that he'd been so blind to her doubts. She must be terrified to have run away like this. Terrified and alone.

He should've known something like this would happen. He'd backed her into a corner, pushed her into this wedding. He'd allowed his own needs, his own desires, to overrule hers.

As dawn streaked the horizon with lavender and pink, he found himself growing ever more concerned.

Where could she be?

His driving became increasingly reckless, his speed gaining as he raced desperately from one possible location to the next. Checking the time, he was nearly swallowed by panic.

There wasn't much time left. They were both supposed to be at the church in a couple of hours. The thought of hurrying back to his family and having to announce that Charlotte had run away filled him with a sick kind of dread. He wouldn't return, he decided, until he'd found her. Until he'd done whatever he could to calm her fears, to reassure her, convince her how much he loved her.

Jason wasn't sure what led him to the beach where he'd proposed to her.

When he saw her car parked haphazardly along the side of the road, he nearly collapsed in relief. A calmness took hold of him and his pulse slowed to an even, steady pace.

He parked behind her and rushed out of his car. The sound of the door closing must have been carried away with the wind, because she didn't turn around or give any indication that she realized he was there.

He paused for a few seconds, looking at her, his heart swelling with gratitude at finding her safe.

Charlotte sat on a log, facing the water. The same log he'd knelt in front of to ask her to marry him. He felt a stab of pain as he remembered that night and how ecstatic he'd been when she accepted his proposal. He didn't expect to feel that good again until they shared in the birth of a child.

Charlotte's shoulders were slumped forward and she seemed mesmerized by the gentle lapping of the water. The wind whipped her hair, which flew wildly about, but she didn't appear to notice. She wasn't wearing a sweater. She must be half freezing, Jason thought, peeling off his jacket.

He watched her for another moment, wondering exactly what he'd say. He'd had hours to prepare for this, hours to come up with the words to tell her how much he loved her and how sorry he was for the way everything had gone. Now he found himself speechless.

She didn't see him until he was almost upon her. When she happened to look up, he saw that her face, ravaged by tears, was as pale as moonlight. She blinked, then frowned as though she couldn't quite believe he was really there.

"Jason?"

"Funny meeting you here," he said, placing his jacket around her shoulders.

"I... How did you find me?"

"It took some effort. If you had any doubts, Charlotte, I wish you'd talked them over with me."

She frowned again. "There wasn't any time... I tried, honestly I did, but you were always so busy and the time went so fast, and now…" The rest of her words faded into nothingness, her gaze avoiding his.

"There's time now," he said, sitting down on the log beside her.

Her eyes widened. "I…can't go through with it."

"Why not?" he asked calmly.

She answered him with a wrenching sob. "Please…I can't. I don't love you…"

Jason tensed. "I don't believe that, Charlotte. There's something else."

"There is… I realize now that it's your family I love. I never had one of my own and it came to me that I was marrying you for all the wrong reasons. I…can't go through with the wedding… I just can't."

Jason felt as if someone had punched him. Hard. "My…family?"

"Yes," she cried. "They're all so wonderful and I… got carried away, thinking that if I married you…Carrie and I would be part of a large, loving family. Then I saw how unfair I was being to *you*…marrying you when I didn't love you."

A cold anger took hold of Jason. An anger rooted in pain and disillusionment.

"It's too bad you didn't think of that sooner, because all this soul searching is a little too late." He grasped her arm and pulled her to her feet. She sagged against him, but he tugged at her and she straightened.

"Jason, please…"

"Shut up, Charlotte. Just shut up before I say something I'll regret." It was no comfort realizing she was the only woman who'd ever brought him willingly to his knees. He'd gone to her in love, a love so strong it had swept away his loneliness. Charlotte was throwing it all back at him now, rejecting his love, betraying him with her last-minute revelations.

Walking out on him at the eleventh hour like this couldn't be considered anything less. Nothing she could've done would have humiliated him more than to leave him standing at the altar.

"I can't be your wife... Don't you understand?"

Her voice was so weak he wasn't sure he'd heard her correctly. Not that it mattered; nothing she could have said would've had any effect on him after her confession. It didn't matter if he could hear her or not. She was mumbling, pleading with him, but he closed off his heart the same way he had his ears.

When they reached his car, he opened the passenger door and deposited her inside. He ran around to the driver's side, not knowing if he could trust her to stay put. He was mildly surprised that she didn't try to escape.

He started the engine and turned on the heater. A blast of warm air filled the car. She didn't seem to notice.

Neither spoke until they were close to the freeway entrance.

"Why are you doing this?" she demanded.

"I don't know," he answered. "But I do know you're going through with this wedding, if it's the last thing either of us ever does."

"But how can you force me to marry you, knowing what you do?"

"It must have something to do with saving my entire family from humiliation," he continued with the same chilly irony. "That family you claim to love so much. Maybe it's because I don't want my mother—who's worked day and night on this wedding for the past three weeks, who's looked forward to this day for years—to become an object of pity among her friends. Maybe it's because I'd have trouble looking my two sisters and their husbands in the eye, knowing they rearranged their entire summer, gave up their vacations, to fly out here for our wedding. Just maybe it's because I have an aversion to being ridiculed myself. I can't really tell you what else would reduce a man to drag a woman who's rejected him to the altar. But make no mistake, Charlotte, you will marry me."

"It isn't that I don't care for you," she whispered through her tears.

"Right. You care so deeply that you decided to go into hiding on our wedding day."

"I know you're angry…"

"You're damn right I'm angry."

"We can't go through with the wedding, Jason! We just can't."

"Oh, but we are, Charlotte."

"What will we do afterward? I mean, once we're married and—"

"Somehow we'll find a way to miss our flight to

Hawaii, then, first thing Monday morning, I'll file for an annulment."

"But it doesn't make sense to go through with the wedding—"

"Yes, my darling Charlotte, it does. It makes a whole lot of sense."

Charlotte was determined to survive the day, although she wasn't sure how she'd manage. She'd been a fool to run off the way she had. A fool and a coward. She was an even bigger fool to think she'd appease Jason's anger by lying.

When she'd left, she hadn't thought about what she was doing to Jason or his family. She hadn't been thinking at all, overpowered instead by her own fears.

On the way back, she tried to tell Jason she was sorry, to apologize for the hurt and humiliation she'd caused, but each time he cut her off, saying he didn't want to hear it.

The ride back to her apartment was like living through the worst nightmare of her life. Jason was so cold, so furiously angry.

He dropped her off at her apartment, took her arm, leveled his steely blue eyes on her and said, "I'll be by to pick you up in forty minutes."

"I can't possibly be ready by then."

"You can and you will. And, Charlotte, don't even think about running away again. Do you understand me?"

Charlotte nodded and almost told him it was bad luck

for the groom to see the bride before the wedding. Then she remembered the whole wedding was a farce, anyway.

"Fine. I'll be ready," she assured him calmly.

She showered, brushed her hair and dressed, but she wasn't conscious of doing any of those things. Carrie was with her, and Mandy, too, both silent and pale. Worried. What she'd done to them was terrible, Charlotte realized. They were both too young to carry this secret, too young to bear the burden of her foolishness.

Neither girl asked her any questions, and for that, Charlotte was grateful. She didn't know what she would've told them if they had.

Leah and Jamie had arrived within minutes of Jason's bringing her home. They were both happy and excited. If her complete lack of emotion bewildered them, they didn't let it show. They chatted excitedly, recalling events at their own weddings, bubbling over with enthusiasm. Charlotte tried to smile, tried to pretend this was the happiest moment of her life. Leah and Jamie seemed to believe it, even if the girls had their doubts.

Jason arrived to escort her to the church, and her future sisters-in-law shooed him away. She wore the beautiful off-white dress Elizabeth Manning had insisted on buying her, and Leah had woven flowers in her hair.

Before she knew it, Charlotte was at the church. The number of guests surprised her. Tears clogged her throat when she reminded herself that she was playing a role.

Tomorrow morning she'd go back to what her life had been before she met Jason Manning. Back to the emptiness. The loneliness.

At the appropriate moment, with organ music swirling around her, she walked dutifully down the aisle, aware every second of Jason standing at the front of the church. His eyes held hers as effectively as a vise, as though he suspected she might try to run even now. And if she tried, she didn't doubt for a second that he'd go after her.

With her morning little more than a vague memory, Charlotte found it ironic that the actual wedding ceremony was so clear to her.

Jason stood at her side, revealing no emotion, and calmly repeated his vows. Charlotte wondered why the minister didn't stop him. It was all too evident from the clipped, angry tone of his voice that he didn't mean what he was saying. He had no intention of loving her, of cherishing her, of allowing her ever to be important in his life. Not after what she'd done. Not after she'd led him to believe her motives were so deceitful. Not after she'd made him think she planned to ridicule him and his family. Whatever love he'd once felt for her was dead. He'd practically told her so himself.

When it was her turn to say her vows, Charlotte's voice was surprisingly strong. She would always love Jason, and she'd always treasure the months they'd shared. The sincerity in her voice must have caught his attention, because he looked at her for the first time since they'd approached the altar. His eyes narrowed scornfully. For a moment she nearly faltered, but decided she wouldn't let him intimidate her.

His eyes seemed to be laughing at her—a mocking laugh that told her she was the biggest hypocrite who'd ever lived. He could think what he wanted, but in her heart she knew the truth.

After the ceremony, they were whisked from the church to the reception at the yacht club.

For Charlotte, the lengthy reception was a thousand times worse than the ceremony. They stood, for what seemed like hours, with the members of their wedding party, while an endless line of guests paraded past.

Everyone was so thrilled for them, so happy, everyone except the two of them. From the moment they'd arrived at the reception, Charlotte was a heart-beat away from dissolving into tears. Heaven knew how she survived the ordeal.

Later they had to cut the cake. The photographer took picture after picture.

"Resist the urge to shove the cake in my face," Jason whispered behind a smile, when she went to feed him a small piece for the camera, "and I'll do the same."

They ate, they danced, they opened gifts. Outwardly they were the perfect couple. Madly in love, solicitous of each other, eager to be alone. Eager to start their lives together.

Only Charlotte and Jason knew the reality beneath the pretense.

Despite herself, Charlotte was impressed by what a brilliant actor Jason was. He refrained from touching her, but when it was unavoidable, his arms were gentle, his look as tender as he could make it, although she knew that he seethed with outrage. She could feel his anger, hidden below the surface, out of everyone's sight but hers. At times Charlotte felt as if that anger would devour her whole.

"Just a few minutes longer," Jason whispered harshly while they were on the dance floor. "Then we can leave."

She relaxed. "Where are we going?"

"Not the airport, so don't worry about it."

"We need to talk."

"No, we don't. Everything's been said. I'll drop you off at your apartment and you can forget this day ever happened."

"But—"

"Like I said, don't worry about it. I'll arrange everything. Once this is over, we won't ever have to see each other again. Needless to say, I'll expect you to find a new place as soon as possible."

She nodded, knowing she'd brought this on herself. But when it was time to go, there was a surprise awaiting both of them. Jason's brothers and brothers-in-law had rented two limousines. The first to take them to the airport, Rich explained, grinning proudly. And the second limousine was so the entire wedding party could follow them and see them off with as much fanfare and enthusiasm as was allowed.

Jason's eyes sought out Charlotte's when she returned from changing her clothes. His gaze assured her not to worry. He wasn't any more willing to spend two weeks in her company than she'd been about going through with the wedding. She was sure he'd find some way to miss the flight.

Except that he didn't.

His mother waited with them at the airline counter, wiping the tears from her eyes as she hugged her son. Carrie was there, too, more relaxed now, excited that she and Higgins would be spending two weeks with Leah and Paul.

Charlotte hugged Jason's mother farewell, tears brimming in her eyes. "No woman ever had a more beautiful wedding," she whispered. "Thank you."

Her father-in-law was waiting when she'd finished, holding out his arms to her as though she were a small child needing reassurance. Nothing could be closer to the truth.

"Eric, thank you," she murmured, as she slipped into his embrace. This might well be the only opportunity she'd have to express her gratitude. Soon enough Jason's parents would know. She wouldn't be able to face them.

"You call me Dad," Eric said, hugging her close. "We already love you like a daughter, Charlotte."

Tears blurred her vision and when she turned, she nearly collided with Jason. He took her by the elbow, his fingers pinching her skin. "You're laying it on a bit thick, aren't you?"

She didn't answer him, couldn't have said a word if she'd tried. They got their boarding passes as everyone watched. They were going to Hawaii, like it or not.

Charlotte realized there was no escape for them, unless they owned up to the truth immediately. Jason didn't look any more pleased than she did, but obviously didn't want to disillusion the family quite so soon.

As he led her into the security area, away from his family, he muttered, "I didn't plan this."

"I know," she said with a helpless sigh. "Oh—my car. I left it at the beach."

"Mandy's getting it for you."

His thoughtfulness surprised her. "Thank you."

"Don't mention it," he said sarcastically. "I wanted it back in the apartment lot so you wouldn't have any trouble leaving again. Next time you can go with my blessing."

Their seats were in business class and they were quickly served glasses of champagne that neither of them drank.

As the plane taxied away from the jetway and toward the airstrip, he closed his eyes, heaved a massive sigh and said, "Don't worry, I'll get us out of this yet."

Charlotte nodded and lowered her gaze. "I'll do everything I can to stay out of your way."

"That would be appreciated."

The flight was five hours, but it seemed closer to fifty. Jason didn't exchange one unnecessary word with Charlotte. At this rate, she didn't know how they'd be able to spend two weeks in each other's company.

Jason must have been thinking the same thing. "I'll see what I can do about arranging a flight back to

Seattle as soon as we land," he told her briskly, without a shred of emotion. No regret, no disappointment, nothing.

Charlotte bit her lip. "I…I didn't pack much of anything…since the suitcase was just for show."

He didn't respond. By the time they landed and collected their luggage, Charlotte was falling asleep on her feet. Apparently Jason suspected as much, since he made some excuse about contacting the airlines from the hotel instead of rushing her onto a return flight. But she wasn't sure if this small kindness was for her benefit or his own, since he couldn't have had much more sleep than she had.

She barely noticed the scenery as the taxi carried them through town. Their hotel was on Waikiki Beach, built on white sands and surrounded by swaying palms.

When they went to check in at the front desk, Charlotte stepped back, letting Jason take care of the necessary paperwork. He was obviously upset about something, but she couldn't tell what.

"Is everything all right?" she asked, as they moved toward the elevator.

"I thought we could get a double room, but…" Jason rubbed a hand across his face, looking weary and defeated. "My parents booked us into the bridal suite."

"Oh." Charlotte didn't fully realize the implications of that until the bellman ushered them, with much fanfare, into the corner suite. There was one bed. A king-size bed that loomed before her.

Charlotte's startled gaze sought-out Jason's as he paid the attendant and closed the door. The fear she'd managed to bury for hours spilled over now, but before she could say a word, he turned to her.

"Don't look so shocked. It isn't as if I intend to make love to you."

"But where will...we sleep?"

He laughed, the sound abrupt. "If you want to call down to the front desk and order a rollaway for the bridal suite, then by all means, be my guest. Frankly, I feel enough of a fool for one day, so I'll leave that option to you."

With no real alternative, she showered, put on an old T-shirt and crawled between the crisp sheets of the bed, making sure she was as far on her side as possible.

She was drifting off to sleep when Jason finished his shower and returned to the bedroom. He stood for several minutes looking down at her. Her heart roared like a crazed animal as she wondered about his intentions. He could force her. Tom had often enough, using her body, leaving her feeling sick and abused afterward. She'd curl up tightly while he shouted how incompetent she was, how unattractive, how lacking. She'd lie there silently as the ugly, demeaning words rained down on her. When he was done with his tirade he'd leave.

The memories made her shiver with revulsion and fear.

"Charlotte."

She didn't answer, pretending to be asleep. Jason

was angry with her, angrier than she'd ever seen him. Eyes closed, she lay still, her heart pounding with dread.

She heard Jason dressing, heard him pause and then, after a moment, heard him turn off the light and leave the room.

Abruptly Charlòtte sat up. He'd left her, walked away just like Tom had, as though he couldn't bear to be in the same room with her. Like Tom, he couldn't wait to be rid of her.

He'd left without a word.

Wasn't that what she wanted? Then why did she feel so alone, so deserted and unloved, so empty inside?

The tears that had threatened most of the day broke free with a low, eerie wail. She tucked her knees against her chest as the sobs overtook her.

She wept for all she'd lost. Jason's love. Any chance of sharing their lives. The dream of having another child. The family she'd never had. It was gone now, crushed by her own hand.

It was too late to try and get any of it back. Jason hated her. She could never recapture what she'd destroyed with her fear. Never rebuild the trust she'd demolished when she'd run away.

She sobbed until the well of grief was emptied. Even that wasn't enough. She tore at the sheets, pulling the blankets from the bed and beating the pillows.

It didn't take long to exhaust what little energy she had, and she fell across the bed sobbing, then fell into a deep, troubled sleep.

* * *

Jason came back to the room an hour later, moving as silently as possible, not wanting to wake Charlotte. He wished he could hate his wife, punish her for what she'd done. She deserved to suffer, didn't she?

But if that was really the case, then why was *he* the one in pain? He saw her climb into bed and curl up, and it was all he could do not to dash across the room and take her in his arms. This woman had betrayed him, and yet he wanted to comfort her.

It was either leave the room or beg her forgiveness for forcing her to endure this day. She wasn't entitled to his forgiveness, he reminded himself, which meant there was only one option. He'd left.

He'd gone for a walk on the beach, which wasn't exactly how he'd expected to spend his wedding night. Not that he was any great shakes as a husband. A hundred times or more he'd gone over his own part in this fiasco. He'd rushed Charlotte into marriage and so had his family, not giving her a chance for second thoughts. Looking back, he understood now that it was the urgency of his mother's idea that he'd found so appealing. Now he understood why.

He'd rushed into marriage with Charlotte because, deep down, he'd been afraid that if she'd had the chance to change her mind, she would. And he'd been right.

Jason didn't know what lunacy had prompted him to make her go through with the ceremony. To avoid embarrassment? Having their marriage annulled the following week would still embarrass him and his family.

There was the problem, too, of returning all the wedding gifts. Eventually he'd have to face people. Make explanations.

He'd taken the easy way out, delaying the inevitable because of his pride.

Charlotte had wanted to cancel the wedding and he'd perversely refused to release her. So now they were stuck in Hawaii on a two-week honeymoon neither of them wanted. Stuck in each other's company, in the bridal suite no less, until he could find a flight back to Seattle.

Once his eyes had adjusted to the dark, Jason made his way across the elegant room. Charlotte was still curled up on the bed, but the sheets and blankets were strewn about as though a storm had raged through.

He discovered a second and a third pillow hurled across the room. One was on the floor, the other dangling from a chair. It looked as if his bride had thrown a temper tantrum.

So she hadn't liked it that he'd left. A smile played across his lips. It was the first time since he'd found her on the beach that she'd displayed any emotion.

The thought of Charlotte losing her temper pleased him, until he remembered she wasn't given to bouts of anger. He felt a pang of concern but brushed it aside—it belonged to the past, to the old Charlotte, the one he'd loved.

Exhausted and depressed, he gazed about the room and noted that the bed was all she'd bothered to disarrange. Everything else in the room remained untouched.

Not knowing what to think, and too tired to care, he quietly stripped off his clothes and slipped beneath a rumpled sheet. It didn't take him long to fall asleep, but his dreams were disturbing and he woke several times before morning.

Not once during the night did Charlotte move. She stayed on her side, facing away from him, never changing her position.

He woke in the morning, the bright sunshine slashing through the bedroom curtains. Charlotte was on her back, already awake. She shifted her head and stared at him with eyes so filled with pain that he hurt just looking at her.

"I lied when I said I didn't love you, Jason," she whispered and a tear rolled down the side of her face. "I do... so very much. I'm sorry...for everything I've done."

He nodded, his throat thick. "I'm sorry, too, Charlotte."

Thirteen

Charlotte closed her eyes because looking at Jason was so painful, knowing he hated her, knowing he'd never really forgive her for what she'd done.

"I lied when I said I wanted to marry you because of your family. I…ran away because I was afraid."

"Of me?"

Her pulse scampered. She should've told him the truth weeks earlier. She'd agreed to be his wife; he had a right to know. But the truth was so easy to put off, so easy to deny. So hard to explain.

There'd been opportunities to tell him, plenty of them, although she'd tried to convince herself otherwise. She'd been too much of a coward to present Jason with the truth. And then, when time ran out, she'd panicked.

"Charlotte?" Jason said in a low voice. "What are you afraid of?"

She couldn't explain that she was, to put it bluntly,

afraid of sex. Of intimacy. That wasn't what a man wanted to hear. Not just Jason, but any man.

He deserved so much more than she was capable of giving him. He deserved a woman who was emotionally whole and healthy. A woman who was physically responsive. Not someone scared and battle-weary and all but dead to her own sexuality.

"I owe you an explanation…."

"I'd say so," he agreed, but his voice was devoid of the previous day's sarcasm, without a trace of anger.

"I meant to tell you sooner. To give you the choice of going through with the wedding or not. But as time went on I—I couldn't…and then it was too late."

"Tell me now."

Charlotte thought back to an age when she'd been innocent, vulnerable and naive. "My mother died while I was in high school. My father had abandoned us years earlier and I don't think my mother ever recovered. If he contacted her at any point after he left, I didn't know about it. She was different after he was gone. It was like she'd given up on life. She loved me, though—I know she did—and she'd been insightful enough to plan for my future."

Jason's hand reached across the bed for hers. Their fingers entwined and Charlotte was grateful for his touch.

"I met Tom my first year of college. He came from another state and was attending classes on a limited scholarship. He was intelligent and good-looking. When he asked me out, I was thrilled. He seemed to like me…."

Later I realized it wasn't me that attracted him, but the insurance money I'd received when my mother died. After a few months, we made love and…and he asked me to marry him. I didn't have any family and…I desperately needed someone. I was too stupid to know why Tom really wanted to marry me. He saw marriage as a way of paying for his education without having to work for it.

"I dropped out of school after one semester and we got married. The money that was meant for my education went toward Tom's while I got a full-time job to pay our living expenses."

Jason's hand flinched, tightening around hers.

"I should've gotten out of the marriage as soon as I figured out he was using me. Instead, I compounded my mistake. I thought if I got pregnant it would make everything better. If Tom didn't love me, surely he'd love the baby."

"You've been so hard on yourself."

"I'll never regret having Carrie. She's been the best thing in my life…but Tom wasn't happy." She hesitated, reliving the terrible scene, so many years past, when she'd told Tom she was pregnant. He'd wanted her to have an abortion, even given her the money. She'd lied and told him she'd done it, hiding her pregnancy until it was too late. He'd been so furious that he'd hit her. The blow had been so hard, it had loosened three of her teeth.

"Go on," Jason prompted.

"I had Carrie and for a while I thought the marriage

might work. Tom liked his little girl and was proud of her."

"You told me Tom was having an affair. When did this happen?"

"It started while I was pregnant. Tom enjoyed sex…and after a while he said I was too fat and ugly to make love to, and everything came to a stop." Charlotte remembered how relieved she was, how grateful because she no longer had to give in to his rough physical demands. She was working a forty-hour week, waiting tables, and was too exhausted at night to satisfy him. He'd been telling her for months that a man needed enthusiasm from his wife during sex, but Charlotte had never seemed able to rouse any. It was like making love to a corpse, he told her.

"I…I never was very good at sex," she continued in a tight voice. "And after Carrie was born, I lost all interest." Actually any pleasure in the physical aspects of their marriage had died months earlier, when Tom had demanded she have an abortion. After Carrie was born, she found herself unwilling to make any effort to please him physically.

"That was when the really bad fights began," she said as evenly as the remembered emotions would allow. "Tom claimed it was his right to make love to me whenever he wanted and…and…" Her throat closed up, forcing her to stop.

"Did he rape you, Charlotte?"

Biting her lower lip, she nodded. Only Tom hadn't called it rape; he'd said it was his right. He'd married her, hadn't he? That meant she'd given him the right to do whatever he wanted with her body the moment she'd signed the marriage document.

Jason moved closer and brought her into his arms, cradling her head against his shoulder, stroking her hair. His chest was heaving and Charlotte knew he was fighting his own anger.

Her eyes glazed over with tears as she struggled to hold back the fear, the memory of the violence, the feeling of powerlessness, the revulsion of those terror-filled episodes. Her breathing became labored.

"I…couldn't satisfy Tom," she admitted in a breathless whisper.

"That has everything to do with Tom—not with you." He paused. "Are you afraid you won't be able to satisfy me?"

She nodded through her tears.

"But, Charlotte," he said, raising himself on one elbow and gazing down at her, "how can you think that? Everything between us has always been so good. Or am I wrong? Haven't you enjoyed the times we kissed?"

She lowered her lashes. "Yes…but they've frightened me."

"I never forced you."

"I…I know that. You've been so patient and gentle. I almost convinced myself I could make love again…that I could erase those nightmare years with Tom and start all over…but I can't. That's why I ran away…that's the real reason, not what I told you earlier."

"Why couldn't you tell me this before?"

She wiped the tears from her face, and swallowed the bittersweet agony of the moment. "Because I love you so much."

Her words were met with a puzzled hesitation. "You wouldn't tell me because you love me?"

She nodded, and hiccuped a sobbing laugh. "It sounds ludicrous, I know, but it's true. Because I couldn't stand to lose you—not that way. Because if we ever did make love, you'd see—you wouldn't want me anymore."

"How could you think that?" Jason asked.

This was the moment she'd dreaded. The moment of truth. She turned her head away, unwilling to look at him, unwilling to let him see her face. A tightness gripped her chest, crushing her, the pressure so intense she could hardly breathe.

"Charlotte?"·

It would've been easier if he hadn't been so gentle. She could deal with his anger and frustration, but not his tenderness. She didn't know how to respond to that in a man.

Shoving aside the blanket and sheet, she sat on the edge of the bed. When he caressed her back, she stood, unable to deal with being touched just then. Her arms were locked around her middle and the aching pressure in her chest rose, settling in her throat. Tears burned her eyes.

"Tell me," he demanded, not unkindly. "Just say it."

"I can't be your wife."

"It's too late for that," he murmured. "You already are."

"I'm not…not in the ways that matter to a man."

"Oh?"

"Don't you understand what I'm saying?" she cried. "Do I have to spell out every degrading detail? Is that what you want? Then fine, I'll say it. I can't be your wife because I can't make love." She gulped in a deep breath. "I'm frigid, Jason. The term might be out of fashion but it still applies."

There was a brief, shocked silence. Then Jason started to laugh.

"Don't you dare laugh at me! Don't you dare laugh." A fury rose inside Charlotte, one that had been years in the making, one so strong there was no holding back. She threw herself at him, arms swinging, feet kicking, fingers clawing, before he had a chance to react.

He caught her by the wrists. "Charlotte…I wasn't laughing at *you*."

She barely heard his words, not that it mattered. She twisted and bucked in his hold. He twisted, too, and with the momentum of his weight they fell together on the bed. He was sprawled over her upper body, his thigh across her legs, holding her down.

Her chest was heaving, her shoulders jerking upward in an effort to escape.

"Charlotte, for heaven's sake, I wasn't laughing at you," he said again.

She gritted her teeth, refusing to answer him.

"Stop struggling, before you destroy any chance of my fathering our future child."

She went still, although the fight hadn't completely left her.

"Now let me explain."

There were too many years of agony inside her, too many insecurities to be soothed away with a few simple words. "No. Just let me go."

"In a minute. Then if you still want me to release you I will. You owe me this much. All right?"

She twisted her head away from him, still refusing to answer.

"I love you, Charlotte. I realized when we first started seeing each other that you'd been badly hurt by your ex-husband. I didn't understand the extent of it until now, but in some ways I think not knowing was for the best. It would have intimidated me in the beginning."

A sob tore through her throat.

"The first time we kissed...I wish I knew how to explain it, but I knew you were different. That moment was different than any I'd ever known before. Kissing you was so good."

Charlotte didn't respond, but she knew he was right. Their kisses *had* been good. Very good.

"It got even better, didn't it?"

She nodded, although only slightly.

"You're not frigid, or whatever term the psychologists prefer now. Not even close. What you are, my love, is afraid, and for a very legitimate reason. You've been sexually abused."

"I'm sexually...damaged. Forever."

"No, not forever. In time you'll heal. We'll heal together." He said it with such conviction, as though they faced only a small problem, when to her it was bigger than both of them. Bigger than even their love.

"But it isn't *you* who...can't make love," she sobbed. "It's me. You're not the one who has to heal...and I don't know if I can."

"We're in this together, Charlotte. Whatever it takes."

"There isn't any reason you should—"

"We can't heal," he interrupted, "unless we try. We can't sweep this under the carpet and ignore it. I'm not so stupid as to believe that all the pain and all the memories will go away simply because we make love and it's as good as our kisses have been."

"I...don't know if I'll ever be able to forget."

Jason rolled away from her, freeing her arms and legs. He stood and raked his hand through his hair. "The decision is yours, and I'll abide by whatever you want. I'm not going to force you to be my wife. I've made some mistakes in this relationship and just now was one of them. I'm sure I'll make more. You should know that."

"I don't understand what you're saying." She sat up and wiped the tears from her burning cheeks, her hands trembling. Jason had moved away from her and was staring out the window.

"Like I said, the decision is yours. If you want me to file for an annulment, then I will. I'll make the arrangements to get us off this island as quickly as possible. As soon as I can, I'll take care of all the legalities. In a few days there won't be anything to bind us together—if that's what you want."

"I see." Her heart filled with mourning.

"But there's something you should understand, Charlotte. If you decide you want to give this marriage a try, there'll be no turning back."

She did understand, and the thought filled her with panic.

"I'm willing to devote myself to you and the marriage, but I'll need the same kind of commitment from you. In other words, you're going to have to *want* to heal. It may mean counseling for you, for us both. We both have to be willing to do whatever it takes."

"I don't know if I could…ever tell anyone else about my marriage to Tom."

"That's your decision, too. If you want to stay my wife, you have to realize that the time will come when we *will* make love—but only when you're ready. And when we do, it'll be good, Charlotte…I promise you that."

"How often?" It was probably a stupid question, but one she needed to know. She might be able to bear it if Jason wanted to make love occasionally. She might be able to overcome the terror if he wasn't too demanding.

"I can't answer that because I don't know."

"More than once a month?"

He turned away from her, but not before she saw his smile. "Yes, Charlotte, more than once a month."

"I see."

"It seems to me that you have some serious thinking to do. Perhaps it would be best if I left for a while. When I come back, you can tell me your thoughts. Does that sound fair?"

She waited until he turned to look at her before she nodded.

So this was what it meant to love someone, Jason thought as he left the hotel and headed for the beach. He felt as though a hole had been carved through the center of his life, and nothing—besides Charlotte—was capable of filling it. He wanted to believe she'd realize he wasn't another Tom. That didn't seem to be the case, however.

He'd felt a glimmer of hope when he'd first started talking, trying to get through to her, soothe her fears. The anger had drained from her eyes as she'd studied him, seeming to measure his words. He'd seen trust gradually replace that anger.

He hoped she'd be willing to give their marriage a chance. He loved her, but he wasn't naive or arrogant enough to believe his feelings for her could, on their own, heal the horror of her experience. She was going to need more than his love, more than his gentleness. Being tender and patient with her wasn't going to wipe out the trauma of having been raped by her own husband. No wonder she was so terrified.

Jason sensed that other things, maybe even worse than those he knew, had happened in her marriage. Things she hadn't told him yet.

Her marriage had been so ugly, so abusive. He

marveled that she'd even considered remarrying. Knowing what he did now, it didn't surprise him that she'd run away at the eleventh hour. It wouldn't surprise him if she decided to go through with the annulment, either.

He'd given her the option, laid everything out on the table for her to examine. His love, his commitment, his willingness to do whatever he could to help her overcome her fears. But in light of what he'd learned, it seemed so little....

A couple of hours later, Jason returned to the hotel to confront Charlotte again. Two hours didn't seem like much time to come to such a monumental decision, but he wanted to be with her.

Perhaps it would be best if he waited for her to come to him, but he quickly rejected that idea as impractical. If he was going to waste precious time debating with himself, he should do it over something important, like how was he going to live without Charlotte. How was he going to let her go, the only woman he'd ever truly loved? Those were the questions he should be asking himself.

Charlotte sat in the darkened room, the drapes pulled against the brightness of the sun, waiting for Jason. Having carefully considered her husband's words, she knew with a clarity that defied explanation what she was meant to do. She *should* remain his wife. *Should* share his bed. *Should* share his life.

The heavy ache in her chest intensified. Fresh tears

moistened her eyes. Jason had offered her his love, his devotion, and his wholehearted commitment. He'd done so with a courage that left her humbled. He was willing to help her heal, but Charlotte didn't know if it would be enough.

There was no guarantee the pain would ever end. No guarantee she'd ever feel whole again. Healing demanded courage. It meant reaching back into the past, into the pain, and reliving the nightmare. Wasn't enduring it *once* enough? Healing meant risking whatever serenity she'd found in the years since her divorce. Healing meant trusting a man again, trusting him enough to freely share her body.

Charlotte closed her eyes, wanting to blot everything out. She was such a coward. A world-class wimp. She knew what she *should* do, but it was so frightening. She wanted to run away, bury her feelings. Hide, the way she'd been doing for years. There was something so comfortable in denial.

There had to be more to life than this choking anger. More than this grief and fear.

With Jason's love there *was* more.

There was hope.

Charlotte must have fallen asleep. When she stirred she saw that the drapes were open and Jason was sitting on the lanai, sipping a glass of orange juice.

"Hello," he said with a smile.

"Hi." She felt a little shy as she slipped out of bed and rubbed her eyes. "What time is it?"

"Afternoon. I imagine you're starved."

Now that he mentioned it, she realized she was hungry. The last food she'd eaten had been at their wedding dinner, and that had been the day before.

"I took the liberty of ordering you lunch."

She smiled and joined him on the lanai. "I slept for so long."

"You needed the rest." He looked so familiar and handsome, sitting there in the sunlight with his baseball cap shading his eyes. His skin was bronzed, and his eyes, as blue as the Hawaiian sky, roamed over her with undisguised love and tenderness. "Listen, Charlotte, I was wrong."

"Wrong?"

"I shouldn't have given you an ultimatum. You're going to need more than a few hours to decide what you want. I made the same mistake earlier by rushing you into a marriage you didn't want and…"

"But I did want this marriage, very badly."

"Did," he repeated in a husky, regretful voice.

"Do," she corrected firmly.

For several minutes, he said nothing. "Even now, knowing what it'll mean?"

"Even now," she said, holding out her hand to him.

Jason held it fast. "I love you, Charlotte Manning."

"I know." Her voice broke, and she struggled not to break down and weep. Someday she'd tell him how close she'd come to walking away from the brightest promise of her life. She'd tell him how she'd finally decided that loving Jason, being his wife, sharing his life wasn't just something she *should* do, but something she *wanted* to do. *Ached* to do, with all her heart. Someday she'd tell him all of this.

"I don't want to live without you."

He reached for her, bringing her onto his lap, his mouth instinctively finding hers. Everything she'd planned to say was caught between two hungry mouths. Trapped between two pounding hearts.

Fourteen

Several months later a storm, a Seattle cloudburst, woke Charlotte. Dawn was on the horizon, but very little light filtered through the gray clouds. The wind beat hard against the windows, rattling them until Charlotte feared they might break.

Gently setting aside the covers, she climbed out of bed and crept into the living room. Higgins was sleeping there, looking worried. She patted his head and offered him reassurances.

She opened the living-room drapes just in time to watch a bolt of lightning rip apart the night. For an hour or so afterward, smiling contentedly, she watched morning creep across the sky. Her life, inside and out, was everything she wanted it to be. Jason had moved into her apartment; they planned to buy a house in the spring. She was taking a break from work, enrolled in an advanced accounting course. Eventually she'd handle all of his bookkeeping and maybe look for a few other clients, too. Yes, life was full of new possibilities.

"Charlotte?" Jason murmured when she returned to bed. He reached for her and without a second's hesitation she slipped into his embrace.

"There's a storm," she whispered.

His smile was lazy, sleepy. "So I hear. Are you frightened?"

"Not anymore." There'd been a time when she would've been terrified, but that time was long past. She felt intensely alive, completely calm. The dangerous storms were gone from her life. She'd survived the raging wind, the drenching rain, the booming thunder. That was all in the past. Her future was holding her in his arms.

She sighed, cuddling close to her husband, suffused with a feeling of profound joy.

"I love you," she whispered.

"I know," he said without opening his eyes. "Believe me, I know."

She slid her arms up his shoulders and brought her mouth to his. He welcomed her kiss, which was slow and deep. Hot excitement poured into her blood. Soon the kiss was no longer slow, but hungry, needy.

Charlotte felt Jason's chest lift with a shuddering intake of breath.

"I want to make love," she said against his lips.

Jason went still. His hand, which was sliding up her thigh, stopped at her hip.

"You're sure?"

It was the first time she'd ever made the request, the first time she'd ever initiated their lovemaking.

"Yes."

Lightning briefly brightened the room, shadows frolicked and danced against the walls, followed by the roar of thunder. The bedroom vibrated with sound.

Jason, ever-sensitive to her moods, paused, but she refused to allow any hesitation. She drew his mouth down to hers and they kissed, until Charlotte's whole body seemed to throb with excitement.

Gently Jason removed her nightgown, pulling it over her head. He'd awakened her to an entire world of sensual pleasure in the months since their marriage, a world she wanted to explore *now*.

He hungrily covered her mouth with his own and her head spun, her nails digging into his back. Abruptly she broke off the kiss, her shoulders heaving. "Jason, please...I want you."

He didn't need any further encouragement....

"Okay, so far?" he asked sometime later.

"Oh, yes," she whispered, smiling her assurance. The pleasure was so keen it was almost beyond bearing.

Lightning flashed and thunder rolled, punctuating their lovemaking. "Jason...oh, Jase," she cried out, her voice a trembling wail of pleasure as her senses caught fire, exploding into a mindless madness. Her body shuddered as she gave herself to the storm, to her husband, to the night.

Afterward, when he, too, had reached completion, they were both panting. Jason gathered her in his arms, and they were silent, words between them unnecessary.

Eventually their breathing steadied.

"I still have trouble believing how good this is," Charlotte whispered. "Making love, I mean."

Jason kissed the crown of her head. "It always has been."

"Not in the beginning."

"It was," he said. "Because you let me try to prove how much I love you."

Charlotte was quiet for a moment as she absorbed his words. Their first attempts at making love, on their honeymoon, had left her frustrated and in tears. She was convinced Jason had made a terrible mistake in marrying her. He wouldn't allow her to criticize herself, though. His patience astonished her and gave her the courage to keep trying.

She'd struggled with her inadequacies, silently condemning herself, but on the seventh night of their stay, they'd broken through the restraints and made beautiful, intoxicating love. Charlotte had wanted everything to be magically different from then on, but that would have been unrealistic. Her fears were unpredictable and continued to be for weeks. But now, four months after their wedding, loving Jason was the most incredible experience of her life.

Tears slipped down Charlotte's cheeks as she recalled the first weeks of their marriage—his gentleness, his unwillingness to give up, his *love*.

"You're crying," he whispered, his lips against her hair.

"You're not supposed to notice."

"But I have. Are you going to tell me why?"

Emotion clogged her throat as she struggled to hold back the tears. "In a minute."

Jason's brow creased with a thoughtful frown. "Is it something that came from your meeting with Bill?"

Bill was her counselor; she saw him twice a week. She shook her head. "You promise you won't laugh?"

"I'll try."

"I'm crying because I'm so happy."

"Happy," Jason repeated slowly. "But if you cry when you're happy, what do you do when you're sad?"

"Cry," she returned with irrefutable logic. "Now aren't you going to ask me *why* I'm so happy?"

"I don't need to. It's obvious."

"It is?"

"Of course. You're married to me."

Charlotte laughed at his mock arrogance. "Carrie cried, too."

"Carrie's *that* happy?"

"It's the reason she's spending the night with a friend. I wanted the evening alone with you."

Jason snickered. "If that's the case, why'd you go to bed at six-thirty?"

"I didn't plan that," she murmured, "but I think it's going to be pretty much the norm for the next few months. I couldn't seem to get enough sleep when I was pregnant with Carrie, either."

"Cute, Charlotte, very cute. You couldn't possibly be—" He stopped cold, his eyes widening.

"It's true," she said, pressing her head to his chest. She smiled as the erratic beat of his heart sounded in her ear.

"How far…?"

"A month."

He shook his head as though in a trance.

"It was inevitable, you know," she told him, happiness spilling from her heart. "How could I not be pregnant? We've been making love for months. And we decided not to use birth control for this very reason."

"Yes, but…"

"When the lovemaking's this good, doesn't it make sense that the result will be equally beautiful?"

Jason kissed her again, his mouth worshipping hers. "I love you so much."

Charlotte sighed and closed her eyes, utterly content. She'd conquered her fears, begun to heal her pain. She'd survived the memories and triumphed over her past.

The future stretched before her, filled with bright promise. She wasn't going to miss a single moment.

* * * * *

SAME TIME, NEXT YEAR

To Beth Huizenga, my friend.
I admire your strength, your romantic heart and
your love of life.

Prologue

James had been warned. Ryan Kilpatrick, a longtime friend and fellow attorney, had advised him to stay clear of the downtown area tonight. The crowd that gathered on Fremont Street between Main and Las Vegas Boulevard was said to be close to twenty thousand.

But James couldn't resist. Although he had a perfectly good view of the festivities from his hotel room window, he found the enthusiasm of the crowd contagious. For reasons he didn't care to examine, he wanted to be part of all this craziness.

The noise on the street was earsplitting. Everyone seemed to be shouting at once. The fireworks display wasn't scheduled to begin for another thirty minutes, and James couldn't see how there was room for a single other person.

A large number of law-enforcement officers roamed

the area, confiscating beer bottles and handing out paper
cups. A series of discordant blasts from two-foot-long
horns made James cringe. Many of the participants wore
decorative hats handed out by the casinos and blew paper
noisemakers that uncurled with each whistle.

James remained on the outskirts of the throng,
silently enjoying himself despite the noise and confusion. If he were younger, he might have joined in the festivities.

Thirty-six wasn't old, he reminded himself, but he
looked and felt closer to forty. Partners in prestigious
law firms didn't wear dunce caps and blow noisemakers. He was too conservative—some might say stodgy—
for such nonsense, but it was New Year's Eve and
staying in his room alone held little appeal.

Impatient for the fireworks display, the crowd started
chanting. James couldn't make out the words, but the
message was easy enough to understand. It amused
him that the New Year's celebration would be taking
place three hours early in order to coordinate with the
one in New York's Times Square. Apparently no one
seemed to care about the time difference.

As if in response to the demand, a rocket shot into the
air from the roof of the Plaza Hotel. The night sky brightened as a starburst exploded. The crowd cheered wildly.

Although he'd intended to stand on the sidelines,
James found himself unwillingly thrust deeper and
deeper into the crowd. Luckily he wasn't prone to claus-
trophobia. People crushed him from all sides. At another
time, in another place, he might have objected, but the
joy of the celebration overrode any real complaint.

It was then that he saw her.

She was struggling to move away from the crowd, with little success. James wasn't sure what had originally attracted his attention, but once he noticed her, he couldn't stop watching. Joyous shouts and cheers rose in the tightly packed crowd, but the young woman didn't share the excitement. She looked as if she'd rather be anywhere else in the world.

She was fragile, petite and delicate in build. He saw that she fought against the crowd but was trapped despite her best efforts.

James soon found himself gravitating in her direction. Within minutes she was pressed up against him, chin tucked into her neck as she tried to avoid eye contact.

"Excuse me," he said.

She glanced up at him and attempted a smile. "I was the one who bumped into you."

He was struck by how beautiful she was. Her soft brown hair curved gently at her shoulders, and he was sure he'd never seen eyes more dark or soulful. He was mesmerized by her eyes—and by the pain he read in their depths.

"Are you all right?" he felt obliged to ask.

She nodded and bit her lip. He realized how pale she was and wondered if she was about to faint.

"Let me help." He wasn't some knight who rescued damsels in distress. Life was filled with enough difficulties without taking on another person's troubles. Yet he couldn't resist helping her.

She answered him with a quick nod of her head.

"Let's get out of here," he suggested.

"I've been trying to do exactly that for the last twenty minutes." Her voice was tight.

James wasn't sure he could do any better, but he planned to try. Taking her by the hand, he slipped around a couple kissing passionately, then past a group of teens with dueling horns, the discordant sound piercing the night. Others appeared more concerned with catching the ashes raining down from the fireworks display than with where they stood.

Perhaps it was his age or the fact that he sounded authoritative, but James managed to maneuver them through the crush. Once they were off Fremont Street, the crowd thinned considerably.

James led her to a small park with a gazebo that afforded them some privacy. She sank onto the bench as if her legs had suddenly given out from under her. He saw that she was trembling and sat next to her, hoping his presence would offer her some solace.

The fireworks burst to life overhead.

"Thank you," she whispered. She stood, teetered, then abruptly sat back down.

"You want to talk about it?" he asked.

"Not really." Having said that, she promptly burst into tears. Covering her face with both hands, she gently rocked back and forth.

Not knowing what to do, James put his arms around her and held her against him. She felt warm and soft in his embrace.

"I feel like such a fool," she said between sobs. "How could I have been so stupid?"

"We're often blind to what we don't want to see."

"Yes, but... Oh, I should've known. I should've guessed there was someone else. Everything makes sense now...I couldn't have been any blinder."

He shrugged, murmuring something noncommittal.

She straightened, and James gave her his pressed handkerchief. She unfolded it, wiped away the tears and then clutched it in both hands.

"I'm sorry," she choked out.

"Talking might help," he said.

She took several moments to mull this over. "I found him with another woman," she finally said. "He wanted me to come to Vegas with him after Christmas, and I couldn't get time off from work. So I said he should go and have fun with his friends. Then...then I was able to leave early this afternoon. I wanted to surprise him on New Year's Eve and I drove straight here. I surprised him, all right."

And got the shock of her life, too, James mused.

"They were in bed together." Her words were barely audible, as if the pain was so intense she found it difficult to speak. "I ran away and he came after me and...and tried to explain. He's been seeing her for some time.... He didn't mean to fall in love with her, or so he claims." She laughed and hiccuped simultaneously.

"You were engaged?" he asked, noting the diamond on her left hand.

She nodded, and her gaze fell to her left hand. She suddenly jerked off the diamond ring and shoved it into her purse. "Brett seemed distant in the last few months, but we've both been busy with the holidays. I noticed he didn't seem too disappointed when I couldn't get time off from work. Now I know why."

It was preferable to learn about her fiancé's roving eye before she married him, but James didn't offer platitudes. He hadn't wanted to hear them himself.

"The problem is, I really love him." She shook almost uncontrollably. "I want to claw his eyes out, and yet I know I'll always love him."

"Are you hoping to patch things up?"

She raised her head. "No. It's over. I told him that and I meant it. I could never trust him again, but you know what?" She hesitated and drew in a deep breath. "I think he was grateful when I broke the engagement. He doesn't want me back—he wants *her.*" She stiffened, as if bracing herself against an attack.

"It hurts right now, but it'll get better in time," James said, squeezing her hand.

"No, it won't," she whispered. "It'll never get better. I know it won't."

James partially agreed with her. Part of him would always belong to Christy Manning. Even now, he had trouble remembering her married name. She wasn't Christy Manning anymore, but Christy Franklin, and her husband was the sheriff of Custer County, Montana.

"Yes, it will, but it'll take a year," James said briskly.

"Not with me. I'll never get over Brett."

"You believe that right now, because the pain's so bad you can't imagine it'll ever go away, but it does, I promise you."

Slowly she turned to study him. "You know? It sounds as if you're talking from experience."

He nodded. "Five years ago the woman I loved broke off our engagement." He laughed derisively. "You see, there was a small problem. She married someone else while she was engaged to me."

"That's terrible," she said with a sigh of righteous indignation. "What kind of woman would do that?"

"It's not as bad as it sounds. You see, her parents are good friends of mine, and I realize now they pressured Christy into accepting my engagement ring. She was fond of me and agreed because she wanted to make her family happy. I don't think she ever realized how much I loved her."

"Do you still love her?"

It might have been a kindness to lie, but James found he couldn't. "Yes, but not in the same way."

"Despite what I know, I can't picture myself not loving Brett." She straightened and wiped the tears from her cheeks. "I suppose I should introduce myself since I've cried all over your shoulder. I'm Summer Lawton. From Anaheim."

"James Wilkens. Seattle."

They exchanged brief handshakes. Summer lowered her gaze. "I wish I could believe you."

"Believe me?"

"That it'll take a year to get over Brett. It doesn't seem possible. We've been dating for nearly five years and got engaged six months ago. My whole life revolved around him."

At one time James's life had revolved around Christy.

"We were apart for less than a week," Summer continued, "and I was so lonely, I practically went through contortions to get to Vegas just so we could be together tonight."

"The first three months are the most difficult," he told her, remembering the weeks after the breakup with Christy. "Keep busy. The worst thing to do is stay at home and mope, although that's exactly what you'll want to do."

"You don't understand," she insisted. "I really love Brett."

"I really love Christy."

"It's different for a man," she said.

"Is it really?" he countered. "A year," he reiterated. "It'll take a year, but by then you'll have worked through the pain."

Her look revealed her doubt.

"You don't believe me?"

"I just don't think it's possible. Not for me. You see, I'm not the type who falls in love at the drop of a hat. I gave everything I had to Brett. It's like my whole world caved in and there's nothing left to live for."

"Shall we test my theory?" he asked.

"How?"

"Meet me back here on New Year's Eve, one year from tonight."

"Here? In this gazebo?"

"That's right," he said. "Right here."

"Same time, same place, next year."

"Same time, same place, next year," he echoed.

One

Summer picked up the mail on the way into her apartment and shuffled through the usual bills and sales flyers. The envelope was there, just as it had been on the first of the month for the past eleven months. A letter from James.

He couldn't possibly have any idea how much she looked forward to hearing from him. The first letter had come shortly after they'd met on New Year's Eve and had been little more than a polite inquiry. She hadn't written him back mainly because she was embarrassed about spilling her heart out to a complete stranger.

His second letter had arrived February first. He told her about the weeks immediately after his breakup with Christy, how the pain had intensified when he'd expected it to lessen. His honesty and generosity touched her heart. It seemed uncanny that her anguish mirrored his so completely. She wrote back then, just a short note to tell him how she was doing, to thank him for writing.

That was how it had started. James would write at the beginning of every month and she'd answer. Gradually their letters grew in length, but were never any more frequent. She liked the formality of exchanging letters, preferring that to the quick and casual convenience of e-mail.

In the year since Summer had met James Wilkens, she'd been tempted to phone him only once. That was the day Brett got married. Ironically, his wife wasn't the girl he'd brought to Las Vegas, but someone he'd met recently. Summer had felt wretched and holed herself up in her apartment with a quart of gourmet ice cream and three rented movies. She'd made it through the day with a little fudge swirl and a lot of grit.

Holding James's letter in her hand, Summer tore open the envelope and started reading on her way into the apartment.

"That's from your lawyer friend, isn't it?" Julie, her roommate, asked. Wearing shorts and a halter top, Julie wandered barefoot through the apartment, munching on a carrot.

Summer nodded, kicked off her shoes and lowered herself onto a padded wicker chair. Her eyes never wavered from the page.

"He wants to remind me of our agreement," Summer said, pleased he hadn't forgotten.

"Agreement?"

"To meet him in Vegas on New Year's Eve."

"Are you going?"

Summer had always planned to follow through on

her promise, although she probably should've thought twice about meeting a stranger. But he wasn't *really* a stranger. She felt she knew James, was comfortable with him. He was a friend, that was all, someone who'd been there when she needed him.

"Are you going?" Julie repeated.

Summer looked up and nodded.

"What's James like?" Julie asked, sitting across from her. The two of them had been close ever since high school and both of them were in the production at Disneyland. Summer had been especially grateful for Julie's unwavering friendship in the past year.

"He's older," Summer said, chewing the corner of her mouth as she tried to recall everything she could about him. "I'd guess he's at least forty. Kind of a stuffed shirt, to tell you the truth. He's about six feet tall and he must work out or something because I remember being surprised by how strong he was."

"Is he handsome?"

Summer had to smile. "You know, I don't actually remember."

"You don't *remember?*" Julie was incredulous. "I realize you were upset, but surely you noticed."

"He has very nice brown eyes and brown hair with some gray in it." She raised her hand to her own hair and wove a strand around her finger. "I'd say he's more distinguished-looking than handsome."

"Is there something romantic going on between the two of you?"

Summer did care for James, but not in the romantic

sense. He'd helped her through the most difficult night of her life. Not only had she clung to him and cried on his shoulder, but he'd stayed with her until the early hours of the morning, listening to her pain, comforting and reassuring her.

"We have a lot in common," was all she'd say to Julie's question about a romance.

"I have a feeling about you and the mysterious James," Julie said, her forehead creased in a frown. "I think you're falling in love."

Love? Not Summer. She'd decided last New Year's Eve that she was finished with love. It sounded melodramatic and a bit ridiculous to be so confident that she'd never love again, but she'd come to that conclusion the minute she found Brett with his girlfriend. Her feelings hadn't changed in the past eleven months.

Although he'd never said as much, she was sure James felt the same way after losing Christy. It'd been six years, and from what she knew about him, there wasn't a woman in his life even now. There wouldn't be a man in hers, either.

This didn't mean that Summer never intended to date again. She'd started going out with other men almost immediately. Pride had prompted her actions in the beginning. Later, she wanted to be able to write James and tell him she was back in the swing of things. He'd applauded her efforts and recounted his own endeavors in that area after Christy had broken off the engagement. As she read his account of various disastrous dates, she'd laughed, truly laughed, for the first time in months.

"You're going to meet James on New Year's Eve, and everything will change," Julie said with a knowing smile.

"What do you mean, everything will change?"

"You won't see him as just a friend anymore," Julie predicted. "You might be surprised to discover there's more to him than you suspect."

"Julie, I told you he's got to be forty years old."

"You're sure of this?"

"No," she said reluctantly. "But…I don't know. I picture James sitting in front of a fireplace, smoking a pipe, with his faithful dog sprawled at his side."

"A basset hound, no doubt."

"No doubt," Summer agreed with a laugh. James was wonderful—no argument about that—but she could never see herself falling for him. Nor would he be interested in someone like her. The man was a distinguished attorney, while she starred in a musical version of *Beauty and the Beast* at Disneyland. Working in the theater wasn't an easy way to make a living, but Summer loved the challenge and the excitement.

"You might be surprised," Julie said again. The tone of her voice suggested that great things were going to happen for her friend this New Year's Eve.

New Year's Eve

Summer freely admitted she was nervous about the rendezvous with James. She got to the gazebo nearly fifteen minutes early and was astonished to find him already there. He was sitting on the bench, the one they'd shared a year earlier. In that moment Summer had a chance to study him with fresh eyes.

The first thing that struck her was that Julie was right.

He was nothing like she remembered. Dignified and proper to the very back of his teeth, but there was something compelling about him. She recalled how Julie had wanted to know if James was handsome. If Summer were to answer that question now, she'd give an unequivocal *yes*. But he wasn't handsome in a Hollywood sense. He certainly wasn't boyishly good-looking like Brett, with his sun-streaked blond hair. But James Wilkens was appealing in a way that spoke directly to her heart. She knew from his letters that this was a man of conscience, a man of integrity, a man of honor. All at once Summer felt as if the oxygen had flown from her lungs.

He saw her then and slowly stood. "Summer?" He sounded equally surprised. His eyes widened briefly.

"Hello, James. I'm early," she said, feeling guilty at being caught staring so blatantly. "I'm always early... it's a family trait."

"I am, too." He grinned. "Usually early, I mean."

Summer had been looking forward to this evening for weeks. There was so much she wanted to say, so much she had to tell him. All at once she couldn't think of a single thing. "The streets are crazy," she said in a hurried effort to make conversation. "I didn't want to risk being late."

"Me, neither," he said. "I hope you don't mind, but I made dinner reservations."

"Thank you." She stepped into the gazebo and sat down next to him.

"So," he said, as if he wasn't sure where to start. "How are you?"

Summer laughed lightly. "A lot better than I was last year at this time. I told you Brett got married, didn't I?"

"You wrote about it."

Summer rarely felt shy, but she did now. She owed James more than she could possibly repay. "Your letters were a godsend," she said, "especially during the first few months. I don't know what I would've done without you."

"You would've done just fine." How confident he sounded, as if there was never a doubt that she'd get over her fiancé's betrayal.

"The first of every month, I'd run to the mailbox. Your letters were regular as clockwork and I counted on them." It had become a ritual for her, an important part of her recovery.

"I enjoyed your letters, too," he said. Fireworks splashed across the night sky, momentarily diverting their attention. "Do you want to join in the festivities?" he asked.

Summer shook her head. "Do you mind?"

He smiled. "Actually I'm just as glad. The crowd got to be a bit much last year."

"I'm so glad you were there," Summer said fervently. "You were like a guardian angel. You helped me so much that night."

"You helped me, too."

"Me? How?" Summer could hardly believe that.

"It's true," James assured her. "Seeing your pain reminded me how far I'd come in the years since losing Christy."

"Was it worse knowing she'd married that sheriff?" Summer asked tentatively. For her, learning about Brett's wedding hurt the most. Friends, under the guise of being kind, were more than happy to relate the details and what they knew about his bride. Every piece of information had cut like a knife.

"Yes."

"Weren't you angry?" she asked. How anyone could treat James in such a shabby manner was beyond her. To be engaged to a man as wonderful as James and then to secretly marry someone else was the most under-handed thing Summer had ever heard of.

"I wasn't angry at first, so much as depressed," he said thoughtfully. "Anger came later. It's the reason I took up squash. I worked out my aggression on the court. It helped."

Summer figured that was a sport an attorney would enjoy.

"It must've been hard finding out Brett was married."

She lowered her gaze and nodded. "Other than the first few weeks after he broke our engagement, the day of his wedding was the worst. It seemed so completely unfair that he should be happy while I was hurting so terribly. If it was ever in me to hate him, it would've been then."

"And now?"

"Now," she repeated. "I certainly don't hate Brett, but I don't love him like I did a year ago. He was a big part of my life, and for a long time my world felt empty without him."

"Does it feel empty now?"

"Not in the least. I'm happy, James, and I didn't believe that would ever be possible."

"Then I was right. It took you a year."

She laughed. "I'm over him and happy to be with you tonight."

"There isn't anyone I'd rather be with on New Year's Eve." He glanced at his watch and stood. "I hope you haven't eaten."

"I didn't. I only arrived a little over an hour ago, and I'm starved." She'd been anxious about their meeting, so her appetite had been nil all day. Her stomach wanted to make up for lost time now.

James led her into the Four Queens Hotel, weaving through the crowds gathered around slot machines and gaming tables. With several thousand people milling around outside, she'd assumed the casinos would be less crowded, but she was wrong.

James took her hand then, gripping it firmly in his own. Summer was surprised by how good that felt. By the time they walked down the stairs to Hugo's Cellar, an elegant, romantically lit restaurant, Summer felt as if she'd survived a riot. So much for all the effort she'd taken with her appearance. She thought she was fortunate to be in one piece.

After a five-minute wait, they were escorted to a booth and presented with elaborate menus. Candles flickered gently, casting dancing shadows on the walls. The noise and bustle upstairs and on the street outside the casino were blessedly absent.

They dined in leisure, shared a bottle of white wine and a calorie-rich dessert. They had so much to talk about—books, movies, world events, their families and more. James asked about her job at Disneyland and seemed genuinely interested in her budding career as an actress.

When she learned he'd recently been appointed a superior court judge to the King County bench, she insisted on ordering champagne to celebrate.

"You should've told me sooner," she said. "It's such wonderful news—so well-deserved."

"It's just temporary," James explained, looking uncomfortable. "I've been appointed to serve out the term of Judge Killmar, who had to retire for medical reasons."

Summer wasn't sure he would've told her if she hadn't asked him about his own hopes and dreams. Only then did he mention it was one of his lifetime goals to serve as a superior court judge.

"You intend on running for the position yourself, don't you?"

"Yes," he said. "But the primary isn't until September, and the election's in November. There're no guarantees."

"You'll win," Summer told him with supreme confidence. Wagging her finger at him, she added, "And don't give me that look. I can't imagine anyone *not* voting for you."

James's eyes met hers. "You're good for my ego," he said. She thought she heard him mutter "too good" under his breath but decided to ignore that.

By the time they'd finished dinner, it was close to twelve. As they made their way out of the casino, someone handed Summer a foil crown and a noisemaker. She donned the hat and handed James the whistle.

The New Year was fast approaching, which meant that her night with James was nearly over. She didn't want it to be.

The crowds had thinned out considerably after the fireworks display. They were standing on the sidewalk outside the Golden Nugget casino when a cheer rose from inside.

"It must be midnight," James commented and ceremoniously blew the noisemaker. "Happy New Year, Summer," he said in a voice so low it was almost a whisper.

"Happy New Year, James."

They stood facing each other, and then, as if this were the moment they'd anticipated all evening, slowly moved toward each other. Summer saw how James's eyes darkened as her own fluttered closed. She wanted this. Needed it.

She sighed audibly as his mouth settled over hers.

Two

Summer was no novice when it came to kissing, but James left her breathless and clinging to him for support. She hadn't expected anything like this. She'd expected them to lightly brush lips and then laugh and wish each other a happy New Year.

It hadn't happened like that.

The instant James's mouth was on hers, she'd gone languid. She was immobile, her arms locked around his neck and her body pressed intimately to his, her lips seeking more.

Summer would've liked James to kiss her again. And again. She didn't want it to end. But she didn't know how to ask him to continue.

Slowly, with what she thought might be reluctance, he released her. She stood there looking at him, arms dangling stiffly at her sides while her face reddened with embarrassment. She considered telling him she wasn't usually this blatant.

"Happy New Year," James said. He didn't sound like himself at all. He cleared his throat and swallowed visibly.

"Happy New Year," she whispered, and stepped away from him.

James reached for her hand and held it in his own. Summer was grateful for his touch. They started walking, with no destination in mind, or none that Summer was aware of. She looked at James, wondering if he felt as confused and uncertain as she did. Apparently he did, because he grew quiet and introspective.

"I believe I'll call it a night," he announced unexpectedly. He checked his watch and frowned. Summer suspected it had been a year since he'd last stayed up past midnight. He was so proper, so serious and sober. Yet she'd enjoyed every minute of her evening with him. They'd talked and laughed, or at least she'd laughed. James had smiled, and she had the impression he didn't do that often, either. Every time he'd grinned, Summer had felt rewarded.

Now she'd ruined everything. She couldn't bear to know what he thought of her. An apology, words of explanation, stumbled over themselves, but she couldn't make herself say them—because she *wasn't* sorry about their kiss. She'd savored it, relished it, and hoped he had, as well.

"I'll call it a night, too," Summer said. She waited, hoping he'd suggest they meet the following day. He didn't.

By the time they returned to the Four Queens,

where they were both booked for the week, Summer was miserable.

"James," she said as they walked across the lobby. Either she apologized now or regretted saying nothing. "I'm sorry. I...don't know what came over me. I don't generally... I can only guess what you must think of me and..."

"You?" He hesitated in front of the elevator. "I was wondering what you thought of *me*. I can only beg your indulgence."

The security guard asked to see their room keys before calling for the elevator. James easily produced his while Summer sifted through the contents of her oversize purse before finding hers.

The elevator arrived, and they both entered. There was no one else inside. Still, James didn't ask to see her again, and Summer's heart grew heavier as they ascended. Her room was on the tenth floor, and his was on the fifteenth.

The silence closed in on them. When the elevator stopped at her floor, the doors slid open, and James moved aside.

Summer glanced at him expectantly. Okay, so he didn't intend to see her again. It made sense, she supposed. A superior court judge wouldn't be interested in dating an actress.

"Good night," she said brightly as she walked out of the elevator.

"Good night, Summer," James said softly.

She hesitated, hoping he'd ask her at the last minute, but he didn't. Discouraged, Summer trudged to her room, unlocked the door and went in. She sat on the edge of her bed, trying to sort out her muddled thoughts.

When Summer had requested a week's vacation, she hadn't planned to spend every available second with James. She knew he'd taken the same length of time, and he'd probably been thinking the same thing.

She slipped off her shoes and wiggled her toes in the thick carpet. If it wasn't so late, she'd call Julie and tell her friend she was right. One evening with James, and she saw him in a completely different light. The moment she'd seen him in the gazebo that evening, she dismissed the father-figure image she'd had in her mind all these months. More than anything, that kiss convinced her James was more than a friend. What became of their relationship would depend on several factors, the most important of which was James himself.

The phone on the nightstand rang, and Summer groped for it. "Hello?"

"Summer, I'm sorry to bother you."

Her heart gave a sigh of relief. "Hello, James."

"I've got a rental car," he said. "I know it might not be something you'd consider fun, but I thought I'd drive over to Hoover Dam in the morning. Would you care to join me?"

"Why wouldn't I consider that fun?" she asked.

"I'm sure there are friends here your own age you'd prefer to spend time with and—"

"Friends? I thought you were my friend."

"Yes, but I was thinking of friends closer to your own age."

His answer irritated her. "I'm not exactly sure what

you're insinuating, but if it is what I think it is, you're wrong, James."

"Listen, Summer, all I want to know is if you'd like to join me in the morning."

That might have been his original question, but she wasn't finished with what she had to say. "I took a week's vacation, and I know you have several days. I don't expect you to entertain me, if that's what you're worried about, because I can find plenty to do on my own."

"I see."

"And yes, there are any number of people my age in Vegas. There would be in any city. If you want my company, fine, but if you'd rather not see me again, I can accept that, too." Not easily, but she'd do it and have a perfectly good week without him.

He was strangely silent.

"James? Are you still there?"

"Yes. Are you always this direct?"

"No, but I didn't want there to be any misunderstanding between us. I value your friendship, and I don't want it ruined because of something silly."

"Nor do I." A short pause followed. "Forgive me for being dense, but I'm not sure I understood your answer. Are you going to Hoover Dam with me or not?"

Summer had waited all evening for this kind of invitation, and now the words were almost anticlimactic. "Would you like me to come?"

"Attorneys do this all the time, you know," he said with a chuckle.

"Do what?"

"Answer a question with one of their own. Yes, Summer, I'd very much enjoy your company."

"Great. When do you want to leave in the morning?"

James told her, and they set a time to meet in the lobby. Summer replaced the receiver and lay back on the bed. She smiled to herself, eager for morning.

James hadn't thought of himself as all that old, since at thirty-seven he was the youngest superior court judge in Washington State. Being with Summer, however, made him feel downright ancient.

She was perfectly named. Being with her was like walking along Green Lake in the middle of August, when the air carried the scent of blooming flowers and sunshine warmed the afternoon. She shone with a summery brightness that made him feel content. More than content. Happy.

James couldn't remember any time he'd smiled more than during their dinner together. She'd told him about playing her role at Disneyland. Her joy and enthusiasm for her job bubbled over like champagne. He could have listened to her all night.

She certainly hadn't done all the talking, however, and to his surprise he'd found himself telling her about the ins and outs of his own position with the court and the upcoming election, which was vital to his career.

His life was very different from hers. While Summer worked in the delightful world of fantasy, he struggled with the often cruel, unjust world of reality.

Naturally he couldn't give her any details about the cases he'd heard, but just talking about his short time on the bench had lifted his spirits considerably. It felt good to share his thoughts with her and he'd enjoyed her opinions and her sometimes unpredictable views.

Then they'd kissed. Talk about sexual chemistry! For the life of him, James couldn't explain what had happened when she'd slipped into his arms. He'd never intended the kiss to become that intense, but once he'd started, nothing could have stopped him.

He'd been afraid his reaction had shocked Summer, but apparently that wasn't the case. Later she'd apologized to him and James hadn't known what to say. She seemed to think she'd done something wrong. She hadn't. The truth was, she'd done everything right.

The next morning James sat down in the lobby to wait for Summer. He was excited about this outing. He'd decided earlier not to invite her, feeling it would be unfair to dominate her time. She was young and beautiful, and he doubted she wanted to spend her vacation with a staid older guy like him.

He'd gone to his hotel room and congratulated himself on not mentioning the trip to Hoover Dam. Ten minutes later he'd talked himself into calling her on the off chance she might be interested.

Well, she'd told him. A smile pulled at the edges of his mouth. Summer had seemed downright angry when he suggested she'd prefer to be with friends her own age.

James liked the idea of being her friend. The operative word being *friend*. He wasn't going to kiss her again—that was for sure.

First, he was afraid of a repeat performance of that

kiss in the street. Secondly, he was way too old for her. He enjoyed her company tremendously, but then any man would. He wasn't going to ruin the bond they'd created; becoming romantically involved, if she even wanted to, would do exactly that.

Summer stepped off the elevator, and James watched as every eye in the place seemed to gravitate toward her. She was stunning. It wasn't the clothes she wore, although the pretty pink pants and matching sweater flattered her. It was Summer herself.

She searched the lobby until she saw him, and then she smiled. James felt as though the sun was beaming directly down on him.

He stood and waited for her to join him. "Did you have breakfast?" he asked.

She nodded. "Hours ago."

"Me, too."

"If you're ready, we can be on our way." All he had to do now was stop staring at her....

A few minutes later, the valet took his ticket for his rental car, and they waited for him to drive the luxury sedan to the back of the hotel. When the car arrived, the young man opened the car door and helped Summer inside. James was almost jealous to have been denied the privilege.

They drove out of Las Vegas in companionable silence. James had studied the map so he knew which freeway to take.

"Do you ever think about her?" Summer asked.

James had no idea what she was talking about. "Who?"

She laughed. "That's answer enough. Christy. Your ex-fiancée."

"Ah yes, Christy." James mulled over Summer's question. "Sometimes. Generally when I'm feeling especially lonely or when I see a couple with kids. That's when I wonder what Christy's and my children would have looked like.

"Do you still think about Brett?" he asked.

She lifted one shoulder in a halfhearted shrug. "Sometimes. It's different with me, though."

"Different?"

"From what you told me about Christy, she went to Montana to help her sister and met someone there."

"She would've broken the engagement right away, but it seemed like a heartless thing to do over the phone." Despite everything James felt a need to defend her. "When she did get back, her mother had arranged for a huge engagement party and I was extremely busy with an important lawsuit. I never blamed Christy for not telling me about Cody right away. She had her reasons."

"*I* blame her," Summer said stiffly. "It was a rotten thing to do."

"You blame Brett, too, don't you?" This was what their conversation was really about, James suspected. Something had happened recently that had hurt her all over again.

"Right before I left," she said in a small voice, "a friend called to tell me Brett and his wife are expecting a baby."

"A friend?" James wondered about that. There

seemed to be a certain type of person who delighted in being the first to deliver bad news.

"I'm going to be twenty-eight next month," she told him.

He smiled. "From the way you said that, one would think you're ready to apply for your retirement benefits."

Summer smiled back. "I suppose I sound ridiculous."

"No, you sound hurt. It's only natural, but that pain will fade in time, as well, especially if you meet someone else and get involved in another relationship."

"You didn't."

James couldn't argue. "It wasn't because I'd dedicated myself to loving Christy for the rest of my life. To be fair, I'm not sure why I never got involved again. It's not like I made the decision not to."

"Do you date?"

"Occasionally." A few months ago, two women had let him know that they'd welcome his attentions. James was flattered and he did enjoy a night out now and then, but he could never seem to dredge up much enthusiasm for either woman.

"What about you?" he asked, then mentally kicked himself. The answer was obvious. Someone like Summer had a long line of men waiting to ask her out.

"I don't date all that often," Summer surprised him by saying, "It's funny, when Brett and I first broke up I saw a different man every night. Within a month I was sick of it, sick of pretending I didn't care, sick of telling everyone about all the fun I was having."

"And now?"

"I haven't been out all month. December is crazy, anyway, with Christmas and family obligations and everything else. In November, I went to a dinner party with a member of the cast, but it was as friends, and it was more a favor to Steve than anything."

Silly as it seemed, James was offended that she didn't count their dinner the night before as a date. He certainly had. Their time together had been the highlight of the year for him.

"My parents want me married," she murmured thoughtfully. "They hinted at it over Christmas."

Now, that was something James could identify with. "My father's a longtime widower and I don't have any siblings. He's been hounding me for years to marry, but his real interest lies in grandchildren."

"I'm not willing to marry just anyone," she insisted.

"I feel the same way."

They glanced at each other and then immediately looked away. Silence again filled the car. James didn't know what Summer was thinking, but he knew where his thoughts were taking him and it spelled trouble.

As they neared the outskirts of Boulder City, James mentioned some of the local facts he'd read. "This is the only city in Nevada that doesn't allow gambling."

"Why?"

"It was built for the men who worked on the construction of the dam. I'd guess it has something to do with making sure the workers wouldn't squander their hard-earned cash on the gaming tables. If that happened, their families would see none of it."

"I wonder if it helped," Summer mused aloud.

The next hour and a half was spent driving over Hoover Dam. They didn't take the tour. The day was windy, and James was afraid Summer's sweater wouldn't be enough protection against the cold.

Once they were back on the Nevada side, they stopped long enough for pictures. James felt the wind as he took several scenic photos of the dam with the digital camera he'd bought last year.

Far more of his shots were aimed at Summer. She was a natural ham and struck a variety of poses for him. He wanted a keepsake of his time with her.

James asked another tourist to get a picture of the two of them together. He placed his arm around her shoulder and smiled into the camera.

"Can you send them to me?" she asked, rubbing her arms in an effort to warm herself.

"Of course," James agreed, pleased that she'd asked.

He turned up the heater when they returned to the car. He noticed that Summer's eyes were drooping about ten miles outside Boulder City. He located a classical-music station on the radio, and the soft strains of Mozart lulled her to sleep.

She woke when they were on the Las Vegas freeway. Startled, she sat up and looked around. "Wow, I must be stimulating company," she said, and smiled.

"I'm accustomed to quiet. Don't worry about it."

"James," she began, then yawned, covering her mouth. "What do you think of women who ask men out on dates?"

"What do I think?" He repeated her question, never

having given the subject much thought. "Well, it seems fine in theory but I can't really say since it's never happened to me."

"Do you view them as aggressive?"

"Not necessarily. I know women invite men out all the time these days."

She smiled, and her eyes fairly danced with excitement. "I'm glad to hear you say so, because I bought two tickets to a magic show. It's this evening at one of the other downtown hotels. I'd enjoy it very much if you went with me."

James had walked into that one with his eyes wide-open. "A magic show," he murmured with pleasure. He hadn't even dropped her off at the hotel yet and already he was looking for an excuse to see her again.

"It's the late show, as it happens, which doesn't start until eleven. You'll come with me, won't you?"

"Of course," he said. If he wasn't driving, James would have pumped his fist in the air.

Although she'd spent nearly the entire day with James, including lunch and a light dinner on the road, Summer counted the hours until they met for the magic show. She was dressing when the phone rang.

"Hello," she said, thinking it could only be James. Her heart began to beat faster.

"Summer, it's Julie."

"Julie!" Summer had tried to call her friend earlier that evening, but she hadn't answered either her cell or the apartment phone. "Happy New Year!"

"Same to you. How's it going with the distinguished attorney?"

Summer sank onto the edge of the bed. "Really well. By the way, he's a superior court judge now."

"Wow. That's great. So you're getting along well," her friend echoed in knowing tones. "Do you still see him as a father figure?"

"No way," Summer said, and laughed. "There's less than ten years between us."

"So." Her friend's voice fell. "Tell me what's been happening."

"Well." Summer wasn't sure where to start, then decided to plunge right in. "He kissed me last night, and Julie, it was incredible. I don't ever remember feeling like this in my life."

"So you'd say there's electricity between you?"

That was putting it mildly. Hoover Dam should produce that much electricity. "You could put it that way."

"This is just great!"

"We went to see Hoover Dam this morning, and tonight we're going to a magic show."

"This sounds promising."

That was how it felt to Summer, as well. "James invited me to drive to Red Rock Canyon with him tomorrow to feed the burros."

"Are you?"

"Of course." It had never occurred to Summer to refuse. She didn't care if he asked her to study goat dung; she would gladly have gone along just to be with him.

"Julie…"

"Yeah?"

"Would you laugh at me if I told you I'm falling in love with this guy?"

"Nope. I've seen it coming for months. You pored over his letters, and for days after you got one, it was James this and James that. I'm not the least bit surprised. This guy must really be something."

Summer's heart sank as she confronted the facts. "He's a judge, Julie. A superior court judge. I'm an actress. We're too different. I live in Anaheim and he's in Seattle. Oh, it's fine here in Vegas, but once we leave, everything will go back to the way it was before."

"You don't want that?"

"No," Summer admitted after some hesitation.

"Then you need to ask yourself exactly what it is you *do* want," Julie said.

Her roommate's words rang in her mind all through the magician's performance. Summer sat beside James and was far more aware of him than the talented performer onstage. There was magic in the air, all right. It sizzled and sparked, but it didn't have a thing to do with what was happening onstage.

After the show, James escorted her to his car, which was parked in a lot outside the casino.

"You've been quiet this evening," James commented.

"I talked to my roommate earlier," she told him when he slid into the driver's seat.

"Does it have something to do with Brett?"

"No," she said, shaking her head for emphasis. When James inserted the key to start the car, she placed her hand on his forearm to stop him. "James," she said softly, "I know this is an unusual request, and I'm sorry if it embarrasses you, but would you mind kissing me again?"

He didn't look at her. "I don't think it's a good idea."

"Why not?"

"Considering what happened the first time, it seems unnecessarily risky."

"I see," she murmured, disappointed.

"Summer, listen," he said impatiently. "You're beautiful and very sweet, but I'm too old for you."

"If you're looking for an excuse, James, you're going to need something better than that." This was the second time he'd brought up their age difference, and it made her mad. "Forget I asked," she said heatedly. "It was a stupid idea."

"That's exactly what I said." He turned the ignition switch, and the engine fired to life.

"You're probably going to tell me you didn't feel anything. Go ahead and lie, but we both know that's exactly what it is—a lie."

James expelled a labored sigh. "I didn't say anything of the sort."

"Then you're afraid."

Summer noticed the way his hands tightened around the steering wheel.

"I prefer to think of myself as cautious."

"Naturally," she mumbled.

What surprised Summer was how much his rejection hurt. No doubt James viewed her as immature and naive. Pushy, as well. She was probably the first woman who'd ever asked him out and the only one who'd sought a kiss.

Shame burned in her cheeks. The sooner they were back at the hotel and she could escape, the better.

The engine revved, but they weren't going anywhere. In fact, James had pulled the car onto the side of the road.

"You might as well know," he muttered, turning off the car. "I've had one hell of a time keeping my hands off you as it is. It doesn't help that you're asking me to kiss you again."

Having said that, he drew her into his arms. His lips were hungry and hard, his kiss long and deep. He broke it off abruptly.

"There," he whispered. "Satisfied now?"

"No," she whispered back, and directed his mouth back to hers.

This time the kiss was slow and sweet. Her mouth nibbled his, and she was completely and utterly amazed by how good it was.

"Summer," he said, "we're going to have to stop."

"Why?" she asked, and her tongue outlined his lips.

James groaned, and she experienced an intense sense of power.

"I don't have a lot of control when it comes to you," he admitted.

"I don't mind."

"I wish you hadn't said that." He kissed her again, deeply, and when the kiss ended, she was clinging to James, mindless of anything but what was happening between them.

James rested his forehead against hers, his breathing uneven. After he'd regained some control, he locked his arms around her and drew her close. For the longest time all he did was hold her.

It felt like heaven to be in James's arms. Summer felt cherished, protected...*loved.*

"I was afraid of something like this," he said quietly.

"Something like what?"

He groaned. "Think about it, would you?"

"I *am* thinking about it. I don't understand the problem. I like it when you kiss me and touch me. I assumed you liked it, too."

"I do," he said. "That's the problem."

"If you say you're too old for me, I won't be held responsible for my actions."

He chuckled at that. "All right," he said, brushing the hair away from her face. "I'm not too old for you in years, but in attitude."

"Well, that's easy enough to change. We'll start first thing in the morning."

"Start what?" he asked, clearly confused.

She kissed him, letting her lips play over his. "You'll see."

Three

James was waiting in the lobby early the following morning. Summer's face broke into a disgruntled look when she saw him. Hands braced on her hips, shaking her head, she walked around him.

"What?" he asked, thinking he might have left part of his shirttail out.

"Where did you say we were going?" she asked.

"Red Rock Canyon."

"Do you always wear a shirt and tie to feed wild burros?"

James wore a shirt and tie to everything. "Yes," he answered.

"That's what I thought. Then I'd like to suggest we stop at a mall first."

"A mall? Whatever for?"

She looked at him as if she questioned his intelligence. "I'm taking you shopping," she announced. "If you have any objections, you'd better voice them now."

"Shopping," James repeated slowly. That was probably his least favorite thing to do. He avoided malls whenever possible. "But why?" he asked innocently. He wasn't giving in without a fight.

"Clothes," she informed him, then added in case he hadn't figured it out, "for you."

He frowned.

"You don't have to do this," Summer said. "I think you look wonderful in a suit and tie, but you'd be far more comfortable in jeans and a T-shirt."

So this was what she meant about altering his attitude. She hadn't mentioned that it involved torturing him by dragging him in and out of stores.

"James?" She gazed up at him with wide eyes. "Are we going to the mall or not?"

It was on the tip of his tongue to tell her he felt perfectly relaxed in what he was wearing. He would've said it, too, if she hadn't blinked just then and her long, silky lashes fanned her cheek. Without much effort this woman was going to wrap him around her little finger. James could see it coming, but he lacked the strength to offer even token resistance.

"How long will it take?" he asked, and glanced at his watch, trying to give the impression that the burros only made their appearance at certain times. They did, but not in the way he was hoping to imply. The minute they suspected visitors had something edible, they appeared.

"We won't be more than an hour," she promised. "Two at most."

He was being fed a line, and he knew it. They'd be lucky to make Red Rock Canyon before nightfall.

"All right," he said with a sigh, wondering how a mature, reasonable male would allow a woman he'd barely met to dictate his wardrobe.

A relationship between them was unrealistic for so many reasons. The age factor, for one. And then she lived and worked in southern California, while his life was in Seattle. He didn't know much about acting, but it seemed to him that if she was serious about her career, California was the place to be. Long-distance relationships rarely survived.

"You won't regret this," she said with a smile.

She was wrong. James already regretted it.

The only shopping mall he knew of in Vegas was the one located on the Strip between two of the largest casino hotels. He drove there and pulled into the underground parking.

When he turned off the ignition, Summer leaned over and kissed him.

"What was that for?" he asked, although he realized he should be counting his blessings instead of questioning them.

"To thank you for being such a good sport."

Little did she know.

To his surprise, Summer stuck to her word. It took less than two hours for her to locate everything she felt he needed. James followed her around like a dutiful child—and discovered he was actually enjoying himself. He let her choose for him, and she did well, generally picking styles he might have picked himself.

"I feel like I squeak when I walk," he said as he led the way back into the underground garage. Almost everything he had on was new. Right down to the running shoes and socks. He'd changed in a washroom at the mall.

"You look twenty years younger," Summer told him.

"In which case, you could be accused of cradle-robbing."

She laughed and slipped her arm through his. She pressed her head against his shoulder, and James derived a good deal of pleasure from having her so close. He was still trying to figure out how he was going to keep his hands off her.

"Sometimes it feels like I've known you forever," she whispered.

James felt the same way. It was as if she'd been part of his life for a very long time. "I have the feeling I'm going to have a huge long-distance phone bill once I get back to Seattle."

Summer closed her eyes and sighed deeply.

"What was that about?" He unlocked the car door and loaded the shopping bags into the backseat.

"I'm grateful, that's all," Summer told him.

"Grateful?" James asked, joining her inside the car.

She was quiet for a moment. "I don't respond to other men this way—the way I have with you. I can't give you a reason or a logical explanation. In the last year, since we've been writing, I've felt close to you.

It's as if you know all there is to know about me. My secrets, my faults, everything.

"That night a year ago, when we met, was probably the most devastating of my life. I don't know what I would've done if it hadn't been for you. Generally I'm the first person to dismiss this sort of thing, but I believe we were destined to meet."

James had wondered about that himself, although he'd always seen himself as a rational man. Of all the people in that massive New Year's crowd, they'd found each other. It had to mean *something*. He didn't doubt that fate, kismet or whatever you wanted to call it, had brought them together.

"I've never experienced the things I do when you kiss me," she confided.

She wasn't alone in that, either. He started the engine and pulled into the traffic that continuously flowed along the Strip. Concentrating on his driving rather than looking at Summer helped him restrain his emotions—and his impulses.

If they'd stayed in the parking garage much longer, James knew they'd have had a repeat performance of the night before.

Kissing her again had been a big mistake. He'd spent half the night fighting off the image of her in bed with him. If he took any more cold showers, the hotel was going to complain about the amount of water he used.

Summer's voice was unsure when she spoke. "I thought that after last evening you wouldn't want to see me again."

James nearly drove the car off the road. "Why would you think that?"

She lowered her gaze to her hands, which were folded primly in her lap. "Well, I behaved so... brazenly."

"You?" She obviously didn't know how close he'd come to losing control. Superior court judges weren't supposed to lose control. James couldn't remember the last time something like this had happened. Probably because it never had...

"It's good to know I'm not in this alone. I don't think I could stand that."

"Trust me, I'm experiencing the same feelings you are," he told her in what had to be the understatement of the century.

"We'll both be going our separate ways in the next few days. Until just now, I didn't know if I'd ever hear from you again."

"We've been in touch all year—why would that end?" He didn't expect anything permanent to develop between them, though; that would be asking too much.

"We can take turns calling each other," she offered. "Maybe exchanging e-mails."

"All right," he agreed.

Summer was silent following that, and he was beginning to recognize quiet moments as a warning. "What's wrong?"

She glanced at him and smiled softly. "I was thinking it would be nice to see each other every once in a while. I hope I don't seem pushy."

Seeing her on a regular basis suited him just fine. They hadn't even gone their separate ways yet, and James was already starting to feel withdrawal symptoms.

"I could fly up and visit you one month, and you could fly down and visit me the next," she suggested, again sounding uncertain.

James's hands tightened around the steering wheel. He suspected that the more often he saw her, the harder it would be to let her go.

"You're not saying anything."

"I was thinking."

"What?"

The complete truth would have embarrassed them both. "I was reviewing my schedule." The primary wasn't until September, but Ralph Southworth, a businessman and longtime friend who'd agreed to head James's campaign, had made it clear long ago: From here on out, James's life wasn't his own. Every place he went, every civic event he attended, would be a campaign opportunity.

"And?"

"February might be difficult for me to get away." His workload had suffered because of this vacation, and another trip, however brief, so soon afterward could cause additional problems.

"That's okay, I can come to you. In fact, I've probably got enough frequent-flyer miles to make the trip free."

"Great. Then I'll try to come to Anaheim in March."

"Wonderful." She lit up like a sparkler on the Fourth of July. Then she hesitated and bit her lower lip. "April might be difficult. Disneyland stays open until midnight during spring break, and we add a second *Beauty and the Beast* show in the evenings. It's hard to get a free weekend then."

"We can work around it." He didn't want to mention that from June onward, his schedule would be impossible. There was no hope of visiting California, and even if she was able to come to Seattle, he couldn't guarantee he'd be able to spend any time with her.

"Yes, we can work around any obstacle," she agreed. But she didn't sound optimistic.

They were outside the city now, driving on a two-lane highway that led to Red Rock Canyon. "I'll be very involved in my campaign this summer." He didn't feel he could be less than honest.

"Summer's the busiest time of year for me, too," she said with an air of defeat. "But we can make this work, James, if we both want it badly enough."

It frightened him how much he wanted Summer, but he was a realist, so he pointed out the obvious. "Long-distance relationships hardly ever work."

"How do you know? You've had several and you speak from experience?"

James resisted the urge to laugh at her prim tone. If memory served him, his first-grade teacher, Mrs. Bondi, had used precisely that voice. Come to think of it, he'd been in love with her, too.

"You'd be shocked by how few relationships I've had," he confessed.

"Do we have a relationship?" Summer asked softly.

James certainly hoped so. "Yes," he answered. And

then, because she seemed to need convincing, he pulled onto a dirt road, behind a ten-foot rock. A trail of red dust plumed behind them.

"Why are you stopping?" she asked.

James wore a wide grin and held out his arms. "It appears to me you need a little reminder of how involved we are." James knew he was asking for trouble. Trouble with a capital *T*. His resistance was about as weak as it could get.

"Oh, James."

"A few kisses is all, understand? I don't have much willpower when it comes to you."

"You don't?" The words were whispered. "That's probably the most beautiful thing you've said to me."

"Has anyone ever told you that you talk too much?" James asked as his mouth swooped down on hers. He kissed her the way he'd been wanting to all morning. No, from the moment he'd watched her approach him in the gazebo.

He kissed her again and again, unable to get his fill. He demanded and she gave. Then she demanded and he gave. He moaned and she sighed. Then and there, James decided he'd do whatever he had to—move heaven and earth, take a red-eye flight—to be with her. He doubted once a month would be enough.

He plowed his hands into her hair and sifted the long strands through his fingers. With their mouths still joined, he lowered one hand to her throat. Her pulse beat savagely against his fingertips.

James had never thought of himself as a weak man.

But with Summer he felt as hot and out of control as a seventeen-year-old in his dad's car.

Reluctantly he dragged his mouth from hers and trailed moist kisses along the side of her neck.

"James."

"Hmm?" He brought his mouth back to hers, kissing her slow and easy. Talking was the last thing on his mind.

She pulled slightly away. "James."

"Yes?" he asked, distracted.

"We seem—" she whispered breathlessly.

His lips returned to her face, lighting on her forehead, her nose, her chin.

"—to have company."

James went still. When he'd left the road, he'd made sure they were out of sight of other drivers. "Company?" he repeated. He could already imagine the headlines. King County Superior Court Judge Caught in Compromising Position in Las Vegas.

"They look hungry."

James's gaze followed Summer's. Burros, five of them, stood outside the car, studying them intently. They were waiting for a handout.

James grinned. At least the burros didn't carry a camera.

Summer smiled, too.

"I brought along a loaf of bread," he said, and reached into the seat behind him.

"Should we get out of the car?" she asked.

"I don't think that's a good idea." He'd read about the burros, but wasn't sure how tame they were.

"Perhaps we should lower the window a bit and feed them that way."

Summer opened her window a couple of inches, far enough to ease a slice of bread out to the eager mouths. Just how eager was something they were to quickly learn.

"Oh!" Summer backed away from the window as a large tongue poked through the small opening.

Soon they were both laughing and handing out the bread as fast as they could. James was going to be sorry when it ran out. Summer certainly seemed to be enjoying herself, and so was he.

When the loaf was finished, they raised the windows. It took the burros a while to realize their food supply had come to an end.

When the burros finally left, James started the engine and pulled back onto the road. They drove for another hour, stopped and toured a visitors' center, taking in the beauty of the countryside.

James felt Summer staring at him as he drove back to the city.

"Now what?" he asked.

"I can't get over the change in you."

"You mean the clothes?"

"Yes. You look like a Jim instead of a James."

James grinned. "There's a difference?"

"Oh, yes, a big one."

"Which do you prefer?" he asked, studying her from the corner of his eye.

His question made her hesitate. "I'm not sure. I like the way Jim dresses, but I like the way James kisses."

"What about how Jim kisses?" The conversation was getting ridiculous.

"Too impatient, I think."

"Really?" He couldn't help feeling a bit miffed. "What's so wonderful about James?"

"His restraint. When James kisses me, it's as if he's holding back part of himself. I have the feeling he's afraid to let go, and it drives me crazy. I want to discover what he's hiding from me. I know this probably sounds a little crazy, but I find James intriguing."

"And Jim?"

She giggled. "Don't tell him, but he's sexy as hell."

"Really?" James was beginning to feel downright cocky.

"He's got that devil-may-care attitude. I have a strong feeling we should be grateful to those burros, because there's no telling what could've happened between us in the canyon."

She was right about that.

"It's those shoes you made me buy," James told her. "The minute I put them on, I had this incredible urge to look for a basketball court and do slam dunks." James loved the sound of Summer's laughter. He'd never been one to tease and joke, but he reveled in her appreciation of his wit.

It was midafternoon when they arrived back at the hotel. After showing the security guard their keys, they stepped into the elevator.

"How about dinner?" he asked, hoping he sounded casual when in reality he felt anything but.

"Sure. What time?"

"Six," he said. Three hours, and he'd be more than ready to see her again. He wanted to suggest they do something until then, but didn't feel he should monopolize her time, although he'd pretty much succeeded in doing that anyway.

"Six o'clock. In the lobby?"

"The lobby," he agreed.

The elevator stopped at her floor, and Summer stared down at her room key. "I'll see you at six."

"Six." They sounded like a couple of parrots.

"Thanks for taking me this morning," she said, easing toward the door. "And for coming to the mall."

"Thank you." He bounced an imaginary basketball and pretended to make a hoop shot.

She smiled, and acting on pure instinct, James lowered his mouth to hers. The kiss was gentle, and when they broke apart, it was all James could do not to follow her to her room.

Summer sat on the end of her bed, trembling. She closed her eyes and tried to relive those last seconds with James and couldn't. Being in his arms was the only possible way to recapture the sensation she experienced each time she was with him.

Julie, her roommate, had known long before Summer had realized it herself. When James had asked her how often she dated, she'd invented an excuse to explain why her social life was nonexistent of late.

But it was really because of his letters.

Hearing from James had become an important part of her life. On the first day of every month she rushed to the mailbox, knowing there'd be a letter from him, each longer than the one before. She'd fallen in love with the man who'd written her those beautiful letters.

Unfortunately she hadn't realized it until she'd seen James. She was worried that she alone experienced all this feeling, all this awareness. But after he'd kissed her, she knew that couldn't be true. He felt it, too.

She smiled to herself, remembering how flustered he'd looked when she'd said they had an audience.

Summer smiled at the memory.

Lying down on the bed, she stared up at the ceiling and soon found herself giggling. She was in love with James. She didn't feel a second's doubt, not the slightest qualm or uncertainty. To think she'd actually believed she'd never love another man after Brett.

She might have drowned in a pool of self-pity if it hadn't been for James. She owed him so much.

As she considered their plans to continue seeing each other, she knew it would be difficult to maintain the relationship, especially since they lived such separate lives.

It would require effort and commitment on both their parts. Summer was willing. She could tell that James wasn't as convinced as she was that they could make this work, but she didn't harbor a single doubt.

Summer dressed carefully for her dinner date with James. She chose a simple sundress with a lacy shawl and pretty sandals.

He was waiting at the same place in the lobby, but he surprised her by not wearing a suit and tie. He'd worn one of the short-sleeved shirts they'd bought that day and a pair of khaki pants. For a moment she barely recognized him. He looked relaxed, as though he hadn't a care in the world.

"James," she whispered when she joined him.

"Jim," he corrected, and grinned. He placed his hand inside his pant pocket and struck a catalog pose.

Summer laughed delightedly.

"I hope you're hungry," James said. He tucked her hand in the crook of his arm and guided her toward the door.

"I'm starved."

"Great. We're about to indulge ourselves in a feast fit for the gods." When they reached the sidewalk of Glitter Gulch, the lights made it as bright as the noonday sun.

"I thought about the conversation we had this afternoon," he announced out of the blue.

"About keeping in touch?"

He nodded. "I'm not sure what we have, the two of us, but whatever it is, I don't want to lose it."

"I don't, either."

"I've only felt this strongly about one other woman in my life."

"I've only felt this way about one other man."

"If I was going to put a name on this…this thing between us…"

"Yes?" she asked when he hesitated. James was a thoughtful man. She didn't mean to rush him, but she wanted him to say what was already on the tip of *her* tongue. Consequently, she had no qualms about leaping in. "I love you, James Wilkens. I want to throw my arms in the air and sing."

He looked at her as if he were actually afraid she'd do exactly that. "What you feel is just gratitude."

"Gratitude," she repeated scornfully. "*Just* gratitude." She shook her head. "I'm capable of knowing my own mind, thank you kindly, and when I say I love you, I mean it."

"I see," James said, and his voice fell.

"You don't have to worry about telling me how you feel, either," she was quick to assure him. It wasn't necessary; his kiss told her everything she needed to know.

"But…"

She stopped in the middle of the crowded sidewalk and pressed her finger to his lips.

"I'm too old for you," he muttered.

She narrowed her eyes.

"But I'm crazy about you, Summer. Call me the biggest fool that ever lived, but it's true."

"Thank you very much."

James chuckled. "I haven't been doing a very good job of hiding how I feel. Maybe that's because I didn't expect to feel like *this*." He splayed his fingers through his hair. "In retrospect, I wonder what I did expect."

"I assumed we'd have dinner that first night and we'd talk about what we said in our letters, and then we'd more or less go our separate ways, me back to my life in California, you back to yours…"

"Really." He arched his eyebrows.

"I wanted Julie to fly in for the weekend, but she refused and I couldn't get her to give me a reason. I know now. She realized what I hadn't—that I'm in love with you. My feelings developed slowly over the past year, and Julie saw it happening." She inhaled a deep breath. "I don't want to lose you, James. We can make this work if we try."

"It's not going to be easy."

As his words faded an idea struck Summer. "Oh, my goodness."

James stopped abruptly. "What is it?"

"James." She clasped his arm as she stared up at him. With every passing second the idea gained momentum. "I just thought of something…wonderful," she said urgently.

"What is it?" His arm circled her waist.

"Oh, James. Kiss me, please, just kiss me."

"Kiss you *here?*" James asked, appalled.

"Never mind." She laughed and, throwing her arms around his neck, she stood on the tips of her toes and kissed him, a deep, lingering kiss that communicated her feelings to him—and his to her.

He stared down at her dumbstruck when she stepped away.

"James," she said breathlessly, "I think we should get married."

"Married." The word was barely audible.

"It makes sense, don't you agree? I know how I feel about you, and you've admitted your feelings for me.

Here we are, both worried about the most ridiculous things, when we already have what's most important. Each other."

Still James didn't say anything. He looked around, and his expression seemed slightly desperate, but that could have been her imagination.

"I can guess what you're thinking," she said with a laugh, "but I've got an answer for every one of your arguments."

"We hardly know each other."

That was a pretty weak argument. "Is that so? You know me better than friends I've had all my life. You've seen me at my worst. You've listened to my pain and my frustrations. There isn't a thing I can't talk about with you."

He frowned, and Summer longed to smooth the lines from his brow and kiss away his doubts.

"Don't look so worried! Honestly, James, anyone would think you were in a state of shock."

"I am." This came through loud and clear.

"But why?" His hesitation took her by surprise. She knew the idea would take some getting used to on James's part. He didn't leap into projects and ideas the way she did. He was methodical and thoughtful and carefully weighed every decision.

"Perhaps I'm assuming something here that I shouldn't," she said slowly. "You don't want to marry me, do you, James?"

Four

Summer was mortified to the very marrow of her bones. Without even trying, she'd managed to make a complete fool of herself. James had never come right out and *said* he was in love with her. But with all their talk about how important they were to each other, she'd naturally assumed he cared as deeply for her as she did for him. She'd assumed he'd want to marry her.

"James, I'm sorry," she said in a weak voice. Past experience had taught her to right wrongs as quickly as possible.

"Summer…"

"Of course you don't want to marry me. I understand. Really, I do," she said and pretended to laugh, but it sounded more like a muffled sob. "Now I've embarrassed us both. I don't know why I say the ridiculous things I do." She tried to make light of it by gesturing with her hands. "I guess I should've warned you that I blurt out the most incredibly awkward stuff. Forget I said anything about marriage, please—otherwise it'll ruin our evening."

James was silent, which made everything ten times worse. She'd rather he ranted and raved than said nothing.

In an effort to fill the terrible silence, she started chattering, talking fast, jumping from one subject to another.

She commented on how busy the casinos were. She talked about the big-name stars performing in town. She mentioned a friend of a friend who'd won the California State lottery, and then brought up air pollution problems in Los Angeles.

"Summer, stop," James finally told her. "It's fine."

She snapped her mouth shut. How she was going to get through the evening without humiliating herself further, she didn't know.

Her stomach was in such a knot that by the time they reached the hotel where the restaurant was located, she felt sure she'd only be able to make a pretense of eating.

The hostess seated them, but Summer got up as soon as the hostess left them.

"If you'll excuse me," she said.

James looked up from his menu.

"I'll be right back." She was hoping that a few minutes alone in the ladies' room would help her regain her composure.

"Summer, wait," James said. "I don't want you to feel bad about this."

She nodded, determined to drop the subject entirely.

"Did you notice they had lobster on the menu?" She didn't actually know if this was true or not.

"It's just that most men prefer to do the asking."

"Of course." And it went without saying that the very proper King County Superior Court Judge James Wilkens wouldn't want an empty-headed actress for a wife.

Summer asked a passing waiter directions for the ladies' room. As she walked across the restaurant, weaving around tables, she felt James's eyes following her.

Once inside the restroom, Summer sat on the pink velvet sofa and closed her eyes. After a number of deep, calming breaths, she waited for the acute embarrassment to pass.

It didn't.

Briefly she toyed with the idea of slipping away, but that would've been childish and unfair to James. His only crime had been his silence, and he'd already explained that was simply his way. Just like making a world-class fool of herself seemed to be hers.

Five minutes later she rejoined him.

He looked up, almost as if he was surprised to see her. "I wasn't sure you'd be back."

"I wouldn't be that rude. It isn't your fault I'm an idiot."

"Stop," he said sharply. "Don't say such things about yourself."

"I can't believe I thought you'd marry someone like me," she said, poking fun at herself. "The girl who always speaks before she thinks and leaps before she looks."

"As a matter of fact, I do plan to marry you." He

announced this while scanning the menu, which he then set aside. He watched her as if he expected some kind of argument. Summer might have offered him one if her throat hadn't closed up, making talking impossible.

The menu slid from her fingers and fell onto the table. Nervously she groped for it.

"Have you decided?" James asked.

She stared at him blankly.

"What would you like to order for dinner?"

"Oh." She hadn't even glanced at the menu. Frazzled as she was, she chose the first thing she saw. "Chicken Dijon," she said.

"Not lobster? It isn't every day one becomes engaged. I think we should celebrate, don't you?"

Somehow she managed a nod.

The waiter came, and James ordered for them both, requesting lobster and champagne. Their server nodded approvingly and disappeared. A moment later he returned with a champagne bottle for James's inspection.

"We'll need to see about an engagement ring," James said as though they were discussing something as mundane as the weather. "I imagine Las Vegas has quite a few good jewelers."

The waiter opened the champagne bottle with a loud pop and poured a small amount into the fluted glass for James to sample. He tasted it and nodded. Soon both their glasses were filled.

Summer breathed easier once they were alone. "James," she whispered, leaning forward. "Are you sure you want to marry me?"

He leaned toward her, too, and a grin slowly formed. "Yes."

"All at once I'm not convinced I'm the right person for you."

"Shouldn't I be the one to decide that?"

"Yes, but...I'd hate to think we're reacting to circumstances that wouldn't repeat themselves in a hundred years."

"Then we'll have a long engagement. We'll both be positive before we take that final step."

"All right." Summer felt only mildly reassured.

"We'll continue to see each other on a regular basis," James told her.

"Yes...we'll need that." She didn't like the idea of being apart so much, but that couldn't be helped.

"I wouldn't want the engagement to be *too* long," Summer said. "I dated Brett for five years, and we were unofficially and then officially engaged almost that whole time. We both know where that ended up."

"Do you wish you'd married him?"

"No," she answered emphatically. "I don't have a single regret. I know you'd never do the things Brett did."

James's eyes brightened with intensity. "It isn't in me to hurt you."

"And I'd never knowingly hurt you," she promised.

"In light of what happened between Christy and me, I'm not fond of long engagements, either."

"Do you regret not marrying her sooner? That way she would've gone to visit her sister as a married woman."

"I've thought about that," James said. "Christy would never have allowed anything to develop between her and Cody if we'd been married. Getting involved with him behind my back was almost more than she could bear."

"I see." Summer figured she could read the writing on the wall. "You wish you'd married her, don't you?"

"No."

His quick response surprised her. "Why not?"

"Christy Manning didn't love me as much as I loved her. I'm sure she would have done her best to be a good wife, and we probably would have grown close over the years, but she would've married me for the wrong reasons."

"The wrong reasons? What reasons?"

"She was trying to make her parents happy."

"Okay," Summer said slowly, still feeling her way carefully around the subject. "So neither of us wants a long engagement. How long is long? A year?"

"That's too long," James said with feeling.

"Six months?"

He hesitated. "That'll make it June."

"June's a nice month," Summer said without any real enthusiasm. "Will you want me to live with you in Seattle?"

"Yes. Is that going to be possible?"

"Of course." She nodded vigorously.

"What about your career?"

She lifted one shoulder. "To tell you the truth, I was getting a little tired of playing Belle anyway. From what I understand, theater in Seattle is thriving. There wouldn't be any problem with me being your wife and an actress, would there? You being a judge and all."

"None that I can think of."

"Good." Summer picked up her fork and ran her fingers along the smooth tines. "My current contract expires in April."

"April," James said. "Can you arrange a wedding on such short notice?"

"You bet I can," she said, grinning. "Oh, James, I can't believe this is happening."

"To be honest, neither can I," he admitted.

Summer had never seen him smile as brightly.

The waiter brought their dinner, and James looked at the man who was a complete stranger and said, "The young lady and I have just become engaged."

Their server smiled broadly. "Congratulations."

"Thank you."

Summer would have added her thanks, but James had shocked her speechless. He wasn't joking; he really meant to follow through with their wedding and he was excited about it. Excited enough to announce their plans to a stranger.

"This hotel has an excellent wedding chapel," the waiter continued. "I gather that more than one celebrity has been married in our chapel."

"Right here in the hotel?" James asked.

"Many of the larger hotels provide wedding services for their guests."

"Don't arrangements have to be made weeks in advance?"

"Not always," the waiter explained. "A lot of people

don't decide which chapel to use until after they arrive. Apparently you can get married with a few hours' notice—if the chapel's available, of course."

"Of course," James murmured.

A look came over him, one she'd seen before. "Our wedding will be in April," she said hastily.

"My very best to both of you." The waiter refilled their flutes with champagne.

"James," Summer said after the server had left their table, "is something wrong?"

"Nothing. What makes you ask?"

"You're wearing an odd look."

"What do you mean?"

"It's a look that says you're not sure you like what you're thinking. Or hearing or seeing. The same one you got when I said we had company in Red Rock Canyon the other day."

"In this case, it's what I'm thinking," he muttered

"You want to call off the wedding?" She should've realized that when James said he wanted to marry her, it was too good to be true. This had to be the shortest engagement in history.

"I don't know where you get the idea that I'm looking for a way out when I'm thinking exactly the opposite. I can only assume impulsive thoughts must be transmitted from one brain to another." He drew in a deep breath and seemed to hold it for a long time. "Would you be willing to marry me now?"

"Now? You mean tomorrow?"

"Yes. Then we'll repeat the ceremony later with family and friends in April."

Speechlessness happened rarely with Summer, and yet James had managed to cause it twice in the same evening. Her mouth dropped open, but no words came out.

"Summer, have I utterly shocked you?"

"Yes," she admitted in a squeaky voice.

James grinned. "I'll admit this is the first impulsive thought I've entertained in years. If you can propose marriage at the drop of a hat, then I should be able to come up with something equally thrilling."

Summer knew she was going to cry now. She could feel the tears welling up in her eyes. She used her linen napkin to dab them away.

"Just remember when we tell the children about this night. You're the one who proposed to me."

"Children." Summer blew her nose. "Oh, James, I'm looking forward to being a mother."

"Then you agree to my plan?"

"Married twice?" Everything was going too fast for her. "I'd want Julie here as my maid of honor."

"Of course. We'll phone her as soon as we're finished dinner. I'll be happy to pay for her airfare."

The tears were back, filling her eyes. These were tears of happiness and relief; she loved him so much. "James, we're doing the right thing, aren't we?"

He didn't hesitate. "Yes. It's what we both want."

"You love me?" He'd never said the words.

His look softened. "Very much."

Her mind whirled with everything they'd need to do. "I'll have to tell my parents. You didn't intend to keep our marriage a secret from our families, did you?"

"No. I'll call my father, as well."

Already Summer could hear her mother's arguments "They're going to think we're crazy."

James grinned again. "Probably."

"What should we do first?" Summer asked as they left the restaurant after dinner.

"I suppose we should find an available wedding chapel."

"Shouldn't we contact our families before we do that?" This was the part Summer dreaded most, and she wanted it over with as quickly as possible.

"But if we have the chapel booked, we'll be able to tell them the time and place," James said.

"Oh, yes." Trust him to be so logical even when he was acting impulsive.

"The ring." James snapped his fingers. "I almost forgot."

"Don't look so concerned. We can pick something out later. A plain gold band is perfect for now. In April we can exchange those for a diamond if you want."

"I'd like you to have my mother's ring."

"I'd be honored to wear it," she said quietly.

He kissed her, and Summer blinked in surprise. It was the first time he'd ever initiated a kiss in public.

Since the waiter had mentioned the wedding chapel at this particular hotel, they tried there first. Summer hadn't expected it to be so easy, but booking their wedding took only a few minutes. The hotel would see to everything, from obtaining the license to the music and flowers. They'd be getting married at seven the next night.

"If I'd known it was this simple," James said as they

walked back to the Four Queens, "I might have suggested it sooner."

Summer pressed her head against his shoulder. They stopped at a crosswalk and waited for the red light.

"I wish you'd kiss me again," she breathed close to his ear.

His gaze found her lips, and he cleared his throat. "I don't think that would be a good idea."

"I suppose you're right," she murmured, but disappointment underscored her words.

"You can call your family from my room."

"Okay," she said, but her mind wasn't on making the dreaded phone call as much as it was on being alone with James.

His thoughts must have been the same because their pace quickened as they hurried across the street and into the hotel.

The elevator ride seemed to take an eternity. As if James couldn't keep himself from touching her in some way, he reached out and brushed a stray curl from her cheek. His knuckle grazed her skin.

"I can't believe you're willing to marry me," he said.

"I feel like the luckiest woman alive."

"You?" He held his hand to his brow. "I want you so much I think I'm running a fever."

"I've got a fever, too. Oh, James, we're going to be so good for each other."

"Don't," he growled.

"Don't?"

"Don't look at me like that, Summer. I'm weak enough where you're concerned. Much more of this, and I'm going to make love to you right in this elevator."

Summer smiled and moved against the back wall. "You're so romantic, James—and I mean that."

"You're doing it again."

"Doing what?"

"Looking at me like you know exactly what I want. Your eyes are telling me you want it as much as I do."

The elevator eased to a stop, and the doors slid open. Summer's heart pounded fast as neither of them made the slightest effort to leave.

"We were going to call our families," she reminded him just as the doors started to close.

James swallowed hard. "Yes, of course."

With precise movements he led the way out of the elevator and down the hallway to his room. She noticed that when he inserted the key his hand trembled slightly, and she loved him all the more for it.

"The phone's over by the—"

"Bed." She completed his sentence, and the word seemed to stick in her throat. She walked across the room and sat on the edge of the mattres, then picked up the phone to dial the familiar number.

It might've helped if she'd taken the time to figure out what to tell her parents. But she was afraid she'd lose her nerve.

She couldn't put into words what she felt for James. She'd never loved anyone this way, this much, and she believed he hadn't, either. They'd each been in love with someone else, and that other person had caused deep pain. This time was different.

She knew, even before they answered the phone, what her mother and father were going to say.

"James," she said, in a panic, banging down the telephone receiver and holding out her arms. "Please, could you kiss me first?"

She glanced over at the man she'd marry in less than twenty-four hours, and his face was a study in raw sexual need. He walked across the room. The bed dipped as his weight joined hers. With loving care he gathered her in his arms and claimed her mouth. The kiss was slow and sensual.

He broke away, and his breath was hard and labored. Eager for the taste of him, the touch and feel of him, she brushed her lips over the curve of his jaw, then brought her mouth back to his.

"Maybe you should call your father first," she whispered when she pulled away.

"All right," he agreed. Reluctantly he sat up and reached for the bedside phone. Summer knelt behind him, wrapping her arms around his waist and pressing her head against his shoulder.

"Dad, it's James," she heard him say.

"Fine…yes, Vegas is just fine." Summer could hear a voice on the other end of the line, but she couldn't make out what was being said.

"I'm calling to let you know I'm getting married."

The voice went silent.

"Dad? Are you still there?"

The faraway voice returned, this time speaking very fast.

"Dad…Dad…Dad." Each time James tried to cut in, he was prevented from saying anything.

In frustration, he held the phone away from his ear. "I think you'd better talk to him."

"Me?" Summer cried. "What do you want *me* to say?"

"Anything."

Summer took the receiver and covered it with her hand. "Just remember this when we talk to my parents."

"I will." He kissed her briefly.

"Mr. Wilkens," Summer said. It sounded as if the line had suddenly gone dead. "My name's Summer Lawton. James and I have known each other a year. I love him very, very much."

"If you've known my son for a year, how is it we've never met?"

"I live in California."

"California?"

"Anaheim. I'm an actress." She might as well give him all the bad news at once. She didn't dare look at James.

"An actress?"

"That's correct."

"You're sure you've got the right James Wilkens? My son's the superior court judge."

"Yes, I know. James and I are going to be married tomorrow evening at seven but we're planning a larger ceremony in April. We felt it was only right to tell you about our plans." Convinced she'd done a miserable job, Summer handed the telephone back to James.

Father and son talked a few moments more, and the conversation ended with James abruptly replacing the receiver. He looked at Summer, but she had the strangest feeling he wasn't seeing her.

"James?"

"He's decided to fly in for the ceremony."

"That's great. I'll look forward to meeting him."

"He's anxious to meet you, as well. He hasn't set eyes on you and already he thinks you're the best thing that's ever happened to me."

Summer laughed and slipped her arms around James's neck. "He could be right."

James grinned up at her. "I know he is."

"I love you, James."

"I know. I love you, too. Now it's time to make that call."

Summer had been delaying the inevitable and knew it. She stared at the phone, expelled a heavy sigh and said, "All right, I'll call my parents. Be prepared, James. They're going to have a lot of questions."

"They couldn't be any worse than my father," he muttered.

"Wanna bet?" Summer punched out the number to the family home a second time and waited. It was the decent thing to do, call her family with the news of her marriage, but if they just happened to be away, out of town themselves, no one would blame her and James for going ahead with the ceremony.

Four rings. Summer was about to hang up.

"Hello," her mother answered cheerfully.

"Mom," Summer said. "It's me."

"I thought you were in Vegas this week with Julie."

"Julie couldn't come."

"You went alone?" Summer could hear the disapproval in her mother's voice.

"I met a friend here. That's the reason I'm calling."

"Your friend is the reason? What's the matter? You don't sound right. You're gambling and you've lost everything? Is that it?"

"Mom, it's nothing like that."

"I never did understand why you'd go back to Vegas after what happened there last year."

"Mom, can I explain?"

"All right, all right."

"I'm calling to tell you—"

"Don't beat around the bush. Just say it."

Summer rolled her eyes. She knew where her flair for drama had come from. "I'm getting married."

Her mother screamed, and the next thing Summer heard was the phone hitting the floor. Her father's voice could be heard in the background, followed by moaning and crying.

"What the hell's going on?" It was her father on the line.

"Hi, Dad," Summer said casually, as if nothing was out of the ordinary. "I called to tell you and Mom that I'm getting married tomorrow evening."

Summer's father said nothing for several seconds. "Do we know this young man?"

"No. But he's wonderful, Dad, really wonderful."

"Like Brett was wonderful?" her mother shouted into the extension.

"Helen, get off the phone. You're too emotional to talk any sense."

"Don't tell me what to do, Hank Lawton. This is our little girl who's marrying some stranger."

"His name's James Wilkens. He's from Seattle and, Daddy, I'm crazy about him."

"He's an actor, isn't he?" her mother demanded. "What did I tell you over and over again? Stay away from actors. But do you listen to me?"

"Mom, James is a judge."

Silence.

"Mom, Dad, did you hear me?"

"What kind of judge? Beauty pageants?" This came from her mother.

Summer almost groaned out loud. "No. Superior court. He was recently appointed to the bench and he'll run for election to his first full term this November."

"A judge, Hank," Helen said softly. "Abby's daughter married that attorney, and we never heard the end of it. Summer's got herself a judge."

"Would you like to talk to James?" Summer offered. It only seemed fair that he talk to her family, since he'd put her on the phone with his father.

"No," her father surprised her by saying. "When I talk to him, it'll be face-to-face. Pack our bags, Helen. We're headed for Vegas."

Five

"Summer," James said patiently when he saw her distress, "what did you expect your family to do?"

"I didn't think they'd insist on coming here," Summer answered. "I wanted it to be just you and me. We can involve our families later, in April. I felt obliged to let my parents know what we were doing—but I didn't expect anything like *this*."

"You don't want them to come?"

"No," she said quickly.

In some ways James could understand her regret. If truth be known, he would've preferred his father to stay in Seattle. As it was, James's time with Summer was already limited, and he didn't want to share with family the precious few days they had left.

"I'm afraid once you meet my mother, you'll change your mind about marrying me," she moaned.

"Honey, it isn't possible."

"My mother—she sometimes doesn't think before she speaks."

"I see." James felt he was being diplomatic by not mentioning that Summer possessed the same trait.

"My dad's really great... You'll like him, but probably not at first." She gazed at James with large, imploring eyes. "Oh, James, he's going to give you the third degree. I'll bet he's having a background check done on you this very minute."

"I don't have anything to hide."

"See, Dad's been working with the seamy side of life for so many years, he suspects everyone."

"He's a policeman?"

Summer nodded. "I don't think he trusts anyone."

"Summer, if twenty-odd years down the road our daughter phones to tell us she's marrying a man neither of us has ever met before, you can bet I'll have a background check done, too."

"You know what this means, don't you?" she said, biting her lip. "We aren't going to have much of a honeymoon."

James chuckled. "Wanna bet?"

Summer grinned.

If this woman's smile could be bottled, James thought, it would be the most potent aphrodisiac ever made. He couldn't look at Summer and not want to make love to her.

"What about Julie?" James said in an effort to get Summer's mind off her parents' imminent arrival.

"Oh—I nearly forgot my best friend." She reached for the phone and called Julie's cell.

Since there were a number of things to do before the

actual ceremony, James walked over to the desk and sat down to write out a list, not wanting to forget anything.

He was only half listening to the conversation between Summer and her roommate when he heard Summer's soft gasp and the mention of Brett, the man she'd once loved. James's ears perked up, and his fingers tightened around the pen.

"What did you tell him?" Summer asked in low tones. This was followed by "Good. Then you're coming? Great. You might want to talk to my parents and see if you can fly in with them. I'm sure they'll be eager to pump you for whatever you can tell them about James." After a few words of farewell, Summer replaced the receiver.

James turned around in his chair, wondering if she'd volunteer the information about Brett.

"Julie's flying in, too. I suggested she catch the same flight as my parents." She seemed self-conscious all at once.

Her eyes avoided his.

"So I heard." James waited, not wanting to approach the subject of her ex-fiancé, hoping she'd save him the trouble.

After an awkward moment, she blurted out, "Julie… Julie said Brett phoned."

James relaxed, grateful she chose not to hide it from him. "Did she find out what he wanted?"

"No. She hung up on him before he got a chance to say."

James had the distinct feeling he was going to like Summer's roommate.

Summer's shoulders moved in an expressive sigh. "I don't think either of us is going to be nearly as happy once our families arrive."

"How bad can it be?" he asked. All he cared about, all that was important, was marrying the woman he loved.

"My mother's going to insist we follow tradition and not see each other all day."

James frowned. He wasn't keen on that idea.

"My dad will keep you occupied with a whole bunch of questions. If you've got the slightest blemish on your record, he'll find it."

"I don't. Trust me, sweetheart, my background's been scrutinized by the very best. Your father isn't going to find anything."

She laughed softly. "In which case, Dad will probably thank you repeatedly for taking me off his hands."

James laughed, too. "Never mind. By this time tomorrow, we'll be husband and wife."

Summer's parents arrived early the following morning with Julie in tow. By chance Summer met them in the lobby on her way down for breakfast. James had called her room an hour earlier, before she was dressed, to tell her he was headed for the coffee shop. Summer had been too nervous to eat then, but had developed a healthy appetite since. She'd need fortification in order to deal with her parents.

"Mom! Dad! Julie!"

They threw their arms around her as if the separation had been ten years instead of a few days.

"I called Adam and told him his little sister's getting married," were the first words out of her mother's mouth. "He's taking time off work and he and Denise are driving in for the wedding."

"Mom," Summer protested, "James and I are having another ceremony later."

"Fine," Helen Lawton said briskly, "Adam will be there, too. Now stop fussing. It isn't like I held a gun to his head and told him he had to come. Your brother *wants* to be here."

"Daddy." Summer hugged her father. Stepping back, she placed her hands on her hips. "James is squeaky-clean, right?"

"How'd you know I had him checked out?"

"You're my father, aren't you?" She slipped her arm around his waist.

"How'd you ever meet a man like this?" Hank Lawton wanted to know. "He's as good as gold."

"Yes, I know. He's wonderful."

James appeared then, coming from the direction of the coffee shop, a newspaper under his arm.

Summer made the introductions, and while Julie and her family checked in to their rooms, Summer and James reserved a table at the coffee shop. They sat next to each other, holding hands.

"Are you ready for all this?" he asked her.

"I don't know." She sighed. "My brother's taking the day off and driving in for the ceremony. I thought we'd have a small, intimate wedding."

"It is small and intimate."

"My brother and his wife have three little kids, who'll probably cry through the entire ceremony."

"I don't mind if you don't," James said and gently squeezed her hand. "I suspect folks will talk about us the same way when we drag our children to family get-togethers."

"Our children," Summer repeated. She felt weak with pleasure at the thought of having a family with James. "I know I've said it before, but I'm looking forward to being a mother."

"Not nearly as much as I am to making you one," he said in a low voice. The teasing light left his eyes. "If you have no objections, I'd like a large family. Maybe four kids?"

"Four." She nodded. "I'd love to have four children. We're going to have a good life, James. I can feel it in my heart. We're going to be so happy."

"I feel that way, too. Being an only child, I was always drawn to large families. I suspect that's why I've been such good friends with the Mannings over the years."

"Christy's family?"

He nodded. "She's the youngest of five."

Her parents and Julie appeared just then, and ever the gentleman, James stood until the ladies were seated.

"I hope you don't mind if we steal Summer away from you for the day," Helen said even before she looked at the menu. "We have a million and one things to do before the wedding."

"We do?" Summer didn't know why she bothered to

protest. She'd realized this would happen the moment her parents announced they were coming.

"First, we need to buy you a dress."

Silly as it seemed, Summer hadn't given much thought to her attire. A nice suit would do, she supposed, something flattering and stylish. The elaborate gown and veil could wait for the April ceremony.

"Then there's the matter of finding a preacher."

"The hotel provides a justice of the peace," James said.

"Do you object to a man of the cloth?" Hank asked sternly.

Summer wanted to leap to her feet and tell James this was a test, but she bit her tongue. Sooner or later her soon-to-be husband would have to sink or swim on his own with her family.

"Not at all. I'd prefer one myself."

Summer had to restrain herself from cheering. James had passed with flying colors.

"I've got the names of several ministers from our pastor in Anaheim." Her father patted his shirt pocket. "We'll leave the women to do their thing, and you and I can find us a proper preacher." His tone implied that his little girl wasn't being married by any justice of the peace.

"What about rings?" Helen asked.

"I thought I'd pick up a couple of plain gold bands for now," James explained. "I'd like Summer to wear my mother's diamond. She can choose the setting at a later date, and it'll be ready before the April ceremony."

Breakfast wasn't the ordeal Summer had expected. Julie sent her curious looks now and then, and Summer knew her friend was waiting for an opportune moment so they could talk.

"We'll meet again at what time?" Helen asked, glancing at her watch.

Summer's father studied his, while Summer and James gazed longingly at each other.

"Six," Helen suggested.

"That late?" Summer protested. They were being cheated out of an entire day. No one seemed to appreciate that her time with James was already limited.

"I'll see to everything," her mother assured everyone. "Hank, all you need to do is get James to the chapel on time."

"Don't worry about my not showing up," James said. "I'm deeply in love with your daughter."

Julie's elbow connected with Summer's ribs. "What did I tell you?" she whispered out of the corner of her mouth.

Julie had more than gloating on her mind, and so did Summer's mother. When they'd finished their coffee, Helen organized a shopping expedition. She made it clear that a suitable wedding dress wasn't the only thing on her list. If her daughter was about to marry a superior court judge, she'd go to him with a complete trousseau.

The minute Summer and Julie were alone in the store, her roommate grabbed Summer's arm. "I heard from Brett again," she whispered.

"Did he phone?"

"No. This time he stopped by the apartment, right before I left for the airport."

"No." Summer closed her eyes, not because she had any regrets or because she harbored any doubts about James.

It was as if Brett possessed some kind of radar that told him when he could cause her the most trouble.

"He's been asking about you. Apparently he talked with a couple of the cast members at Disneyland. Steve and Karen? Do those names sound familiar?"

"Yes." Summer clenched her fists. "I can't tell you how much this irritates me."

"You? The man's been making a pest of himself all week. According to Brett, you're pining away for him." Julie made a melodramatic gesture, bringing the back of one hand to her forehead. "You've been unhappy ever since the two of you split up—he says."

"Oh, puhleese."

"That's what I told him."

"If I was pining for anyone," Summer said, "it was for James."

"Exactly. I told Brett that, too."

"Thanks."

"I explained, with a great deal of satisfaction, that you're involved with someone else now, and he should stay out of your life."

"Good grief, he's married and about to become a father. The man has no principles." The thought of Brett trying to reestablish their relationship while his wife was pregnant with their child made Summer sick to her stomach. "I'm glad to be rid of him."

"You couldn't be getting married at a more opportune time. I'm telling you, Summer, from the way Brett argued with me, your marriage is about the only thing that'll convince him it's over."

"You did tell him I'm getting married, didn't you?"

"Yes, but he wouldn't believe me. He accused me of fabricating the whole thing."

"Girls, girls." Helen returned with a salesclerk.

"I wonder how long it'll be before she considers us women?" Summer asked her friend under her breath.

By evening Summer felt more like a French poodle than a bride. She'd been shampooed, her nails polished, her hair curled, her body massaged and moisturized. She'd been in and out of more clothes than a New York fashion model. And she was exhausted.

The idea of a white suit for the wedding was one of the first ideas to go. Before Summer could argue, she was draped in satin and silk from head to toe.

"You look absolutely stunning," Helen said.

Summer wasn't sure she could trust her mother's assessment. Her eyes went to Julie.

"She's right."

"But what about April?"

"What about it?" Helen's hands flew into the air. "You'll wear the dress twice. Big deal. No one needs to know."

She tried another arguement. "It's so much money."

"My baby girl only gets married once."

Well, no. She'd be getting married twice—to the same man, but still, there were going to be two ceremonies.

Julie arranged the veil and the long train for the photographer who was on his way, then handed Summer the intricate gardenia bouquet. "If you're going to throw that, just be sure and aim it my way."

Summer smiled. "You got it."

"Not yet, I haven't," Julie reminded her.

A knock sounded at the door, and Helen answered it. Summer didn't pay any attention, assuming it was the photographer her father had hired.

A few minutes later, Helen introduced the tall, balding man. "Summer, this is James's father, Walter. You should've told me he was a retired superior court judge himself."

Summer would have been happy to, had she known.

"My, oh, my," Walter said as he entered the room. He stood in front of Summer, hands on his hips, and he slowly shook his head. "And where did my son meet such a beauty?"

"Here in Vegas," Summer said. "A year ago."

"I was about to give up hope for that son of mine. It seemed to me he'd settled a little too comfortably into bachelorhood. This comes as a very pleasant surprise."

"I'm so glad you came to meet me and my family, especially on such short notice."

Walter withdrew a thick cigar from the inside of his suit pocket and examined the end of it. "Wouldn't have missed it for the world."

Walter sat down and made himself comfortable. After a moment he returned the cigar to his inside pocket. "I quit smoking five years ago and I still miss it. Every now and then I take one out and look at it, just for the thrill."

Summer could see she was going to like James's father.

"To be frank, I didn't think that boy of mine possessed this much common sense."

"He's a judge," Summer said, eager to defend her husband-to-be.

"When it comes to the law, James is one of the finest men on the bench. He seems to be worried about the November election, but as far as I can see, he won't have a problem. No, what I'm talking about is something else entirely."

Summer felt like sitting down, too. Both her mother and Julie had mysteriously disappeared, and since the photographer had yet to show up, she decided to relax.

"Have you seen James?" she asked, missing him dreadfully.

"Oh, yes."

"How is he?" She folded her hands, wondering what James was thinking and if he was sorry he'd gotten involved in all this. Everything had seemed so uncomplicated when they discussed it the night before.

"He's pacing in his room."

"Pacing," she repeated, certain this was a bad sign.

"It's just as well this wedding's going to happen less than an hour from now. I don't think your father and brother could keep James away from you much longer than that."

Summer smiled in relief.

"Never thought I'd see the day my boy would fall head over heels in love like this."

"But he was engaged before. I know about Christy Manning."

"Ah, yes, Christy. She's a dear girl, and James had strong feelings for her, but deep down I believe what he found so attractive about Christy was her family. There's quite a difference between the love James has for you and what he felt for Christy Manning. As you'll recall, he was content to stay engaged to Christy for a good long while. But you… He's marrying you so fast, my head's spinning. His, too, from the looks of him. You've thrown him for quite a loop."

"I love James, too," Summer said with feeling, "very much."

"Good. I hope the two of you will seriously consider making me a grandfather soon. I'm hoping for a grandchild or two to spoil."

"We'd like to have four."

"Four." Walter nodded, looking pleased. "But you're worried about something."

"Yes," she said softly, wondering how he knew. "My biggest fear is that I'm not the right kind of wife for James. I'm afraid I might inadvertently harm his career."

"What makes you think that?"

"I have this tendency to speak my mind."

"I find that refreshing."

"You will until I put my foot in my mouth and embarrass James. To give you an example…" She hesitated, not sure she should continue, then realized she couldn't very well stop now. "I'm the one who suggested we get married."

"Really?"

"It just…came out. It seemed like a brilliant idea at the time…you know how good things can sound until you've thought them through. Well, anyway, James stared at me like he'd swallowed his tongue."

Walter burst out laughing. "Forgive me, my dear. Continue, please."

"Naturally I felt like a fool. Mainly because James didn't say anything and didn't say anything and didn't say anything, and I was convinced I'd ruined everything."

"He said nothing, did he?"

"Well, he did mumble something about preferring to do the asking himself."

"And you clammed up."

"Oh, quite the opposite. I started talking at hurricane speed until he told me it was fine and I needn't worry. And then, after I'd fallen all over myself telling him how sorry I was, he said he thought it was a good idea. James came up with the idea of a ceremony now and then one in April."

"He did?" Clearly this was news to his father.

"Yes." Summer grinned sheepishly. "He said something about impulsive thoughts being contagious."

"There's more to the boy than I assumed."

There was another knock at the door, and the photographer let himself inside.

"I'd better get back to James," Walter said. "It's been a delight meeting you, Summer. I don't have a shred of doubt that you're the best thing to come into my son's life for a very long time. Make him happy, Summer, make him very happy."

"I intend to do my best."

"And while you're at it, teach him how to laugh."

Summer nodded. "I'll try." She had a sneaking suspicion they had plenty to teach one another.

James looked at his watch for the third time that minute. No one seemed to understand that he *needed* to see Summer. Needed to talk to her, find out about her day, tell her about his.

If he'd had even an inkling that their wedding was going to cause such a big commotion, he would never have agreed to contact their families.

James liked Summer's parents, but he'd prefer to spend his time with her. Alone.

"We can go into the chapel now," Hank Lawton said.

James was so grateful he felt like cheering. According to his calculations, the ceremony would take approximately twenty minutes, thirty at most. They'd sign the marriage certificate, and the rest of the night would be theirs. He couldn't tolerate any more of these separations, however brief. The next time Summer left his sight would be at the airport.

He saw her family in the small chapel, her brother's children wide-eyed and excited as the organ music rose triumphantly. He noticed that the wedding chapel was almost full and wondered for just a moment who the other guests were.

James went to stand in front with the minister, Reverend Floyd Wilson. James had rented the tuxedo because it seemed odd for the father of the bride to be wearing one and not the groom. Now, however, the shirt seemed too tight around the collar. He resisted the urge to insert his finger and give himself a little extra breathing space.

It was then that Summer appeared.

James felt as if someone had smashed him in the knees with a bat. Never in all his life had he seen anyone more beautiful. His heart beat so hard he thought it might pound straight through his chest.

Her dress was silk and lace with pearls, as traditional a wedding gown as any he'd seen. One would think Summer was a debutante and this a society wedding.

When she joined him at the altar and placed her arm in his, James felt this was the proudest moment of his life. He knew they'd repeat the ceremony in a few months, but nothing would match the blend of humility and pride he experienced right then.

Her brother, Adam, was kind enough to serve as his best man, while Julie, of course, was the maid of honor.

The ceremony itself was a blur. James's full concentration was on the woman at his side. He knew she was feeling the same emotions he was when she began to repeat her vows.

Summer's voice shook slightly, and she sounded close to tears. His arm tightened around hers as the minister said, "I now pronounce you husband and wife. You may kiss your bride."

James didn't need to hear that twice. Carefully he gathered Summer close, sighing when their lips met in the tenderest, sweetest kiss of his life.

She clung to him. "Oh, James, how soon can we get rid of everyone?"

He'd entertained that very question from the moment Summer's mother had taken her away that morning.

"Soon," he promised. Heaven only knew how they were going to cope with being separated for the next four months. "After dinner."

They were hit with a barrage of birdseed on their way out the door. They laughed and tried to catch it in their outstretched hands.

"Pictures," Helen insisted, and when Summer groaned, she added, "Just a few more. That's all."

"Mother, you'll get plenty of pictures later."

"I want some now," her mother insisted. But "some" turned out to be at least a hundred by James's estimation.

They signed the marriage license, and James took the opportunity to kiss his bride. "I don't ever want to spend another day like this one," he whispered.

"Me, neither," she said, then giggled. "But you're

going to get something out of it. Mother bought me this cute little black nightie."

James could feel the hot blood circle his ears and... other places. "Your mother bought you a nightie?"

"She said it's her wedding gift to you."

"I'll thank her later."

"Wait until you see what Julie got us," she whispered.

"I have the feeling it isn't a toaster," he said wryly.

Summer laughed. "No. She picked it out when Mom wasn't looking. You do like tassels, don't you?"

"Tassels?"

"Shh." Summer looked around to be sure no one was listening. "I'll save them for after the honeymoon."

"Why?"

"Because, my darling husband, they cover—" She stopped abruptly.

"Yes?" he coaxed.

"Husband," she said the word as if saying a prayer. "James, you're my *husband*."

"I know. And you're my wife." It hit him then, too. The beauty of it, of belonging to each other, of the word itself.

Their families all seemed to return at once.

"I don't know about anyone else," Helen Lawton was saying, "but I'm starved."

There was a chorus of agreement. They trooped into the hotel's elegant restaurant and ordered dinner and champagne, although Summer could barely eat and had trouble following the conversation.

"We'll say good-night, then," James announced the

minute they could leave without being rude. "Thank you all for making this the most incredible day of my life."

"It's still early," Helen protested.

"Helen," Hank snapped. "Think about it."

"Oh, yes, sorry." Helen's face brightened, and she smiled apologetically at James.

"Will we see you in the morning?"

"Helen!" her husband growled.

"I'm just asking, Hank. What harm is there in asking?"

"I don't know, Mom. What time is your flight?"

James didn't listen to the answer, although he supposed he should have. As it was, he had a hard time hiding his impatience. He and his wife—his wife— would only have two more days together. Luckily that was two days and *three* nights. Their flights were leaving within a half hour of each other, and then it would be a whole month before he saw her again.

"All right, then, darling," Helen said, hugging Summer, "we'll see you both in the morning."

The entourage left, and James was alone with Summer at last.

"Are we going to my room or yours?" she asked, smiling up at him.

"Neither. I rented the honeymoon suite here for the rest of our stay. Your mother packed your suitcase and had it sent over."

"You think of everything." She reached up and removed the wedding veil and shook her head, freeing her curls. "I can't tell you how anxious I am to get out of this dress."

James chuckled as he led the way to the elevator. "Not nearly as anxious as I am to get you out of it."

"Who were all those guests?" she asked him when they stepped inside the elevator car.

"I thought they were friends of your family."

"I've never seen them before in my life."

James shrugged. "Me, neither."

"You know what? I'll bet my mother invited them. She couldn't bear to have us married in an empty chapel."

James fingered his room key. "Are you hungry?"

"No."

"Good. Let's go work up an appetite."

Summer smiled and moistened her lips with the tip of her tongue. "I have a feeling you aren't talking about racquetball."

James cleared his throat. He wanted her so much his body trembled with the strength of his need. "You're right about that."

Six

James astonished Summer. She didn't know what to expect from him as a lover, but it wasn't this. They'd made love no less than three times during their wedding night, and Summer woke the following morning to find him standing at the foot of their bed, fresh from the shower.

His nude body glistened in the early-morning light. Droplets of water dripped from his hair and onto the dark curls that covered his chest.

"Good morning, Mrs. Wilkens."

Summer smiled and stretched her arms high above her head, arching her back. The sheet slipped away, exposing her breasts.

"Good morning, James." She saw that he was fully aroused and slowly lifted her gaze to his. Already her body was responding to him, throbbing with readiness and need. James's eyes narrowed as they focused on her.

Wordlessly she knelt on the bed and held out her arms to him. She smiled, thinking someone should've warned her about this man before they were married. At this rate, they'd both be dead within a week.

He walked over to the side of the bed, kissed her once, twice, and then knelt beside it.

All her life Summer had never experienced such power. Or such love. Her breathing grew slow and shallow. She half closed her eyes in pleasure at the simple touch of his hand.

James groaned, and Summer recognized his meaning. He couldn't wait any longer. Neither could she. She threw her arms around his neck and slowly lay back against the bed, bringing him with her.

She smiled contentedly as they began to make love. All of a sudden her eyes flew open. "James, you forgot—"

"It'll be all right," he assured her breathlessly. "Just this one time."

She didn't want him to stop. Not now. "Okay."

James reached his climax soon after she experienced hers. A harsh groan tore from his throat, and his powerful body shuddered.

His shoulders still heaving, he gathered her in his arms and spread soft, delicate kisses over her face. He started to move away from her, but she wouldn't let him.

"Not yet," she pleaded. "I want to be a part of you."

"You are. You always will be. You could travel to Mars, and my heart would be with you." He brushed the damp hair from her forehead. "I can't believe you love me."

"I do, so much my heart feels like it's about to burst wide open. Will it always be like this?" she asked. "Two weeks ago, you were someone whose letters I looked forward to. This week you're the most important person in my life."

James kissed the tip of her nose. "It's only going to get better from here on out."

"Better?" She laughed delightedly. "I can't imagine it."

In one uninterrupted movement James rolled onto his back, taking her with him so she was sprawled across his chest. Across his heart. "I can't, either. Summer, I love you."

"Good." She pressed her head against his shoulder. "But what about—"

"I'll remember next time," he promised. "The last thing we need now is an unplanned pregnancy."

"I'm pretty sure this is my safe time, so don't worry."

James kissed her neck. "I suppose we should get dressed and meet everyone for breakfast."

"I suppose," she agreed, but neither of them showed any signs of moving.

"It won't be so bad," James whispered.

They'd been married less than twenty-four hours and already Summer could read her husband's thoughts. "Being separated? It's going to be terrible. I don't know how I'll last four months without you."

"Four months." He made it sound like an eternity.

"James, where do you live?"

He gave her a puzzled look. "Seattle. You know my address."

"But is it an apartment? A condo? A town house or what?"

"A house."

Summer liked the idea of that.

A slow grin spread across his face. "I must've known I was going to meet you. This is a big house on Queen Anne Hill with seven bedrooms."

"James!"

"It's a lovely older home. I'm quite proud of the garden. I hope you'll like it."

"I love it already."

"You haven't seen it."

"No, but I saw the look on your face when you talked about it. The house is going to be perfect for us, just perfect."

His eyes grew dark. "*You're* perfect."

"I hope we'll always love each other as much as we do at this moment." Summer laid her head on his chest and sighed.

Time had never passed more quickly for James. He'd dreaded leaving Summer almost from the moment they'd met again on New Year's Eve. It was as though Seattle was another world, one he wasn't that eager to return to. Not when it meant having to say goodbye to Summer.

His wife of two days was unusually quiet as they packed their suitcases on Saturday morning, the day of their departure. When she found him watching her, she offered him a reassuring smile.

The bellboy carried their luggage to the lobby. While James was checking out of the hotel, he noticed Summer twisting the plain gold band around her finger. His own felt awkward and heavy, and he wondered if she was experiencing any regrets. For his own part, he didn't have a single one.

Having returned the rental car earlier, James ordered a car. He and Summer held hands as they rode silently to the airport.

He wanted to assure her it wouldn't be so bad, but that would've been a blatant lie. Every minute he was away from her was a minute too long. He wanted to be sure she understood how much he loved her, how crucial she was to him. But the backseat of a limo with a driver listening in didn't seem the most appropriate place to tell her those things.

Nothing would ever be the same for either of them, and they both knew it.

The car dropped them off, and since they were flying on different airlines, they separated to check in their luggage and receive their seat assignments.

James finished first and caught sight of Summer hurrying through the crowd toward him. Even from that distance he sensed her sadness. He met her halfway and they went through security together.

"My flight leaves from Concourse B," she said, looking down at her ticket. Her voice was small and tight.

"Mine's Concourse A."

"What time's your flight?"

She already knew, but apparently needed to hear it again. "Ten-thirty," James told her.

"My departure's at ten."

He was perfectly aware of what time her plane left. "I'll walk down to Concourse B with you."

"You can't, James, you might miss your own flight."

Frankly he didn't give a damn. "Then I'll catch the next one."

"I'll worry. James, really, I'm a big girl. I can find my way around the airport."

"I didn't say you couldn't," he snapped, surprising himself.

Summer looked up at him, her eyes brimming with tears. She turned and walked away from him and headed for Concourse B.

James followed and wanted to kick himself. He wouldn't see his wife for weeks and here he was, apparently doing his utmost to start an argument. No doubt there was some psychological reason for his attitude. He'd examine what was happening later, but at the moment he was more concerned about saying goodbye to her properly.

Summer arrived at her gate and walked over to the window. James could see her plane and knew it wouldn't be more than a few moments before the boarding call was announced.

"I'm sorry, sweetheart." He rested his hands on her shoulders and closed his eyes.

"Me, too."

He frowned. She'd done nothing wrong. "For what?"

"Oh, James," she whispered brokenly, slipping her arms around his waist. "I'm going to be so lost without you."

"It's going to be hard." He wasn't willing to pretend otherwise. "I'll phone as often as I can."

"Do you have my work schedule?" she asked.

"Yes. Do you have everything you need?" They'd gone over the details a dozen times.

"No. I need you, James."

His hold on her tightened. He wondered if they were afraid they'd lose the magic. Afraid that once they returned to their respective lives, everything would change.

Her flight number was announced, and James tensed. It wouldn't be long before he saw her, he promised himself. He'd try for a week, two at the most. A few minutes later her row was called.

"That's you," he said reluctantly.

"I know."

But neither of them made a move to break apart.

Summer was the last one to board the plane, and James had to tear through the airport in order to catch his own flight. If anyone had suggested even ten days ago that the dignified James Wilkens would race through an airport so he could spend a few extra minutes with a woman, he would have scoffed. He wasn't scoffing now.

He arrived in the nick of time and collapsed into his seat, his heart racing.

Between dashing through airports and hours spent

making love, Summer would be the death of him yet. He smiled as he snapped his seat belt into place. If he was to die that very moment, he'd leave this earth a happy man.

James's house had never seemed so empty. By the time he got home, it was dark and shadowy. His first mistake had been stopping at the office on his way back from the airport. After he arrived in Seattle, he'd spent what remained of the day working through the memos, briefs and case histories. No one else was in, so he was able to accomplish quite a bit, catching up on some of his backlog. He'd do anything he had to so he could arrange time away as soon as possible.

Summer was never far from his thoughts.

Once he reached his house, suitcase in hand, he was exhausted. He switched on the light in the kitchen, put down his bags and set his briefcase on the walnut table in the breakfast nook.

He hadn't eaten since that morning, and a look inside the refrigerator reminded him he'd been away all week. He'd need to order out or microwave something from the freezer.

Deciding against both, he heated a can of soup, ate, then showered. He'd showered that morning, but Summer had been in the stall with him and neither one had seemed particularly concerned about washing.

James stood in front of the mirror in the steamy bathroom and wiped off some of the condensation, then stared at his reflection. He didn't look all that different from the man he'd been a week ago. But he *was* different.

Unable to delay talking to Summer, he dressed quickly and headed for his book-lined den.

Having memorized her apartment and cell phone numbers, James called her at home.

Summer answered on the first ring. "Hello."

"Hello, darling."

"James!"

"I would've called sooner, but I went to the office. I needed to clear off my desk."

"Did you check your calendar?"

"First thing. I can fly down on a Saturday morning in two weeks, but I'll need to be back Sunday afternoon. That doesn't give us much time."

"No," she agreed, "but we'll make the most of it." Her relief was evident. "I was afraid once you looked at your schedule you'd find it impossible to get away."

"I don't care what it takes, I'll be in California in two weeks."

"Wonderful. I traded weekends with a friend so I can come to you in February. My mother's already started to plan the wedding. She's left a message with the secretary at the Moose Hall. It's a very nice building."

"Your mother's enjoying every minute of this, isn't she?"

Summer laughed. "Yes. But the one who surprises me most is my dad. I don't know what you said or did, but my dad thinks you walk on water."

It was his turn to laugh.

Then they were both silent. They'd spent nearly every minute of the previous week together. They'd discussed everything there was to discuss. Yet neither was willing to break the connection.

An hour later they were still on the phone. They hadn't spoken more than a few words between whispered promises and deep sighs. They'd shared a few secrets and memories, some of them very private. Very intimate...

In their next conversation, he'd let Summer know he couldn't handle much more of that.

"I've gotten together with a group of businessmen and spread the word," Ralph Southworth was saying.

James sat in his office, gazing into the distance. As always, his thoughts were fifteen hundred miles to the south with Summer. He barely heard his campaign manager. In eight days he'd be with his wife. The last six had been the purest form of torture.

He lived for the times he could phone her. Because she performed in the last show of the night, he couldn't reach her until after ten, and more often than not they spoke until past midnight.

"There's a dinner party this Friday night at the Morrisons'," Ralph announced.

James didn't comment.

"You're going, aren't you?"

"You mean to the Morrisons'?"

Ralph Southworth looked at him oddly. "Who else do you think I mean?"

James shrugged. Ralph was a good man, a bit abrasive at times, but sincere and hardworking. According to people James trusted, Ralph Southworth was the best man for the job of getting James elected to the superior court.

"What's with you lately, James?" Ralph asked abruptly. He pulled out a chair and sat down across from James's desk.

Ralph was nothing if not direct. "What makes you ask?"

"Something's not right. Ever since you got back from vacation, you haven't been the same."

James considered telling Ralph the truth. Part of him was eager to share the news of his marriage. Marrying Summer was nothing to be ashamed of—the opposite, in fact—but arrangements for the second ceremony were already being made. If he was willing to face the truth, James would have to admit he wasn't keen on explaining his sudden marriage, especially to the man who'd frowned on his vacation in Vegas. He preferred to leave things as they were and invite Ralph to the wedding in April. So far, he'd told no one about Summer and for the time being even left his wedding band at home.

"Have you ever been in love?" he asked, unable to resist.

Ralph shook his head adamantly. "Never, and proud of it."

James's eyebrows shot to his hairline. "I see."

"Women have ruined more than one good man.

Don't be a fool, James. Don't do anything stupid at this point. Unless it's with someone who can help you politically, of course. Now, if you told me you were seeing Mary Horton…"

"Who?"

"Mary Horton—never mind, she's not your type. All I can say is that if you're going to fall for someone now, just make sure it's a woman who can help you politically."

"She can't."

Ralph tossed his hands in the air. "Somehow, I knew you were going to say that. Listen. Keep your head screwed on tight and your pants zipped up. The last thing we need now is a scandal, understand?"

"Of course. Summer's not like—"

"Her name is *Summer?*" Ralph rolled his eyes expressively. "James, listen to me. You've asked me to run your campaign, and I'm glad to do it, but I'm telling you right now, getting involved with a woman named Summer is asking for trouble."

"Don't you think you're being unfair?"

"No. Where'd you meet her?"

"Vegas."

Ralph's mouth thinned. "Don't tell me she's a show girl," he muttered.

"No—but she's an actress."

A muscle leapt in his friend's jaw. "Don't say anything more. Not a single word. I've got high blood pressure and don't want to know any more than you've already told me."

"Summer has nothing to do with you," James said, finding it difficult to quell his irritation. Ralph made Summer sound like…like a mistake.

"Don't you remember a certain congressman who got involved with a stripper a few years back?"

"Summer isn't a stripper!"

"It ruined him, James. Ruined him. I don't want the same thing to happen to you."

"It won't. Furthermore, I won't have you speaking about her in those terms." In light of Ralph's reaction, James didn't think now was the time to announce they were already married. "If you must know, I intend to marry her."

"Great. Do it after the election."

"We've decided on April."

"April!" Ralph barked. "That's much too soon. Listen, you're paying me big money to run this campaign. You want my advice, you've got it. What difference would a few months make?" He paused, waiting for James's response. "Will you do that one thing?"

"I don't know."

"Are you afraid you'll lose her?"

"No."

"Then put off the wedding until after the election. Is that so much to ask?"

"I'm not sure which is worse," Julie said, applying bright red polish to her toenails, "this year or last."

"What do you mean?" Summer asked.

"You." She swirled the brush in the red paint and started with the little toe on her left foot. "Last year, after you broke up with Brett, you moped around the apartment for months."

Summer laughed. "This year isn't much better, is it?"

"Not that I can see. Listen, I understand how much you miss James. The guy's hot. No wonder you fell for him. If the situation was reversed, you can bet I'd be just as miserable. The thing is, you won't be apart for long. April's right around the corner."

Summer folded her arms and leaned against the back of the sofa. "I didn't know it was possible to love someone as much as I love James."

"If the number of times he calls you is any indication, I'd say he feels the same about you."

"He works so hard." Summer knew that many of James's late-night calls came from his office. She also knew he was putting in extra-long hours in order to free up time he could spend with her.

"Summer, he'll be here in a few days."

"I know."

"You haven't told him about Brett?" Julie asked.

Summer's nails bit into her palms. "What good would it do? James is fifteen hundred miles away. Brett hasn't got a chance with me. Unfortunately he doesn't seem ready to accept that. But he's going to get the same message whenever he calls."

"By the way, when James visits, I'm out of here."

"Julie, you don't need to leave. We can get a hotel room—really, we don't mind."

"Don't be ridiculous. This is your home. You'd be more relaxed, and both of you have been through enough stress lately."

Summer was so grateful it was all she could do not to weep. It was the stress, she decided, this tendency to be over emotional. "Have I told you how glad I am that you're my friend?"

"Think nothing of it," Julie said airily.

"I mean it, Julie. I don't know what I would've done without you these last weeks. I feel like my whole world's been turned upside down."

"It has been. Who else goes away for a week and comes home married? Did you think James had lost his mind when he suggested it?"

"Yes," she admitted, remembering the most fabulous dinner of her life. "I don't think he's done anything that impulsive his whole life."

Julie grinned. "Until he met you."

"Funny, James made the same comment."

The phone rang just then, and Summer leapt up to answer it on the off chance it was James.

"Hello," she said breathlessly.

"Summer, don't hang up, please, I'm begging you."

"Brett." Her heart sank. "Please," she told him, "just leave me alone."

"Talk to me. That's all I'm asking."

"About what? We have absolutely nothing to say to each other."

"I made a mistake."

Summer closed her eyes, fighting the frustration.

"It's too late. What do I have to say to convince you of that? You're married, I'm married."

"I don't believe it." His voice grew hoarse. "If you're married, then where's your husband?"

"I don't owe you any explanations. Don't phone me again. It's over and has been for more than a year."

"Summer, please…please."

She didn't wait to hear any more. His persistence astonished her. When she'd found him with another woman, he'd seemed almost glad, as though he was relieved to be free of the relationship. In retrospect, Summer realized that Brett had fallen out of love with her long before, but had lacked the courage to say anything. Later, when he'd married, and she learned it wasn't the same woman he'd been with in Vegas, she wondered about this man she thought she knew so well, and discovered she didn't know him at all.

His behavior mystified her. After loving Brett for six years, she expected to feel *something* for him, but all the feeling she could muster was pity. She wanted nothing to do with him. He'd made his choice and she'd made hers.

"Brett? Again?" Julie asked when Summer joined her in the living room.

Summer nodded. "I hope this is the end of it."

"Have you thought about having the phone number changed?"

"That's a good idea. And I'm going to get call display, too."

Julie studied her for a moment. "Are you going to tell James why we've got a new phone number?"

"No. It would only worry him, and there's nothing he can do so far away. Brett doesn't concern me."

"Maybe he should."

Summer arrived at the Orange County airport forty minutes before James's flight was due, in case it came in early. Every minute of their day and a half together was carefully planned.

The only negative for Summer was the brunch with her parents Sunday morning. Her mother had several questions about the wedding that she needed to discuss with James. Summer begrudged every minute she had to share James; she knew she was being selfish, but she didn't care.

Julie, true to her word, had made a weekend trip to visit a family member, an elderly aunt in Claremont.

By the time James's plane touched down, she was nearly sick to her stomach with anticipation. As soon as he stepped out of the secure area, he paused, searching for her.

Their eyes connected and in the second before he started toward her, her heart seemed to stop. Then it began to race.

When they'd parted in Las Vegas, it felt as if everything had come to an abrupt standstill. Now she could see him, could *feel* him, for the first time since they'd parted two weeks ago.

Dashing between the other passengers, she ran toward him. James caught her in his arms and crushed her against him. His hands were in her hair, and his mouth hungrily sought hers.

His embrace half lifted her from the ground. She clung to him, fighting back a flood of emotion. Unexpectedly tears filled her eyes, but she was too happy to care.

James broke off the kiss, and Summer stared up at him, smiling. It was so good to see him.

"What's this?" he asked, brushing his thumb across the moisture on her cheeks.

"I guess I missed you more than I realized."

"You're beautiful," he said in a low voice.

"I bet you tell all the women that," she joked.

"Nope, only the ones I marry."

Summer slipped her arm around his waist, and together they headed toward the luggage carousel. "I packed light."

"Good." Because it felt so good to be close to him, she stood on the tips of her toes and kissed his cheek. "You'll be glad to hear Julie's gone for the weekend."

"Remind me to thank her."

"She's been wonderful."

"Any more crank calls?"

Summer had almost forgotten that was the excuse she'd given him when she'd had her phone numbers changed. "None." And then, because she was eager to change the subject, she told him, "I've got every minute planned."

"Every minute?"

"Well, almost. Mom and Dad invited us over for brunch in the morning. I couldn't think of any way to get out of it."

"It might be a good idea to see them."

"Why?"

James frowned, and she noticed the dark circles under his eyes. He was working too hard, not sleeping enough, not eating properly. That would all change when she got to Seattle. The first thing she'd do was make sure he had three decent meals a day. As for time in bed, well, she didn't think that would be a problem.

"There might be a problem with the wedding date," he said reluctantly.

Summer halted midstep. "What do you mean?"

"April might not work, after all." He paused. "It doesn't matter, does it? We're already married."

"I know, but..."

"We can talk about it later, with your family. All right?"

She nodded, unwilling to waste even one precious minute arguing over a fancy wedding when she already wore his ring.

Seven

For years James had lived an impassive and sober life. He'd never considered himself a physical man. But three weeks after marrying Summer, making love occupied far more of his thoughts than it had in the previous thirty-odd years combined.

"How far is it to your apartment?" he asked, as they walked to her car.

Summer didn't immediately respond.

"Summer?"

"It seems to me we have a few things to discuss."

"All right," he said, forcing himself to stop staring at her. She had him at a distinct disadvantage. At the moment he would have agreed to just about anything, no matter where the discussion led—as long as they got to her place soon. As long as they could be alone...

"I want to know why there's a problem with the wedding date."

He should've realized. "Sweetheart, it has more to

do with your parents than you and me. Let's not worry about it now."

"You want to delay the wedding, don't you?"

"No," he responded vehemently. "Do you honestly think I'm enjoying this separation? I couldn't be more miserable."

"Me, neither."

"Then you have to believe I wouldn't do anything that would keep us apart any longer than necessary." James glanced at her as she drove. He was telling the truth, although not, perhaps, the whole truth. Time enough for that later, he thought. He was worried about Summer. She seemed pale and drawn, as if she weren't sleeping well or eating right. This situation wasn't good for either of them.

After fifteen minutes they arrived at her apartment building. He carried in his suitcase and set it down in her small living room, gazing around.

Summer's personality seemed to mark each area. The apartment was bright and cheerful. The kitchen especially appealed to him; the cabinets had been painted a bold yellow with red knobs. Without asking, he knew this was her special touch.

She led him into her bedroom, and he stopped when he noticed the five-foot wall poster of her as Beauty posing with the Beast. She looked so beautiful he couldn't take his eyes off it. He felt a hint of jealousy of the man who was able to spend time with her every night, even if it was in costume.

His gaze moved from the picture to the bed. A

single. He supposed it wouldn't matter. The way he felt just then, they'd spend the whole night making love anyway.

He turned toward his wife. She smiled softly, and in that instant James knew he couldn't wait any longer. His need was so great that his entire body seemed to throb with a need of its own.

He held out his hand, and she walked toward him.

If he had any regrets about their time in Vegas, it was that he'd been so eager for her, so awkward and clumsy. Tonight would be slow and easy, he'd promised himself. When they made love, it would be leisurely so she'd know how much he appreciated her. They'd savor each other without interruption.

"Summer, I love you." He lifted the shirt over her head and tossed it carelessly aside. His hands were at the snap of her jeans, trembling as he struggled to hold back the urgency of his need.

He kissed her with two weeks' worth of pent-up hunger, and all his accumulated frustration broke free.

He eased the jeans over her slender hips and let them fall to her feet, then released her long enough to remove his own clothes. As he was unbuttoning his shirt, he watched her slip out of her silky underwear. His breath caught in his throat.

When James finished undressing, they collapsed on the narrow bed together. And then he lost all sense of time....

* * *

Summer woke to the sound of James humming off-key in the kitchen. The man couldn't carry a tune in a bucket, as her dad liked to say. Smiling, she glanced at her clock radio—almost 6:00 p.m. She reached for her housecoat and entered the kitchen to find him examining the contents of her refrigerator.

"So you're one of those," she teased, tying the sash of her robe.

"One of what?" He reappeared brandishing a chicken leg.

"You get hungry after sex," she whispered.

"I didn't eat on the plane, and yes," he said, grinning shyly at her, "I suspect you're right."

She yawned and sat on the bar stool. "Anything interesting in there?"

"Leftover chicken, cottage cheese three weeks past its expiration date, Swiss cheese and an orange."

"I'll take the orange." She yawned again.

"Have you been getting enough sleep?" He peeled the orange and handed it to her, frowning. It wasn't his imagination; she was pale.

"More than ever. I seem to be exhausted lately. All I do is work and sleep."

"Have you seen a doctor?"

"No. I'm fine," she said, forcing a smile. She didn't want to waste their precious time together discussing her sleeping patterns. She ate a section of the rather dry orange. "I better shower and get dressed."

"For the show?"

She nodded, sad that part of her weekend with James would be spent on the job, but there was no help for it. It was difficult enough to trade schedules in order to fly up to Seattle.

"I'm looking forward to seeing what a talented woman I married."

"I hope I don't disappoint you."

"Not possible." He shook his head solemnly.

"James," she said, staring down at the orange. "Do you ever wonder what's really there between us?"

He tossed the chicken bone into the garbage. "What do you mean?"

"Sometimes I'm afraid all we share is a strong physical attraction. Is there more?"

He swallowed; the question seemed to make him uncomfortable. "What makes you ask that?"

"In case you haven't noticed, we can't keep our hands off each other."

"What's wrong with that?"

"I think about us making love—a lot. Probably more than I should. You're a brilliant man. I'm fairly sure you didn't marry me because I challenge you intellectually."

"I married you because I fell in love with you."

He made it sound so uncomplicated.

"I love the way a room lights up when you walk into it," he said. "When you laugh, I want to laugh, too. I've never heard you sing or seen you perform on stage, but there's music in you, Summer. I sensed it the first night we met.

"Just being with you makes me want to smile. Not that you're telling jokes or doing pratfalls or anything— it's your attitude. When I'm with you, the world's a better place."

Summer felt her throat tighten.

"Like your father, an attorney or a judge can develop a jaded perspective in life. It's difficult to trust when the world's filled with suspicion. It's difficult to love when you deal with the consequences of hate every day. Perhaps that's been my problem all along."

"Not trusting?"

"Yes. You came to me without defenses, devastated, vulnerable, broken. I'd been hurt, too, so I knew how you felt because I'd experienced those same emotions. I'd walk through the fires of hell before I'd allow anyone to do that to you again." He walked over and held out his hand. "It's more than just words when I say I love you, Summer. It's my heart, my whole heart."

She gripped his hand with both of hers.

"If you're afraid our relationship is too much about sexual attraction, then maybe we should put a hold on anything physical for the rest of the weekend. Instead, we'll concentrate on getting to know each other better."

"Do you think it's possible?" She gave him a know-ing look, then leaned forward. The front of her robe gaped open, and Summer watched as he stared at her breasts, then carefully averted his eyes.

"It's possible," he said in a low voice. "Not easy, but possible."

"I need to take a shower before I leave for work." She

slipped off the stool and started to walk away. Then she turned, looked over her shoulder and smiled seductively. "Remember what fun we had in the shower, James?"

James paled. "Summer," he warned through clenched teeth. "If we're going to stay out of the bedroom, I'll need your help."

She turned to face him full on. "The shower isn't in the bedroom."

"Go have your shower," he said stiffly. "I'll wait for you here."

"You're sure?" She released the sash and let the silk robe fall open.

He made a sound that could mean various things— but he didn't make a move. Feeling slightly disappointed, Summer walked slowly into the bathroom and turned on the shower.

She'd just stepped inside and adjusted the water when the shower door was pulled open.

Naked, James joined her there. "You know I can't resist you," he muttered.

"Yes," she said softly. "I can't resist you, either."

Summer and her mother were busy in the kitchen at the Lawton family home. James sat in the living room with his father-in-law, watching a Sunday-morning sports show.

James didn't have the heart to tell Hank that he didn't follow sports all that much. And he sure wasn't going to admit he found them boring.

"Helen's going to be talking to you later," Hank said, relaxing during a spell of uninterrupted beer commercials. "She's having trouble getting a decent hall for the wedding reception in April. The church is no problem, mind you, but finding a hall's become pretty complicated."

"Summer said something about the Moose Hall."

"That fell through. I'll let Helen do the explaining."

"Does Summer know this?"

"Not yet. Couldn't see upsetting her. The girl's been miserable ever since she got back from Vegas. You want my opinion?" He didn't wait for a response. "You should take her to Seattle with you now and be done with it. It's clear to me the two of you belong together."

James wished it was that easy.

"I know, I know," Hank said, scooting forward to the edge of his chair as some football players ran back onto a muddy field. "She has to fulfill her contract. Never understood where the girl got her singing talent."

"She's fabulous." Summer's performance had shocked James. Her singing had moved him deeply and her acting impressed him.

Hank beamed proudly. "She's good, isn't she? I'll never forget the night I first went to see her perform at Disneyland. It was all I could do not to stand up and yell out, 'Hey, that's my little girl up there.'"

"There's such power in her voice."

"Enough to crack crystal, isn't it? You'd never suspect it hearing her speak, but the minute she opens her mouth to sing, watch out. I've never heard anything like it."

James had come away awed by her talent. That she'd willingly walk away from her career to be his wife, willingly take her chances in a new city, humbled him.

"She could go all the way to the top."

Hank nodded. "I think so, too, if she wanted, but that's the thing. She loves singing, don't get me wrong, but Summer will be just as happy humming lullabies to her babies as she would be performing in some hit Broadway show."

James's heart clutched at the thought of Summer singing to their children.

"Helen's mother used to sing," Hank said, but his eyes didn't leave the television screen. He frowned when the sports highlights moved on to tennis. "Ruth didn't sing professionally, but she was a member of the church choir for years. Talent's a funny business. Summer was singing from the time she was two. Now, Adam, he sounds like a squeaky door."

"Me, too." All James could hope was that their children inherited their mother's singing ability.

"Don't worry about it. She loves you anyway."

James wasn't quite sure how to respond, but fortunately he didn't have to, because Helen poked her head in at that moment.

"Brunch is ready," she said. "Hank, turn off that blasted TV."

"But, Helen—"

"Hank!"

"All right, all right." Reluctantly Hank reached for the TV controller and muted the television. His wife didn't seem to notice, and Hank sent James a conspiratorial wink. "Compromise," he whispered. "She won't even know."

James sat next to Summer at the table. "This looks delicious," he said to Helen. His mother-in-law had obviously gone to a lot of trouble with this brunch. She'd prepared sausages and ham slices and bacon, along with some kind of egg casserole, fresh-baked sweet rolls, coffee and juice.

Helen waited until they'd all filled their plates before she mentioned the April wedding date. "The reason I wanted to talk to the two of you has to do with the wedding date." She paused, apparently unsure how to proceed. "I wasn't too involved with Adam's wedding when he married Denise. I had no idea we'd need to book the reception hall so far in advance."

"But I thought you already *had* the place," Summer wailed.

"Didn't happen, sweetheart," Hank said. "Trust me, your mother's done her best. I can't tell you how many phone calls she's made."

"If we're going to have the wedding you deserve," her mother said pointedly, "it'll need to be later than April. My goodness, it takes time just to get the invitations printed, and we can't order them until we have someplace *nice* for the reception."

"How much later?" was James's question.

Helen and Hank exchanged looks. "June might work, but September would be best."

"September," Summer cried.

"September's out of the question." With the primary in September, James couldn't manage time away for a wedding. "If we're going to wait that long, anyway, then let's do it after the election in November." The minute he made the suggestion, James realized he'd said the wrong thing.

"November." Summer's voice sagged with defeat. "So what am I supposed to do between April and November?"

"Move up to Seattle with James, of course," Hank said without a qualm.

"Absolutely not," Helen protested. "We can't have our daughter living with James before they're married."

"Helen, for the love of heaven, they're already married. Remember?"

"Yes, but no one knows that."

"James?"

Everyone turned to him. "Other than my dad, no one knows I'm married, either."

Summer seemed to wilt. "It sounds like what you're saying is that you don't want me with you."

"No!" James could hear the hurt and disappointment in her voice and wished he knew some way to solve the problem, but he didn't. "You know that isn't true."

"Why is everything suddenly so complicated?" Summer asked despondently. "It seemed so simple when James and I first decided to do things this way. Now I feel as if we're trapped."

James had the same reaction. "We'll talk about it and get back to you," he told his in-laws. Both were content to leave it at that.

After brunch he and Summer took a walk around her old neighborhood. Their pace was leisurely, and she didn't say anything for a couple of blocks. She clasped her hands behind her back as if she didn't want to be close to him just then. He gave her the space she needed, but longed to put his arm around her.

"I know you're disappointed, sweetheart. So am I," he began. "I—"

"This is what you meant about problems with the April date, isn't it? The election."

"Yes, but…"

"I feel like excess baggage in your life."

"Summer, you *are* my life."

"Oh, James, how did everything get so messed up?"

"It's my fault," he muttered, ramming his fingers through his hair. "I was the one who suggested we go ahead with the wedding right away."

"Thank heaven. I'd hate to think how long we'd have to wait if you hadn't."

"I was being purely selfish and only a little practical. I knew I wouldn't be able to keep from making love to you much longer."

"And you're traditional enough—*gentleman* enough— to prefer to marry me first," she suggested softly.

"Something like that." She made him sound nobler than he was. He'd married her because he wanted to. Because he couldn't imagine *not* marrying her.

"As you said, the problem is the election. I had no business marrying you when I did. Not when I knew very well what this year would be like."

"The campaign?"

He nodded. "I've never been a political person, but it's a real factor in this kind of situation."

"I thought judges were nonpartisan."

"They are, but trust me, sweetheart, there's plenty of politics involved. I want to be elected, Summer, but not enough to put you through this."

She was silent again for a long moment. "One question."

"Anything."

She lowered her head and increased her pace. "Why didn't you tell anyone we're married?"

"I told my campaign manager you and I were engaged." James hesitated, selecting his words carefully.

"And?"

"And he asked me to wait until after the election to go through with the wedding. He had a number of reasons, some valid, others not, but he did say one thing that made sense."

"What?"

"He reminded me that I'm paying him good money for his advice."

"I see." She gave a short laugh that revealed little amusement. "I don't even know your campaign manager and already I dislike him."

"Ralph. Ralph Southworth. He isn't so bad."

"What will we do, James?"

"I don't know."

"Do you want me to wait until after the election to move to Seattle?"

"No," he said vehemently.

"But you have to consider Ralph's advice."

"Something like that." They walked past a school yard with a battered chain-link fence. It looked as if every third-grade class for the past twenty years had made it his or her personal goal to climb that fence.

"I've been thinking about this constantly," James told her. It had weighed down his heart for nearly two weeks, ever since his talk with Ralph. "There are no easy solutions."

"We don't need to decide right now, do we?"

"No." Actually James was relieved. At the moment he was more than willing to say the heck with it and move Summer to Seattle in April.

"Then let's both give it some thought in the next few weeks."

"Good idea." He placed one arm around her shoulders. "I've worked hard for this opportunity to sit on the bench, Summer, but it's not worth losing you."

"Losing me?" She smiled up at him. "You'd have a very hard time getting rid of me, James Wilkens, and don't you forget it."

James chuckled and kissed her lightly. It was a bittersweet kiss, reminding him that in a matter of hours he'd be leaving her again. Only this time he didn't know exactly when he could be with her again.

Summer rubbed her face against the side of his.

"Not so long ago, I had to practically beg you to kiss me in public."

"That was before you had me completely twisted around your little finger." The changes she'd already wrought in his life astonished him. "I don't know what I did to deserve you, but whatever it was I'm grateful."

"Your flight leaves in less than five hours."

"I know."

"I suppose we should go back to the apartment." She looked up at him and raised her delicate eyebrows. "That's plenty of time for what I have in mind."

"Summer..."

"Yes, James?" She batted her eyelashes at him. He grinned. She managed to be sexy and funny simultaneously, and he found that completely endearing.

They made their farewells to her family and were soon on their way back to the apartment. There was time to make love, he decided, shower and pack. Then he'd be gone again.

Summer must have been thinking the same thing because she said, "We always seem to be leaving each other."

James couldn't even tell her it wouldn't be for long. They parked in the lot outside her apartment, but as soon as they were out of the car James knew something wasn't right. Summer tensed, her gaze on the man climbing out of the car next to theirs.

"Summer?" James asked.

"It's Brett," she said in a low voice.

"Brett?" It took James a moment to make the connection. "*The* Brett?"

Her nod was almost imperceptible.

"What's he want?"

"I don't know."

Apparently they were about to find out. He was big—football-player size—and tanned. He wore faded cutoff jeans, a tank top and several gold chains around his neck.

"Hello, Brett," Summer said stiffly.

"Summer." He turned to James. "Who's this? A friend of your father's?"

"This is my husband. Kindly leave. We don't have anything to say to each other."

"Your husband?" Brett laughed mockingly. "You don't expect me to believe *that,* do you?"

"It's true," James answered. "Now I suggest you make yourself scarce like the lady asked."

Brett planted his muscular hands on lean hips. "Says you and what army? No way am I leaving Summer."

"As I recall, you already left her," James said smoothly, placing himself between Summer and the other man. "I also remember that you got married shortly afterward. And didn't I hear, just recently, that you and your wife are expecting a baby?"

"We're separated."

"I'm sorry to hear that. Unfortunately Summer and I are now married and she's not interested in starting anything with you."

"I don't believe that," he muttered stubbornly.

"Oh, honestly, Brett," Summer said, not concealing her impatience. "Are you such an egotist you actually think I'd want you back?"

"You love me."

"Loved," she said. "Past tense."

"Don't give me any bull about you and granddaddy here."

"Granddaddy?" she snapped. "James is ten times the man you'll ever be." She pushed in front of James and glared at her former fiancé. "You know what? Every day of my life I thank God we ended our engagement—otherwise I'd never have met James. He's taught me what loving someone really means. Which is something *you* don't have a clue about."

James had Summer by the shoulders. "It won't do any good to argue with him," he told her. He looked at Brett, who was red-faced and angry. "I think it would be best if you left."

"Stay out of this," Brett growled.

"We're married," James said, trying to add reason to a situation that was fast getting out of hand. "Nothing you say is going to change that."

Brett spit on the ground. "She's nothing but a whore anyway."

James would've walked away for almost anything. But he refused to allow anyone to speak in a derogatory way about Summer. He stepped toward Brett until they were face-to-face. "I suggest you apologize to the lady."

"Gonna make me?"

"Yes," James said. He'd been a schoolboy the last time he was in a fistfight, but he wasn't going to let this jaded, ugly man insult his wife.

Brett's hands went up first. He swung at James, who was quick enough to step aside. The second time James wasn't so fortunate. The punch hit him square in the eye, but he didn't pay attention to the pain since he was more intent on delivering his own.

"James!" Summer repeatedly screamed his name. James could vaguely hear her in the background, pleading with him to stop, that Brett wasn't worth the trouble.

The two men wrestled to the ground, and James was able to level another couple of punches. "You'll apologize," he demanded from between clenched teeth when Brett showed signs of wanting to quit.

Blood drooled from Brett's mouth, and one eye was swollen. He nodded. "Sorry," he muttered.

James released him just as the police arrived.

Eight

Summer wouldn't have believed James was capable of such anger or such violence. Part of her wanted to call him a fool, but another part wanted to tell him how grateful she was for his love and protection.

His left eye was badly swollen, even with the bag of ice she'd given him. James had refused to hold it to his face while he talked to the police.

His black eye wasn't the only damage. His mouth was cut, and an ugly bruise was beginning to form along his jaw. Brett was in much worse shape, with what looked to be a broken nose.

After talking to both Brett and James and a couple of witnesses, the police asked James if he wanted to press charges. James eyed Brett.

"I don't think that'll be necessary. I doubt this…gentleman will bother my wife again. Isn't that right?" he asked, turning to Brett.

Brett wiped the blood from the side of his mouth. "I didn't come here looking for trouble."

"Looks like that's what you got, though," the police officer told him. "I'd count my blessings and stay away." He studied him for a moment, then asked, "Want to go to the hospital?"

"Forget it. I'm out of here," Brett said with disgust. He climbed inside his car and slammed the door, then drove off as if he couldn't get away fast enough.

"He won't be back," Summer said confidently. She knew Brett's ego was fragile and he wouldn't return after being humiliated.

"You're right, he won't," James insisted darkly, "because you're filing a restraining order first thing tomorrow morning."

Summer nodded, wishing she'd thought of doing it earlier.

"This isn't the first time he's pestered you, is it?"

Summer lowered her gaze.

"He's the reason you had your phone number changed, isn't he?"

She gave a small nod.

"Why didn't you tell me?"

"What could you have done from Seattle?"

"You should have told me. I could at least have offered you some advice. For that matter, why didn't you tell your father?"

James was furious and she suspected she was about to receive the lecture of her life. When nothing more came, she raised her eyes to her husband—and wanted to weep.

His face was a mess. His eye was completely swollen now. It might have been better if she could've convinced him to apply the ice pack. Anyone looking at him would know instantly that her husband the judge had been involved in an altercation—and all because of her.

The police left soon afterward.

"Can I get you anything?" Summer asked guiltily as they entered the apartment.

"I'm fine," he said curtly.

But he wasn't fine. His hands were swollen, his knuckles scraped and bleeding. All at once he started to blur, and the room spun. Everything seemed to be closing in on her. Panic-stricken, Summer groped for the kitchen counter and held on until the waves of dizziness passed.

"Summer? What's wrong?"

"Nothing. I got a little light-headed, that's all." She didn't mention how close she'd come to passing out. Even now, she felt the force of her will was the only thing keeping her conscious.

James came to her and placed his arm around her waist, gently guiding her into the living room. They sat on the sofa, and Summer rested her head against his shoulder, wondering what was wrong with her.

"I'm so sorry," she whispered, fighting back tears.

"For what?"

"The fight."

"That wasn't your fault."

"But, James, you have a terrible black eye. What will people say?" She hated to think about the speculation he'd face when he returned to Seattle, and it was all on account of her. Perhaps she should've told him that Brett was bothering her, but she hadn't wanted to burden him with her troubles.

"Everyone will figure I was in a major fistfight," James teased. "It'll probably be the best thing to happen to my reputation in years. People will see me in an entirely new light."

"Everyone will wonder...."

"Of course they will, and I'll tell them they should see the other guy."

Summer made an effort to laugh but found she couldn't. She twisted her head a bit so she could look at him. The bruise on his jaw was a vivid purple. She raised tentative fingers to it and bit her lip when he winced.

"Oh, James." Gently she pressed her lips to the underside of his jaw.

"That helps." He laughed and groaned at the same time.

She kissed him again, easing her mouth toward his. He moaned and before long, they were exchanging deep, hungry kisses.

"I refuse," James said, unbuttoning her blouse but having difficulty with his swollen hands, "to allow Brett to ruin our last few hours together."

She smiled and slid her arms around his shoulders. "Want to have a shower?" she breathed.

"Yes, but do you have a large enough hot-water tank?"

Summer giggled, recalling their last experience in

her compact shower stall and how the water had gone cold at precisely the wrong moment.

The sound of the key turning in the lock told Summer her roommate was home. She sat back abruptly and fastened her blouse.

"Hi, everyone." Julie stepped into the living room and set her suitcase on the floor. "I'm not interrupting anything, am I?" Her gaze narrowed. "James? What on earth happened to you?"

James didn't expect his black eye to go unnoticed, but he wasn't prepared for the amount of open curiosity it aroused.

"Morning, Judge Wilkens." Louise Jamison, the assistant he shared with two other judges, greeted him when he entered the office Monday morning. Then she dropped her pencil. "Judge Wilkens!" she said. "My goodness, what happened?"

He mumbled something about meeting the wrong end of a fist and hurried into his office. It was clear he'd need to come up with an explanation that would satisfy the curious.

Brad Williams knocked on his door five minutes later. His fellow judge let himself into James's office and stared. "So it's true?"

"What's true?"

"You tell me. Looks like you've been in a fight."

"It was a minor scuffle, and that's all I'm going to say about it." James stood and reached for his robe, eager to escape a series of prying questions he didn't want to answer. He had the distinct feeling the rest of the day was going to be like this.

And he was right.

By the time he pulled out of the parking garage that evening, he regretted that he hadn't called in sick. He might've done it if a black eye would disappear in a couple of days, but that wasn't likely, so there was no point in not going in. He checked his reflection in the rearview mirror. The eye looked worse than it had the previous day. He pressed his index finger against the swelling and was surprised by the pain it caused. Still, he could live with the discomfort; it was the unsightliness of the bruises and the questions and curious glances he could do without.

Irritated and not knowing exactly whom to blame, James drove to his father's house. He hadn't been to see Walter in a couple of weeks and wanted to discuss something with him.

His father was doing a *New York Times* crossword puzzle when James let himself into the house. He looked up from the folded newspaper and did a double take, but to his credit, Walter didn't mention the black eye. "Hello, James."

"Dad."

James walked over to the snifter of Scotch Walter kept on hand and poured himself a liberal quantity. He wasn't fond of hard liquor and rarely indulged, but he felt he needed something potent. And fast.

"It's been one of those days, has it?"

James's back was to his father. "You might say that."

He took his first sip and the Scotch burned its way down his throat. "This stuff could rot a man's stomach."

"So I've heard."

Taking his glass, James sat in the leather chair next to his father. "I suppose you're wondering about the eye."

"I'll admit to being curious."

"You and everyone else I've seen today."

"I can imagine you've been the object of more than one inquisitive stare."

"I was in a fistfight."

"You?"

"Don't sound so surprised. You're the one who told me there'd be times in a man's life when he couldn't walk away from a fight. This happened to be one of those."

"Want to talk about it?" His father set aside the paper.

"Not particularly, but if you must know, it was over Summer."

"Ah, yes, Summer. How is she? I'm telling you, son, I like her. Couldn't have chosen a better mate for you if I'd gone looking myself."

James smiled for the first time that day. "She's doing well. I was with her this weekend." James raised the Scotch to his lips and grimaced. "We had brunch with her parents."

"Helen and Hank. Good people," Walter commented.

"There's a problem with the April wedding date—

on their end and mine. Helen suggested we wait until September. I said November, because of the election."

"Do you want that?" Walter asked.

"No. Neither does Summer."

"Then the hell with it. Let her finish out her contract with Disneyland and join you after that. You've already had a wedding. I never could understand why you wanted two ceremonies, but then I'm an old man with little appreciation for fancy weddings. What I *would* appreciate is a couple of grandkids. I'm not getting any younger, you know, and neither are you."

"Do away with the second ceremony?"

"That's what I said," Walter muttered.

James closed his eyes in relief. Of course. It made perfect sense. He'd suggested a second wedding because he thought that was what Summer wanted, but if he asked her, James suspected he'd learn otherwise. The wedding was for her parents' sake.

"How'd you get so smart?" James asked his father.

"Don't know, but I must be very wise," Walter said, and chuckled. "I've got a superior court judge for a son."

James laughed, feeling comfortable for the first time all day.

"Stay for dinner," his father insisted. "It's been a while since we spent any real time together. Afterward you can let me beat you in a game of chess, and I'll go to bed a happy man."

"All right." It was an invitation too good to refuse.

* * *

When James got home after ten, the light on his phone was blinking. He was tempted to ignore his messages.

He felt tired but relaxed and not particularly interested in returning a long list of phone calls. Especially when he suspected most of his callers were trying to learn what they could about his mysterious black eye.

The only person he wanted to talk to was Summer. He reached for the phone, and she answered on the second ring.

"I just got in," he explained. "Dad and I had dinner."

"Did you give him my love?"

"I did better than that—I let him beat me at chess."

She laughed, and James closed his eyes, savouring the melodic sound. It was like a balm after the day he'd endured.

"How's the eye?" she asked next.

"Good." So he lied. "How was the show today?"

"I didn't go in. I seem to have come down with the flu, so my understudy played Belle. I felt crummy all day. When I woke up this morning, I just felt so nauseous. At first I thought it was nerves over what happened with Brett, but it didn't go away, so I had to call in sick."

"Have you been to a doctor?"

"No. Have you?"

She had him there. "No."

"I'll be fine. I just want to be sure I didn't give you my flu bug while you were here."

"There's no sign of it," he assured her.

They must have talked for another fifteen minutes, saying nothing outwardly significant yet sharing the most important details of their lives. Their conversation would have gone on a lot longer, had someone not rung his doorbell.

It was Ralph Southworth. His campaign manager took one look at James and threw his arms dramatically in the air. "What the hell happened to you?"

"Good evening to you, too," James said evenly.

Ralph rammed all ten fingers through his hair. "Don't you listen to your messages? I've left no fewer than five, and you haven't bothered to return one."

"Sit down," James said calmly. "Do you want a drink?"

Ralph's eyes narrowed as he studied James's face. "Am I going to need it?"

"That depends." James pointed to the recliner by the large brick fireplace. He'd tell Ralph the truth because it was necessary and, knowing his campaign manager's feelings about Summer, he suspected Ralph *would* need a stiff drink. "Make yourself at home."

Instead, Ralph followed him into the kitchen. "I got no less than ten phone calls this afternoon asking about your black eye. You can't show up and then say nothing about it."

"I can't?" This was news to James, since he'd done exactly that. "I thought you were here to discuss business."

"I am." Ralph frowned when James brought an

unopened bottle of top-shelf bourbon out of a cabinet. "So I'm going to need that."

"Yes."

"I met with the League of Women Voters and I've arranged for you to speak at their luncheon in July. It's a real coup, James, and I hope you appreciate my efforts."

"Yes," he murmured. "Thanks."

"Now tell me about the eye. And the bruises."

"All right," James said, adding two ice cubes to the glass. He half filled it with bourbon and handed it to his friend. "I got hit in the face with a fist more than once."

"Whose fist?"

"Some beach bum by the name of Brett. I don't remember his last name if I ever heard it."

Ralph swallowed his first sip of liquor. "Does the beach bum have anything to do with the woman you mentioned?"

"Yeah."

The two men stared across the kitchen at each other.

"Were the police called?" Ralph demanded.

It took James a moment to own up to the truth. "Yes."

Ralph slammed his hand against the counter. "I should've known! James, what did I tell you? A woman's nothing but trouble. Mark my words, if you get involved any further with Spring…"

"Summer!"

"Whatever. It doesn't matter, because her name spells just one thing. Trouble. You've worked all your life for this opportunity. This is your one shot at the bench. We both know it. You asked me to manage your campaign and I agreed, but I thought it would be a team effort. The two of us."

"It is." James wanted to hold on to his seat on the bench more than he'd ever wanted anything—other than to marry Summer. He also felt he was the best man for the position. To get this close and lose it all would be agonizing.

"Then why," Ralph asked, palms out, "are you sabotaging your own campaign?"

"I'm not doing it on purpose."

"Stay away from this woman!"

"Ralph, I can't. I won't."

Ralph rubbed his face with both hands, clearly frustrated.

"Summer's in California, but I plan on bringing her to Seattle as soon as I can arrange it. Probably April."

"Tell me you're joking."

"I'm not." James figured he should admit the truth now and be done with it. "We're married."

"What?" Ralph pulled out a chair and sank into it. "When?"

"Over New Year's."

"Why?"

"It was just…one of those things. We fell in love and got married. We were hoping for a more elaborate ceremony later, but I can see that's going to be a problem."

"You want to know what's the real problem, James? It's the marriage. Why didn't you tell me right away?"

"I should have," James said, sorry now that he hadn't.

"But when you told me you'd never been in love, I didn't think there was much of a chance you'd understand."

"What you've done is jeopardize your entire campaign."

Somehow he doubted that. "Aren't you overreacting?"

"Time will tell, won't it?" Ralph asked smugly.

James decided to ignore that. "If anything, Summer will be an asset. She's lovely and she's good at connecting with people. Unfortunately her contract with Disney doesn't expire until April."

"That's right," Ralph said sarcastically. "I forgot, she's a showgirl."

"A singer and an actress and a very talented one at that," James boasted.

"An actress, a showgirl, it's all the same."

"Once she's finished with her contract, I want her to move in with me."

"Here in Seattle?" Ralph made it sound like a world-class disaster.

"A wife belongs with her husband."

"What about the beach bum?"

James frowned. "We don't have to worry about him. He's gone for good."

"I certainly hope so. And while we're making out a wish list, let's add a couple of other things. Let's wish that your worthy opponent doesn't find out about this little skirmish between you and Summer's previous lover-boy. And let's make a great big wish that he doesn't learn that the police were called and a report filed."

"He won't," James said confidently, far more confidently than he felt.

"I hope you're right," Ralph said, and downed what was left of his bourbon in one gulp. The glass hit the counter when he put it down. "Now tell me, what kind of damage did you do to the beach bum?"

"You didn't tell him, did you?" Julie said when Summer set the telephone receiver back in place.

"No." She sighed reluctantly. She rested her hand protectively on her stomach.

"A man has the right to know he's going to be a father," Julie said righteously. She bit into an apple as she tucked her feet beneath her on the sofa.

Summer closed her eyes. Even the smell of food or the sound of someone eating made her sick to her stomach. In the past two months she'd seen parts of toilets that weren't meant to be examined at such close range. She hadn't kept down a single breakfast in weeks. The day before, she'd wondered why she even bothered to eat. Dumping it directly into the toilet would save time and trouble.

"How long do you think James is going to fall for this lie about having the flu?"

It had been more than a month since she'd last seen him, and in that time Summer had lost ten pounds. Her clothes hung on her, and she was as pale as death. She seemed to spend more time at the doctor's office than she did at her own apartment. Her biggest fear was that being so ill meant there was something wrong with the baby, although the doctor had attempted to reassure her on that score.

"Why haven't you told him?" Julie wanted to know.

"I just can't do it over the phone." Besides, she remembered James mentioning that a pregnancy now would be a mistake. Well, she hadn't gotten this way by herself!

She knew exactly when it had happened, too. There was only the one time they hadn't used protection.

"When are you going to see him again?"

Summer shook her head. "I don't know."

"You talk on the phone every night. He sends you gifts. I can't think of anyone else who got six dozen red roses for Valentine's Day."

"He's extravagant…."

"Extravagant with everything but his time."

"He's so busy, Julie. I never realized how much there was to being a judge, and he really cares about the people he works with. Not only the people who stand before him, but the attorneys and his staff, too. Then there's the election…."

"So, go to him. He's just as unhappy without you."

"I've got three weeks left on my contract, and—"

"Do you really suppose no one's figured out that you're pregnant? Think about it, Summer. You came back from Vegas all happy and in love, and two weeks later you're heaving your guts out after every meal. No one expects you to perform when you feel this crummy."

"But…"

"Do everyone a favor and—" Julie stopped when there was a knock at the door. "Is anyone coming over tonight?"

"No." Summer laid her head back against the sofa and drew in several deep breaths, hoping that would ease her nausea.

"It's for you," Julie said, looking over her shoulder as soon as she'd opened the door. "It's Walter Wilkens."

Summer threw aside the blanket and scurried off the sofa, anxious to see her father-in-law. "Walter?" What could he possibly be doing here? "Come inside, please."

The refined, older gentleman stepped into the apartment. "Summer?" He gazed at her, his expression concerned. "James said you'd been ill with the flu, but my dear…"

"She looks dreadful," Julie finished for him. Her roommate took another noisy bite of her apple. "I'm Julie. We met at the wedding. Summer's roommate and best friend."

Walter bowed slightly. "Hello, Julie. It's nice to see you again."

"Sit down, please," Summer said, motioning toward the only chair in the house without blankets or clean laundry stacked on it.

"Would you like something to drink?" Julie asked.

"No…no, thank you." He cleared his throat. "Summer, my dear." He frowned. "Have you been to a doctor?"

"Yup," Julie answered, chewing on her apple. "Three times this week, right, Summer?"

"Julie," she snapped.

"Are you going to tell him or not?"

Summer tossed the tangled curls over her shoulder and groaned inwardly. "I don't have much choice now, do I?" She met Walter's eyes and realized her lower lip was trembling. She was suddenly afraid she might burst into tears. Her emotions had been like a seesaw, veering from one extreme to another.

"Summer, what is it?" Walter prodded.

"I'm pregnant," she whispered. She smiled happily all the while tears streamed down her cheeks.

Walter bolted out of his chair. "Hot damn!"

"Other than me, you're the first person she's told," Julie felt obliged to inform him. "Not even her own family knows, although her mother would take one look at her and guess."

"James doesn't know?"

"Nope." Again it was Julie who answered.

"And why not?"

"A woman doesn't tell her husband that sort of thing over the phone," Summer insisted. "Or by e-mail." She needed to see his face, to gauge James's reaction so she'd know what he was really thinking.

"She's been sicker than a dog."

"Thank you, Julie, but I can take it from here."

"I can see that," Walter said, ignoring Summer.

"What brings you to California?" Summer asked cordially, looking for a way to change the subject.

"A business trip. I thought James might have mentioned it."

If he had, Summer had missed it. She had a feeling she'd been doing a lot of that lately.

"Well, my dear," Walter said, sitting back in his chair and grinning broadly. "This is a pleasant surprise."

"It was for me, too."

"I can just see James's face when you tell him."

"He probably won't know what to do, laugh or cry."

"He'll probably do a little of both."

Walter himself was laughing, Summer noticed. He hadn't stopped smiling from the moment he'd heard the news.

"Everything's always been so carefully planned in James's life," Walter said, still grinning. "Then he met you and bingo. He's a husband, and now he's about to be a father. This is terrific news, just terrific."

"James might not find it all that wonderful," Summer said, voicing her fears for the first time. "He's in the middle of an important campaign."

"Don't you worry about a thing."

"I *am* worried. I can't help it."

"Then we're going to have to do something about that."

"We are?" Summer asked. "What?"

"If my son's going to become a father, you should tell him, and the sooner the better. Pack your bags, Summer. It's about time you moved to Seattle with your husband where you belong."

"But…"

"Don't argue with me, young lady. I'm an old man and I'm accustomed to having my own way. If you're worried about his campaign, this is how we fix that. You'll be introduced to the public as his wife and we're going to put an end to any speculation right now."

Nine

Something was wrong with Summer. James had sensed it weeks ago. He would have confronted her and demanded answers if she hadn't sounded so fragile.

There was that business with the flu, but exactly how long was that going to last? When he asked her what the doctor said, she seemed vague.

Part of the problem was the length of time they'd been apart. He hadn't meant it to be so long. Summer had intended to come to Seattle, but that had fallen through, just as his last visit to California had. Neither of them was happy about it, but there was nothing James could have done on his end. He was sure that was the case with her, too.

James paced in his den, worrying. When he had to mull over a problem, that was what he did. Lately he'd practically worn a path in the carpet. He felt helpless and frustrated. Despite Ralph's dire warnings, he wished he'd brought Summer back to Seattle. This separation was hurting them both.

His greatest fear was that she regretted their marriage.

Their telephone conversations weren't the same anymore. He felt as if she was hiding something from him. They used to talk about everything but he noticed that she steered him away from certain topics now. She didn't want to talk about herself or her job or this flu that had hung on for few weeks. They used to talk for hours; now he had the feeling she was eager to get off the line.

James wondered about Brett, but when he asked, Summer assured him she hadn't seen or heard from him since the fight.

The fight.

His black eye had caused a great deal of speculation among his peers. James had never offered any explanation. Via the grapevine, he'd heard Ralph's version and found it only distantly related to the truth. According to his campaign manager, James had been jumped by gang members and valiantly fought them off until the police arrived.

When James confronted Ralph with the story, the other man smiled and said he couldn't be held accountable for rumors. Right or wrong, James had let it drop. He was eager to put the incident behind him.

James certainly hadn't expected married life to be this lonely. He'd never felt this detached from the mainstream of everyday life, this isolated. Missing Summer was like a constant ache in his stomach. Except that a store-bought tablet wasn't going to cure what ailed him.

His desk was filled with demands. He felt weary. Unsure of his marriage. Unsure of himself.

He went into the kitchen to make a cup of instant coffee when he saw a car turn into his driveway and around to the backyard.

His father.

He wondered why Walter would stop by unannounced on a Sunday afternoon. James wasn't in the mood for company—but then again, maybe a sounding board was exactly what he needed. Other than his father, there was no one with whom he could discuss Summer.

The slam of a car door closing was followed almost immediately by another. James frowned. Dad had brought someone with him. Great. Just great.

He took the hot water out of the microwave, added the coffee granules and stirred briskly. There was a knock at the back door.

"Come in, the door's open," he called, not turning around. He didn't feel like being polite. Not today, when it felt as if the world was closing in around him.

He sipped his coffee and stared out the window. The daffodils were blooming and the—

"Hello, James."

James whirled around. "Summer?" He couldn't believe she was really there. It was impossible. A figment of his imagination. An apparition. Before another second passed, James walked across the kitchen and swept her into his arms.

Laughing and sobbing at once, Summer hugged him close.

Then they were kissing each other. Neither could give or get enough.

Walter stood in the background and cleared his throat. "I'll wait for the two of you in the living room," he said, loudly enough to be sure he was heard.

As far as James was concerned, his father might as well make himself comfortable. Or leave. This could take a while.

Summer in his arms was the closest thing to heaven James had ever found. Not for several minutes did he notice how thin and frail she was. The virus had ravaged her body.

"Sweetheart," he whispered between kisses. He paused and brushed back her hair to get a good look at her.

She was pale. Her once-pink cheeks were colorless, and her eyes appeared sunken. "Are you over the flu?"

She lowered her eyes and stepped away from him. "I…you'd better sit down, James."

"Sit down? Why?"

Her hands closed around the back of a kitchen chair. "I have something important to tell you."

He could see she was nervous and on the verge of tears. The worries that were nipping at his heels earlier returned with reinforcements. Summer had more than a common flu bug.

"Just tell me," he said. A knot was beginning to form in his stomach. Was she ill? Was it something life threatening? The knot twisted and tightened.

"I don't have the flu," she whispered.

Whatever it was, then, must be very bad if his father had brought her to Seattle.

"How serious is it?" he asked. He preferred to confront whatever they were dealing with head-on.

"It's serious, James, very serious." Slowly she raised her eyes to his. "We're going to have a baby."

His relief was so great that he nearly laughed. "A baby? You mean to tell me you're pregnant?"

She nodded. Her fingers had gone white, and she was watching him closely.

James took her in his arms. "I thought you were really sick."

"I have been really sick," she told him crisply. "Morning sickness. Afternoon sickness. Evening sickness. I…I can't seem to keep food down…. I've never been more miserable in my life."

"I suspect part of her problem has been psychological," Walter announced from the doorway. "The poor girl's been terribly worried about how you were going to take the news."

"Me?"

"My feelings exactly," Walter said. "The deed's done, what's there to think about? Besides, you've made me an extremely happy man."

"A baby." James remained awestruck at the thought.

"Now tell him your due date, Summer—he'll get a real kick out of that."

"September twenty-third," Summer announced.

Everyone seemed to be studying him, waiting for a reaction. James didn't know what to think. Then it hit him. "September twenty-third? That's the date of the primary."

"I know. Isn't it great?" Walter asked.

"How long can you stay?" James asked, taking Summer's hands in his own.

Summer looked at Walter.

"Stay?" his father barked. "My dear son, this is your wife. I brought her to Seattle to live with you. This is where she belongs."

"You can live with me?" A man could only take in so much news at one time. First, he'd learned that his wife didn't have some life-threatening disease. Then he discovered he was going to be a father. Even more important, he was going to have the opportunity to prove what kind of husband he could be.

"Yes. I got out of my contract for medical reasons, and Julie's getting a roommate. So…everything's settled."

James pulled out the chair and sat Summer down. Then he knelt in front of her and took her hands in his. "A baby."

"You're sure you don't mind?"

"Of course he doesn't mind," Walter said, "and if he does I'll set up an appointment with a good psychiatrist I know. This is the best news we've had in thirty years."

"When did it happen?" James asked.

Summer laughed at him. "You mean you don't remember?" She leaned toward him and whispered, reminding him of the one episode the morning after their honeymoon night.

"Ah, yes," James said, and chuckled. "As I recall, I was the one who said one time wouldn't matter."

"I don't suppose there's anything to eat in this house?" Walter asked, banging cupboard doors open and shut.

"Why have you been so ill?" James wanted to know. It worried him. "Is it routine?"

"My doctor says some women suffer from severe morning sickness for the first few months. He's been very reassuring. I try to remember that when I'm losing my latest meal."

"Is there anything that can help?"

"She's got what she needs now," Walter said.

Summer laid her head on his shoulder. "I was worried you'd be upset with me."

"Why would I be upset when the most beautiful woman in the world tells me she's having my baby?" He reached for her hand and pressed her palm over his heart. "Notice anything different?" he asked.

She shook her head, giving him a puzzled look.

"My heart's racing because I'm so excited. Because I'm so happy. We're going to have a baby, Summer! I feel like I could conquer the world."

He wanted his words to comfort her. The last thing he expected was that she'd burst into tears.

"But you said a baby would be a mistake right now," she reminded him between sobs.

"I said that?"

"He said that?" Walter glared at James.

"I don't remember saying it," James told him. "I'm

sorry, my love. Just knowing we're going to have a baby makes me happier than I have any right to be."

"Damn straight he's happy," Walter tossed in, "or there'd be hell to pay. I should've been a grandfather two or three times over by now. As far as I'm concerned, James owes me."

"I'll try and make it up to you," James promised his father with a grin.

Summer couldn't remember ever being so hungry. She'd been with James a week and had settled so contentedly into her new life it was almost as if she'd always been there.

"Would you like another piece of apple pie?" James asked. "Better yet, why don't we buy the whole thing and take it home with us?"

"Can we do that?" Summer was sure her appetite must be a source of embarrassment to him. They were at a sidewalk restaurant on the Seattle waterfront. Summer couldn't decide between the French onion soup and the Cobb salad, so she'd ordered both. Then she'd topped off the meal with a huge slice of apple pie à la mode.

"I'll ask the waitress," James said as though it was perfectly normal to order a whole pie for later.

"Have I embarrassed you?" she asked, keeping her voice low.

James's mouth quivered. "No, but I will admit I've rarely seen anyone enjoy her food more."

"Oh, James, you have no idea how good it is to be able to eat and keep everything down. I felt a thousand times better this past week than I did the whole previous two months."

"Then Dad was right," he said.

"About what?"

"The psychological effects of the pregnancy were taking their toll along with the physical. In other words, you were worried and making yourself more so. I could kick myself."

"Why?"

"For not guessing. You have to forgive me, sweetheart, I'm new to this husband business."

"You're forgiven."

"Just promise me one thing. Don't keep any more secrets from me, all right?"

She smiled. "You've got yourself a deal."

"James?" A striking-looking couple approached their table.

"Rich and Jamie Manning." Sounding genuinely pleased, James stood and exchanged handshakes with the man. Then he turned to Summer. "These are good friends of mine, Rich and Jamie Manning. This is my wife, Summer."

"Your wife?" Rich repeated, doing a poor job of hiding his surprise. "When did this happen?"

"Shortly after New Year's," James explained. "Would you care to join us?"

"Unfortunately we can't," Rich said. "The babysitter's waiting. But this is great news. I hope there's a good reason I didn't get a wedding invitation."

"A very good one." James grinned. "I've been meaning to let everyone know. But Summer just moved here from California."

"Well, the word's out now," Jamie said, smiling at her. "Once Rich's mother hears about it, she'll want to throw a party in your honor." Jamie and her husband shared a private, happy look.

"I'd better call your parents before I alienate them completely," James said.

"I'll be seeing you soon," Rich said and patted James's shoulder as he passed by. "Bye, Summer."

James was silent for a moment, and Summer wasn't sure if he was glad or not that his friends had stopped to talk. She didn't think he intended to keep their marriage a secret, yet he hadn't made a point of introducing her around, either.

"Is there a problem?" she asked.

"No. It's just that I was hoping to give you some time to regain your strength before you met my friends."

Summer's gaze followed the couple as they made their way toward the front of the restaurant.

"They're happy, aren't they?"

"Rich and Jamie?"

Summer nodded.

"Yes." He relaxed in his chair. "They came to see me a few years back with perhaps the most unusual request of my career." He smiled, and Summer guessed he must've been amused at the time, as well.

"What did they want?"

"They asked me to draw up a paper for a marriage of convenience."

"Really." That seemed odd to Summer. Although she'd just met the couple, it was clear to her that they were in love.

"They'd come up with some harebrained scheme to have a baby together—by artificial insemination. Rich would be the sperm donor."

"Did they have a baby?"

"Yes, but Bethany was conceived the old-fashioned way without a single visit to a fertility clinic."

Summer shook her head. "This doesn't make any sense to me. Why would two healthy people go to such lengths to have a child? Especially when they're perfectly capable of doing things…the usual way?"

"It does sound silly, doesn't it?"

"Frankly, yes."

James leaned forward and placed his elbows on the table. "Jamie and Rich had been friends for years. Since their high school days, if I recall correctly. Jamie couldn't seem to fall in love with the right kind of man and, after a couple of disastrous relationships, she decided she was giving up dating altogether."

"I love the tricks life plays on people," Summer said, licking melted ice cream off her spoon. She looked across the table at the remnants on James's plate. "Are you going to eat that?" she asked.

He pushed the plate toward her.

"Thanks," she said, and blew him a kiss. "Go on," she encouraged, scooping up the last bits of pie and ice cream. "What happened?"

"Apparently Jamie was comfortable with her decision,

except that she wanted a child. That's when she approached Rich about being the sperm donor."

"Just between friends, that sort of thing?"

"Exactly. At any rate, Rich didn't think it was such a bad idea himself, the not-marrying part. He'd had his own ups and downs in the relationship department. But the more he thought about her suggestion, the more problems he had with being nothing more than a sperm donor. He suggested they get married so their child could have his name. He also wanted a say in the baby's upbringing."

"And Jamie agreed to all this?"

"She wanted a child."

"So they asked you to draw up a contract or something?"

"Yes, but I have to tell you I had my reservations."

"I can imagine."

"They have two children now."

"Well, this so-called marriage of convenience certainly worked out," Summer told him.

"It sure did."

While she was looking around the table for anything left to eat, she noticed that James was studying her. "How are you feeling?" he asked.

"A thousand times better." She smiled and lowered her voice so he alone could hear. "If what you're really asking is if I'm well enough to make love, the answer is yes."

He swallowed hard.

"Shall we hurry home, James?"

"By all means."

He paid the tab and they were gone. "You're sure?" he asked as he unlocked the car door and helped her inside.

Sitting in the passenger seat, Summer smiled up at her husband. "Am I sure? James, it's been months since we last made love. I'm so hot for you I could burst into flames."

James literally ran around the front of the car. He sped the entire way home, and Summer considered it fortunate that they weren't stopped by a traffic cop.

"Torture…every night for the last week," James mumbled as he pulled into the driveway. "I couldn't trust myself to even touch you."

"I know."

Her time in Seattle hadn't started out well. The first morning, she'd woken and run straight for the bathroom. James helped her off the floor when she'd finished. He'd cradled her in his arms and told her how much he loved her for having their baby.

Her first few dinners hadn't stayed down, either. But each day after her arrival, the nausea and episodes of vomiting had become less and less frequent. Now, one week later, she was almost herself again.

He left the car and came around to her side. When he opened the door, she stepped out and into his embrace—and kissed him.

James groaned and swung her into his arms.

"What are you doing?" she asked.

"Carrying you over the threshold," he announced. "You've been cheated out of just about everything else when it comes to this marriage."

"I haven't been cheated."

"You should've had the big church wedding and—"

"Are we going to argue about that again? Really, James, I'd rather we just made love."

He had a problem getting the door unlocked while holding her, but he managed. The minute they were inside, he started kissing her, doing wonderful, erotic things that excited her to the point of desperation.

Summer kicked off her shoes.

James kissed her and unsnapped the button to her skirt. The zipper slid down. All the while he was silently urging her toward the stairs.

Her jacket went next, followed by her shirt.

She made it to the staircase and held out her hand. James didn't need any more encouragement than that. They raced to the bedroom together.

Summer fell on the bed, laughing. "Oh, James, promise you'll always love me this much."

"I promise." He tried to remove his shirt without taking off his tie, with hilarious results. Arms clutching her stomach, Summer doubled over, laughing even harder. It was out of pure kindness that she climbed off the bed and loosened the tie enough to slip it over his head. Otherwise, she was afraid her normally calm, patient husband would have strangled himself.

"You think this is funny, do you?"

"I think you're the most wonderful man alive. Will you always want me this much?"

"I can't imagine not wanting you." And he proceeded to prove it....

* * *

James was half-asleep when he heard the doorbell chime. He would have ignored it, but on the off chance it was someone important, he decided to look outside and see if he recognized the car.

Big mistake.

Ralph Southworth was at his door.

James grabbed his pants, threw on his shirt and kissed Summer on the cheek. Then he hurried down the stairs, taking a second to button his shirt before he opened the door. "Hello, Ralph," he said, standing, shoes and socks in hand.

Ralph frowned. "What the hell have you been— never mind, I already know."

"Summer's here."

"So I gather."

"Give her a few minutes, and she'll be down so you can meet her," James told him. He sat in a chair and put on his shoes and socks. "What can I do for you?"

"A number of things, but mainly I'd…" He hesitated as Summer made her way down the stairs. Her hair was mussed, her eyes soft and glowing.

"Ralph, this is my wife, Summer," James said proudly, joining her. He slipped his arm around her shoulders.

"Hello, Summer," Ralph said stiffly.

"Hello, Ralph."

"When did you get here?"

"Last week. Would you two like some coffee? I'll make a pot. James, take your friend into the den, why don't you, and I'll bring everything in there."

James didn't want his wife waiting on him, but something about the way she spoke told him this wasn't the time to argue. That was when he saw her skirt draped on a chair, and her jacket on the floor.

"This way, Ralph," he said, ushering the other man into the den.

He looked over his shoulder and saw Summer delicately scoop up various items of clothing, then hurry into the kitchen.

"Something amuses you?"

James cleared his throat. "Not really."

"First of all, James, I have to question your judgment. When you told me you married a showgirl—"

"Summer's an actress."

Ralph ignored that. "As I was saying, your judgment appears to be questionable."

This was a serious accusation, considering that James was running for a position on the superior court.

Ralph's lips were pinched. "It worries me that you'd marry some woman you barely know on the spur of the moment."

"Love sometimes happens like that."

"Perhaps," Ralph muttered. "Personally I wouldn't know, but James, how much younger is she?"

"Not as much as you think. Nine years."

"She's unsuitable!"

"For whom? You? Listen, Ralph, I asked you to manage my campaign, not run my life. I married Summer, and she's going to have my child."

"The girl's pregnant, as well?"

"Yes, the baby's due September twenty-third."

Ralph's lips went white with disapproval. "Could she have chosen a more inconvenient date?"

"I don't think it really matters."

"That's the primary!"

"I'm well aware of it."

"Good grief, James." Ralph shook his head. "This won't do. It just won't. Once people learn what you've done, they'll assume you were obligated to marry the girl. The last thing we need now is to have your morals questioned."

"Ralph, you're overreacting."

"I can't believe you brought her here, after everything I said."

James gritted his teeth. "She's my wife."

Ralph paced back and forth for a moment or two. "I don't feel I have any choice," he said with finality.

"Choice about what?"

"I'm resigning as your manager."

Summer appeared just then, carrying a tray. "Coffee, anyone?"

Ten

Summer settled easily into life with James. She adored her husband and treasured each moment that they were together.

Her days quickly began to follow a routine of sorts. She rose early and, because she was feeling better, resumed her regular workout, which included a two-mile run first thing in the morning.

James insisted on running with her, although he made it clear he didn't like traipsing through dark streets at dawn's early light. But he wasn't comfortable with her running alone, so he joined her, protesting every step of the way.

James was naturally athletic, and Summer didn't think anyone was more surprised than he was by how enjoyable he started to find it. After their run, they showered together. Thankfully James's hot-water tank was larger than the meager one back in her Orange County apartment.

This was both good and bad. The negative was when

James, a stickler for punctuality, got to court late two mornings in a row.

"You shower first," he told her after their Monday-morning run.

"Not together?" she asked, disappointed.

"I can't be late this morning."

"We'll behave," she promised.

James snickered. "I can't behave with you, Summer. You tempt me too much."

"All right, but you shower first, and I'll get us breakfast."

Ten minutes later, he walked into the kitchen, where Summer was pouring two glasses of orange juice. He wore his dark business suit and carried his briefcase, ready for his workday.

"What are your plans?" he asked, downing the juice as he stood by the table. He sat down to eat his bagel and cream cheese and picked up the paper.

"I'm going to send Julie a long e-mail. Then I thought I'd stop in at the library and volunteer to read during storytime."

"Good idea," he said, scanning the paper.

Summer knew reading the paper was part of his morning ritual, which he didn't have as much time for since her arrival. She drank the last of her juice and kissed his cheek.

"I'm going upstairs for my shower," she told him.

"All right. Have a good day."

"I will. Oh, what time will you be home tonight?" she asked.

"Six or so," he mumbled absently and turned the front page.

Summer hesitated. His schedule had changed. Rarely did he get home before eight the first week after she'd moved in. It seemed that every night there was someone to meet, some campaign supporter to talk to, some plan to outline—all to do with the September primary, even though it was still months away.

In the past week James had come directly home from the courthouse. Not that she was complaining, but she couldn't help wondering.

"What about your campaign?" she asked.

"Everything's under control," was all he said.

Summer wondered.

All at once James looked up, startled, as if he'd just remembered something. "What day's your ultrasound?"

"Thursday of next week. Don't look so worried. You don't need to be there."

"I *want* to be there," he stated emphatically. "Our baby's first picture. I wouldn't miss it for the world. Besides, I'm curious to find out if we're going to have a son or daughter."

"Don't tell me," she said. "I don't want to know."

"I won't," he said, chuckling. He reached out to stroke her abdomen. "I can't believe how much I love this little one, and he isn't even born yet."

"He?" she asked, hands on her hips in mock offense.

"A daughter would suit me just fine. Actually Dad's hoping for a granddaughter. It's been a long time since there's been a little girl in the family."

Summer pressed her hand over her husband's. She'd never been this happy. It frightened her sometimes. Experience had taught her that happiness almost always came with a price.

Walter joined them for dinner Wednesday evening. From the moment she'd met him, Summer had liked her father-in-law.

"Did you know Summer could cook this well when you married her?" Walter asked when they'd finished eating.

She'd found a recipe for a chicken casserole on the Internet and served it with homemade dinner rolls and fresh asparagus, with a fresh fruit salad made of seedless grapes and strawberries. For dessert she picked up a lemon torte at the local bakery.

"Summer's full of surprises," James told his father. His eyes briefly met hers.

"What he's trying to say is no one knew how fertile I was, either."

"That's the best surprise yet," Walter said. He dabbed the corner of his mouth with his napkin in a blatant effort to hide a smile.

"It certainly is," James put in.

Walter studied her. "How are you feeling these days?"

"Wonderful."

"What's the doctor have to say?"

"That I'm in excellent health. The baby's growing by leaps and bounds. I haven't felt him move yet, but—"

"Him?" James and Walter chimed in simultaneously.

"Or her," she retorted, smiling. She stood and started to clear the table.

"Let me do that," James insisted.

"I'm not helpless, you know," Walter added.

Both men leapt from their chairs.

"Go have your coffee," Summer told them. "It'll only take me a few minutes to deal with the dishes."

Walter shrugged, then looked at his son. "There are a few things I need to discuss with James," he said.

"Then off with you." She shooed them out of the kitchen.

James poured two cups of coffee and took them into the living room. He paused in the doorway and looked over his shoulder. "You're sure?"

"James, honestly! Go talk to your father."

Although she didn't know Walter well, she sensed that something was on his mind. Throughout the meal she'd noticed the way he watched his son. James was acting odd, too.

Walter wanted to discuss the campaign, but every time he'd introduced the subject, James expertly changed it. He did it cleverly, but Walter had noticed, and after a while Summer had, too.

She ran tap water to rinse off the dinner plates before putting them in the dishwasher, and when she turned off the faucet she heard the end of James's comment.

"…Summer doesn't know."

She hesitated. Apparently the two men didn't realize how well their voices carried. She didn't mean to eavesdrop, but it did seem only fair to listen, since she was the topic of conversation.

"What do you plan to do about it?" his father asked.

It took James a long time to answer. "I haven't decided."

"Have you tried reasoning with him?"

"No," James answered bitterly. "The man said he has doubts about my judgment. He's insulted me, insulted my wife. I don't need Southworth if he's got an attitude like that."

"But you will need a campaign manager."

"Yes," James admitted reluctantly.

So *that* was what this was about. Summer leaned against the kitchen counter and closed her eyes. Ralph had resigned, and from the evidence she'd seen, James had, too. Resigned himself to losing, even before the election. It didn't sound like him.

"What's the problem?" Walter asked as if reading Summer's mind.

James lowered his voice substantially, and Summer had to strain to hear him. "He disapproves of Summer."

"What?" Walter had no such compunction about keeping quiet. "The man's crazy!"

"I've made a series of mistakes," James said.

"Mistakes?"

"With Summer."

The world collapsed, like a house falling in on itself. Summer struggled toward a chair and literally fell into it.

"I should never have married her the way I did,"

James elaborated. "I cheated her out of the wedding she deserved. I don't know if her mother's forgiven me yet. The last I heard, her family's planning a reception in November. By then the baby will be here and, well, it seems a little after the fact."

"You can't blame Summer for that."

"I don't," James remarked tartly. "I blame myself. In retrospect I realize I was afraid of losing her. So I insisted on the marriage before she could change her mind."

"I don't understand what any of this has to do with Ralph," Walter muttered.

"Ralph thinks Summer's too young for me."

"Nonsense."

"He also seems to think I've done myself harm by not letting everyone know immediately that I was married. Bringing Summer here to live with me now, pregnant, and saying we've been married all along, is apparently too convenient to believe."

"It's the truth."

"You and I know that, but there's already speculation."

"So? People will always talk. Let them. But you've got to do something about getting this campaign organized. There are worse things you could be accused of than marrying in secret or getting Summer pregnant before your wedding day. As far as I'm concerned, Southworth's looking for excuses."

"I refuse to subject Summer to that kind of speculation," James said stubbornly.

"Have you talked this over with her?"

"Not yet…"

"You haven't?"

"I know, I know." The defeatist attitude was back in James's voice. "I've put it off longer than I should have."

After that, Summer didn't hear much more of the conversation between father and son. Their marriage had hurt her husband; it might have robbed him of his dreams, cheated him out of his goals.

The phone rang long before she had time to gather her thoughts. "I'll get it," she called out to James, and reached for the extension in the kitchen. Her hand trembled as she lifted the receiver.

"Hello," she said, her voice weak.

"Hello," came the soft feminine reply. "You don't know me. My name's Christy Manning Franklin."

"Christy…Manning?" Summer said, stunned. She hadn't recovered from one shock before she was hit with another. "Just a moment. I'll get James."

"No, please. It's you I want to talk to."

"Me?"

"From your reaction, I'd guess James has mentioned me."

"Yes." Summer slumped down in a chair and closed her eyes. "You and James were engaged at one time."

"That's right. I understand you and James recently got married."

"Three months ago," Summer said, embarrassed by how weak her voice still was. "In Las Vegas," she added a little more loudly.

"I hope you'll forgive me for being so forward. I

talked it over with Cody—he's my husband—and he said since I felt so strongly about it I should call you."

"So strongly about what?"

"About you…and James. I'll always regret the way I treated James. He deserved a lot better, but I was younger then. Immature in some ways. At one time I thought I was in love with him. I knew he loved me, and my family thought the world of him. Then I met Cody." She hesitated. "I didn't phone to tell you all this. I'm sure James filled in the details."

"Why did you call?" Summer was sure that under other circumstances she might have liked Christy Franklin.

"I wanted to tell you how happy I am that James found someone to love. I know it's presumptuous of me but I wanted to ask a favor of you."

"A favor?" The woman had a lot of nerve.

"Love him with all your heart, Summer. James is a special, special man and he deserves a woman who'll stand by his side and love him."

"I do," she said softly.

"For quite a while I despaired of James ever getting married. I can't tell you how pleased I was when Mom phoned to tell me Rich and Jamie had met you. Cody and I want to extend our very best wishes to you both."

"Thank you."

"I know it's a lot to ask, but I do hope you'll keep Cody and me in mind when you count your friends. There's a place in my heart for James. He's been a friend to our family for years. He was a tremendous help to Paul when Diane died, and again later when he married Leah. James helped Rich and Jamie, too, and he's been a good friend to Jason and Charlotte, as well. We're all indebted to him one way or another."

"I do love him so much." She was fighting back tears and not even sure what she was crying about. The fact that Ralph Southworth had resigned as James's campaign manager because of her? Or that James's ex-fiancée still cared for him deeply?

Summer had just replaced the receiver when James stepped into the kitchen. He stood with one hand on the door.

"Who was that on the phone?" he asked.

Summer met his look straight on, waiting to read any emotion. "Christy Franklin."

"Christy?" he repeated. "What did she want?" He looked more surprised than anything.

"She called to give us her and Cody's best wishes. She said it was high time you were married and she can hardly wait to meet me."

"Really?"

"Really."

"And what did you tell her?"

Summer grinned. "I said she's to keep her cotton-pickin' hands off my husband."

James chuckled, obviously delighted by her possessive attitude. "You aren't going to get much of an argument from me."

"Good thing," she said, and slid her arm around his waist. Together they joined his father.

* * *

"I don't understand it," Summer muttered. She sucked in her stomach in order to close her skirt. "I can barely zip this up. It fit fine just last week."

"Honey, you're pregnant," James said matter-of-factly.

"Three months. I'm not supposed to show yet."

"You're not?" James's eyes left the mirror, his face covered with shaving cream. He carefully examined her rounded belly.

"Tell me the truth, James. If you were meeting me for the first time, would you guess I was pregnant?"

He frowned. "This isn't one of those trick questions, is it?"

"No."

"All right," he said, then cleared his throat. He seemed to know intuitively that she wasn't going to like the answer. "You do look pregnant to me. But then you *are* pregnant, so I don't understand what the big deal is."

"I'm fat already," she wailed, and felt like breaking into tears.

"*Fat* is not the word I'd use to describe you."

"If I'm showing at three months, can you just imagine what I'll look like at nine?"

His grin revealed pride and love. "I'd say you'll look like the most beautiful woman in the world."

"No wonder I love you so much," she told her husband, turning back to the closet. She sorted through the hangers, dismissing first one outfit and then another.

"Where are you going that you're so worried about how you look?" James asked.

Summer froze. "An appointment." She prayed he wouldn't question her further. She'd arranged a meeting with Ralph Southworth, but she didn't want James to know about it.

"Okay. Don't forget tonight," he reminded her. "We're going to the Mannings' for dinner."

"I won't forget," she promised. "Eric and Elizabeth, right?"

"Right. Knowing Elizabeth, she'll probably spend the whole day cooking. She's called me at least five times in the past week. She's anxious to meet you."

"I'm anxious to meet them, too." But not nearly as anxious as she was about this meeting with Southworth. In setting up the appointment, Summer hoped to achieve several objectives. Mainly she wanted Ralph to agree to manage James's campaign again. And she wanted to prove to James that he didn't need to protect her from gossip and speculation.

James left for court shortly after he'd finished shaving. Summer changed into the outfit she'd finally chosen, a soft gray business suit with a long jacket that—sort of—disguised her pregnancy. She spent the morning doing errands and arrived at Ralph's office at the Seattle Bank ten minutes ahead of their one-o'clock appointment.

She announced her name to the receptionist and was escorted into Southworth's office a few minutes later.

Ralph stood when she entered the room. He didn't seem pleased to see her.

"Hello again," she said brightly, taking the chair

across from his desk. She wanted it understood that she wouldn't be easily dissuaded.

"Hello," he responded curtly.

"I hope you don't object to my making an appointment to see you. I'm afraid I may have, uh, misled your secretary into thinking it had to do with a loan."

"I see. Are you in the habit of misleading people?"

"Not at all," she assured him with a cordial smile, "but sometimes a little inventive thinking is worth a dozen frustrating phone calls."

Southworth didn't agree or disagree.

"I'll get to the point of my visit," she said, not wanting to waste time, his or hers.

"Please do."

"I'd like to know why you've resigned as my husband's campaign manager."

Southworth rolled a pencil between his palms, avoiding eye contact. "I believe that's between James and me. It has nothing to do with you."

"That isn't the way I understand it," she said, grateful he'd opened the conversation for her. "I overheard James and his father talking recently, and James said something different."

"So you eavesdrop, as well?"

He was certainly eager to tally her less than sterling characteristics.

"Yes, but in this case, I'm glad I did because I learned that you'd resigned because of me."

Southworth hesitated. "Not exactly. I questioned James's judgment."

"About our marriage?" she pressed.

Once again he seemed inclined to dodge the subject. "I don't really think…"

"I do, Mr. Southworth. This election is extremely important to James. *You're* extremely important to him. When he first mentioned your name to me, he said you were the best man for the job."

"I am the best man for the job." The banker certainly didn't lack confidence in his abilities. "I also know a losing battle when I see it."

"Why's that?"

"Mrs. Wilkens, please."

"Please what, Mr. Southworth? Tell me why you question James's judgment. Until he married me, you were ready to lend him your full support. I can assure you I'll stay right here until I have the answers to these questions." She raised her chin a stubborn half inch and refused to budge.

"If you insist…"

"I do."

"First, you're years younger than James."

"Nine years is hardly that much of a difference. This is a weak excuse and unworthy of you. I do happen to look young for my age, but I can assure you I'm twenty-eight, and James is only thirty-seven."

"There's also the fact that you're a showgirl."

"I'm an actress and singer," she countered. "Since I worked at Disneyland, I hardly think you can fault my morals."

"Morals is another issue entirely."

"Obviously," she said, finding she disliked this man more every time he opened his mouth. It seemed to her that Ralph Southworth was inventing excuses, none of which amounted to anything solid.

"You're pregnant."

"Yes. So?"

"So…it's clear to me, at least, that you and James conveniently decided to marry when you recognized your condition."

Summer laughed. "That's not true, and even if it were, all I need to do is produce our marriage certificate, which I just happen to have with me." Somehow or other she knew it would come down to this. She opened her purse and removed the envelope, then handed it to the man whom her husband had once considered his friend.

Southworth read it over and returned it to her. "I don't understand why the two of you did this. No one meets in Vegas, falls in love and gets married within a few days. Not unless they've got something to hide."

"We're in love." She started to explain that she and James had known each other for a year, but Ralph cut her off.

"Please, Mrs. Wilkens! I've known James for at least a decade. There had to be a reason other than the one you're giving me."

"He loves me. Isn't that good enough for you?"

Southworth seemed bored with the conversation. "Then there's the fact that he kept the marriage a secret."

Summer had no answer to that. "I don't really know why James didn't tell anyone about the wedding," she admitted. "My guess is that it's because he's a private man and considers his personal life his own."

"How far along is the pregnancy?" he asked, ignoring her answer.

"Three months," she told him.

"Three months? I don't claim to know much about women and babies, but I've had quite a few women work for me at the bank over the years. A number of them have had babies. You look easily five or six months."

"That's ridiculous! I know when I got pregnant."

"Do you, now?"

Summer drew in her breath and held it for a moment in an effort to contain her outrage. She loved James and believed in him, but she refused to be insulted.

"I can see we aren't going to accomplish anything here," she said sadly. "You've already formed your opinion about James and me."

"About you, Mrs. Wilkens. It's unfortunate. James would've made an excellent superior court judge. But there's been far too much speculation about him lately. It started with the black eye. People don't want a man on the bench who can't hold on to his own temper. A judge should be above any hint of moral weakness."

"James is one of the most morally upright men I know," she said heatedly. "I take your comments as a personal insult to my husband."

"I find your loyalty to James touching, but it's too little, too late."

"What do you mean by that?" Summer demanded.

"You want your husband to win the election, don't you?"

"Yes. Of course." The question was ludicrous.

"If I were to tell you that you could make a difference, perhaps even sway the election, would you listen?"

"I'd listen," she said, although anything beyond listening was another matter.

Southworth stood and walked over to the window, which offered a panoramic view of the Seattle skyline. His back was to her and for several minutes he said nothing. He seemed to be weighing his words.

"You've already admitted I'm the best man to run James's campaign."

"Yes," she said reluctantly, not as willing to acknowledge it as she had been when she'd first arrived.

"I can help win him this September's primary and the November election. Don't discount the political sway I have in this community, Mrs. Wilkens."

Summer said nothing.

"When James first told me he'd married you, I suggested he keep you out of the picture until after the election."

"I see."

"I did this for a number of reasons, all of which James disregarded."

"He...he really didn't have much choice," she felt obliged to tell him. "I turned up on his doorstep, suitcase in hand."

Ralph nodded as if he'd suspected this had been the case. "I can turn James's campaign around if you'll agree to one thing."

Her stomach tightened, knowing before the words were out what he was going to say. "Yes?"

"Simply disappear for several months. Stay away from Seattle, and once the November election is over, you can move back into his house. It won't matter then."

She closed her eyes and lowered her head. "I see."

"Will you do it?"

"Summer, I'm sorry I'm late." James kissed her soundly and rushed up the stairs to change clothes.

He was late? She hadn't noticed. Since her meeting with Ralph Southworth, Summer had spent what remained of the afternoon in a stupor. She felt numb and sad. Tears lay just beneath the surface, ready to break free.

This decision should've been far less difficult. She could give her husband the dream he'd always wanted or ruin his life.

Five minutes later James was back. He'd changed out of his suit and tie and wore slacks and a shirt and sweater. "Are you ready?" he asked.

"For what?"

"Dinner tonight with the Mannings. Remember?"

"Of course," she said, forcing a smile. How could she have forgotten that? James was like a schoolboy eager to show off his science project. Only in this case, *she* was the project. She still wore her gray suit, so after quickly brushing her hair and refreshing her makeup, she considered herself ready—in appearance if not in attitude.

He escorted her out the front door and into his car, which he'd parked in front of the house. "You haven't had much campaigning to do lately," she commented.

"I know."

"What does Ralph have to say?" she asked, wanting to see how much James was willing to tell her.

"Not much. Let's not talk about the election tonight, okay?"

"Why not?"

"I don't want to have to think about it. These people are my friends. They're like a second set of parents to me."

"Do they know I'm pregnant?"

"No, but I won't need to tell them, will I?" He gently patted her abdomen.

"James," she whispered. "When we get home this evening, I want to make love."

His gaze briefly left the road and he nodded.

The emptiness inside her could only be filled with his love.

"Are you feeling all right?"

She made herself smile and laid her head against his shoulder. "Of course."

"There's something different about you."

"Is there?" Just that her heart felt as if it had been chopped in half. Just that she'd never felt so cold or alone in her life. Southworth had asked her to turn her back on the man she loved. He'd asked that she leave and do it in such a way that he wouldn't follow. He'd asked that she bear her child alone.

When they got to the Manning home, James parked his car on the street and turned to Summer. He studied her for an intense moment. "I love you."

"I love you," she whispered in return. She felt close to tears.

James helped her out of the car. They walked to the front porch, and he rang the doorbell. When she wasn't looking, he stole a kiss.

A distinguished older gentleman opened the door for them. "James! It's good to see you again."

"Eric, this is my wife, Summer."

"Hello, Summer." Instead of shaking her hand, Eric Manning hugged her.

They stepped inside, and all at once, from behind every conceivable hiding space, people leapt out.

They were greeted with an unanimous chorus of "Surprise!"

Eleven

Summer didn't understand what was happening. A large number of strange people surrounded her. People with happy faces, people who seemed delighted to be meeting her.

"Elizabeth," James protested. "What have you done?"

The middle-aged woman hugged first James and then Summer. "You know how much I love a party," she told him, grinning broadly. "What better excuse than to meet your wife? I'm the mother of this brood," she told Summer proudly, gesturing around the room. There were men, women and children milling about. "You must be Summer."

"I am. You must be Elizabeth."

"Indeed I am."

Before she could protest, Summer was lured away from James's side. The men appeared eager to talk to James by himself. Summer looked longingly at her husband. He met her eyes, then shrugged and followed his friends into the family room.

Soon Summer found herself in the kitchen, which bustled with activity. "I'm Jamie. We met the other day in the restaurant," Rich's wife reminded her.

"I remember," Summer told her, stepping aside as a youngster raced past her at breakneck speed.

"These two women with the curious looks on their faces are my sisters-in-law. The first one here," Jamie said, looping her arm around the woman who was obviously pregnant, "is Charlotte. She's married to Jason. He's the slob of the family."

"But he's improving," Charlotte told her.

"When's your baby due?"

"July," Charlotte said. "This is our second. Doug's asleep. I also have a daughter from my first marriage, but Carrie's working and couldn't be here. I'm sure you'll get a chance to meet her later."

"Our baby's due in September," Summer said, ending speculation.

The women exchanged glances. "You're just three months pregnant?"

Miserable, Summer nodded. "I think something must be wrong. The first couple of months I was really sick. I'm much better now that I'm in Seattle with James. But I'm ballooning. Hardly any of my clothes fit anymore."

"It happens like that sometimes," Elizabeth said with the voice of experience. "I wonder…" Then she shook her head. "I showed far more with Paul, my first, than

I did with Christy, my youngest. Don't ask me why nature plays these silly tricks on us. You'd think we have enough to put up with, dealing with men."

A chorus of agreement broke out.

Elizabeth took the hors d'oeuvre platter out of the refrigerator. "The good news is I was blessed with three sons. The bad news is I was blessed with three sons." She laughed. "My daughters are an entirely different story."

"I don't know what to expect with this baby," Summer told everyone, pressing her hand to her stomach. "We didn't plan to get pregnant so soon."

"I'll bet James is thrilled."

Summer smiled and nodded. "We both are."

"This is Leah," Jamie said, introducing her other sister-in-law, who'd just entered the kitchen. "She's Paul's wife. Paul's the author in the family."

"He's very good," Leah said proudly. "His first book was published last year, and he's sold two more."

"That's great!"

"Let me help," Jamie insisted, removing the platter from Elizabeth's hands. She carried it to the long table, beautifully decorated with paper bells and a lovely ceramic bride-and-groom centerpiece.

"I've been waiting for a long time to use these decorations," Elizabeth said disparagingly. "My children didn't give me the opportunity. It all started with the girls. Neither one of *them* saw fit to have a church wedding. Then Rich married Jamie and Paul married Leah, again without the kind of wedding I always wanted."

"Jason and Charlotte were the only ones to have a big wedding," Leah explained. "I don't think Eric and Elizabeth have ever forgiven the rest of us."

"You're darn right, we haven't," Eric said, joining them.

"They made it up to us with grandchildren, dear," his wife interjected. "Now, don't get started on that. We're very fortunate."

Summer couldn't remember the last time she'd sat down at a dinner table with this many people. A rowdy group of children ate at card tables set up in the kitchen. Twin boys seemed to instigate the chaos, taking delight in teasing their younger cousins. The noise level was considerable, but Summer didn't mind.

More than once, she caught James watching her. She smiled and silently conveyed that she was enjoying herself. Who wouldn't be?

There were gifts to open after the meal and plenty of marital advice. Summer, whose mood had been bleak earlier, found herself laughing so hard her sides ached.

The evening was an unqualified success, and afterward Summer felt as if she'd met a houseful of new friends. Jamie, Leah and Charlotte seemed eager to make her feel welcome. Charlotte was the first to extend an invitation for lunch. Since they were both pregnant, they already had something important in common.

"A week from Friday," Charlotte reminded her as Summer and James prepared to leave. She mentioned the name of the restaurant and wrote her phone number on the back of a business card.

"I'll look forward to it," Summer told her and meant it.

It wasn't until they were home that she remembered her meeting with Southworth. She didn't know if she'd be in Seattle in another week, let alone available for lunch.

Sadness pressed against her heart.

James slipped his arm around her waist. He turned off the downstairs lights, and together they moved toward the stairs. "As I recall," he whispered in her ear, "you made me a promise earlier."

"I did?"

"You asked me to make love to you, remember?"

"Oh, yes…" Shivers of awareness slid up and down her spine.

"I certainly hope you intend to keep that promise."

She yawned loudly, covering her mouth, fighting back waves of tiredness. "I have no intention of changing my mind."

"Good." They reached the top of the stairs, and he nuzzled her neck. "I wonder if it'll always be like this," he murmured, steering her toward their bedroom.

"Like what?"

"My desire for you. I feel like a kid in a candy store."

Summer laughed, then yawned again. "I enjoyed meeting the Mannings. They're wonderful people."

"Are those yawns telling me something?" he asked.

She nodded. "I'm tired, James." But it was more than being physically weary. She felt a mental and emotional exhaustion that left her depleted.

"Come on, love," James urged gently. He led her into the bedroom and between long, deep kisses, he undressed her and placed her on the bed. He tucked her in and kissed her cheek.

The light dimmed, and Summer snuggled into the warmth. It took her a few minutes to realize James hadn't joined her.

"James?" She forced her eyes open.

"Yes, love?"

"Aren't you coming to bed?"

"Soon," he said. "I'm taking a shower first."

A shower, she mused, wondering at his sudden penchant for cleanliness.

Then she heard him mutter, "A nice, long, *cold* shower."

James had been looking forward to the ultrasound appointment for weeks. He'd met Dr. Wise, Summer's obstetrician, earlier and had immediately liked and trusted the man, who was in his late forties. David Wise had been delivering babies for more than twenty years, and his calm reassurance had gone a long way toward relieving James's fears.

The ultrasound clinic was in the same medical building as Dr. Wise's office. He'd said he'd join them there, although James wasn't convinced that was his regular policy. Still, he felt grateful.

Summer sat next to him in the waiting room, her face pale and lifeless. She hadn't been herself in the past few days, and James wondered what was bothering her. He didn't want to pry and hoped she'd soon share whatever it was.

They held hands and waited silently until Summer's name was called.

It was all James could do to sit still as the technician, a young woman named Rachel, explained the procedure.

Summer was instructed to lie flat on her back on the examining table. Her T-shirt was raised to expose the bump that was their child. As James smiled down on her Dr. Wise entered the room.

A gel was spread across Summer's abdomen. It must have been cold because she flinched.

"It's about this time that women start to suggest the male of the species should be responsible for childbearing," Dr. Wise told him.

"No, thanks," James said, "I like my role in all this just fine."

Dr. Wise chuckled. Rachel pressed a stethoscope-like instrument across Summer's stomach, and everyone's attention turned toward the monitor.

James squinted but had trouble making out the details on the screen.

"There's the baby's head," Dr. Wise said, pointing to a curved shape.

James squinted again and he noticed Summer doing the same.

"Well, well. Look at this," the physician continued. "I'm not altogether surprised."

"Look at what?" James studied the screen intently.

"We have a second little head."

"My baby has two heads?" Summer cried in alarm.

"Two heads?" James echoed.

"What I'm saying," Dr. Wise returned calmly, "is that there appear to be two babies."

"Twins?"

"It certainly seems that way." As the ultrasound technician moved the instrument across Summer's abdomen, Dr. Wise pointed to the monitor. "Here's the first head," he said, tracing the barely discernible round curve, "and here's the second."

James squinted for all he was worth just to see one. "Twins," he murmured.

"That explains a lot," Dr. Wise said, patting Summer's arm. "Let's run a copy of this for you both," he said, and Rachel pushed a series of buttons.

Within minutes they had the printout to examine for themselves. While Summer dressed, James studied the picture.

"Twins," he said again, just for the pleasure of hearing himself say it. He turned to Summer and smiled broadly. "Twins," he repeated, grinning from ear to ear.

She smiled, and James thought he saw tears in her eyes.

"It won't be so bad," he said, then immediately regretted his lack of sensitivity. He wasn't the one carrying two babies, nor would he be the one delivering them. "I'll do whatever I can to help," he quickly reassured her.

She gave him a watery smile.

"Say something," he pleaded. "Are you happy?"

"I don't know," she admitted. "I'm still in shock. What about you?"

"Other than the day I married you, I've never been happier." He couldn't seem to stop smiling. "I can hardly wait to tell my father. He's going to be absolutely thrilled."

Summer stared at the ultrasound. "Can you tell? Boys? Girls? One of each?" Strangely, perhaps, it hadn't occurred to her to ask Dr. Wise.

James scratched his head. "I had enough trouble finding the two heads. I decided not to try deciphering anything else."

They left the doctor's office and headed for the parking garage across the street.

"This calls for a celebration. I'll take you to lunch," he said.

"I was thinking more along the lines of a nap."

James grinned and looked at his watch. "Is there time?"

"James," she said, laughing softly. "I meant a *real* nap. I'm exhausted."

"Oh." Disappointment shot through him. "You don't want to celebrate with a fancy lunch?"

She shook her head. "Don't be upset with me. I guess I need time to think about everything."

That sounded odd to James. What was there to think about? True, Summer was pregnant with twins, but they had plenty of time to prepare. As for any mental readjustment, well, he'd made that in all of two seconds. The twins were a surprise, yes, but a pleasant one.

"This news has upset you, hasn't it?" he asked.

"No," she was quick to assure him. "It's just that... well, it changes things."

"What things?"

She shook her head again and didn't answer. James frowned, not knowing how to calm her fears or allay her doubts. She didn't seem to expect him to do either and instead appeared to be withdrawing into herself.

"You don't mind if I tell my dad, do you?" he asked. If he didn't share the news with someone soon, he was afraid he'd be reduced to stopping strangers on the street.

She smiled at him, her eyes alight with love. "No, I don't mind if you tell Walter."

He walked her to where she'd parked and kissed her, then walked the short distance back to the King County Courthouse. His thoughts were so full of Summer that he went a block too far before he realized what he'd done.

In his office, the first thing he did was reach for the phone.

His father answered immediately. "You'll never guess what I'm looking at," he told Walter.

"You're right, I'll never guess."

"Today was Summer's ultrasound," James reminded him. Hiding his excitement was almost impossible.

"Ah, yes, and what did you learn?"

James could hear the eagerness in Walter's voice. "I have the picture in front of me."

"And?"

"I'm staring at your grandchildren right this second."

"Boy or girl?"

James couldn't help it. He laughed. "You didn't listen very well."

"I did, too, and I want to know—what do we have? A boy or a girl?"

"Could be one of each," James informed him calmly.

"Twins!" Walter shouted. "You mean Summer's having twins?"

"That's what I'm telling you."

"Well, I'll be! This is good news. No, it's great news. The best!"

James had never heard Walter this excited—practically as excited as he was himself.

It wasn't every day that a man learned he was having not one baby but two!

Summer didn't go directly home. Instead, she drove around for at least an hour, evaluating the situation between her and James. She loved him so much. The thought of leaving him, even when she knew it was the best thing for his career, brought her to the verge of tears.

What she wanted was to talk with her mother, but her parents were vacationing, touring the south in their motor home. They weren't due back for another month. Summer received postcards every few days with the latest updates and many exhortations to look after herself and their unborn grandchild. Wait till she told them it was grand*children*, she thought with a brief smile.

This vacation was good for them, but she really needed her mother now.

Without realizing she knew the way, Summer drove to the Manning family home. She parked, wondering whether she was doing the right thing.

It took her a full five minutes to gather up enough nerve to get out of the car, walk up the steps and ring the bell.

Elizabeth Manning answered the door. Her face lit up with warmth. "Summer! What a lovely surprise."

"I hope I haven't come at an inconvenient time."

"Not at all," Elizabeth said, ushering her in. "I was making meatballs. It's Eric's favorite. Today's his bowling day, so he's out just now. Can I get you a cup of tea?"

"No, thank you."

Elizabeth sat down in the living room.

"Would it be all right if we talked in the kitchen?" Summer asked after an awkward moment.

"Of course."

"I…I'm aware that you barely know me, and it's an imposition for me to drop in like this."

"Not at all. I'm delighted to see you again."

"I…my parents have a motor home," Summer said, wishing now she'd thought this through more carefully before she approached James's friends. "They're traveling across the south."

"Eric and I do quite a bit of traveling in our own motor home. We visit Christy and her sister, Taylor, at least once a year. Montana's become like a second home to us." She dug her hands into the bowl of hamburger and removed a glob of meat. Expertly she formed it into a perfect round shape.

"I really just wanted to thank you for everything you did the other night," Summer said. "The party for James and me…"

She suddenly decided she couldn't burden this woman with her troubles. She would've welcomed advice, but felt uncomfortable discussing her problems with someone who was little more than a stranger to her.

"When you know me better," Elizabeth was saying, "you'll learn that I love throwing parties. James has always been a special friend to our family, and we were so happy to find out about his marriage. Naturally we wanted to celebrate."

Summer nodded. "I didn't think it was possible to love anyone so much," she confessed, and then because tears began to drip from her eyes, she stood abruptly. "Listen, I should go, but thank you. I'll see myself to the door."

"Summer," Elizabeth called after her. "Summer, is everything all right?"

Summer was in her car by the time Elizabeth appeared in the doorway. She hurriedly started the engine and drove off, sure that she'd done more harm than good with her impromptu visit.

Wiping away tears, Summer went home. She walked into the house and up the stairs, then lay down on the bed and closed her eyes.

She had to leave, but she didn't know where to go. If she didn't do it soon, she'd never find the courage. Only minutes earlier, she'd declared to James's family friend how deeply she loved her husband. That was the truth, so doing what was best for him shouldn't be this difficult.

But it was.

Sobbing and miserable, Summer got up from the bed and pulled a big suitcase from the closet. She packed what she thought she'd need and carried it down to the car.

At the last minute she decided she couldn't leave without writing James. She sat at his desk for several minutes, trying to compose a letter that would explain what she was doing and why. But it was all so complicated, and in the end she simply said he was better off without her and signed her name. She read it twice before tucking it in an envelope.

Tears streamed down her cheeks. It wouldn't be so bad, or so she attempted to convince herself. The babies would be less than two months old when the election was over, and then she'd be free to return.

If James wanted her back.

James had seldom been in a better mood. He sat in the courtroom, convinced he must be grinning like a fool.

His assistant didn't know what to think. During a brief recess, he waltzed back to his office to phone Summer, whistling as he went.

His wife might not have wanted to celebrate with lunch, but their news deserved some kind of festivity. Dinner at the Space Needle. A night on the town.

While he was in his office, he ordered flowers for Summer with a card that said she'd made him the happiest man alive. Twice. He wondered what the florist would make of *that*.

The phone rang four times before voice mail kicked in. James hung up rather than leave a message. He'd try again later. Summer was probably resting; he hoped the phone hadn't disturbed her.

"Judge Wilkens?" Mrs. Jamison, his assistant, stopped him as he was leaving his office.

"Yes?"

"Your father phoned earlier. He wanted me to let you know he's been to the toy store and purchased two giant teddy bears. He also asked me to tell you he'll be dropping them off around six this evening. And he said he made dinner reservations in case you hadn't thought of it."

"Great." James laughed and discovered his assistant staring at him blankly.

"See this," James said, taking the ultrasound picture from inside his suit pocket. "My wife and I just learned we're having twins."

"Your wife? Twins for you and Summer. Why, Your Honor…" Her mouth opened, then shut, but she recovered quickly. "Congratulations!"

"Thank you," James said. Then, checking his watch, he returned to the courtroom.

The afternoon was hectic. James was hearing the sad case of a man who, crazed with drugs and alcohol, had gone on a shooting rampage. He'd killed three people and injured seventeen more. The case was just getting underway but was sure to attract a lot of media attention. James knew the defense was hinging its case on a plea of temporary insanity.

A door opened at the rear of the courtroom. James didn't look up, but out of the corner of his eye, he saw a lone figure slip into the back row. Whoever it was apparently didn't want to be recognized. She wore a scarf and large sunglasses.

Twice more James found his gaze returning to the figure in the back of the courtroom. If he didn't know better, he'd think it was Summer.

Whoever it was stayed for quite a long time. An hour or more. He wasn't sure when the woman left, but James couldn't help being curious.

His best guess was that the woman was a reporter.

When he was finished for the afternoon, James returned to his office and removed his robe. His secretary brought in a stack of phone messages. The one that seemed most peculiar was from Elizabeth Manning. She'd never called him at court.

Leaning back in his chair, he reached for the phone. "Hello, Elizabeth," he said cheerfully. It was on the tip of his tongue to tell her his and Summer's good news, but she cut him off.

"You'd better tell me what's wrong. I've been worried sick all afternoon."

"Worried? About what?"

"You and Summer."

Sometimes she baffled him. "I don't have a clue what you're talking about. I will tell you that Summer and I were at the doctor's this morning and found out she's pregnant with twins."

"Congratulations." But Elizabeth seemed distracted. "That can't be it," she mulled aloud. "She was here, you know."

"Who?"

"Summer."

"When?"

"This afternoon. Listen to me, James, there's something wrong. I knew it the minute I saw that girl. She was upset and close to tears. At first I thought you two might've had an argument."

"No…" James frowned. "What did she say?"

"She talked about her parents traveling in their motor home. I suppose I should've realized she wanted to discuss something with me, but I started chattering, hoping she'd relax enough to speak her mind."

"Tell me everything that happened."

"After the part about her parents' vacation, she said she'd come to thank me for the party, which we both knew was an excuse. Then she apparently changed her mind about talking with me and started to cry. Before I could stop her, she was gone."

"Gone? What do you mean gone?"

"The girl literally ran out of the house. I tried to

catch up with her, but with my bad leg, that was impossible."

"She drove off without another word?"

"That's right." Elizabeth sounded flustered. "What could be wrong, James?"

"I don't know. I just don't know. She was fine this morning." Or was she? James had no idea anymore. "I'll give you a call this evening," he assured Elizabeth. "I'm sure everything's okay."

"I hope so. Summer was very upset, James. Oh. That's odd...."

"What is?"

"I remember something else she said, and it was after this that she started to cry."

"What was it?" James asked anxiously.

"She told me how much she loved you."

A few minutes later, when he'd finished speaking to Elizabeth, James was more confused than ever. He tried calling Summer again—but again there was no answer. He left the office abruptly, without a word to his staff.

When he got to the house he burst through the front door. "Summer!" he shouted, his heart racing.

He was greeted with silence.

He raced up the stairs, taking them two at a time. He searched every room but couldn't find her.

What confused him further was that her clothes still hung in her closet, but one suitcase was missing. Surely if she was planning to leave him, she'd have taken more things. The only items that seemed to be missing were hcr toothbrush, slippers and a book about pregnancy and birth.

Baffled, he wandered back downstairs. He scouted out thc kitchen and the other rooms. The last place he looked was in his den. There he found an envelope propped against the base of the lamp.

James tore open the letter. It was brief and it made no sense. All he understood was that she'd left him. He had no idea why, other than that she seemed to think she was doing what was best for him.

He immediately called her cell. No answer.

A sick feeling attacked his stomach. He sat numbly at his desk for what could've been minutes or hours; he'd lost track of time. The next thing he knew, the doorbell chimed. He didn't get up to answer. A moment later the door opened on its own and his father came into the house.

"You might've let me in," he grumbled, setting one huge teddy bear in the chair across from James. "I'll be right back." He returned a couple of minutes later with the second bear.

"How'd you get in?" James asked, his voice devoid of emotion.

"You gave me a key, remember?"

He didn't.

"What's going on around here?" Walter asked. "Where's my daughtcr-in-law who's giving me twin grandkids?"

"Apparently Summcr has dccidcd to leave me. She's gone."

Twelve

"Gone?" Walter protested. "What do you mean, gone?"

"Gone, Dad," James said bitterly, "as in packed-a-suitcase-and-walked-out-the-door gone."

His father quickly sat down. "But…why?"

James couldn't answer that; silently he handed Walter the brief letter Summer had left him.

Walter read it, then raised questioning eyes to James. "What's this supposed to mean?"

"Your guess is as good as mine."

"You must've said something," Walter insisted. "Think, boy, think."

"I've done nothing *but* think, and none of this makes sense. I thought at first that she was upset about the twins. I realize now that whatever it is has been worrying her for some time."

"What could it be?"

"I don't know. I'd hoped she'd tell me."

"You mean to say you didn't ask?"

"No."

Walter glared at him in disbelief. "That's the first thing I learned after I married your mother. She never told me a thing that I didn't have to pry out of her with a crowbar. It's a man's duty, a husband's lot in life. When you didn't ask, Summer must've assumed you didn't care. She probably figures you don't love her."

In spite of his heavy heart, James smiled. "Trust me, Dad, Summer has no fear of speaking her mind, and as for my loving her, she couldn't have doubted that for an instant."

"She loves you." Walter's words were more statement than question.

"Yes," James said. He felt secure in her love. Or he had until now.

"Where would she go?"

This was the same question he'd been debating from the moment he discovered her letter. He shrugged. "No idea."

"Have you tried her cell?"

"Of course," he snapped. "She turned it off."

"Did you contact her parents?"

He would have, but it wouldn't help. James rubbed his face, tired to the very marrow of his bones. "They're traveling across the Southwest in their motor home. Half the time they don't have cell phone coverage."

"What about friends she's made since the move?"

"They're more acquaintances than friends. She's planning to volunteer at the library, but she's only mentioned the children's librarian in passing."

"I see." Walter frowned. "What about the Mannings?"

"She went over to talk to Elizabeth earlier this afternoon. Elizabeth phoned me and said Summer started to cry and then left in a hurry."

Walter's look was thoughtful. "Sounds as if she was trying to reach out for help."

"The only other person I can think of is her former roommate, Julie. I'll call her now."

"Julie, of course," his father said as if he should've thought of her himself.

James looked up the number and spoke to Julie's new roommate for several minutes.

"Julie's contract with Disney was up at the same time as Summer's," he said as he hung up. "Now that I think about it, Summer did say something about Julie being on tour with a musical group."

"So she'd be staying in hotels. Unlikely Summer would go to her."

James closed his eyes. His wife had walked out on him into a cold, friendless world.

"What about her brother?"

After another quick call, James shook his head. "Adam and Denise haven't heard from her. All I did was scare them," he said grimly.

"Did you check the airlines?"

"Where would she go?" James asked, losing his patience.

"I don't know," Walter admitted reluctantly. He began pacing.

His movements soon irritated James. "For heaven's sake, will you kindly sit down?"

"I can't sit here and do nothing."

"Yes, you can and you will," James insisted, making a decision. "I'll take the car and drive around, see if I can find her. You stay here by the phone in case she calls or we hear something."

"Okay. Check in with me every half hour."

James nodded. As he climbed into the car, he felt as if he was setting out on a journey without a map. Essentially he was, he thought as he drove through the narrow neighborhood streets. Try as he might, he couldn't figure out where she'd go. He tried to put himself in her shoes. Alone in a strange city with few friends.

The only thing he could do was ask God to guide him.

The wind blew off Puget Sound and buffeted Summer as she stood at the end of the pier. The waterfront was one of her favorite places in all of Seattle. Not knowing where else to instruct the taxi to take her, she'd had the driver bring her here.

She loved to shop at the Pike Place Market. Every Saturday morning James came down to the waterfront with her, and they bought fresh fruit and vegetables for the week. He'd been wonderfully patient while she browsed in the tourist shops that stretched along the waterfront. Some of their happiest moments in Seattle had been spent on this very pier.

How she hated to leave this city. It was as if everything in her was fighting to keep her in Seattle. Her husband was here, her home, her very life.

The instant she'd walked into James's large house,

she'd experienced a powerful sense of homecoming. She'd never said anything to her husband—he might think her reaction was silly—but Summer felt that his house had always been meant for them together.

She'd like to think that somewhere in James's subconscious he'd known he was going to fall in love and marry. The house had been his preparation for her entry into his life.

Tears blinded her eyes. She didn't want to focus on her unhappiness, so she turned her attention to the water. The pull of the tide fascinated her. The dark, murky waters of Elliott Bay glistened in the lights overhead. A green-and-white ferry chugged into the terminal.

Summer closed her eyes, willing herself to walk away. Except that she didn't know where she'd go. One thing was certain; she couldn't spend the night standing at the end of the pier. She'd need to find herself a hotel. In the morning her head would be clearer and she could make some decisions.

She was about to reach for her suitcase when she sensed someone approaching. Not wanting company, even the nonintrusive sort, Summer turned away from the railing. She kept her eyes lowered, but that didn't prevent her from recognizing James.

He sauntered to the railing several feet from where she stood. Wordlessly he stared into the distance.

Summer wasn't sure what she should do. She couldn't very well walk away from him now. It had been difficult enough the first time. She didn't have the strength to do it again.

"How'd…how'd you find me?" she asked.

He continued to stare into the distance. "Lucky guess," he finally said in cool tones.

Summer doubted that James felt lucky being married to her just then. He was furious with her. More furious than she'd ever seen him.

She wanted to explain that she was a detriment to his career, but couldn't force the words through her parched throat.

The tears that had flowed most of the day returned. She brushed them away with her fingertips.

"Was I such a bad husband?" he demanded in the same chilling tone.

"No," she whispered.

"Did I do something so terrible you can't forgive me for?"

Sobbing, she shook her head.

"You've fallen out of love with me," he suggested next.

"Don't be ridiculous," she cried. If she'd loved him any more than she already did, her heart couldn't have stood it.

"Then tell me why you walked out on me."

"My letter…"

"…explained nothing."

"I…I…" She was trembling so much she couldn't speak.

James walked over to her and reached for her suitcase. "We're going back to the house and we're going to talk about this. Then, if you're still set on leaving, I'll drive you to the airport myself. Understand?"

All she could manage was a weak nod.

Thankfully, he'd parked the car close by. Summer felt disoriented. Maybe she shouldn't be this happy that James had found her, but she was. Even if he was angry with her, she was grateful he was taking her home.

James opened the car door for her and set her suitcase in the backseat. He didn't speak so much as a single word on the drive home.

When they pulled into the driveway, Summer saw Walter's car.

"Your father's here?"

James didn't answer her. Nor did he need to. Walter was already out the door.

"Where'd you find her?" he asked, bolting toward them.

"The waterfront."

"Sit down, sit down," her father-in-law murmured, guiding Summer inside and into a chair. She felt she was about to collapse and must have looked it, too.

"Now what the hell is this all about?" James said roughly.

"You can't talk to her like that," Walter chastised. "Can't you see the poor girl's had the worst day of her life?" He turned to Summer, smiling gently. "Now what the hell is this all about?"

Summer looked from one man to the other. "Would it be all right if I spoke to James alone?" she asked her father-in-law. She couldn't deal with both of them at the same time.

It looked for a moment as if Walter wasn't going to leave. "I suppose," he agreed with reluctance. "I'll be in the other room."

"Walter," Summer said, stopping him on his way out the door. "I take it the two teddy bears are your doing."

He nodded sheepishly. "The car's loaded with goodies. I'm afraid I got a little carried away."

"These babies are going to love their grandpa."

Walter grinned, then walked out, closing the door.

James stood by the fireplace, his back to her. Summer suspected he was preparing a list of questions. She wasn't even sure she had all the answers; she wasn't sure she wanted him to ask them. She decided to preempt his interrogation.

"I…I went to see Ralph Southworth," she said in a quavering voice.

James whirled around. "You did *what?*"

"I…I overheard you and your father talking not long ago and I learned that Southworth resigned as your campaign manager."

"So he's what this is all about," James said thoughtfully. His eyes hardened. "What happened between the two of us had nothing to do with you."

"James, please, I know otherwise. I…I knew from the start that Ralph disapproved of me. I'm not sure why, but it doesn't matter."

"No, it doesn't. Because Southworth doesn't matter."

Summer didn't believe that. "Afterward, it seemed like you'd given up on the election. In the last two weeks you haven't made a single public appearance. When I ask, you don't want to talk about it and—"

"There are things you don't know."

"Things you wouldn't tell me."

James sat across from her and leaned forward,

elbows on his knees. He didn't say anything for several minutes.

"What was I supposed to think?" she cried when he didn't explain. "Being a judge is the most important thing in the world to you. You were born for this.... I couldn't take it away from you. Don't you understand?"

"You're wrong about something. Being a superior court judge means nothing if you're not with me. I guarantee you, my career's not worth losing my wife and family over."

"I was going to come back," she whispered, her eyes lowered. "After the election..."

"Do you mean to say you were going to deliver our babies on your own? Do you honestly think I wouldn't have turned this city upside down looking for you?"

"I...didn't know what to think. Ralph said—"

"Don't even tell me." A muscle leapt in his jaw. "I can well imagine what he said. The man's a world-class idiot. He saw you as a liability when you're my greatest asset."

"If you truly believe that, then why did you throw in the towel?"

"I haven't," he told her. "I took a few days to think about it and decide who I'll ask to manage the rest of my campaign. It seems there are several people who want the job."

"But Southworth said he could sway the election for you.... He claims to have political clout."

"He seems to think he does," James said tightly.

"We made a deal," she whispered, lowering her gaze.

"What kind of deal?"

"Southworth agreed to manage your campaign if I left Seattle until after the election."

James snickered. "It's unfortunate you didn't check with me first."

"Why?"

"I don't want Southworth anywhere near my campaign."

Summer bristled. "You might've said that earlier."

"True," James admitted slowly. "But I wanted everything squared away before I announced that I'd changed campaign managers."

"So, who did you choose? Who's your new manager?"

"Eric Manning. He's not only an old friend, he was a successful businessman and he's very well connected." He shook his head. "I should've asked him in the first place."

"James, that's wonderful! I like him so much better than Ralph."

James reached for her hands and held them in his own. "What you don't understand is that I wouldn't have taken Southworth back under any circumstances. First of all, I won't allow any man to talk about my wife the way he did. It's true I made some mistakes when we first got married. I blame myself for not publishing our wedding announcement immediately. Frankly, I didn't think of it."

"I didn't, either. And remember, we were talking about an April ceremony back then." Summer wasn't willing to have him accept all the blame.

"You're my wife, and I couldn't be prouder that

472
Debbie Macomber

someone as beautiful and talented as you would choose to marry me. Ralph made it sound as if we should keep you under wraps until after the election, which is utterly ridiculous. I'm angry with myself for not taking a stand sooner."

"What about the election?" She didn't care to hear any more about Southworth.

"I'll get to that in a minute. When Southworth said he questioned my judgment, I realized what a fool I'd been to listen to the man for even a minute."

"But—"

"Let me finish, sweetheart. The best thing I ever did in my life was marry you."

"It was impulsive and—"

"Smart," he said, cutting her off. "I don't need South-worth to win this campaign for me. He had me convinced I did, but I know otherwise now."

"What about his political friends?"

"That's a laugh. A man as narrow-minded and self-righteous as Ralph Southworth can't afford the luxury of friends. He has none, but he doesn't seem to know it. If he hadn't decided to leave my campaign, I would've asked him to resign."

It was a good thing Summer was sitting down. "You mean to say I went through all that grief and left you for *nothing?*"

"Exactly."

"Oh."

James gathered her in his arms. "Summer, whatever I am, whatever I may become, I'm nothing without you."

Summer sobbed into his shoulder.

"Winning the election would be an empty victory if you weren't standing at my side. I want you to share that moment with me. I love you, Summer, and I love our babies, too."

"Oh, James, I've been so unhappy. I didn't know what to do."

"Don't ever leave me again. It was like I'd lost my mind, my heart—everything—until I saw you standing at the end of that pier."

Summer tightened her arms around him.

Walter tapped on the door. "Can I come in yet?"

"No," James growled.

"So have you two settled your differences?"

"We're working on it," Summer called out.

"Then I'll leave you to your reunion."

"Good night, Dad," James said in what was an obvious hint for his father to leave.

"'Night, kids. Kiss and make up, okay?"

"We're going to do a lot more than kiss," James whispered in her ear.

"Promises, promises, promises," she murmured.

"You can bet I'll make good on these."

Thirteen

"This is my wife, Summer," James said, his arm around her thick waist. Although she was only six months pregnant, she looked closer to nine.

"I'm so pleased to meet you," the older woman said.

"Who was that again?" she whispered to James.

"Emily Rohrbaugh, president of the League of Women Voters."

"Oh. I don't know how you remember all these names. I'm impressed."

"I'm more impressed that you can remember all your lines in *Beauty and the Beast*," he said. "But here's my little trick for recalling names. I try to tie them in with something else," James told her. "Some kind of object or action."

"Rohrbaugh is something of a challenge, don't you think?" Summer raised her eyebrows.

"Roar and baa," he said under his breath. "Think of

a lion and a lamb. A lion roars and a lamb goes *baa*. Rohrbaugh."

Summer's face lit up with a bright smile. "No wonder I married you. You're brilliant."

"I bet you won't have a problem remembering Emily the next time you meet."

"I won't."

"She's a good friend of Elizabeth Manning's," James said, feeding his wife a seedless grape. It was a test of his restraint not to kiss her afterward. One would assume his desire for her would fade after all these months; if anything, quite the opposite had occurred. She was never more beautiful to him than now, heavy with their children.

"Elizabeth Manning?" Summer repeated. "I didn't think she'd be the political type."

"She isn't," James said. They mingled with the crowd gathered on the patio of an influential member of the state senate. "But the two of them have been friends since high school."

"I see."

"Do you need to sit for a while?"

"James," she groaned. "Stop worrying about me."

He glanced down at her abdomen. "How are Mutt and Jeff?"

She circled her belly with both hands. "I swear these two are going to be world-class soccer players."

James chuckled, reaching for an hors d'oeuvre from one of the several platters set around the sunny patio. He gave it to Summer.

"James, I don't believe I've met your wife."

James recognized the voice—William Carr, the president of the Bar Association. He quickly made the introductions. He never worried about Summer saying the wrong thing or inadvertently embarrassing him. She had a natural way about her that instantly put people at ease. She was charming and open and genuine. These political functions weren't her idea of a good time, but she never complained. She seemed eager to do whatever she could to aid his campaign and had proved to be the asset he knew she would be.

"I'm very pleased to meet you," she said warmly as they exchanged handshakes.

The obvious topic of conversation was Summer's pregnancy, which they discussed but only briefly. She managed to deftly turn the conversation away from herself, and soon Carr was talking about himself, laughing over the early days when his wife was pregnant with their oldest child.

After ten minutes or so, Summer excused herself.

"She's an excellent conversationalist," William Carr commented as she walked away.

James did his best to hide a smile. It amused him that Carr could do most of the talking and then act as if Summer had been the one carrying the discussion.

"It seems strange to think of you as married," the attorney said next.

"When I'm with Summer, I wonder why I ever waited so long."

Carr shifted his weight from one foot to the other.

"If I'd given you advice before you were appointed to the court, it would've been to marry."

"Really?" This came as a shock to James.

"You're a fine young man, and I expect great things from you. Just between you, me and the fence post, I think you're doing an excellent job."

"I hope so," James said, but there were some who weren't as confident as William Carr. Generally those under the influence of Ralph Southworth. To James's surprise, Southworth had managed to prejudice several supporters against him.

"You remind me of myself thirty years back," Carr told him.

James considered this high praise. "Thank you."

"But you needed a little softening around the edges. You came off as strong and unbending. Not a bad thing for a judge, mind you, but being a little more human wouldn't have hurt."

"I see." James didn't like hearing this but knew it was for his own good, however uncomfortable it might be.

"It's easy to sit in judgment of others when you live in an ivory tower."

James frowned uncertainly. "I don't understand."

"Until you married Summer, your life was a bit... sterile. Protected. If you don't mind my saying so... A married man knows how to compromise. I imagine you've done things to make your wife happy that you wouldn't normally do."

He nodded.

"In my opinion, marriage matures a man. It helps him sympathize and identify with his fellow humans."

"Are you trying to tell me I was a stodgy stuffed shirt before I married Summer?" James asked outright.

William Carr seemed taken aback by his directness, then grinned. "Couldn't have said it better myself."

"That's what I thought." James reached for a tiny crab puff.

"By the way, I wanted to congratulate you on a job well done. That multiple homicide was your first murder trial, wasn't it?"

"Yes." To be honest, he was happy it was over. The ordeal had proved to be exhausting for everyone involved. The jury had found the young man guilty, and after careful deliberation, James had pronounced the sentence.

His name and face had appeared on television screens every night for weeks. It went without saying that a lot of people were watching and waiting to see how he'd rule. Liberals were looking for leniency, and hard-liners wanted the death penalty. James had agonized over the sentence.

There were more victims than the ones who were shot during those hours of madness. Three families had lost loved ones. Seventeen others would always carry the mark of a madman's gun. Innocent lives had been forever changed.

James had delivered a sentence he felt was fair. He didn't try to satisfy any political factions, although the outcome of the election could well rest on his judgment.

He'd sentenced the killer to life without the possibility of parole, with mandatory psychiatric treatment.

It would've been impossible to keep everyone happy, so his decision had been based on what he considered equitable for all concerned. Some were pleased, he knew, and others were outraged.

"Thank you," James said, "I appreciate your vote of confidence."

"The decisions won't get any easier," William Carr told him. The older man grabbed a stuffed green olive and popped it in his mouth.

"The bar will be taking their opinion poll about the time your wife's due to have those babies of yours."

James knew that whether or not the results were published was at the discretion of the bar. The vote could sway the November election.

Summer returned just then, looking tired. Despite her smile, William Carr seemed to realize this. He wished them his best and drifted away.

"Are you ready to leave?" James asked.

"No," she protested. "We've barely arrived."

"We're going." His mistake was in asking her; he should've known to expect an argument.

He made their excuses, thanked the host and hostess and urged Summer toward their parked car. Her progress was slow, and he knew she was uncomfortable, especially in the heat.

"Charlotte's due in two weeks," she said when he helped her inside. She sighed as she eased into the seat. The seat belt barely stretched all the way around her.

James paused. "What's that comment about Charlotte about?"

"I envy her. Look at me, James!"

"I am looking at you," he said, and planted a kiss on her cheek. "You're the most beautiful woman in the world."

"I don't believe you," she muttered.

"You'd better, because it wouldn't take much to convince me to prove it right here and now."

"James, honestly."

"I am being honest."

She smiled, and he couldn't resist kissing her a second time.

After they got home, Summer sat outside in the sunshine. She propped her feet on a stool, and her hands rested on her stomach.

James brought her a glass of iced tea.

She smiled her appreciation. "You spoil me."

"That's because I enjoy it." He sat down next to her. "I don't suppose you've thought about packing up and leaving me lately?"

Summer giggled. "Once or twice, but by the time I finished dragging out my suitcases, I was too tired to go."

"You're teasing."

"Of course I'm teasing."

"Speaking of suitcases, do you have one ready for the hospital?"

"Aren't we being a little premature?"

"Who knows what Mutt and Jeff are thinking."

James's hand joined hers. It thrilled him to feel his children move inside her. "And this time you might want to take more than your toothbrush, a book and your bedroom slippers."

"That goes to show you the mental state I was in."

"Never again," James said firmly.

Summer propped her head against his shoulder and sighed. "Never again," she agreed.

The day of the September primary, Summer woke feeling sluggish and out of sorts. Getting out of bed was a task of monumental proportions. She felt as if she needed a forklift.

James was already up and shaved. He'd been watching her carefully all week. To everyone's surprise, including her doctor's, Summer hadn't delivered the twins yet. She'd read that twins were often born early. But not Mutt and Jeff, as they'd been affectionately named by James.

"Most babies aren't born on their due dates, so stop looking so worried. This is *your* day." She sat on the edge of the bed and pressed her hand to the small of her back.

James offered her his arm to help her upright. "How do you feel?"

"I don't know yet." The pain at the base of her spine had kept her awake most of the night. It didn't seem to go away, no matter how often she changed her position.

"When are we voting?" she asked.

"First thing this morning," James told her.

"Good."

"Why is that good?" he asked anxiously. "Do you think today's the day?"

"James, stop! I'm in perfect health."

"For someone nine months pregnant with twins, you mean."

Summer swore that somehow, God willing, she'd make it through this day. James was so tender and endearing, but she didn't want him worrying about her during the primary.

They gathered, together with Walter, at the large Manning home for the election results that evening. Summer was pleased for the opportunity to be with her friends.

Jason and Charlotte, along with their toddler and infant daughter, Ann Marie, were among the first to arrive. Many of the friends who'd worked so hard on James's campaign showed up soon after, shortly before the first election results were announced.

Summer planted herself in a chair in the family room and didn't move for an hour. The ache in her back had intensified.

Feeling the need to move about, she made her way into the kitchen. She was standing in front of the sink when it happened. Her eyes widened as she felt a sharp, stabbing pain.

"James," she cried in panic, gripping the counter. Water gushed from between her legs and onto the floor. "Oh, my goodness."

"Summer?" James stood in the doorway, along with at least ten others, including Elizabeth Manning.

"I'm sorry," she whispered, looking at James. "But I think it might be time to take me to the hospital."

She saw her husband turn and stare longingly at the election results being flashed across the screen. "Now?"

Fourteen

"James…I'm sorry." The pain that had been concentrated in the small of her back had worked its way around her middle. Summer held her stomach and closed her eyes, surprised by the intensity of it.

"Sorry," James demanded, "for what?" He moved quickly and placed his arm around her shoulders.

"You'd better get her to the hospital," Elizabeth advised.

"I'll phone the doctor for you," Eric added.

James shouted out the number he'd memorized, and five or six Mannings chanted it until Eric found a pad and pen to write it down.

Summer felt as if everyone wanted to play a role in the birth of their twins.

"Toss me the car keys, and I'll get the car as close to the front door as I can," Jason Manning shouted.

James threw him the keys, and Jason hurried out the front door.

"What about the election returns?" Summer asked, gazing at the television.

"I'll get them later," James said as if it meant nothing.

"I'll leave messages on your cell phone," Charlotte volunteered, "and James can call us when he has an update on Summer and the babies."

Summer bit her lip at the approach of another contraction. It hurt, really hurt. "James." She squeezed his hand, needing him.

"I'm here, sweetheart. I won't leave you, not for anything."

Jason reappeared, and the small entourage headed for James's car. It was parked on the grass, close to the front door, the engine running.

"The doctor said you should go directly to the hospital," Walter said breathlessly. "He'll meet you there."

"Don't worry, Summer, this isn't his first set of twins," Elizabeth said in a reassuring voice.

"True, but they're mine," James said.

"James?" Summer looked at her husband and noticed how pale he'd suddenly become. "Are you all right?"

He didn't answer for a moment; instead, he helped her inside the car and strapped her in. Before long he was sitting next to her, hands braced on the steering wheel. Summer saw the pulse in his neck pounding.

"It's going to be fine," she whispered. "Just fine."

"I'll feel a whole lot better once we get you to the hospital."

"Call us," Charlotte shouted, standing on the steps, waving.

Summer waved back, and no fewer than fifteen adults crowded onto the Mannings' front porch, cheering them on.

"James, are you okay to drive?" Summer asked when he took off at breakneck speed. He slowed down and stayed within the speed limit, but there was a leashed fear in him that was almost palpable.

"I'll be okay once we get you to the hospital."

"The birthing process is perfectly natural."

"Maybe it is for a woman, but it isn't as easy for a man."

With her hands propped against her abdomen, Summer smiled. "What's that supposed to mean?"

"I don't know if I can bear to see you in pain," he said, wiping his face as they stopped for a red light.

"It won't be too bad."

"Hey, you saw the films in our birthing class. I don't know if I'm ready for this."

"You!" she said, and giggled.

James's fingers curled around her hand. 'This isn't a laughing matter. I've never been more frightened in my life. No, only once," he amended. "The night I came home and found you gone."

"The babies and I are going to be just fine," she said again. "Don't worry, James, please. This is your night to shine. I'm just sorry Mutt and Jeff chose right now to make their debut."

"At the moment, the election is the last thing on my mind. None of it matters."

"You're going to win the primary," she insisted. Summer knew the competition had been steep, and Ralph Southworth had done what damage he could, eager to prove himself right.

"We're almost at the hospital," James said, sounding relieved.

"Relax," she said, and as it turned out, her words were a reminder to herself. The next contraction hit with unexpected severity, and she drew in a deep breath trying to control the pain.

"Summer!"

"I'm fine," she said breathlessly.

James pulled into the emergency entrance at Virginia Mason Hospital and raced around the front of the car. He opened the door, unsnapped the seat belt and lovingly helped her out.

Someone rolled a wheelchair toward her, and while Summer sat and answered the questions in Admitting, James parked the car.

She was on the maternity floor when he rejoined her, looking pale and harried.

"Stop worrying," she scolded him.

James dragged a chair to the side of her bed and slumped into it. "Feel my heart," he said and placed her hand over his chest.

"It feels like a machine gun," Summer said, smiling. She moved her hand to his face and cupped his cheek.

"I need you so much," James whispered.

Summer couldn't speak due to a strong contraction. James clasped her hand and talked to her in soothing tones, urging her to relax. As the pain ebbed, she kept her eyes closed.

When she opened them, she found James standing by the hospital bed, studying her. She smiled weakly and he smiled in return.

Dr. Wise arrived and read her chart, then asked, "How are we doing here?"

"Great," Summer assured him.

"Not so good," James said contradicting her. "I think Summer needs something for the pain, and frankly I'm not feeling so well myself."

"James, I'm fine," Summer told him yet again.

"What your husband's saying is that he needs help to deal with seeing you in pain," the physician explained.

"Do something, Doc."

Dr. Wise slapped James affectionately on the back. "Why don't we let Summer be the one to decide if she needs an epidural? She's a better judge than either one of us."

"All right." But James's agreement came reluctantly.

For Summer the hours passed in a blur. Her labor was difficult, and she was sure she could never have endured it if not for James, who stood faithfully at her side. He encouraged her, lifted her spirits, rubbed her back, reassured her of his love.

News of the primary filtered into the room in messages from Charlotte and various nurses, who caught snippets on the waiting room TV. In the beginning Summer strained to hear each bit of information. But as the evening wore on, she became so consumed by what was happening to her and the babies that she barely heard.

She lost track of time, but it seemed to her that it was well into the wee hours of the morning when she was taken into the delivery room.

James briefly left her side and returned a few minutes later, gowned in surgical green. He resembled a prison escapee, and she took one look at him and laughed.

"What's so funny?"

"You."

James drew in a deep breath and held Summer's hand. "It's almost time."

"I know," she breathed softly. "Ready or not, we're about to become parents. I have the feeling this is going to be the ride of a lifetime."

"It's been that way for me from the night I met you."

"Are you sorry, James?"

"Sorry?" he repeated. "No way!" Leaning over, he kissed her forehead. "My only regret is that I didn't marry you that first New Year's."

"Oh, James, I do love you."

Dr. Wise joined them. "Well, you two, let's see what we've got here, shall we?" He grinned at James. "Congratulations, Your Honor. You won the primary. This is obviously a night for good news."

Two months later Summer woke to the soft, mewling cry of her infant daughter. She climbed silently out of bed and made her way into their daughters' nursery.

There she found James sitting upright in the rocker, sound asleep with Kellie in his arms. Kerrie fussed in her crib.

Lifting the tiny bundle, Summer changed Kerrie's diaper, then sat in the rocker next to her husband and offered the hungry child her breast. Kerrie nursed eagerly and Summer ran her finger down the side of her baby's perfect face.

Her gaze wandered to her husband and she felt a surge of pride and love. The election had been that night, and he'd won the court seat by a wide margin. During the heat of the last two weeks of the campaign, James had let her compose and sing a radio commercial for him. Summer had been proud of her small part in his success, although she didn't miss life on the stage. Her twin daughters kept her far too busy for regrets.

James must have felt her scrutiny because he stirred. He looked up and saw Summer with Kerrie.

"I might as well feed Kellie, too," she said. Experience had taught her that the minute one was fed and asleep, the other would wake and demand to be nursed. Her twin daughters were identical in more than looks. Even their sleep patterns were the same.

James stood and expertly changed Kellie's diaper.

When Kerrie finished nursing, Summer swapped babies with him. James gently placed his daughter on his shoulder and patted her back until they heard the tiny burp.

"Why didn't you wake me?" Summer asked.

"You were sleeping so soundly."

"It was quite a night, Your Honor," she said, looking over at her husband. "I couldn't be more thrilled for you, James. Your position on the bench is secure."

"I couldn't have done it without you," he told her.

"Don't be ridiculous."

"It's true," he said with feeling. "You and Kerrie and Kellie. The voters fell in love with the three of you. Those radio commercials you sang were the talk of the town. I'm the envy of every politician I know."

"Because I can sing?"

"No, because you're my wife." His eyes were dark, intense. "I'm crazy about you, Summer. I still can't believe how much you've given me."

"I love you, too, James." Summer closed her eyes. It had started almost two years ago in Vegas, when it felt as if her heart was breaking. Now her heart was filled to overflowing. Life couldn't get any better than it was right then, she decided.

But Summer was wrong.

Because the best was yet to come.

* * * * *

REQUEST YOUR
FREE BOOKS!

2 FREE NOVELS
FROM THE ROMANCE/SUSPENSE
COLLECTION PLUS 2 FREE GIFTS!

YES! Please send me 2 FREE novels from the Romance/Suspense Collection and my 2 FREE gifts (gifts are worth about $10). After receiving them, if I don't wish to receive any more books, I can return the shipping statement marked "cancel." If I don't cancel, I will receive 4 brand-new novels every month and be billed just $5.49 per book in the U.S. or $5.99 per book in Canada, plus 25¢ shipping and handling per book plus applicable taxes, if any*. That's a savings of at least 20% off the cover price! I understand that accepting the 2 free books and gifts places me under no obligation to buy anything. I can always return a shipment and cancel at any time. Even if I never buy another book from the Reader Service, the two free books and gifts are mine to keep forever.

185 MDN EF5Y   385 MDN EF6C

Name _____ (PLEASE PRINT) _____

Address _____ Apt. # _____

City _____ State/Prov. _____ Zip/Postal Code _____

Signature (if under 18, a parent or guardian must sign)

Mail to The Reader Service:
IN U.S.A.: P.O. Box 1867, Buffalo, NY 14240-1867
IN CANADA: P.O. Box 609, Fort Erie, Ontario L2A 5X3

Not valid to current subscribers to the Romance Collection,
the Suspense Collection or the Romance/Suspense Collection.

Want to try two free books from another line?
Call 1-800-873-8635 or visit www.morefreebooks.com.

* Terms and prices subject to change without notice. N.Y. residents add applicable sales tax. Canadian residents will be charged applicable provincial taxes and GST. Offer not valid in Quebec. This offer is limited to one order per household. All orders subject to approval. Credit or debit balances in a customer's account(s) may be offset by any other outstanding balance owed by or to the customer. Please allow 4 to 6 weeks for delivery. Offer available while quantities last.

Your Privacy: Harlequin is committed to protecting your privacy. Our Privacy Policy is available online at www.eHarlequin.com or upon request from the Reader Service. From time to time we make our lists of customers available to reputable third parties who may have a product or service of interest to you. If you would prefer we not share your name and address, please check here. ☐

BOB08R

DEBBIE MACOMBER